NOT IN KANSAS ANYMORE

He was lying on the shag carpet, playing with his cat, Felix, when he got a sudden urge to look at the crystal. Sipping the wine and getting quite drunk, he put the crystal between himself and the cat. Felix's eyes opened wide and the animal backed cautiously away, emitting a low growl. The poor kitty was terrified of the yellow eyes which danced around and stared back.

The wine bottle was almost empty when Lew spilled the rest on the carpet. "Damn!" he said, and noticed that the cat's eyes in the crystal were moving, seemingly of their own volition.

He held Felix up to the crystal; and the cat hissed loudly and vanished, sucked into the depths of light.

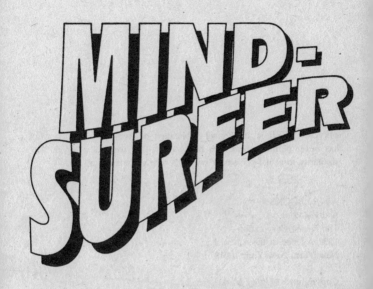

MIND-SURFER

MARK LEON

AVON BOOKS • NEW YORK

MIND-SURFER is an original publication of Avon Books. This work has never before appeared in book form. This work is a novel. Any similarity to actual persons or events is purely coincidental.

AVON BOOKS
A division of
The Hearst Corporation
1350 Avenue of the Americas
New York, New York 10019

First AvoNova Printing: January 1995

AVONOVA TRADEMARK REG. U.S. PAT. OFF. AND IN OTHER COUNTRIES, MARCA REGISTRADA, HECHO EN U.S.A.

Printed in the U.S.A.

RA 10 9 8 7 6 5 4 3 2 1

CONTENTS

This is for Dice

Acknowledgment

Special thanks to Jim Hankinson, friend and professor, for the title.

1

~~~~~~~~~~

Encounters

Lew Slack pulled the final copy of the report from the printer and headed for the conference room. He walked in, full of confidence, and handed it to his boss. Leaning forward, ready to explain some of the subtle details which he had added at the last minute, he was casually rebuffed. "Thank you, Lew, that will be all."

Lew left, instantly deflated. His work was critical to the decisions of the men sitting in that room. But once they had his data he was forgotten.

"What's wrong?" Susan, the boss's secretary, asked him.

"Nothing!" he snapped, more at himself than at her. "You know what I am?" he continued. "Just a glorified file clerk."

"No one knows the computer system like you do," Susan said, sympathetically.

"And no one wants to know," he said. "They use me to generate data. The only time they remember where it came from is when something goes wrong."

"Cheer up, Lew," Susan said. "It's almost lunchtime."

Walking in the sunlight, Lew tried to convince himself that he was fortunate to be outside, free, not cooped up in a meeting under fluorescent lights. But it was futile. All he felt was frustration and alienation.

Sipping his coffee, he reflected on his wasted life. The thoughts were all familiar ones. "Had I only finished graduate school, had I not wasted so much time on fruitless dreams, had I only known then what I know now . . ."

The coffee was terrible. The headline in the paper was

about AIDS, which only reminded him that remaining single all those years was a mistake. There was no more advantage to it. The era of free love was over.

He finished his sandwich and went back outside, determined to take a long lunch as compensation for the morning's humiliation.

A man spoke to him. "Why so glum, chum?"

Lew was annoyed by the intrusion. What business did anyone have with his despair?

"I said what's the problem?" the stranger insisted as Lew continued to walk.

"I don't have any spare change," Lew said, looking at the man for the first time. He was surprised to see a well-tailored, white-haired old man, obviously in no need of money. The face shocked him. It was handsome and somehow familiar.

The old guy just laughed. "God bless you then, sonny," he said and handed Lew a crystal.

"No thanks," Lew said.

"No problem," the man said, and proceeded to drop the crystal into Lew's coat pocket. Before Lew could protest, his benefactor was on his way, showing unusual quickness for one his age.

Back at the office Susan looked worried. "He wants to see you," she said.

"Alright," Lew answered and strode in through the double doors, where his boss was seated behind the wooden desk, looking out the window.

"You wanted to see me."

"Where were you?" Mr. Phelps asked, without turning around.

"Lunch," Lew answered.

"Long lunch," Phelps said, swiveling around in his chair to look Lew in the eye.

"Sorry. Did you need me?"

"No. But we might have." Phelps leaned way back in his chair and folded his hands across his bulging stomach.

"I'll be more careful . . ." Lew started to say and then faltered. "Look," he spoke up again, "you take two-hour lunches all the time."

"Executive privilege," Phelps said, oblivious to his abuse of the term.

Lew sensed an opening. "That's what I want to talk to you about," he said, sitting down in front of the desk and leaning forward. "I think I could make a significant contribution if my status were upgraded. I really do. I should have been in that meeting today. My job is too important. I don't just keep data, I analyze it. I guess I am saying that I should be an executive too."

Phelps laughed. "You hardly look the part," he said.

Lew blushed while he looked down at his canvas shoes and faded blue jeans. "I can wear a suit," he said, flustered.

"Yes, Lew, I suppose you can. Listen. I'll think about it and get back to you. But I'm very busy right now, so . . ."

Lew got up. "Thanks," he said.

Susan looked up from her terminal as Lew stalked out of the office, blind to her concerned expression.

Alan Fain stepped onto a San Francisco pier. The Pacific crossing in the tramp steamer had been difficult. He stood for a few seconds, getting his land legs back and brushing the dust from his old, gray flannel suit. "Mistel Fain, Mistel Fain." The boat captain, an ancient-looking Oriental man, was trying to get the passenger's attention.

Fain took a deep breath. "What?" he said finally.

"Your bags are still on board."

Fain patted his breast pocket to make sure he still had his wallet and passport. "Keep them," he replied, and started away. After a few steps he stopped and called back to the captain, "Which way to the airport?"

The creased face broke into a smile, revealing a mouth half-full of dubious-looking teeth, and the shoulders came up in a shrug.

"Thanks," Fain said. He took another deep breath and strode on down the pier, looking straight ahead.

After he purchased his ticket at the airport, Alan rushed to the nearest newsstand. He found what he wanted, a paperback entitled *Kybal* by Hermes Trismegistus. He quickly bought it and began skimming the contents, smiling occasionally, and once laughing so loud that he drew stares. "Sorry," he said to a woman nearby. "I've been away." He closed the book and slid it into his coat pocket. Shutting his eyes, he sat up straight and sank into deep samadhi meditation. His even breathing and obvious concentration brought more strange looks. Two hours later, exactly boarding time, he stood up, stretched, and headed for his gate.

Lew remembered the crystal that evening as he took off his coat. It felt good in his hand. He regarded it over supper, where it stood on his dining table. The thing was a narrow, hexagonal pyramid, about six inches tall with a sharp point. The red tones from his wine danced in the crystal, and Lew decided it was a pleasing centerpiece.

Dinner finished, he poured another glass of wine, palmed the crystal, and moved to the sofa. He held it up to the light, admiring the sharpness of the reflections and refractions.

Something moved. He looked closely; the image was no trick of the light. There was a face looking back, not his face. Her lips were moving; she was beautiful, and Lew again had the eerie sense that she was someone he should recognize.

"What?" Lew whispered involuntarily.

"Who are you?" she asked, her voice suddenly audible. Lew dropped the crystal on the coffee table. Several minutes later he picked it up, but there were no more faces.

He slept fitfully. About 3:00 A.M. he heard footsteps on his stair. There was the sound of a key in his lock.

Lew rolled over and pretended to be asleep. Soon he felt a body slide in next to him. It was Pamela, clad only in thin cotton panties.

"Lew," she said, "are you asleep?"

He didn't move. She moved closer.

Lew put his hand behind him and slid it under her elastic waistband. She giggled softly and made a similar move of her own.

Pamela was up early. "Lew," she whispered in his ear, "it's time to get up." She handed him a cup of coffee.

"Ungh!" he groaned. It was cold in his drafty, garage apartment.

"How can you stand to walk around naked like that?" he asked. "It's cold."

"I like it," she said. "What's the matter? Don't *you* like it?"

"I don't like anything this early in the morning," he said. "The coffee is good though."

"Thanks a lot!" she said, and pulled her long red hair around to the front, letting it cover her pale, creamy breasts. Then she covered the red patch between her legs with both hands.

Lew took another sip of coffee and put the cup down on the spool table beside his low bed. "Come here," he said.

"No." She laughed.

Lew dragged himself out of bed, shivering. Before he could get to her she had run into the kitchen. He caught her around the waist and pulled her to him, pressing into her softness from behind.

"My, Lew," she said. "What's this?"

"Nothing," he said.

"Feels like something," she said.

"Yeah," he sighed.

"Look at the suit!" Susan said and whistled as Lew walked into the office. "What's the occasion?" she asked.

"I just felt like it," Lew snapped.

"OK," Susan said. "It looks nice."

"Thanks," Lew said, extremely self-conscious.

"It's a herringbone, isn't it?" Susan asked.

"Yeah," Lew said, brushing a wide lapel. "English wool."

Susan giggled as Lew walked on to his office. "Did you see that suit?" she asked the receptionist. "It must be thirty years old!"

Lew sat down at his desk and logged on. The system appeared to be functioning normally, so he leaned back in his chair, propped his feet up on his desk, and opened the newspaper.

The phone rang. "Slack," Lew said.

"A call for you on line one, Lew." It was Susan. "Must be one of your new girlfriends," she added with a giggle.

"OK. Thanks." Lew punched one, expecting to hear Pamela's voice.

"Lew?" a soft feminine voice asked. It was definitely not Pamela.

"Yeah. Who is this?" he asked.

"Who are you?" she said mysteriously. Suddenly Lew recognized the voice of the woman in the crystal.

"Who is this?" he asked anxiously. "Really?" His heart was beating fast.

"Wouldn't we all like to know the answer to *that* one?" she said. "You will come won't you?" she asked, sounding a little anxious herself.

"Come where?"

"Just come," she said and hung up.

"Damn!" Lew muttered. He threw the paper into the mess of reports and manuals on his desk. Then he got up and grabbed his coffee cup. There was mold growing on the black sludge in the bottom. He wandered out into the hall, rinsed his cup out, and went back to the front office.

"Fresh pot, Lew," Susan said. "Just for you." She winked.

"Thanks," he said, and poured a cup.

"Anything wrong?" Susan asked. "You look a little pale."

"That phone call," Lew said, "—it was weird. I feel so weak all of a sudden."

"It must have been Sheila," Susan said, with mock mystery.

"How did you know her name?" Lew shot back, almost spilling his coffee.

"Take it easy, Lew. It was just a joke. I got the name out of this book." Susan held up the book she had been reading. The cover art featured a powerful, bare-breasted woman with wild hair and a bow.

"What is *that* about?" He found the image both highly erotic and frightening.

"It's called *Goddess Power*," Susan said self-consciously. "It tells how to get in touch with your own inner goddess."

"How's it going?" Lew could not quite keep the sarcasm out of his voice, although he regretted it immediately. He knew Susan as someone who was sensitive and suffered from low self-esteem. He picked the book up, hoping his feigned interest would make up for his little barb. He was immediately struck by the uncanny resemblance of the mythic female on the cover to Susan. "She looks like you," he said, trying to sound amused, but in truth he was a bit shaken by the weirdness of it.

"So everyone tells me," Susan said as Lew handed the book back.

"Who is she supposed to be?" Lew asked. "She looks like a New Age version of Diana, the goddess of the moon and the hunt."

"According to the book her name is Psylene," Susan said,

blushing a little. "She is the wild and free spirit who supposedly dwells in each woman. Sheila is her daughter—her creation actually. Psylene uses the erotic power of Sheila to overpower men. I was just joking. It's interesting, but I really don't think I'm the goddess type . . ."

"Don't be so sure . . ." Lew began.

"Oh Lew!" It was Mr. Phelps.

"Yes?" Lew answered, moving toward the large, double doors.

"Can I see you for a minute?"

"Sure," Lew said. He walked in and sat down.

"Where did you get that suit?" Phelps asked.

"Oh," Lew said uneasily, "I . . ."

"I haven't seen anything like that since I was in college," he said.

"Yeah," Lew said, "I guess it is a little out of style. It belonged to an old friend of mine. We roomed together in college. He disappeared over twenty years ago. Went to Asia or something."

"It's well preserved though, except for a few moth holes," Phelps said. "Anyway, how is the new database going?"

"Fine," Lew said. "Just a few minor bugs left. It should be ready by the end of the month."

"Good," Phelps said. "We're really counting on it."

"No major problems that I can see," Lew said.

"That's all I wanted." Phelps was already turning his attention back to the reports on his maple desktop.

"Uh, Mr. Phelps?" Lew said.

"Yes?" Phelps looked up, peering out, over his reading glasses. "What is it?"

"Well, have you thought about what I said yesterday?"

"What's that?" Phelps mumbled, and took off his glasses. He leaned back in his big, swivel chair. The sun coming through the window at his back reflected off his bald head. "Oh yes," he said. "Yes, I remember. Lew, have you ever read Castaneda?"

"Who?" Lew asked.

"Carlos Castaneda. You know. The Don Juan books."

"Oh yeah," Lew said. "The Mexican sorcerer. I read a few. It all turned out to be a hoax, didn't it? I mean, Don Juan never was a real person, was he?"

"Oh I don't know that it matters much," Phelps said. "There was a beautiful little piece in one of those books about power spots."

"Power spots?" Lew said.

"Yes. A man needs to find his power spot, the place that is right for him, where he can gather personal power. I have found mine." He folded his hands across his belly and leaned farther back.

"Right," Lew said. "But I don't see what that has to do with my future here."

"But it has everything to do with it," Phelps said. "I know you aren't happy. But maybe you just haven't found your spot. These things take time. Some people never find their place. But you need to try. Take some risks in life. I guess what I am saying is that maybe you aren't in the right place here."

"Exactly," Lew said. "I need a promotion."

"A promotion won't change things, Lew," Phelps said and leaned forward, lowering his voice. "You need to experiment. *Really* change. Strike out on your own."

"You mean . . . I'm fired?" Lew said.

"Not until the new database is complete." Phelps laughed. "Just a little joke," he said when he noticed Lew wasn't smiling. "No, of course not. You're doing a superb job. I'm just trying to help. A little friendly advice is all." He grabbed his reading glasses and sat back up. It was clear that the interview was over.

Lew stood up slowly and turned to leave.

"Think about it Lew," Phelps said.

"I will," Lew said hollowly as he walked out.

"Oh Lew," Phelps called.

"Yes?"

"Shut the door, please. Thank you."

"How'd it go?" Susan asked.

"Power spots," Lew said.

"What?" Susan asked.

"Think about it," he said as he walked by.

Lew met Pamela for lunch. "Nice," she said, leaning across the table and fingering the wool lapel of his suit.

"Don't you make fun of me too," he said.

"I *like* it," she said. "Why so defensive?"

"Things aren't going too well," Lew said.

"What's wrong?"

"Job," he said. "Everything. I'm just not happy."

"Why?" she asked.

"I'm almost forty," he said.

"So?"

"So nothing has happened yet in my life. Not like it was supposed to anyway."

"It never does," she said. Lew didn't notice how nervous she suddenly was. "Lew?" she asked.

"Yeah?" He cut into his remaining enchilada.

"When are we getting married?"

He froze. "Pamela, I thought we had agreed not to talk about that for a while."

"Neither one of us is getting any younger," she said.

"I can't deal with that right now. Not on top of everything else," he said.

"But don't you see? You can't separate it from everything else. Maybe what you need is change, commitment. I know I do. Lew, I want to have a baby before it's too late." She reached across the table and put her hand on his.

Lew looked up. "OK," he said. "You're right. We do need to talk about it. But not right now, please. Just not right now. Weird things have been happening."

"What things?"

"Well, yesterday an old guy gave me this crystal." He pulled the crystal out of his pocket and held it to the light. It sent dazzling rays of color through the water glasses on the table.

The waitress was about to pour more water for Lew when the colors distracted her. She gasped and dropped the pitcher on the floor.

She rushed back into the kitchen muttering underneath her breath. The hostess came over to apologize and clean up the mess. "Sorry, *senor*," she said. "Lisa is so superstitious. You know some of our help . . . well . . ."

Lew knew in fact that most of the help consisted of illegal aliens from across the Rio Grande. That was why the food was so good. "What was that she said?" Lew asked.

"Oh nothing." The hostess smiled. "There—it is all fine now, *qué non*?"

"Yeah," Lew said. "But what did she say, really?"

"Just superstition," the hostess said. "You know, *curandero* stuff. Sorcery. She thinks she saw magic in your glass there."

"This crystal?" Lew asked, holding it up.

"Yes," the hostess said. "Forget it. Enjoy your dinner."

"Let me see that," Pamela said. She hefted the thing in her hand. "It's big and incredibly symmetric. If it's real, it could be worth a lot of money."

"I think there *is* something strange about it," he said. "Last night I thought I saw a face in it, a woman. I swear she spoke to me. And then today, at work, I got a phone call. It was the same voice! I don't believe in any of this New Age stuff, crystal magic or pyramid power, but *something* is going on." He idly picked up the check.

"Lunch is on me," Pamela said, snatching the check from him.

"Thanks, Pamela," he said. "We'll have dinner tomorrow, OK? Then we'll talk. I promise."

"Why not tonight?" she asked.

"Dinner with Dr. Cline, remember?" he said.

"Oh that's right," she said. "Give my regards to the doctor. And Lew, I wouldn't worry too much about that crystal. I'm sure the phone call was just a wrong number."

"And the face?"

"How much wine did you have?" She laughed.

"Yeah," he said. "I guess so. But the waitress won't come near our table now."

"Superstition," Pamela said.

Lew was walking to his car when Pamela stopped him. "Hey!" she yelled, "isn't that Alan's old suit?"

Lew turned around, looking like a character from an old movie. "Yeah," he said. "I'm surprised you remember."

"How could I ever forget Alan Fain?" she said. "How long has it been now? Since he disappeared."

"Twenty years," Lew said.

"We were just kids—" she said wistfully, "crazy, dreamy kids back then."

"We didn't think so at the time," Lew said.

"Why did he do it?" she asked.

"I don't know," Lew said. "But Alan never did anything without a good reason."

*   *   *

Lew worked late, optimizing search algorithms for the new database. By the time he got home it was half past seven and time to dress for his dinner engagement with Dr. Cline. His cat followed him as he hurried up the rickety, wooden stairs. Lew stroked the kitty while he pondered his wardrobe, finally deciding just to change his tie. He carefully knotted a green bow tie, paying close attention to the symmetry of the silk as it took shape underneath his collar. Cline, a physicist, was a bit eccentric; he would appreciate the outfit. Lew admired himself in the mirror. It pleased him that he could still fit into the suit of a slim, athletic, young man.

The dull, baby blue and white tones of the '57 Ford's finish glowed warmly in the pastel light of the evening sunset as Lew rolled into the long circular driveway. He sat for a few seconds, staring into his rearview mirror. His hair had started to recede a little, and wrinkles were beginning to show around his eyes. Why, he wondered, did he feel constantly compelled to take inventory on himself, as if he were a commodity for sale?

Dr. John Cline greeted him warmly at the door. It was a large, heavy oak door with impressive fittings. The rooms inside were spacious and well appointed. Lew had always admired his friend's tastes. His anxiety began to fade as he anticipated the meal; Cline always served good wine.

"The wife and kids are away," Cline remarked as they entered the dining room. "So it's just us."

"Great," Lew said. He noticed that his friend was getting heavier.

Midway through the meal, Cline asked Lew about Pamela. "When are you two going to get married?"

Lew set his wineglass down and stared up at the chandelier. "I don't know," he said.

"What are you waiting for?" Cline asked pointedly. "A sign from above?"

"Maybe," Lew said.

"Don't hold your breath," Cline said. He set his glass down and carefully wiped the corners of his mouth with his linen napkin. "This is *it*, man. Right here. Now." The light cast angular shadows on Cline's face that made him seem more stern than usual.

"That's easy for you to say," Lew said. "You have it all . . . all this." Lew made a sweeping gesture with his fork, a piece of steak speared neatly on the end, at all Cline's luxury.

"How do you think I got it?" Cline asked. "I faced reality early in life. You don't have any more time to waste with your head in the clouds. You are pushing forty, man. What are you waiting for? A miracle?"

"Maybe," Lew said. "Maybe I am." A dreamy look had come into his eyes. He held his glass out and Cline poured some more wine. Lew looked back at the starry, glittering spokes of the chandelier, as if his miracle might come from there.

A few moments later Cline asked, "How's the job?"

"I just got turned down for a promotion," Lew said in a tone that indicated he did not want to talk about his job.

"Why?" Cline sounded concerned.

"Not aggressive enough, I guess," Lew said. "Oh hell! I really don't give a damn about that job! So what if most of the junior executives are younger than I am! So what if they are mostly incompetent! It is just a stupid *job*!"

"I would say that it is one of the few things you have going for you right now, Lew," Cline said, seriously. "A lot of young, sharp, aggressive kids would practically kill to get your job."

"I don't care," Lew said with a forced sneer.

Cline shook his head slowly. "Still the firebrand, Lew. After all these years. But think about this. Such rebellious nonconformity is tolerated by society much more readily in the young. The angry *young* man is something of a cherished figure, protected to a degree, even encouraged. But the facade begins to wear thin with the onset of middle age."

"It's not a facade," Lew said.

"Yes. I know." Cline sighed. "That's what worries me. But let's have some coffee and relax."

When they were seated comfortably in the living room, Lew on the sofa, and Cline in his leather reclining chair, the physicist said, "Sugar?" He proceeded to put several teaspoons in his coffee.

"No," Lew said. He leaned forward to avail himself of the refreshment. He poured just enough cream to transform the black liquid in the cup to a dark brown.

When Cline finished his coffee, he rose and walked into the adjacent study. He returned carrying a paperback book. Before he resumed his comfortable seat he placed the book on the coffee table. "You should have a look at this. It is more your type of thing than mine really."

They both poured more coffee from the thermal dispenser. Lew noted the cover of the book. It was black with a gold symbol in the center. The symbol was a caduceus, the coiled staff of Mercury, messenger of the gods.

He opened the book. The title page read, *Kybal: True Alchemy for the True Seeker*. The author was listed as Hermes Trismegistus. "What's this?"

"My book. Just published," Cline said.

"You *wrote* this? *You* are Hermes Trismegistus?" Lew asked, incredulous, looking back at the name on the title page.

"No, no." Cline laughed. "That's just the pen name. You know, Hermes Trismegistus is supposedly the original alchemist. No one knows if he ever really existed. Most 'authentic' texts on the subject are attributed to him, at least in part. I collaborated with a professor out in California."

The blurb on the back read, "Finally a book that reveals the secret of the philosophers' stone and the elixir of life! Find the key to the authentic experience of self. Learn how consciousness is broadcast throughout the universe on waves that travel faster than light. Understand the quantum of thought, the nouon, a subatomic particle that is immaterial yet more real than matter."

It also promised to show the "sincere reader" how to receive and decode the cosmic waves of consciousness. Supposedly this would enable one to meet his or her sexual opposite, achieve perfect sexual fusion with him or her, travel to realms of pure thought, and other nonsense.

Lew closed the book. "How could you, a scientist, seriously mess around with stuff like this?" he asked. "And what do you mean, 'It's more my sort of thing than yours'?"

"Don't kid me, Lew," Cline said. "You're a dreamer. Always were. That's your problem, too many possibilities floating around in your head. You have never been willing to accept the limits of being human."

"And this"—Lew held up the book—"shows how to transcend those limits? I really can't see you writing something like this."

"I wouldn't have if I hadn't met my collaborator. At first I thought he was just a nut. His theories were so bizarre. But he convinced me that they had a certain elegance even if they were utterly fantastic. He needed my help to lend credibility to the project. It sounded like fun, so I agreed on the condition that we would write under an assumed name. This sort of thing would not go over well in the scientific community."

"What are these theories?" Lew asked.

"Read the book." Cline smiled. "He has postulated atomic particles of thought, the quanta of cognition. People receiving communications from other realms instantaneously, that sort of thing."

"That reminds me," Lew said. He reached into his pocket and pulled the crystal out. "Look at this. What do you think it is?"

Cline took it and held it up to the light. "This is interesting. I'd like to check it out. The refractive properties are highly peculiar. Listen, I've got some equipment in the basement. I know it's late, but I would really like to do an NMR on this thing."

Cline's lab was impressive. Years of working on lucrative defense contracts had made it possible for the doctor to buy some sophisticated toys. Cline looked up from the spectral graph that he had been studying for some ten minutes. "I really don't know what to say. This thing"—he touched the crystal—"is not matter."

"Not matter?" Lew said, puzzled.

"Not in the conventional sense," Cline said. "I've double-checked and cross-checked the data. There is nothing wrong with the equipment. The thing has structure but not *atomic* structure. It is crystal*like*, but the lattice symmetry is completely foreign, unlike anything I know. There is absolutely no nuclear resonance. Unbelievable really. It is as if it were constructed of some new kind of material altogether." He was silent for a few moments, just staring at the piece, where it stood next to his data. "Where did you get it?" he finally asked.

"An old man gave it to me," Lew said.

"Who? What old man?"

"I don't know. I thought he was a bum at first, until I got a good look at him. He just dropped it in my pocket and walked away."

"Can I keep it for a while? I'd like to run some more tests," Cline said.

Lew started to agree but checked himself. "I don't know why," he said finally, "but I just can't part with it right now. It seems that I've grown rather attached to it."

"Alright," Cline said. "But you may have something that could revolutionize science here. It could be worth a lot of money if handled properly."

"Right now I am more interested in revolutionizing myself," Lew said.

"Right," said Cline. "Well it is late."

Lingering at the door, Lew said, "Sometimes I think that the reason I haven't really done anything yet is because I have an important mission that only someone without family and career responsibilities can perform. I got a mysterious phone call today from a woman. I think it has something to do with the crystal . . ."

"You really should meet the professor," Cline said.

"Who?" Lew snapped out of his reverie.

"My coauthor. This business with the crystal and the phone call—it's just his cup of tea. Too far out for me. I'll lend you the book. Maybe you can get something out of it."

Cline returned with the book and handed it to Lew, saying, "That suit's a real antique. Where did you get it?"

"It belonged to Alan. When we were roommates in college."

"Alan Fain! Of course! That suit was old when he used to wear it. It was his father's wedding suit. What are you doing with it?"

"It's a long story," Lew said, sounding very tired.

"Do you think Alan is still alive?"

"Yes," Lew said.

"He was the most brilliant man I ever knew," Cline said, wistfully.

Something about those parting words kept Lew from turning on the radio as he drove home. He cruised in silence, reflecting on his future.

Lew shivered in his apartment. He lit the old gas heater and stood in front of it, warming his ass. The phone rang.

"Hello?" Lew said.

"Lew?" It was her again.

"Who is this!" Lew said. "What do you want!" He was surprised at the anger in his voice. She started to cry.

"Lew, I'm scared. I really think I need your help." She was sobbing softly.

"How can I help you?" Lew asked, regretting his anger. "Don't cry. Please."

"Just come."

"Come where?" he asked.

"I have to go now, Lew. I'm sorry. I really have to go." The line went dead.

Lew paced furiously and slammed his fist into his palm. "Damn! Who is she?"

He opened the door at the sound of his cat scratching; the poor thing had a torn ear from a vicious cat fight. Lew picked it up and began stroking it distractedly.

The calls had awakened feelings long since buried, intimations of something beyond the ordinary, unfulfilled promises of the fantastic. And in the light of something truly mysterious the book on his sofa, the *Kybal*, with all its funny markings and arcane lore, appeared silly.

Later, restless and unable to sleep, Lew flopped down on his beat-up old sofa and picked it up. It intrigued and irritated him to know that Cline had written part of it. He turned to the section on philosophy. "Philosophically the Western conception of the universe began as a unity of thought and being. The Greeks stretched this metaphor in an attempt to account for the many entities and beings which confront us in actual existence. Later philosophical developments pushed it farther, postulating an original unity which allows fragmentation into the many, within the framework of time, and finally finds resolution at the end of time, outside of time, as the *One*."

He laid the book down on the coffee table. In principle he thought such books were ridiculous, exploitive of gullible, dissatisfied people. The *Kybal* professed to lay the innermost secrets of the ancient alchemists open to the sincere practitioner. But it also claimed that the true meaning of the text would be hidden from the reader who did not possess the "key" to the "right" reading of the text.

How convenient, he thought. The book could mean anything to anyone, absolving the authors of any responsibility
whatsoever.

Lew had a sudden, strange urge to smoke. How long had
it been since his last cigarette? One year? Two? He and Alan
used to smoke. Many a night they had stayed up late, talking
about the quest for higher consciousness, comrades in what
seemed like a great, metaphysical adventure. "Who knows
where he is now?" Lew wondered. Alan, who had said so
long ago, "You know Lew, the *One* is merely our feeble
expression for that vast being of which we are only infini-
tesimally small atoms . . ." He had dropped out of school and
disappeared shortly after that pronouncement. All efforts to
locate him had failed.

As Lew descended his rickety old stairs into a night lit by
a full moon, he recalled something else Alan had said. "To
a male the Universe is female." It was back on a beautiful
spring day, when it still seemed like anything was possible,
and Alan had said it with impish authority, as if he were a
comical guru. Lost in reflection, Lew hardly noticed when he
reached the all-night, convenience store.

"Can I help you?" The night checker sounded irritated. Lew
slipped back into the present and his purpose.

"Pack of Camel regulars," he said.

As the young girl turned to get the cigarettes, Lew said,
"Does the Universe have gender?"

"What?" She turned suddenly.

"Sex. Do you see the Universe as male or female?" he
blurted out.

"Listen," she said, slamming the pack down on the counter,
"I don't know what's wrong with you, but if you want those
cigarettes you had better pay for them. I'm not alone. My boss
is in back. He's an ex-marine."

"Fuck the marines," Lew said without thinking. "Hey, take
it easy," he added quickly when he saw the look of fear on
her face. "Just a joke. I'm doing cosmic research." He handed
her a bill.

"Well do it somewhere else," she said. "That kind of stuff
scares me."

"Sorry," Lew muttered as he walked out.

He fumbled with the pack and managed to extract a cigarette after walking half a block. He rounded a corner and instinctively increased his pace as he passed a dark alley.

"Need a light?" A voice came out of the alley. Suddenly Lew was face-to-face with a tall man in a suit.

"No thanks," Lew said, but the man had already flicked his heavy metal lighter and was holding the flame in front of Lew's face. Lew wanted to run, but a strange authority in the voice made him lean forward, ready to accept the light.

"Good God, man!" the stranger said. "You can't do that!"

"Do what?" Lew said, alarmed. The man had jerked the cigarette from his mouth.

"You can't light this end!" he said. He turned the cigarette around and offered it to Lew. "You have got to smoke the label, the blue Camel imprint. Otherwise it is the . . ."

"Curse of the camel," Lew said softly, recalling the old college smoking maxim, a secret shared by his own inner circle of friends. He looked closely as he accepted the light, this time on the "right" end of his cigarette. The man's features came alive in the dim flicker of the lighter's flame.

"Alan!" he exclaimed. "Alan Fain! My God!"

"No," Alan said, "just an ordinary mortal like yourself. How are you, Lew?"

They stared at each other for a few moments.

"Well?" Alan finally said.

"Well what?" Lew responded.

"What the hell are you doing in my suit?"

Lew threw his arms around Alan. It was the most spontaneous thing he had done in years. Suddenly it seemed as if all his problems had begun when Alan had disappeared so many years ago. He felt momentarily as if his savior had arrived out of the wilderness.

2

A Person Is a Good Place to Hide

"I don't believe it!" Alan exclaimed as they walked down Lew's driveway. The yellow streetlight, filtering through the mist, gave all objects an eerie, spectral sort of illumination.

"What?" Lew stopped next to Alan, about ten paces back from the old Ford parked in the driveway.

"The Ford!" Alan sounded euphoric. "You still have the Ford!"

"I nearly traded it for a Honda," Lew said.

Alan was walking around the car, tracing the chrome, reveling in memory. "Man!" he said, finally. "It's a living piece of history. A Honda? You couldn't."

"I didn't."

Later, when they were settled comfortably inside, Alan got up to go to the bathroom. Lew was suddenly embarrassed at the dismal state of his apartment. He hoped that Alan would not notice the mold growing on the shower curtain and the cobwebs in the corner. He quickly got up and pulled the underwear off the bed. They were Pamela's, and he paused briefly to rub them lightly across his cheek before he threw them in the closet.

"Excuse the mess," Lew said, as Alan emerged.

Alan just shrugged while settling back onto the sofa.

Lew sunk back into the green, overstuffed chair.

"So?" Lew said. The silence bothered him; Alan didn't seem to mind.

"So," Alan responded. "So it is. So it is."

"I mean . . ." Lew began, and faltered.

"Where have I been all these years?" Alan said.

"Yeah," Lew said self-consciously, looking down at the worn shag carpet.

"Not so easy, Lew. Not so easy," Alan said. He appeared calm and comfortable in his gray flannel suit. Lew was cold. "So what about you, Lew? What have you been up to?"

"Well, I've been here. More or less. Graduated from college a few years after you . . . left. There was nothing much doing in the way of jobs. I had some real lousy ones. Finally lucked out, accidentally got into computers. That's what I do now. But . . ."

"But what?"

"Hell, Alan. I can't compress twenty years into a few words!"

"Exactly," Alan said. "All in good time. All in good time."

"How about some wine?" Lew asked, getting up and walking into the kitchen. He returned with a bottle of Pinot Noir. "Romanian," Lew said. "It's cheap, but good."

Opening the bottle seemed to break the tension. He poured. "To the times that never were and all the times to come," he said, raising his glass.

Alan seemed happy with the toast. He cautiously sipped his wine while regarding his surroundings. The room was large enough to accommodate a king-size bed in one corner, the green, overstuffed chair next to the bed, and the sofa along the wall opposite the bed. In front of the sofa was a coffee table made from two old Coca-Cola crates, a pair of two-by-fours, and several pine boards. Between the bed and the overstuffed chair was a small spool table, which doubled as a nightstand for the bed and tea table for the chair.

Alan was looking down at his wineglass, which he supported with both hands in his lap. "Anyone else from the old days still around?" he asked.

"Well there's Cline," Lew said. "John Cline. He is *Doctor* Cline now, highly respected physicist. He does government work mostly. That is the money comes from the government. He consults for several large companies on weapons systems."

"Cline never was much of an idealist." Alan laughed. "What about Pamela Fine?"

"Yes," Lew said. "She's still here. Funny thing about that. We were always good friends, but I was never attracted to her. Then about two years ago, after I managed to extract myself from a pretty nasty affair with a married woman, something happened. Pamela and I were having lunch—I just looked into those green eyes and saw something I had never seen before. Well, anyway, we are practically engaged now."

"Oh," Alan said. He looked down and finished off his wine. Then he reached for the bottle and quickly poured another glass. Lew didn't notice, but for the first time since the encounter Alan was clearly uneasy. "Well . . . congratulations. I'm sure you two will be very happy."

"You know something about Pamela that was really peculiar?" Lew said.

"What's that?"

"Well, I probably shouldn't be telling you this, but when I started seeing her, you know, dating or whatever it is you call it nowadays, she was a virgin. Imagine that. A thirty-six-year-old virgin."

"And now?" Alan asked tensely.

"What do you think?" Lew smiled.

"Right," Alan said. "Right." He quickly drained his glass again. "Well, enough about you. I suppose you would like to know where the hell I have been."

"Well, yeah," Lew said.

Alan leaned forward. "I said it's not so easy to tell. But I will try. Some of it, at least is simple. Deceptively simple. You remember what I used to say about personhood?"

"No," Lew said.

"A person is a good place to hide," Alan said, with the faraway look of recollection in his eyes.

"Oh yeah, I remember that," Lew said. "You once suggested that our true identities choose to hide in 'personhood,' that is, what we think of as people, but are really masquerades."

"Do you remember the rest of it?" Alan prompted, raising his eyebrows and eyeing Lew over the wineglass.

"Yeah. Yeah, I think I do," Lew said. "You said that before a true self hides inside a 'person' he leaves clues. Or plants them, so that at some future point in time the true self can rediscover or remember itself."

"Well, I have been hiding all these years," Alan said. "And I have just found my first clue. So now I am back."

"Looking for more clues?" Lew asked warily.

"Yeah. I think so," Alan said. "Listen." He calmly reached for the wine bottle. "Reality was for me, in fact, a drag." Alan shook his head. He inhaled deeply on the Camel burning between his fingers. "Somebody should investigate, do a study," he continued.

"What do you mean?" Lew asked, puffing lightly on his cigarette.

"Where have all the good things gone?" Alan asked. It was rhetorical.

"Yeah," Lew said.

"I took it seriously, Lew, the quest for meaning." He sighed.

"Do you regret it?" Lew asked. "I mean . . . now?" he added quietly.

"When a man is desperate, he looks for miracles," Alan said, ignoring Lew's question. "I always admired those old Tibetan gurus we used to read about, those yogis up in the Himalayas. So I went there. It wasn't easy, but I found some of the authentic boys, some of the real heavy dudes. I chose to stay for a while. It was far too painful to face what had happened in the 'real world.' All the idealism of our youth was gone, evaporated back into the limitless possibility from which it sprang. I guess you could say, Lew, that the endless days of meditation in the high, secluded reaches of the Himalayas became my person. And . . ."

"A person is a good place to hide," Lew finished the sentence for Alan.

Lew got up and turned off the harsh, overhead lights. Then he lit a candle and resumed his seat. Alan's story was completely fantastic, but Lew believed it. "Did you ever . . . ?" He didn't quite know how to phrase the question.

"Ever what?" Alan asked.

"Reach anything, achieve enlightenment," Lew said, finally.

"Once I did. Only for a moment, but that moment changed my life. That was ten years ago. It took ten years of meditating to get there and ten years after the fact to get me down off those mountains and back here. But yes, I found it."

"Oh," said Lew, feeling jealous.

"And lost it," Alan said. "I got so bitter, that's why I stayed ten years too long. Trying to get it back. I tried even the most bizarre methods. We used to go down to the icy, mountain lake waters at midnight. We students would sit naked while the masters dipped sheets in the water and draped them across our shoulders. The student who dried the most sheets by dawn was proclaimed most adept in the 'yoga of the psychic heat.' I was never any damn good at it. I froze my ass off is what I did. Anyway, I finally realized that I was just playing games. It was time to move on.

"But I learned something valuable. Remember how we used to speculate that supernormal realities were locked inside our heads, and that the right trigger could open you up, cause you to experience such a reality? We tried drugs, of course, which worked for a while. When the drugs stopped working people looked all over for some other key to a greater reality.

"The unstated assumption is that all experience is inside our heads and nothing of 'life' exists out there." Alan's arms opened wide as if to embrace the whole cosmos. "But don't you see!" He became excited. "That view leads nowhere; it's a nihilistic view of reality. Isn't it more edifying, more fun to believe that our brains are like radios tuned to certain life frequencies being universally broadcast. Then the right mind-manifesting trigger, whether it's a drug, computer software, or yogic meditation, is simply like a *transducer* existing for a short time in the radio receiver, the brain that is, and enabling it to tune in to frequencies we normally can't receive. Life is *out there*, Lew. Not in here." Alan tapped his skull and smiled.

"Maybe that is what I was searching for," he continued. "Confirmation that something exists beyond myself. Those old gurus sure know it. My personal teacher explained it to me using a metaphor. He said that life is an eternal wave, broadcast throughout the cosmos. We are all surfers on that wave. If you could ever catch the ultimate wave, get that one last ride into eternity . . ." Alan sounded wistful, as if he were trying to remember something.

"What if everything in this room and, 'out there' "—Lew made a sweeping gesture—"is really just an organically engendered hallucination? We used to speculate about that, remember?"

"Of course I remember," Alan said, thoughtfully. "It could be the case. It just could be. But so what? What matters is still precisely this and only this, 'What does it mean to you?' " Alan pointed the lit end of his cigarette directly at Lew.

Lew looked away, poured another glass, and fumbled with a cigarette. "Things have only gotten worse in the 'real world,' " he said, lighting up and shaking his head. "Still no room in reality for much of anything other than the rat race of work and mortgage payments.

"Cline says that I have never been willing to accept the limits of being human," Lew continued. "He said that tonight, actually. I had dinner with him. He has a fine big house, lovely wife, and two kids."

"Yeah." Alan laughed. "John never had any doubts about those limits. He's one of the lucky ones. He's right, you know. People like us have it so much harder because we have never been able to accept the limitations as they are commonly understood. Or, more precisely, we haven't commonly understood them. But at the heart of the issue is this: Why should Cline or the president of the United States or some guru in Tibet have the authority to define the limits?"

"Exactly!" Lew said. This was the old Alan he had known and loved.

"I'm tired, Lew," Alan said.

"Well, I've got the softest sofa in the state," Lew said.

Pamela was late, grading calculus exams that night. It was eleven when she pulled into her driveway. The mail consisted of the usual junk, except for one postcard with familiar handwriting.

She was about to file it without reading it, as she had done with countless others, until she noticed the postmark. It was from San Francisco. She gasped, and put the card on her dining table. She did not read it until she had eaten dinner. Then she turned the card over: "Pamela, I'm back and coming home. Will you see me?" signed, "The man in the gray flannel suit."

She went to her study and opened a file drawer; it was filled with postcards, all from India or Tibet, all with cryptic mes-

sages she had long since stopped reading because they hurt
and made no sense. She pulled out a handful and idly thumbed
through them. "Dried my first sheet last night," said one. "It
matters not if each atom occupies its own space or shares. Is
space quantized, darling?" And "Stop the train of thought or
ride it to the very end. It is all the same: Eternal bliss, my
love!"

Suddenly she was crying. She put all the cards, including
the new one, back and slammed the drawer. "Damn!" she said.
"Damn you, Alan Fain!"

Lew was too drunk to hear the familiar sounds on his steps,
but not Alan. When the door opened he pulled the blankets
over his head. As she passed she did not even look in the
direction of the sofa, where he watched as she undressed in
the moonlight. Her body was the same, supple and creamy
pale. The breasts hung a little lower, and her hips were slightly more full than he remembered, but even in the moonlight
he could see those green eyes flash with the old fire.

It was like that the last time he saw her twenty years ago.
He held her close after she had made herself naked in front
of him for the first time, offering herself to him for what they
both knew could be the last time. How he now regretted his
refusal! "No," was all he said, but it had taken everything he
had to say it.

"I'll wait for you then," she said.

"No you won't. I don't know if I'm coming back." Alan
brought himself back to the present, where Pamela was sliding into bed beside his best friend. He rolled over and willed
his breath to the rhythm of sleep. Years of hard discipline
made that possible but could not prevent the painful dreams
that came.

"Lew," Pamela whispered.

"Ummm." Lew rolled over, and Pamela smelled the heavy
breath of alcohol.

"Never mind," she said, softly. "Just hold me."

She was up early as usual, making coffee in the nude when
someone said, "Good morning, Pamela."

She turned with a start and dropped the filter, spilling fresh
coffee grounds down her smooth belly. "My God!" she said.
"Alan!"

"Let me help." He bent down to pick up the filter, and could not keep from looking up at her thighs and the downy, red tuft between her legs. She backed off, covering herself.

"Sorry," he said, standing up quickly and looking away as he handed her the filter.

"Oh Alan!" she rushed forward and embraced him. He pulled her close and hugged.

"What's going on?" Lew said, standing at the kitchen door in his underwear and scratching his stomach. Pamela quickly ran to the closet and grabbed a robe.

"Sorry, Lew," Alan said.

"No problem," Lew said. "You two are old friends. Pamela always runs around in the buff. My head is killing me." He groaned.

"Let me make the coffee," Alan said. He put the water on.

"Lew, why didn't you tell me?" Pamela asked accusingly.

"Tell you what?"

"That Alan was back!"

"Oh," Lew said. "I guess I wasn't in any condition to tell you much of anything last night."

Pamela reached inside her robe and dug a coffee ground from her navel. She dropped it into the filter and shot Alan a sharp glance. He met her gaze and held it for a moment before she quickly looked away.

When Lew was dressed, he said, "I have to go in today. Project that can't wait. Why don't you drive me to work, Alan? You can have the car. If Pamela will take the day off, she can show you around the old city."

"You know I can't cancel classes," she said.

"Offer's still good," Lew said. "About the car I mean . . ."

Alan had some trouble with the car. "No cars at the ashram," he explained, "but I'll get the hang of it again. Where does Pamela work?" he asked, as Lew was getting out in front of the downtown, glass building.

"Junior college," Lew said. "She teaches math. It's a comedown for her. She once had bright prospects, could have become another Einstein according to some people."

"Yeah," Alan sighed. "I'll bet."

"We'll all get together for dinner, OK?" Lew asked.

"Sure." Alan fumbled the clutch, burning rubber as he shot

into traffic. Lew watched a near miss with a cab and then went inside.

Susan looked uneasy as Lew passed by the front office. "Slack! Is that you?" It was Phelps. Susan shrugged her shoulders as Lew shot her a questioning glance and went into the boss's office.

"Where the hell have you been?" Phelps said. "It's almost nine."

"Same time I always come in," Lew said. "We agreed. Remember?"

"Oh." Phelps looked nervous. "Well, cancel the agreement. From now on it is eight sharp. And what happened to the suit?"

"It didn't seem to make much difference," Lew said.

"Coat and tie. Starting tomorrow," Phelps said.

"Does this mean I get the promotion?" Lew asked.

"Who said anything about a promotion? We have a new contract is all. You're the only man qualified for it, I'm afraid. The requirements were very specific. We were lucky to get this thing, too. It's worth a lot of money, so I hope"—Phelps looked Lew in the eye and lowered his voice—"that you can handle it."

"What?" Lew said. "Handle what?"

"Our contact will be here shortly," Phelps said. "He'll explain everything. That's all."

Alan drove back to Lew's apartment. He was pacing when the phone rang. He grabbed the receiver anxiously. "Hello? What? You're here! When? Tonight? Well sure, alright.

"Listen, there is a new complication," Alan said. "It's Pamela. Remember the woman I told you about? I thought I was beyond all that, but . . ."

There was a chuckle at the other end of the line and then, "The redhead? I know what you mean. I could never resist that extra texture, that fire down below . . ."

"It's not just that!" Alan said. "I still love her!"

"I'm sure."

"Well?" Alan asked.

"Well what?"

"So what do I do?"

"Why ask me?"

"You're the one who got me back here. I was perfectly encapsulated back in the high Himalayas until you showed up! I'm asking you for advice, man! Help!"

"Yes, I understand. These sexual matters are often more complicated than one might suppose from a distance. I don't know that there is much of anything I can tell you, though. When you say you love her that just about rules out all conventional analysis."

"Thanks," Alan said.

"We'll talk about it tonight."

"We can't," Alan said. "Not if Lew is there. He and Pamela are . . ."

"Oh that's right," the voice chuckled again. "Interesting."

Lew was steaming in his office. He was trying to get the nerve to go tell Phelps what he really thought when his phone rang. "Lew?" It was Phelps.

"Yeah," he said, not bothering to conceal his contempt.

"The contact is here. Meet us in the conference room. And Lew?"

"What?"

"Try not to be so sullen."

Lew walked into the conference room, where Phelps and another man were talking. He cleared his throat and the two turned around. Lew gulped when he saw the contact. It was the old man who had given him the crystal. After introductions, the old guy winked at Lew and put his finger to his lips.

"The professor is from Sofia Systems," Phelps said when they were seated around the big table. "I told him about you, Lew, and we both agreed that this project is just your kind of thing. Right, professor?"

Before the old man could say anything, Lew blurted out, "It doesn't have anything to do with defense, does it? I won't work on bomb projects!"

Phelps turned red. He was furious and trying not to show it. "I'm sure whatever *moral* objections you may have are of no interest to the professor," he said.

"On the contrary," the professor said. "I completely concur with Mr. Slack. It is of the utmost importance that each of us is able to give full commitment, moral and otherwise. Without that, I'm afraid the project hasn't the slightest chance of success. If there is any question about that, then I am wasting my time here." He looked directly at Phelps.

"No question at all!" Phelps said quickly. "Right, Lew?" When Phelps turned to Lew, the professor caught Lew's eye. Lew smiled in spite of himself.

"Just what is the project?" Lew asked.

"Not so easy. Not so easy to explain," the professor said. "Mr. Phelps, I don't quite know how to put this—you are the president of the company, but we at Sofia Systems have run this thing on a strict 'need to know' basis."

Phelps just looked at the professor, not comprehending.

"And the only person here who needs to know more about the specific nature of project Asklepios is Lew," the professor continued.

Slowly it dawned on Phelps, and he clearly did not like it. "Of course," he said. "I'm an old army intelligence man myself." He forced a smile. "If I can be of any further assistance . . ." he added with extreme difficulty.

"Thank you," the professor said with easy authority. "That will be all for now."

When they were alone, the professor leaned forward and said in a low voice, "There is an old saying . . ."

"What?" Lew asked.

"Money talks and bullshit walks."

Four hours later Lew was back in his office, alone and hungry. He called his place and Alan answered. "Lew," Alan said. "I'm glad you called. What are you doing tonight?"

"Well, I thought we would all get together for dinner," Lew said.

"Lew, I didn't tell you everything last night."

"What didn't you tell me, Alan."

"I didn't come down from the Himalayas voluntarily. I would have stayed there indefinitely if I hadn't met someone."

"Who?" Lew asked.

"He was there doing research," Alan said. "On consciousness. He worked extensively with my guru on some of the concepts we discussed last night—you know—the idea that

life and consciousness are broadcast throughout the cosmos
as a kind of wave . . . the Asklepian wave, I think he calls
it. But that's beside the point. He took an interest in me and
convinced me that it was time to come back, recast my lot
with the living so to speak."

"Yeah," Lew said—he was beginning to have an uneasy
feeling, as though he had heard all about it already. "So
what?"

"So he's here."

"Who is here?"

"My friend, my *benefactor* I guess you could call him,"
Alan said. "He wants to meet you tonight. I told him it was
OK. It's all set if you're up for it. He's agreed to meet us at
his favorite restaurant. It's expensive and it's on him."

"Sure," Lew said. "But right now I've got to get lunch. Are
you interested? I could meet you downtown."

"No thanks, Lew," Alan said. "I've got some things I want
to do."

Lew sat for a few moments, staring at his monitor. It was
just too much. He grabbed his jacket and started out.

Phelps stopped him at the elevator. "I have been instructed
by the professor that from now on you keep your own hours,"
the boss said tightly. "It is highly irregular, but I don't care so
long as we keep him happy."

"Coat and tie?" Lew said with a vicious smile.

"You wear what you please." Phelps nearly choked on the
words. "But Lew . . ."

"Yes?"

"You screw this thing up and it's your ass." He stalked
off.

Alan continued to pace in Lew's apartment. Finally he
grabbed the phone book and got the number for the mathematics office at the junior college. "Pamela Fine, please," he
said to the receptionist.

"She won't be in today, sir. I believe she is ill."

"Do you have her home number?"

"I'm sorry sir. We are not allowed to give that information
over the telephone."

Alan looked it up and dialed.

"Hello." It was Pamela.

"Pamela," Alan said.

"What?"

"I've got to see you."

"No," she said.

"But I love you!"

"What good can it possibly do?"

"Please?"

She was sitting in her living room when he arrived. "Sit over there," she said, indicating a chair on the other side of the coffee table.

"Did you get my cards?" he asked.

"Yes. Lew and I are getting married, Alan."

"Do you love him?"

"What business is that of yours? You disappear for twenty years and then all of a sudden . . ."

"Do you love him?"

She said nothing.

"Because we had something that has only grown stronger for me," he said and approached her.

"That kind of love is over!" she said getting up quickly and moving away. "We were kids! Crazy, passionate kids. I waited for a long time. But then I grew up, Alan. Love is a choice. I am thirty-eight years old. I want to have a baby! I want a life! Lew and I have made that choice together, and you aren't any part of it."

"Do you love him?" Alan persisted, following her. "The way I love you. The way I think you loved me. Say yes and I will leave. Say yes and I will never mention it again." He was very close to her now. He could smell her, and it nearly made him swoon with memories of twenty years past. "That kind of love isn't over for me. It never will be. Tell me it isn't over for you."

"Oh Alan," she sighed and looked up at him, mouth open, lips moist.

He kissed her.

Lew called. Pamela answered from her bed, Alan asleep beside her. She instinctively pulled the sheet over her breasts as she picked up the receiver. "Pamela?"

"Hello, Lew," she said.

"Are you alright? I called your office and they said . . ."

"Yes, I'm fine. Just tired."

"Listen, about dinner tonight. Alan wants me to meet an important friend of his. I know you wanted a dinner alone so we could talk, but . . ."

"It's OK," she said. "You two go on without me."

"Are you sure? Don't you want to come?"

"No. I need to rest."

"Pamela?"

"Yes."

"I love you."

"Yes."

"I really do think I want to get married. Have that baby," he said.

"Alright, Lew. We'll talk about it later."

"Are you sure you're alright?"

"Yes. I'm just very tired."

Alan insisted that they dress for dinner. "The professor has expensive tastes," he said. The only real suit Lew had was Alan's old herringbone. "It's a little big on you," Alan pointed out as he put the finishing touches on his tie. Alan's shoulders were slightly broader than Lew's.

"Close enough," Lew said.

On the way to the restaurant Alan said, "So you and Pamela are getting married?"

"Well I haven't formally proposed," Lew said. "But yeah, I'm committed now."

The professor was waiting for them at a corner table. Seated next to him was Dr. Cline. Both men wore tuxedos.

"Oh no!" Lew muttered to himself when he saw the white-haired old man for the second time that day, although he was not really surprised.

"Good evening, gentlemen." The professor stood. "We all know each other, so I will pass on the introductions, although I think it has been a long time for Alan and Dr. Cline."

Alan and Cline shook hands. "My God!" Cline said. "I, for one, never expected to see you again. You're certainly looking fit."

"Good to see you, John," Alan said. "It *has* been a long time."

When they were seated Alan said, "I don't understand.

You two have already met?" He looked at Lew and then the professor.

"It is a small world," the professor said merrily as he poured wine for everyone. "Lew and I are working together. My company, Sofia Systems, has contracted with Lew's outfit. That is, in fact, what brings me to town." He proposed a toast. "Here's to old friends and new!"

Lew was silently staring at Dr. Cline. "And you, John?" he said finally. "What is your association with Sofia Systems?"

"None," Cline said cheerfully. "But the professor here is my coauthor. Remember the book I showed you?"

"This one," Alan said, pulling his paperback copy of the *Kybal* from his coat pocket.

"Yes," Cline said. "That one."

"I see," said Lew, looking at the professor, who was calmly studying the menu.

"I recommend the veal," the professor said, "although I hear the fish is excellent."

Plates full and a second bottle opened, the professor said, "This gathering is more than a social event. I apologize for the haste and the mystery. It really is quite straightforward. I explained the nature of project Asklepios to Lew this morning at his office. Dr. Cline and Alan are both aware of certain specifics. But I thought a meeting of the minds would be both fruitful and enjoyable." He carefully cut a small slice of tender, white veal.

Lew had just taken a bite of his steak when the professor suddenly said, "Lew, hand me the crystal."

"This, gentlemen," the professor said, having stood the crystal on the white tablecloth, "is no mystery. This is what the ancient alchemists all sought. Crystallized thought, pure *nous*, the philosophers' stone!"

Pamela sat at her desk. She was past tears now as she shuffled through the stack of postcards. Some two hundred in all, about one a month. She remembered how frantic she had been when Alan first missed a month. But years passed. Finally, after thirteen years of waiting and reading, she made a conscious decision to put them out of mind, read no more, file them away.

They had decided to keep their love secret. Why, she could

not remember, if she ever knew; it seemed right at the time.
There was to be no mention of Alan to anyone while he was
on his quest.

For Pamela the mysteries of life were tangible things that
existed in the immediate present. She did not understand what
it was about men that compelled them to look elsewhere. Alan
was an extreme case, but even Lew, in his mediocre manner,
lived as if there were something to attain, some new state—
as if he might arrive there one day and find what it was he
needed. *What a waste!* she thought, *to let life slip by like that,
never suspecting that it was right in front of you all along*.

She made a little postcard house and blew gently on the
structure. It quietly collapsed. *Like my careful plans for a life*,
she thought.

"Any questions?" The professor smiled as he studied his
cheesecake. Alan said nothing; Cline was too engrossed in his
apple pie.

"Just one," Lew said.

"What's that?"

"Why me? My experience is limited, and I have never done
theory of any kind. I am strictly an applications man."

"So am I," the professor said. "So am I. Results come from
doing, not thinking. When I was in Tibet I gathered my final
corroborating data from the adept who was Alan's special
teacher in these matters. I immediately recognized him as a
man who knew how to get results. I don't know how much
he told you, but Alan Fain has had remarkable experiences in
the application of the most rarefied and refined techniques of
intellection.

"I knew it was time to put together a team to coordinate
my efforts, bring a lifetime of research to fruition. Dr. Cline
I already knew from our literary collaboration. Alan assured
me that there was at least one other man who shared his passion for the quest. And that, Lew, is far more important than
any degree or résumé." He held Lew's gaze for a moment, and
Lew again had the uneasy feeling that he should recognize this
old man.

"One more thing," Lew said. "I am taking some risks here,
getting involved in this thing."

"I can't lie to you about that," the professor said, looking down at the check, which he held lightly just over his napkin. "There are risks. Calculated risks which I believe are worth taking, but . . ."

"I don't mean that kind of risk," Lew said. "I'm talking about my job. My career. If this thing fails, I'm fired. Now that I plan to get married soon, and hopefully have a child, security suddenly takes on a new dimension of importance."

The professor laughed, which Lew found extremely irritating. "I wouldn't, any one of us, worry too much about that," he said, dropping the check and reaching into the inside pocket of his tux jacket. "Project Asklepios is very well funded. Before I forget I would like to give you each an advance." He opened a leather wallet and pulled out some checks, which he proceeded to pass around.

Alan merely glanced at his and put it away. Lew gawked at the amount—$10,000. He looked at Cline, who gave a sly, knowing nod, then at the professor, who observed, "A drop in the bucket, gentlemen. This calls for a last toast." He raised his glass and waited for the others to reciprocate. "To project Asklepios!" he said, smiling at Lew.

The professor's glass slipped from his fingers as it met Lew's. For the first time Lew saw the professor slightly ill at ease. The spilled wine did not seem to bother him, but he had some difficulty retrieving the glass. His fingers were a little stiff. "Old injury," he said. Lew glimpsed a long scar on the professor's wrist. He rubbed it slightly before pouring himself another glass. Lew felt a burning desire to ask about the scar, but the cuff of the professor's sleeve fell back into place, removing the wound from sight. Lew kept quiet since the professor was obviously anxious to have the incident forgotten.

"Do you think he's legitimate?" Lew asked Alan as they drove home.

"Yes," Alan said. "The professor knows what he's doing. Whatever the outcome, there will be some interesting results. I wouldn't have come back if I didn't think so."

The professor turned his Jaguar sedan toward Cline's home. The doctor was waiting for him when he arrived. "Everyone's asleep," Cline whispered at the door. They went down to his basement laboratory.

"You still have my original specifications?" the professor asked when they were seated.

"Yes, I do," Cline said. "I can build it, but . . ."

"Will it work?" the professor asked.

"I'm still not sure what it is supposed to do," Cline said.

"The nouancer will just allow us to amplify the action of the crystal. We should be able to access nouspace with precision. It should make it possible to pick up extremely subtle nouonic vibrations and, eventually, to penetrate nouspace itself. I am most excited by that prospect. It is, as far as I'm concerned, the whole thrust of project Asklepios," the professor said.

"That's another thing," Cline said. "If I understand correctly, you plan to send Lew into this 'nouspace.' "

"Yes."

"Well, frankly . . ." Cline said, "I like Lew. He's bright, has potential, always has, but do you really think he can handle it?"

"If we do our part, Lew can do his. Rest assured," the professor said. "That is the one thing of which I am certain." Cline, lethargic from the food and drink, failed to notice the twinkle in his colleague's eyes.

"*Nous*," Alan said. They were back in Lew's apartment, moonlight flooding the room. "It is the ancient Greek word for 'intellect.' But it can denote any mental phenomenon, logical analysis, imagination, dreaming . . ." His voice trailed off as if he were beginning to dream.

"This *nouspace*," Lew said suddenly, causing Alan to snap out of his meditation. "The professor hinted that you had been there."

"So they tell me," Alan said. "My guru claimed that I was not yet advanced enough in my mental control to retain unbroken consciousness through the transition back to ordinary space-time. He insists that I went there on several occasions, but I have no recollection of it."

"If this thing is so valuable," Lew said, holding the crystal up where it split a moonbeam, casting creamy colors on the sofa and Alan's face, "why would he anonymously drop it in my pocket like that?"

"The professor is prone to dramatics," Alan said. "And I think it was part of the experiment. The nouonic pulse, or the Asklepian wave as he sometimes calls it, resonates in the crystal, but without the amplification of the nouancer it is an extremely subtle effect. Had you been looking, expecting something unusual, it is possible the interference of your own thought processes would have completely blocked any real resonance from nouspace."

"And now . . ." Lew said, staring hard at the thing in his hand.

"Now that the gulf has been breached," Alan said, "there is an affinity established between your own unique mental 'fingerprint' and certain entities in nouspace."

"I really can't believe it," Lew said.

"It doesn't matter. I told you that reality is 'out there,' not trapped inside our skulls. This is proof."

"So I am to be a receiver for these Asklepian vibrations," Lew said. "Merely a tool for scientific research. I am being used, Alan. Why couldn't he have given the thing to someone else?" Lew said.

"You can stop now, if you choose," Alan said.

"But I can't choose," Lew said. "And he knows it."

"What about Pamela?" Alan asked.

"What about her?" Lew said.

"Are you still going to marry her?"

"I can't explain it," Lew said, "but now that I'm on the verge of the unknown I truly feel, for the first time in my life, compelled to marry, have kids, settle down to a quiet, normal life."

"But is it fair?" Alan asked.

"What do you mean?"

"Fair to Pamela. Things could go wrong. You may even be gone for a period of time," Alan said.

"I guess it is myself that I'm really concerned with right now," Lew said, "not her."

3

Eternity Road

"What we need from you," the professor was explaining to Lew in his office, "is a device driver." They were drinking the professor's coffee. He insisted that the stuff Susan made was swill.

Lew leaned way back in his chair with his feet propped up on the desk. "I can write device drivers," he said. "No sweat."

"This isn't for a printer or a disk drive," the professor said. "This is software for a machine that has yet to be built, the Asklepian nouancer. But you can get started. I've written a pre-compiler which will allow you to test your code on the existing hardware." He patted the terminal on Lew's desk. "Success will finally depend on speed. Your main job will be to optimize certain search algorithms. Are you up to it?"

"One of my specialties," Lew said.

"I thought so. The pre-compiler and skeleton code are already on your system, filed under 'nous.' "

Lew was leaving for lunch when Susan stopped him. "Aren't you even going to sign out?" she asked.

"No more of that." Lew grinned. "Boss's orders."

"I haven't seen you all morning," she complained. "Not even for coffee." Lew usually stopped to chat with Susan around ten o'clock, when she would make a fresh pot of coffee. It was an informal arrangement, one of those things that helped them both get through the day.

"The professor brought his own today," Lew said. "Some kind of gourmet stuff."

"Oh," she said. "There is something strange about that old guy."

"He's a genius," Lew said. "And he just may be my ticket out of this dump. By the way, how is the goddess business going? Have you found your 'wild woman' yet?"

Lew keenly felt how the change in his status and his teasing hurt Susan's feelings. The camaraderie between them was threatened. But he was also thrilled by a new coldness. It gave him a wicked sense of power to snuff out the old sympathy that had made them friends. He would not let it bring him down. *Too bad about all the Susans of the world*, he thought as he walked away.

That night at dinner Pamela was distracted; it was difficult for her to focus on what Lew was saying. "This thing came along at just the right time." He said. "Don't you see? We can get married, buy a nice big house, have a kid . . . after the successful completion of the project, of course."

"Lew," she said, "how do you know the money will still be there when the project is over?"

"Have some faith, Pamela!" he said. "That's what's wrong with you! You can never see beyond what is ordinary and practical!"

She was shocked at his sudden anger—it was not the Lew she knew.

And he sensed a subtle change in her. "What is it? Don't you want to marry me now? Now that I am about to be successful? Are you *threatened* by it . . ."

"Oh Lew." She quickly looked away to conceal her hurt.

"I'm sorry," he said. "Things are happening so fast. I . . ."

"It's OK." She recovered quickly. "Let's just not talk about it for a while."

She didn't invite him in, said she needed to be alone for a while. He tried not to worry about it as he drove home.

Alan was stretched out on the couch, reading from the *Kybal*, when Lew walked in. "Listen to this," Alan said. "The original creative act of the *One* produces the first great derived reality, nous, intellect, or spirit—from this again comes soul, which forms and orders the entire physical Universe.

"Nous is eternal. The levels of being are not spatially separate or cut off from each other. They are really distinct but all intimately present in every part of the Universe and each one of us. To ascend through soul to intellect and intellect to the *One*, we do not have to travel in space to another world, but we must wake to a new kind of awareness."

Lew pulled the crystal out of his pocket. "This thing is starting to affect me," he said.

"How?" Alan put the book down.

"It's hard to describe, but I have a new sense of power. It is as if I can read minds . . . almost. What was impossible is now easy, or so it seems. I don't know, Alan. It's weird."

"Well it should be," Alan said thoughtfully. "What you have there is pure, crystallized intellect, nous."

"But what *is* it?" Lew asked, putting it down on the coffee table.

"Well I would have said that it isn't any *thing*, in the material sense, at all," Alan said. "But the professor has proved me wrong there." He touched the crystal.

"And who is she—the woman I saw?"

"A figment of your imagination," Alan said.

"She was not!" Lew said furiously. "I saw her! I spoke to her!"

"Hey take it easy," Alan said. "You don't understand. According to the professor, a figment of the imagination is as real as you or I, it just exists in a different place, nouspace."

"Sorry," Lew said, "but that is absurd. To suppose that any thought, any flight of fancy is a real thing somewhere else, in nouspace or whatever."

"Yeah . . . probably absurd . . ." Alan said.

Pamela idly shuffled the postcards on her desk.

How charming, she thought. *Alan spent twenty years of his life floating in and out of various transcendental dream states and these postcards are the result.*

In order to shut herself off from it all she turned back to her work, pure mathematics. She loved mathematics not so much for its logic, but for its seductive beauty. While it never deceived, as so much in life did, it teased and enticed. For the one who knew how to probe it, mathematics was a beautiful labyrinth, full of mystery and occasional delights.

Somewhat of an anomaly as a woman in mathematics, she was even more so because of her chosen field, singularity groups.

They were hers. She had discovered them and written her dissertation on the subject. It won her instant recognition as a bright, new talent. Unfortunately that was all. Singularity groups were now regarded as mildly interesting, certainly an excellent subject for a Ph.D. dissertation, but good for little else, a mathematical dead end. She could have easily taken up a more lucrative field, possibly computer applications, but she refused to compromise her work for a career.

When no university would hire her she took a job at the local junior college and quietly continued her research. Had she been a man, things might have turned out differently . . . but she wasn't and glad of it.

"In a sense it is the difference between thought and idea," the professor said. Lew was only half listening. "Thoughts flutter about all the time; an idea is something else."

"How so?" Lew asked lazily.

"An idea is composed of many thoughts," the professor said, "but not in a random way. An idea is a highly structured aggregate of thoughts, bound together by an essential relationship which is, paradoxically, the idea itself."

"What has that got to do with the software I'm supposed to write?" Lew asked.

"As the crystal resonates to your mental activity," the professor said, "it will transmit your thoughts to the nouancer, which will have the capacity to amplify those thoughts. But mere amplification of thought isn't enough. You have only to stop and examine the random flow of thoughts in your mind at any point to appreciate that. Most of it is rather useless. Ask Alan; he has spent years doing just that, examining in minute detail the stream and flux of his own mind. Amplification will only produce a lot of gibberish. Interesting gibberish, no doubt, but not what we are after."

"What are we after?" Lew asked.

"Nous," the professor said. "Real intellect. Unprocessed, amplified thought is merely the by-product of real intellectual activity and exists on the fringes of nouspace. We want to penetrate to the heart of nouspace itself."

"And where is that exactly?" Lew asked.

"To say it is nowhere is to misrepresent things," said the professor. "The question makes no sense; you might as well ask what color is five o'clock? Where is an idea? Just because you cannot give it space-time coordinates—does that mean that a thought is 'nowhere'? Hardly. The 'where' of a thought is, in some sense, more real, more concrete, than the 'where' of your head.

"Anyway, the point is that without your software we will certainly get some interesting results. You will be able to hear what goes on inside your mind with startling clarity. But it won't take you anywhere, certainly no closer to the source than you already are. Your software will process raw thoughts, sort, file, and reconstitute them into *ideas*. And idea is the fundamental unit of language. I have incorporated a semiotic extrapolation algorithm into the software, one that will allow the contents of nouspace to manifest as syntactically correct English. We can then *hear* the nouscape, read it like a book, and hopefully guide you there."

"How is Cline doing?" Lew asked.

"The nouancer is almost ready to test," the professor said. This made Lew uneasy. He was having trouble with the software. It was too advanced; the professor had incorporated technique and theory in the skeleton code that pushed the art of programming into the next century.

"You'll do just fine," the professor said, sensing Lew's uneasiness. "Give it some time. It will sort out and practically write itself if you stick with it.

"One more thing, Lew," the professor said as he was leaving.

"What's that?"

"Now that you have an opening into nouspace, via the crystal, you may notice subtle changes. For example, I wouldn't be surprised if you felt you had new mental powers."

"Yes . . ." Lew said, warily.

"Don't let it go to your head. We have a long way to go yet. You will only jeopardize the project if you start showing off, not to mention the damage you could cause."

"Damage?" Lew asked.

"Just be careful. Try to maintain some balance, some humility."

*   *   *

Phelps sponsored a company happy hour that evening, something he had not done in a long time. Free drinks and free food brought about half the office staff out after work. Lew was there.

"How's the project going, Lew?" Phelps asked, slurping a beer.

"Fine," Lew muttered.

"Don't get me wrong," Phelps said. "I'm not trying to pry. The professor assures me you are doing an excellent job. I'm just curious. Rumor has it that this could be something big, revolutionary."

Lew eyed Phelps coldly. He wondered why he had ever felt threatened by the man. "Oh it's big," Lew said, sipping his beer.

"Can you just give me a little hint? When this thing is all over, you're going to be a pretty big man around here," he said.

"*If* I'm still here," Lew said.

"Oh we want you to stay!" Phelps said anxiously. "I know morale hasn't been very good lately. That's why I had this little party. We want to keep people happy. Our *good* people that is." He tried a sly wink which failed and looked like a nervous tic.

At one time Lew might have been sympathetic at this point, shown a little friendliness. But he felt ruthless. He set his beer down on the table and moved closer to Phelps. He put his arm around the man and said, "We *are* on the verge of something big."

"Oh." Phelps was uneasy, unsure whether he was being taken into confidence or being had.

"Yes. We are building a cosmic radio," Lew said, his eyes boring into his boss. "This is the real thing. And there may not be room for tired, old managers who read Castaneda when we are done. You might have to find a new power spot." Then he threw his head back and laughed hard, loud and long. It was a wicked sound, and he loved it. Phelps was completely devastated, on the verge of tears.

Lew picked up his beer and chugged it, unaware of Susan's presence next to him. He tossed the empty on the table and started to leave when she caught his eye. "Lew," she said, "what's happened to you?" He looked down and rapidly walked out.

He picked up a six-pack on the way home. Alan was stretched out on the sofa when he walked in. "Why don't you get a job?" he said, meaning it to be funny but sounding hostile instead.

"I can get a place of my own." Alan said. "I've got money . . ."

"I'm sorry," Lew said. "I didn't mean it that way. I was just kidding. Have a beer." He tossed a can toward the couch.

"I don't know what it is," Lew said, popping a top. "I feel so powerful, like I can do anything. The old limits no longer apply. It's kind of scary. Pamela senses it. I think she's backing away from me. Would you try to talk to her for me?"

"She won't talk to me either," Alan said. "I think I remind her too much of the past."

"Oh," Lew said. Much later, after Alan fell asleep, Lew opened a bottle of wine. He knew he was drinking too much, but he convinced himself that he needed it.

He was lying on the shag carpet, playing with his cat, Felix, when he got a sudden urge to look at the crystal. He put it between himself and the cat. Felix's eyes opened wide and the animal backed cautiously away from it, emitting a low growl.

Lew grabbed the cat with one hand and picked up his glass of red wine with the other. Sipping the wine and getting quite drunk, he started playing a game with the cat and the crystal. He would hold Felix's face in front of the reflective surface until the poor kitty became terrified of the yellow eyes which danced around and stared back. Then he would hold the cat close and speak to it, saying things like, "Please remember, kitty-kat, that there are those of us who disagree with you about the eating of raw mice, about the bizarre sexual practices of felines, and many other things. Please remember that a human is just as credible an animal as you." The cat would respond with a lazy stretch and Lew would collapse in hysterical laughter onto the floor.

This went on until the bottle was almost empty and Lew spilled the rest on the carpet. "Damn!" he said, and noticed that the cat's eyes in the crystal were moving, seemingly of their own volition. He held Felix up to the crystal; and the cat hissed loudly and vanished, sucked into the depths of light and nous.

"Felix! Felix!" Lew called, not believing his eyes. Then he lay down and cried. "You stupid fool!" he kept muttering over and over again to himself.

"The nouancer is ready to test," Cline said. The professor nodded.

"What about the software?" Cline asked.

"Lew is having some difficulty," the professor said.

"I was worried about that."

"Well I'm not," the professor said. "What Lew doesn't realize is that the code I gave him is nearly complete. There's very little he has to do. He's just overwhelmed right now by the complexity of it."

"Then why have him worry with it at all?" Cline asked.

"Because I want Lew to have some understanding of the system," the professor said. "I could have done it all myself, but the more he knows about how all this works, the better."

"Oh. More brandy?" Cline poured another round.

"I am worried about something else, though," the professor said, holding his glass in both hands.

"What is that?"

"I've had some experience with this myself. Lew is beginning to get that dangerous look in his eye. As his thought processes become more attuned to the Asklepian wave, through the influence of the crystal, he is liable to become unbalanced."

"Unbalanced?"

"Yes. Overconfident. He will develop a new, more refined mental prowess. That much is real. But the temptation to use it to fight old battles which are no longer relevant may become too great. I think it's already happening. Once it starts, the process can accelerate rapidly. Lew could endanger the entire project."

"How?"

"By doing something really stupid," the professor said.

"So?"

"So we may have to act faster than I had planned. We will test the hardware tomorrow—without the software, and if Lew doesn't finish with his part soon, I will have to do it myself."

*   *   *

Lew felt terrible, hung over, and sick about his beloved cat, Felix, as he drove to work. Susan stared at him as he walked by without saying anything. Phelps called to apologize.

"Apologize for what?" Lew asked, remembering his own shabby behavior at the happy hour.

"For prying yesterday evening," the boss said. "I know you can't talk about the project for security reasons."

All Lew's guilt evaporated in anger at Phelp's weakness. The man should be furious with him; instead, he was sucking up, trying to curry favor. It took all his remaining self-control to say, "No need to apologize, Mr. Phelps. We all have our jobs to do. You do yours, and I will do mine."

"Exactly." Phelps sounded relieved. "And Lew?"

"Yes?"

"The board meets tomorrow. Can you come?"

"Me?"

"They want to hear about Asklepios, and I can't tell them very much."

"OK," Lew said.

"Lew . . ." Phelps continued nervously, voice cracking, "I hope that . . . what I mean to say is that I'm not real popular with some of the major shareholders. If you could say something good . . . about management, I mean . . ."

"Don't worry," Lew said. "I won't rock the boat."

"Thank you, Lew. Thank you so much."

"Sure," Lew said, hiding his revulsion at the man's spinelessness.

The phone rang again. It was Susan. "There is someone out here to see you, Lew," she said, coldly.

"Who is it?"

"A Mr. Alan Fain."

"Send him back," Lew said and hung up.

Alan wanted to see the computer code. "I was into math, before I left, remember?" he said. "I guess I missed all this computer stuff, though."

Lew printed the section of code that he was working on, the most perplexing piece. Alan didn't understand the programming language, but when Lew drew a diagram of the encapsulated data structures and algorithms, Alan said, "Hey! That looks like a singularity group."

"A what? Isn't that Pamela's field?" Lew asked.

"Pamela?" Alan asked, surprised.

"Yeah," Lew said. "She discovered them; that was her Ph.D. dissertation. How do you know anything about them?"

"I don't know," Alan said, scratching his head. "Now that you ask me, I can't recall having ever studied them. Curious . . ." Alan again felt as if he should remember something. He closed his eyes, but after a few moments of intense concentration he gave up. "Hopeless," he muttered. He looked up and shook his head. "But none of that matters right now." His voice suddenly brightened. "Look at this." Alan diagrammed the elementary singularity group and explained the basic algebraic structure. "So it looks to me," he concluded, "that all you have to do is map the canonical homomorphism onto this structure, take the resulting factor group, and the identity element will be the hash key you are looking for."

"Incredible," Lew said, "but I think you're right."

"I didn't see Felix this morning, Lew," Alan said.

Lew looked down at the code on his desk. "He's alright," he said in forced tones. "You know tomcats. They disappear for days, sometimes weeks. He's done it before."

Alan called Pamela after he left Lew's office.

"It is over," she said.

"How? How can you say that, after . . ."

"It was wonderful, Alan," she said. "But that kind of love is too unpredictable. It's fine for kids, but . . ."

"So you're going to marry Lew," he said.

"Maybe."

"Pamela, what do you know about singularity groups?" Alan asked suddenly.

She balked at the question. "Singularity groups? Why do you ask? I know practically everything there is to know about them. I discovered them."

"When?"

"When what?"

"When did you discover them?"

"When I was in graduate school. About twelve years ago. Why?"

"And before that, no one had ever heard of them?"

"That's right."

"Thanks," he said. "And I wish you and Lew the best, Pamela. Really."

They all met that evening in Cline's basement for the test.

"Give me the crystal, Lew," the professor said.

"Interesting," Alan said. "No wires to the brain, electrodes, or anything like that."

"Movie stuff," the professor said, as he carefully slid the crystal into the front of the nouancer. It looked much like a conventional, stereo amplifier/radio receiver. The paneling around the crystal socket and dial was polished mahogany. He plugged a set of ordinary-looking headphones into a jack and handed them to Lew.

"Now Lew," the professor was saying, "as I explained, without the software this thing is going to give us raw, unprocessed thought. Your thought. Try not to worry about what you hear. Try to remain detached. A lot of it is stuff from the subconscious that may be frightening, sexy, or plain boring. If at all possible, stay objective and remember that this is just a test. Alan will tell you that it isn't easy, but it can be done."

"Yeah," Alan said. "Cultivating a detachment from your own jumble and flow of thoughts is a primary goal of Tibetan yoga. It is difficult, but I've done it."

"Then why isn't Alan your guinea pig?" Lew asked, testily. He was frightened and did not want it to show.

"Is it really safe?" Cline asked. "I wouldn't want anything to go wrong . . . down here, I mean."

"You mean what if *my* brains went spewing all over *your* lab?" Lew shot back. "That would be a nasty mess for *you*, wouldn't it?"

"Shut up!" the professor snapped. He got very close to Lew. "Now listen to me, Lew. We need Alan here as a backup and possible contact. He is the only one who can follow you if that becomes necessary. This test is perfectly safe. No one is going to get hurt. But you have got to get a grip on yourself. Things are happening fast, I know. But there is still important work to be done."

"Sorry," Lew said. "Did Alan tell you about the code?"

"No." The professor backed off.

"I think we have it. The hash key is an unusual algebraic structure. I'll run my first tests tomorrow," Lew said.

The professor looked at Cline and smiled. Cline still looked nervous. "Excellent," the professor said. "Now, shall we begin? Just sit in that armchair, Lew. Make yourself comfortable. Close your eyes if you like. Dr. Cline, could you shut off the overhead lights? Too much glare. Good.

"Now, when I turn the machine on, relax. I want to run it for five minutes, but if at any time, for any reason, you want us to stop, Lew, just raise your right arm. Alright?"

Lew put the headphones on. It was surprisingly pleasant. He felt the ebb and flow of his own mind in a new, tangible way. He drifted into it with ease. The feeling was that of flowing down a long, lazy river, except that the stream seemed to be flowing toward, rather than away from, its source.

Without software to drive the nouancer's semiotic filter, the Asklepian pulse could not be translated into actual language. Eventually speakers would be installed to enable the researchers to hear what was happening.

But for now, the effects were invisible to all but Lew:

"Float upstream."

"I am, am, am, am . . ."

"Hah. Hah. Laughter is the key, Lew. Where is the door?"

"Alan, are you here?" He saw a figure come and glide mysteriously across the waters of his mindstream before disappearing, a ghostly shape that felt like Alan Fain.

"Lew, Lew? You will come won't you? Lew, Lew?" It was the girl of the crystal. "Call me Sheila, Lew." She pronounced it "She-La."

The current had a definite rhythm; it was the rhythm of breath. In-out, in-out. As Lew was able to focus more on his breathing he could visualize the nouscape more clearly. It was densely organic, lush; the air bristled with fecundity of life. He saw a forest. The trees were so tall and thick that only filtered sunlight reached the matted ground. There were musty smells and large fungi. Wildness called him with a lustful longing, beckoning him to lose himself in the midst of it.

"Grrr!" What was that? It sounded like a cat. "Felix!" Lew's mind called out, "Felix! Here, kitty!" A magnificent feline appeared, parting the thick growth on the shore of his thoughts. It was the size of a panther, except that it was not a panther. It was a jet black house cat, unmistakably Felix, a very great and noble Felix.

He heard a voice. It sounded like the professor. He turned to see the old man standing on the shore of the river. *I know you*, Lew thought. *I have always known you . . .*

"Easy, Lew." It was the professor. He held Lew's face in both hands. "You got rather tense there at the end. Just take a few deep breaths and relax."

After Lew had recovered sufficiently they retired to the den, where Cline served tea. "Now, Lew," the professor said easily. "Can you describe what happened?"

"It felt as if I were drifting—on a river, but the river was my own mind, or rather the thoughts of my mind and it was flowing upstream not down. She was there! Sheila is her name. And . . . oh No! Felix, my cat."

"What?" The professor seemed concerned.

"Felix disappeared last night," Alan said.

"Listen, Lew," the professor said. "What happened to Felix? Do you know anything about it?"

"Well . . ." Lew looked guiltily down at his feet. "Felix and I were playing last night. I was drunk and teasing the cat with his reflection in the crystal. But I never thought . . ."

"What happened to the cat, Lew?" the professor asked.

"He vanished into the crystal," Lew said.

"Oh no," the professor said. "Well, that's that. We'll just have to make the best of it."

"What?" Cline inquired.

"Lew's affinity for nouspace is now quite strong," the professor said. "The Asklepian pulse resonates in his mind. A creature like Felix, an ordinary house cat, hasn't got a very strong intellectual sense of self. In the presence of Lew's mind and an open window into nouspace, the crystal, he was blown through that window like a feather on a breeze."

"But he was huge," Lew said. "As big as a panther."

"Yes," the professor said. "What exists of Felix now is something greater than Felix; it is your idealized version of Felix. You unwittingly projected an exalted image of the cat into nouspace—you *thought* the poor thing there. And now I'm afraid he may be a bit of a problem for us, but other than that I would say that the experiment was a success. With your software, Lew, we will be ready for the real thing."

"But I saw you, too," Lew said, looking curiously at the professor. "And I *recognized* you—from somewhere else. Who are you?"

The professor laughed, but it was more forced than his usual chuckle. "Common occurrence," he said. "Like déjà vu. You recognized me because you know me. But the feeling that you know me from before, or in some deeper sense, is an illusion, an aftereffect of seeing so much of your intellectual activity in such vivid detail. You are apt to make many new associations, put things together that don't necessarily belong."

Late that night Lew was aroused from a deep sleep by the telephone. "Lew, it's Sheila."

"Sheila?" Lew said, half awake.

"Lew?"

"What?"

"I'm carrying your child, Lew."

"You're what? But that is impossible. How . . ."

"Don't you want to see your baby, Lew?"

"But I haven't even met you."

"Not yet," she agreed.

"So how . . ."

"Don't worry about time. Things past mingle with things future—to make the present. I feel your life inside me, Lew. Please come. You will come?" She hung up.

"My child?" Lew muttered, and fell back to sleep.

Lew dressed casually for the board meeting, jeans and running shoes. His sense of new power was keener since the test. He felt close to a religious experience. He could read each gesture, easily decipher the meaning of every action, spoken or otherwise.

"Would you say that Mr. Phelps has taken a *conservative* approach toward management?" the chairman asked Lew.

"Yes," Lew said.

Lew felt he was onto an important truth. He realized that anything could be communicated with any word. The way he phrased that "yes," for example. And the way he looked the chairman in the eye. Phelps was squirming because of it.

There was no reason for it. He pitied his boss. Lew saw Phelps for just what he was, an ordinary man who was now fighting for his dignity. But he was enjoying this new ability to shape lives with a word, a nod.

After the meeting, in the hall, Phelps said, "I appreciate what you said in there, Lew," knowing that the way it was said would likely be his undoing.

Lew looked away. His head hurt. "Sure," he said.

When Phelps called him in, after the board had left, Lew was not surprised at what he heard. "You are now in charge of Asklepios, Lew. You will be your own boss on this one. I'm leaving at the end of the month. Early retirement. Looking forward to it really, I . . ."

"Who's going to take your place?" Lew asked.

"Oh, younger man, I guess. Probably some fool with an MBS, Ph.D., or whatever—I can't keep up with all these degrees." He tried to make light of it, but he was struggling to hold back the tears. "Good luck, Lew." They shook. Lew's hand was cold, Phelps's clammy.

Susan could no longer contain herself. She went back to Lew's office. "You little son of a bitch!" she said.

This threw Lew completely off-balance. He started to say, "Watch it, I'm a supervisor now," but he was suddenly confused.

"Why, Lew? Why? I just want to know why. I know the old man didn't always treat you with respect. I know you thought you were underpaid. But I think you should know something. He admired you."

"Admired?" Lew asked, a little scared. He had never seen Susan really angry. But there was something else. The woman glowed with a newfound fierceness. She seemed to revel in it.

"Yes. Admired. He admired your 'free spirit,' as he used to call it. 'That Lew,' he said to me one time, 'he is one bright guy, and what he lacks in ambition, he makes up for in spirit.' Phelps couldn't afford to go to college, Lew. He had to work it the hard way. And I suppose it left some scars. Maybe he isn't the most sensitive guy in the world. But he was just doing the best he could. And I'll tell you something else. He was going to give you a big raise at the end of the month."

"Like hell," Lew said. "I asked him."

"See for yourself!" she said and flung a file down on his

desk. It was dated the previous week. There was clearly a promotion for him at the end of the month.

"Why didn't he tell me?" Lew wondered aloud.

"That was his style," she said. "Don't give anything away, don't show your hand until you have to. He took some hard knocks along the way, things you will never know about. But then I guess you don't care. And I guess I never really knew you."

Lew felt naked in front of Susan, ashamed. "Don't judge me too harshly, Susan. This is one rough, old world."

"Oh Lew," she said emotionally. "What *has* happened to you? I never thought I would hear that kind of cheap crap from Lew Slack." She turned to leave.

Lew remembered something and said quickly, "You were right about Sheila. That is her name."

This stopped Susan in her tracks. The remark puzzled her at first, but then she remembered the phone call. The expression on her face when she turned around shocked Lew. It was not the Susan he had known who said with cool authority, "I would be careful about Sheila if I were you, Lew."

Before he could respond she was gone.

The professor stopped by. "What the hell is going on, Lew?" he asked.

"Meet the new exec," Lew said, and stuck out his hand.

"Oh, no," the professor sighed, brushing Lew's hand away and sitting down. "I warned you about this."

"What?"

"Don't play dumb!" the professor said sharply. "You know what I am talking about. You have got a taste, a glimmer of what it is like to have real intellect under real control and look what you have done. Giving yourself a meaningless job title at the expense of another's life is such a waste!"

The professor sat down to compose himself. "Oh well," he sighed finally, "what's done is done. Let me see the code. We have to act really fast now."

"Why?"

"Because you are out of control. You could screw up the entire project. We need some secrecy and the kind of stunt you pulled this morning is bound to attract a lot of attention, not to mention what it's doing to your judgment."

"My judgment?"

"Is shot," the professor said. "Now let's see the code." He was pleased with what he saw. "Yes. Excellent. The algebraic application of Alan's singularity factor group is something I had not thought of. It will be even faster than I anticipated. I need to make a few changes, but we should be ready to go by tomorrow."

"Tomorrow?"

"Yes. I think the first thing you should do as a manager is give yourself a long vacation."

Lew met Pamela for lunch. "Don't you want to do something special tonight, Lew?" she asked.

"Yeah," he said. "Let's get married."

"Don't be silly. That's not what I mean."

"What then?"

"It's your birthday," she said.

"Wow! I actually forgot. So much has been happening. What do you want to do?" he asked.

"Why don't you come over?" she said. "I'll make dinner."

"And then," he said intensely, grabbing her wrist, "we can talk about the future. You will be married to one of the world's most powerful men. Perhaps the most renowned name in history when the final book is written." He had a skull-like grin on his face.

She jerked her arm away. "What are you talking about, Lew? What is this nonsense?"

"Something that is long overdue," he said, with a faraway look. "I'm discovering my true self."

"Well I'm not so sure I like it," she declared.

"You will. All women eventually gravitate to power." He laughed.

"That's not very funny, Lew. And it is sexist."

"Sexist," he said. "The universe is filled with polarization: positive-negative, matter-energy, male-female; so why is 'sexist' necessarily bad?"

"You know what I mean!" she said, hotly. "I've got to get back to work, Lew."

"Yeah," he said. "I don't, but I'll see you tonight."

After work Susan drove straight to her apartment and unplugged her phone. She went into her bedroom, which was beginning to look like a small, pagan temple. After selecting a tape of smooth, synthesized sitar music she lit some incense. She positioned herself comfortably on the floor, using some well-placed cushions and opened the book, *Goddess Power*. After several minutes of reading, she leaned her back against the wall and closed her eyes.

The images came more quickly this time. They were so vivid that they made her gasp. "This is really happening!" the chattering part of her mind kept saying. She silenced these mental distractions, using the techniques she had been practicing. This allowed her to merge more freely with the strange, new landscape. She found herself walking through a jungle, wild with color. She was naked from the waist up. The steamy, vegetable heat felt good on her breasts. She carried an elaborately carved bow, and there was a quiver of arrows slung over one shoulder.

She emerged into a clearing. She stopped and stared in wonder at a large, metal sundial. The light reflected by its polished surface seemed brighter than the sun itself. "I know this place," she whispered.

A few minutes later Susan opened her eyes and stretched. She was beginning to feel confident in her newfound abilities. The guided imagery, she now understood, was more than a relaxation technique. It was a door to a new world. The really strange thing for Susan was that it was a world she had always known, where she felt at home.

It was a sense of longing and dissatisfaction with her life that had motivated her to seek something else, something more. Now that she had indeed found it, the vague, initial yearnings had grown into a single resolve—she was going to make this new world her own. She would have it the way she had never been able to have anything before—totally and without compromise. A smile crept across her face, and it transformed Susan from a demure, mildly attractive female into a woman with a powerful and unsettling beauty.

Lew walked into a surprise party at Pamela's. Alan and Dr. Cline were there.

Alan was sitting on the couch, strangely quiet. Lew hustled

Pamela into the kitchen. "We have to talk . . ." he said.

"Lew," she said. "You've changed."

"Sshh." He pulled her close and kissed her. She jumped back, and when he opened his eyes he saw Alan standing in the doorway.

"Do you love him?" Alan asked.

"Alan, don't," she said.

"Now what is this all about?" Lew asked, looking at the pair.

"Tell him, Pamela," Alan said.

"Tell me what!" Lew felt a violent passion surging through him.

Pamela glared at Alan for a moment. "I told you it was over, Alan," she said.

"I'm sorry," Alan said, deflated. "Listen, Lew. I have always been in love with her. She loved me once. I just can't stand by and . . ."

"She's mine, Alan," Lew said venomously.

"No she is not!" Pamela said. "Not anymore! I don't belong to either one of you!"

"Just one thing, Alan," Lew said, softly.

"What?"

"Did you sleep with her?"

"Oh Lew!" Pamela said. "You bastard!"

He pushed her back, harder than he intended. She hit the pantry and fell to the floor. Alan rushed to help her.

"Well?" Lew nearly yelled. "Did you?"

Alan just looked up from where Pamela was gasping for breath. "Yes," he said. "I did. You're really sick, you know that?"

Lew grabbed Alan by his lapels and hauled him up with a strength that surprised both of them. "Funny, Alan," he said softly, "but when I first met you, all those years ago, I had a feeling that we might do battle one day."

The fight that ensued was a silent affair, like a dance at first. The two men grappled for position and moved slowly around the kitchen. Cline watched, afraid to intervene. Pamela stood by the pantry, not believing her eyes.

Alan was breathing in a rhythmic way, drawing strength from his pranayam, the yogic practice of breath control. Lew was pumped with adrenaline and his newfound psychic energy.

"John," Pamela said, "someone is going to get hurt. Call for help."

At that moment Alan released Lew's left hand in an attempt to go for his neck. Lew easily eluded the hold and reached into his coat pocket. He pulled out the crystal. The sharp point flashed in the light before he plunged it deep into Alan's right side.

Alan collapsed on the tile floor, blood gushing from his wound.

"Oh my God, Lew," Pamela gasped. Lew stood there over Alan, clutching the bloodstained crystal in his hand.

"Put the telephone down, Doctor." It was the professor, standing in the kitchen doorway. He said it with such authority that no one questioned him. "Now, you and Pamela get him to the couch. Put a compress on to slow the bleeding. Wait for me on the porch, Lew."

"Don't call an ambulance," the professor said to Pamela. "If he goes to the hospital, he will die. I promise you that."

"What about him?" She gestured to Lew, who was standing on the porch, shivering.

"Don't let's judge him too harshly," the professor said. "He's got more than he can handle right now." He left them. No one noticed that he took the birthday cake.

"Quickly, Lew," he said outside. "Into my car."

"I've done murder," Lew said hollowly as they drove away in the Jag.

"Don't worry about it," the professor said, absently scraping some icing off the cake with his finger. Free hand on the wheel, he slowly savored the sweet, white frosting as they sped quietly into the night.

"This is a bad business," Cline said, standing over Alan and wringing his hands. "Do you think we should call the police?"

"No," Pamela said. "The professor is right. He may be a son of a bitch, but he is right."

"How can you be sure?"

"He should be dead by now," she said, looking at Alan. "As much as I distrust that old man, I don't think he would be a willing accomplice to murder. He has got something else in mind; a criminal investigation would only get in his way."

"He's stopped bleeding," Cline said, kneeling by Alan. "He's breathing, but very slowly."

"He appears to be in coma," she said, covering him with a thick quilt.

After a long while the professor spoke. "Give me the crystal, Lew." It was warm, despite Lew's cold grip, and it was still smeared with Alan's blood. The professor slid the crystal into the nouancer; the device was installed in his dash, the polished wood surface blending in with the elegant, English paneling of the car.

"That was really brilliant programming, Lew," the professor said. "Just brilliant. To use such an esoteric piece of algebra, singularity groups! I wish I had thought of it myself!"

"It was Alan's idea," Lew said.

"I didn't really explain fully about all this," the professor said. "What you hear on this thing"—he patted the dash— "are really not your own thoughts. Rather, what comes across are the contents of nouspace, *inflected* by your own mind. We needed three ingredients to make it work. The crystal, the nouancer, powered by your software, and a sympathetic human intelligence. Your having the crystal for a while has conditioned your mind so that you are now that sympathetic intelligence. You have, of course, noticed the internal changes in your consciousness."

"Alan is dead," Lew said.

"Regrettable," the professor said.

"Alan is dead!" Lew screamed. "And you call it regrettable!"

"What would you call it? Not regrettable? Listen, Lew, it wasn't your fault. Now our only hope is to go ahead with the project. Trust me."

Lew noticed that they were stopped, and it was lighter, dawn already?

"Then let's go," Lew said bitterly.

"This is where I get off," the professor said. He opened the glove box. "There's a small thermos of excellent coffee, and"—he pulled out a copy of the *Kybal*—"this book, which you may find useful."

"You knew this was going to happen," Lew said suddenly. "You knew that I wouldn't be willing to go off alone on your mad adventure unless I were truly desperate . . ."

"But you already were, 'truly desperate,' as you say. You just didn't know it. Now you know, which is a better state. It is always preferable to know rather than exist in a state of ignorance. Wouldn't you say? Here, have some cake. After all, it *is* your birthday." He chuckled, helping himself to more frosting.

"You are mad," Lew said. "Mad as a hatter." He was staring out the windshield. They were stopped in the middle of a highway. It was perfectly straight, and there were no cars to be seen. "Where are we?"

"This is the road in. I can't go any farther," the professor said. "All I can tell you is to turn the nouancer on, listen, and keep your eyes on the road and your hands on the wheel."

"How will I get back?" Lew almost whispered.

"That I don't know."

"You don't know or you don't care?"

"I'm counting on your return," the professor said. "We all are. I think you will make it back. Keep your head."

"And just where is it that I am going?" Lew asked.

"It's more 'here' than here." The professor smiled. "You know there is *something* out there, something more—so go!" He extended his hand. Lew took it very slowly. It was sticky from the cake. "And good luck." The professor got out and began walking away, into the mist.

"Wait! Wait!" Lew was yelling, but by the time he got out, the professor was gone and the fog was getting thicker.

He sat down behind the wheel. Pamela's cake was still slightly warm from the oven. It smelled good. He ate a piece and poured some coffee. The food and drink had an intoxicating effect; he almost forgot his disastrous birthday party.

Settling back into the leather bucket seat, he had the curious sensation that his mind was just another sense, like taste. He reached out and turned the dial. The nouancer came on with a pop that reverberated through his ears and central nervous system. The only thing he heard was a soft roar, like the ocean sound one hears in a shell. It was quiet, soothing. Lew turned the key, and the big twelve-cylinder engine came to life.

He turned the dial on the nouancer. The speakers came alive

with music. It sounded vaguely familiar, classical. But as soon as he thought it classical he detected random jazz elements and then rock chord progressions.

He put the car into gear and slowly accelerated. It felt good to be moving forward.

The professor had steered him right, he decided; all his anxiety and distrust began to disappear in the rhythm of the road, the delicious coffee, and beautiful music.

Then a male announcer's voice interrupted, "Professor . . . what was his name? You know, the old man with the metaphysical theories about nouspace?"

"Yeah that's the one," a sexy feminine voice said. "I think he's really *hot* if you know what I mean."

"No, I don't, but then I'm no expert on those matters like you. He got off to an inauspicious start for such a brilliant, sexy scholar, didn't he?"

"Oh? How's that?"

"Wasn't he the one—I'm sure I'm not mistaken—who did the original work on the stinkless fart?"

Lew exploded in an hysterical outburst of laughter, spewing a mouthful of coffee onto the dash. Simultaneously the Jag took off with an alarming burst of acceleration. Lew glanced at the speedometer. The needle was quivering wildly at the top end of the scale. Stars were streaming past the windshield in long streams and sheets of white light.

The car veered. Lew lost and regained his grip on the wheel, trying desperately to stay on the road. He nearly had things under control when his front, right tire blew. The Jag plowed off the road and slammed sideways into a post.

It was quiet. Lew was sprawled across the passenger seat; the door on that side was smashed in.

The fog was still thick. A smoky, yellow light pervaded everything. It was a soft, pastel glow which seemed slightly brighter straight ahead, down the road.

Lew got out to inspect the damage. The road was cobblestone laid out in an endless variety of geometric patterns as far as the eye could see, giving the illusion of life and movement in the surface. The light reflecting off the various hues of stone added to this illusion. It was hypnotic, and had the effect of drawing one's attention ahead, down the road.

He walked off the road around to the other side of the Jag

to see what he had hit. It was pole with a sign attached—a street sign. The white letters on green background would have been a familiar sight in almost any American town. He could just see the first few letters. The impact of his Jag had twisted the pole so that he had to walk farther around to read it.

It was loose. There was a breeze from the direction he had come, a warm, wild summer breeze like the Mediterranean sirocco winds. It was gone as soon as he noticed it, running wildly on toward the horizon, but it left the sign flapping. It knocked rhythmically against the pole.

Lew sniffed the air, which still carried a wild, sweet scent from the wind. Then he looked back at the sign, still amazed. It read, "Eternity Road," and made him shiver slightly.

4

Soft Fire

Pamela had learned patience over the years. She had learned to inure herself to boredom, tedious technical work, and people who would never appreciate her intelligence or passion. But the present situation strained her resources to the utmost. Her fiancé had gone mad and possibly murdered her lover, who now lay comatose in the back bedroom.

"I know you don't trust the professor," Cline said, "but I think he's right about Alan. The best we can do is keep him safe and hidden."

Chips and dip were still on the coffee table. A beer cooler stood on the floor. The trappings of Lew's tragic birthday party seemed to sit in silent judgment as the evening crept into night.

"Shouldn't we *do* something?" Pamela asked, not expecting Cline to answer.

"We should wait for Lew. That is all any of us can do." The voice came from the porch. It was the professor. Cline got up and let him in.

"How can Lew possibly help?" Pamela threw up her hands. "He has gone utterly mad!"

"Has he?" the professor asked in a tone of voice that made Pamela want to kill him. He remained standing just inside the door.

"I know this is difficult for you," he went on, "but have some faith."

"Faith?"

"Yes, faith. Now listen, Pamela. Alan's condition will not change so long as he is not disturbed. I cannot stay here. My situation is already . . . compromised, too attenuated."

What the hell did he mean by that? Pamela wondered.

"Be patient," he continued. "Our destinies are, for better or worse, intimately connected with Lew."

"Where is Lew?"

"I can't *tell* you where he is. But soon enough you will begin to understand." That was the last thing he said to her. She watched, speechless, as he walked away into the night.

"Who *is* he?" Pamela asked Cline.

"I have my suspicions." Cline said. "But that's not important. I doubt that we will see him again, anyway. We should check on Alan."

Alan's condition was stable. He was ashen and cool, breathing about once a minute. The wound in his side was not healing, but it did not fester; it remained, just a hole into his liver. The organ was actually visible and slightly torn.

"Call me if you need anything." Cline, sensing that Pamela needed to be alone, had let her walk him to the door.

"Thanks, John. I will." She gave him a little hug.

After Cline left, her analytical mind began a spontaneous inventory of her feelings. She decided that she felt little grief, just bewilderment, strain, and a desire to be free from it all, to live a simple, uncomplicated life. But it was too late for that, and she knew it. She guessed she had always known it, and that is what made her special. She also decided that she was tired of being special.

She went into the kitchen. She idly licked some birthday cake icing from the mixing bowl. It was late but she was a night person, and it did not seem like a good time for sleeping. She sat down at the kitchen table and began to work.

Most people are intimidated by mathematics, and so do not understand how it can be a soothing, therapeutic practice. At the advanced level on which Pamela worked, mathematics allowed one to escape into a purely "metaphysical" realm. Yet unlike the metaphysics of philosophy or literature, there was nothing fuzzy about it. The mathematical universe is infinitely mysterious and, at the same time, infinitely intelligible. Pamela characterized mathematics as a burning passion which also cools. She called it the "soft fire," and took refuge there whenever she could.

Her progress that night surprised her. In one hour she found the solution to a problem that had eluded her for years. It brought her one step closer to isolating the canonical singularity group.

She had proved the existence of such a thing many years ago. Finding it was another matter. The task had seemed hopelessly complicated, until now. And if she could do it, she knew that the established mathematical community could no longer ignore her work, no longer dismiss it as eccentric and irrelevant.

The incredible thing about singularity groups was their relation to physics and philosophy. They were structures which linked gravitational singularities, black holes as they were popularly known, to personal identity.

Personal identity, she thought. *Who am I? Who is Lew, the professor, or anyone?* Her animosity toward the professor faded. She sensed that he was not really responsible for what had happened. If anyone was, it was Lew. The professor was just playing a role in which he had little choice. *Maybe it is all of us*, she thought. *We are all trapped inside a story—no way out.*

She worked for another hour but failed to come up with anything significant. "So close, yet so far . . ." she said aloud, and got up to stretch. Suddenly a great tiredness came over her. She wandered into her bedroom and pulled her dress over her head. She looked at herself in the mirror. *Not bad*, she thought. Her fatigue manifested itself as a strange eroticism, and staring at her body intensified the feeling. Her hand slipped between her legs. Oddly she thought neither of Lew nor Alan. Even so, the heat of arousal became intense and Pamela lay back on her bed with a soft moan. Her climax was followed almost immediately by a deep, restful sleep.

5

The Curse of the Camel

Lew inspected the flat. The half-open hood would not close properly. Nouspace, if that was where he was, surprised Lew. The fog had lifted enough to reveal lush vegetation on either side of the road. The odors were warm and organic. Lew, startled by a clicking noise, turned around and froze at the sight.

It was a skeleton that moved with a bone-jangling grace. It was coming toward Lew, who slowly backed away. The creature stopped by the blown tire and shook its head. The slow motion was accompanied by more pops and clicks from the exposed vertebrae.

"Blowout," it said. It proceeded to walk around to the rear of the car, where it opened the trunk. Lew watched in amazed terror as the thing pulled the spare and jack and set to work.

"That should do it," it said, tightening the last lug nut. "Too bad about the door though," it added, looking at the smashed side.

Lew just stared. "Good God, man, speak. You're making me nervous," the thing said.

"No," Lew said.

"Suit yourself." It walked around to the driver's side and peered into the car. "Aha!" it said, and extended a long, white, bony digit to the birthday cake, still sitting on the console. The finger swiped a glob of icing. Soon the thing was grabbing handfuls of cake and stuffing them into its mouth. His movements were fluid and easy, actually pleasing to the eye if one could ignore the strangeness of it.

"So where you from, stranger?" he asked, plunging a huge wad of cake and icing between his grinning jaws. "I say where you from?" he repeated when Lew failed to respond.

"I don't know," Lew said.

It chuckled a little between bites. The cake was almost gone. When Lew could bring himself to look at the thing he thought he saw some color begin to appear on the bleached bones. Sure enough, a film of capillaries and what looked like connective tissue were beginning to form. Lew continued to look on, mesmerized by the sight. With the last few bites blood began to pump through the growing mass of arteries. Then muscle, lined with nerve and vein, attaching to bone. Finally skin, dark-complexioned skin with olive tones of the Mediterranean.

Lew looked up at the face. It was a face now, gaunt, but a real face, with black eyes and long, narrow nose. "There," he said, "that's better." He picked up the plate and licked the last traces of icing with a brand-new tongue.

"It *is* better this way," he said. "A little meat on the bone." He slapped his thigh and laughed with surprising resonance. Then he stuck out a lean but fleshy hand and introduced himself, "Hermes Trismegistus."

"Lew Slack," Lew said, and they shook.

Trismegistus laughed quite hard at the sound of Lew's name. "Good one," he said. "My name means the 'three times great,' you know?" he added with a chuckle.

"My name doesn't mean anything," Lew said, blushing from both embarrassment and anger.

"Don't be so sure," Trismegistus said, scanning the interior of the Jag. "You got any coffee?"

Lew got in the car and opened the glove box. He pulled out the thermos and the paperback book.

"Ah!" Trismegistus said. "What kind of nonsense do they attribute to me these days?" He snatched the book out of Lew's hand. "You have no idea what history will do to a good name." He thumbed through the book, sometimes laughing, sometimes shaking his head. Then he gave it back. "Actually not a bad piece of work," he said. "Several blatant errors and lies, but all in all it seems a creditable representation of my work."

"Where are we?" Lew asked, pouring coffee.

"In between," the man answered, gratefully accepting the coffee.

"Between where?"

"I suppose you think you came from what people usually call 'reality'?" Trismegistus said.

"Yeah. Although I am really not sure anymore."

"Good. That's a good first step. Anyway, your former life is back that way." Trismegistus turned to look back at a thick fog bank. It appeared to be moving slowly toward them. "Up ahead, down the road, is potential."

"Potential?"

"More or less. The possible is actually as real as the actual. What actualizes is just your own commitment. I suspect you were not very committed to anything back there?"

"No," Lew said, "I suppose I wasn't."

"That is why you ended up here. Anyone who doesn't choose eventually ends up here. You are lucky."

"Why?

"Because you really have no idea what you are doing here. That is good. If you did . . ."

"If I did, what?"

"Never mind. But now you at least have the chance to go forward and find out what is possible, and if you really can be anything."

"I don't understand."

"Good."

"Can I ever get back?" Lew asked, looking at the fog.

"Try it."

Lew walked toward the fog. It was about twenty yards behind them and rolling very slowly in their direction. It was cool as the mist began to swirl around him. It grew cold extremely fast. Lew felt an icy blast—the severe cold brought him to his knees, shivering. He stood up in a panic. Not sure which way led back, he bolted.

"See what I mean," Trismegistus said when Lew, gasping for breath, stumbled back to the car. "You don't want to go that way." He had seated himself inside the Jag, behind the wheel. "Shall I drive?" he asked.

"But . . ." Lew started to speak.

"Look," Trismegistus cut him off, pointing back toward the icy mist. It was moving faster now. In a matter of seconds it would engulf them.

"No!" Lew said. "Move over. I'll drive!" The big man obliged him.

Trismegistus opened a vent. "Ah! It is good to breathe aether again!"

"Aether?" Lew asked.

"What else? It is the cosmic aether that pervades all levels of existence from the subatomic to the galactic. It is the medium of all life and thought in the Universe. Good stuff." He inhaled deeply.

"What's this?" Trismegistus asked, pointing at the nouancer.

Lew turned it on. Some weird music filled the Jag. "That's an Asklepian nouancer," Lew said. "It . . . processes thought, or something like that. Is aether the medium of the Asklepian wave?" he asked.

"Indeed," Trismegistus said, as he reached out and extracted the crystal from the front panel. "And this?"

"Crystallized nous," Lew said.

"Primitive," he said, fingering the crystal and scraping off flakes of dried blood. "I don't need to ask what this is," he said, holding one flake between thumb and forefinger and peering suspiciously at Lew, who looked quickly away.

"No need for that, Lew," Trismegistus said. "Whatever it is you have done, I'm sure I've done worse. Murder probably. It is the most common. Who was it? Friend?" He put the crystal back and the music returned.

"Yeah," Lew said, gripping the wheel and staring hard at the distant horizon.

"All men are outlaws, you know," Trismegistus said after a short silence.

"And women?" Lew asked.

"Who knows?" Trismegistus said solemnly. "But I suspect that the men were in bondage wherever you came from."

"Yeah." Lew thought about his office and Phelps and all the other offices, bosses, bad coffee, and short lunch breaks.

"Not that women have it any easier," Trismegistus said as if he could see Lew's thoughts. "Man's slavery is also woman's burden. But men and women *are* different. The truth must be faced . . . eventually."

"What truth?"

"Men are essentially outlaws. It is their nature to want to live beyond limits—all limits. The problem is that the law is the law and most men are very clumsy lawbreakers. That is what makes the difference between misery and happiness—whether or not you can skillfully break the rules." Trismegistus looked at Lew.

"I wasn't very skillful," Lew said sadly.

"Don't worry about it," Trismegistus said.

They drove in silence for some time. Trismegistus finished the coffee. Lew was grateful for the long, straight road. It helped him forget.

He noticed something up ahead. It was a figure standing by the road. "What's that?" Lew asked.

"Hitchhiker probably," Trismegistus said.

Sure enough the figure resolved itself into a man, standing with his thumb out. "Should I stop?" Lew asked.

Trismegistus just shrugged.

Lew made up his mind to leave the stranger by the road, but the closer he got, the more compelled he felt to stop. He screeched to a halt about twenty yards past the man. Looking in the rearview mirror, he saw a bearded face break into a grin and start running toward them.

"Thanks!" The young man got in behind them. He was lean and wearing Indian-style clothing. His face was covered with a magnificent growth of beard.

"Do I smell coffee?" he asked when they were underway.

"Sorry." Trismegistus said. "All gone. Where you headed?"

"Nowhere. Just out for a tour." The young man extended his hand. "I'm Sharma."

"Just call me Herman," Trismegistus said, shaking hands. "This here is Lew."

"Do I know you, Lew?" Sharma asked.

"No," Lew said.

"I guess not," Sharma said. "You remind me of someone I once knew. Anyway, what I'm really after is the answer to a big question."

"What's that?" Herman asked.

"Is the entire phenomenological universe merely a complex thought?"

"Whose thought?" Herman said.

"Ah! For us Buddhists, that is hardly a problem," Sharma said. "Mind is mind, it matters not whose. Such niceties are illusion, sheer phantasmagoria, as it were."

"For us alchemists," Trismegistus said, "it is the crux of the problem. The true goal of alchemy has little to do with making gold, as is commonly thought. No, the real gold is the self; the taste of true, individualized self is the elixir of life."

"And my masters will say that no real individualized self exists," Sharma said pleasantly.

"And what do you say?" Trismegistus asked.

"I haven't made up my mind," Sharma answered. "I suspect that the argument may be pointless, but . . ."

Sharma was interrupted by a loud voice from the nouancer, "Don't touch that dial! Ladies and gentlemen, it is that time again. Yes it is time for us to play a selection from our *religious experience* jukebox . . ."

"Oh God, I hate this," Trismegistus said. "These things are popularized and commercialized out of all recognition. They take a sublime experience and turn it into something to sell soap."

"That's life," Lew said.

"Shhh!" Sharma said. "Let's see what it is."

"Every week we play a selection from our vast library of distilled religious experiences," the announcer said. "What will it be? Christian, Buddhist, Hindu, or perhaps the ancient Persian fire faith of Zoroaster?

"I feel like a real Hindu today, folks. In fact, that is the name of this track. So sit back and relax, get in the groove—meditate while I play one of my favorite oldies, the golden sitar sound of Baba Bum Rap playing 'Like a Real Hindu.' "

"Oh boy," Sharma said, with a naive enthusiasm that clearly disgusted Trismegistus. The hitchhiker sat back, very still, and closed his eyes.

The car filled with sitar music and the exotic smells of India—sandalwood, lotus blossom, and saffron. The intoxication of it filled Lew's mind with pictures of many beings passing through thousands, millions of incarnations. There were epic battles between good and evil where godlike creatures took part. He saw the blue-skinned Krishna perform miracles and save the world from the forces of darkness.

The vision became more personal and he experienced a rapid succession of life-forms from the microbe to the *arhant* or saint. His struggle was long and filled with every conceivable kind of suffering. But his duty was clear: devotion to Brahma the uncreated creator of the world. Such devotion, he felt certain, would eventually bring release from the long, painful cycles of birth and death. He yearned for this release with all his being. It was the one, great elusive desire, this longing. It was a desire itself more desirable than the object of any other passion. Just as he was on the verge of final awakening into that state which is beyond suffering, as he was about to experience *moksha*, the eternal bliss of release, the record ended. He opened his eyes with a feeling of both joy and inconsolable loss. He also realized that Trismegistus was holding the wheel. The big man gave Lew a critical look.

"Sorry," Lew said, taking the wheel. "Guess I got carried away."

Sharma continued to sit as if in a trance.

Embarrassed as he was, a strange, violent kind of peace lingered in Lew. He stared out the window at the hills beyond the road.

"Stop the car!" Sharma suddenly opened his eyes and yelled with earsplitting force.

Lew slammed on the brakes, throwing Trismegistus into the dash. The big Jag screeched to a halt.

"I have a wonderful meditation spot in those hills," Sharma said, brightly, pointing out the window to his left.

"Huh?" Lew looked back and blinked at the man.

"Would you like to come with me? It is no great distance, and the quality of the meditations I get from sitting on those cliffs is superb. I would be happy to show you."

Trismegistus sat back up. He was rubbing his forehead but appeared to be OK. "By all means go. I'm sure it will be an *edifying* experience for Lew," he said sarcastically. "You won't mind if I choose to wait here. I'm sure there is plenty of other drivel I can listen to." He reached out and fiddled with the dial on the nouancer.

"Well . . ." Lew said. Something about the young man was compelling. Lew found himself following as Sharma scampered out of the car.

Lew did not expect the massive growth which confronted the two as they hiked off the road. He felt disoriented, like a miniature man in a tropical herb garden. The variety in shape, size, and color of the flora was stunning.

Sharma knew his way well, pressing forward through the tangle at a steady pace. His long, Indian-style shirt, a *coorta*, picked up pollen and scent from the contact. The narrow, cream-colored pajama trousers hugged his ankles, contrasting sharply with his brown, sandaled feet, which pressed the densely packed jungle floor, leaving soft imprints in the layers of decaying vegetable matter.

Lew followed with more difficulty, sometimes losing sight of his guide as big leaves and fronds snapped back in place behind Sharma's advance. Lew's running shoes were a little too spongy for the already-soft terrain; he lost his footing more than once and nearly sprained an ankle. His jeans were too heavy, and the denim quickly became damp from sweat and the steamy atmosphere.

Gradually the growth thinned as they moved to higher ground. Lew was then able to discern a path, and the surface was harder. He tired rapidly as the rate of ascent increased. Panting and at the point of exhaustion, he nearly bumped into Sharma, who had stopped. "We are almost there," Sharma said. "See the ridge up ahead." He pointed to a jagged outcrop of rock set off by giant trees.

When they arrived, Sharma stood surveying the valley. It was magnificent. The road ran long and straight before disappearing into the distant horizon. In the other direction the road simply vanished into the low-lying clouds. Directly across from the cliff where they stood the other side of the valley rose in a majesty of organic color and form.

"Ah!" Sharma stretched his arms and breathed deeply. His long-flowing beard moved in the breeze. "Nothing like the *prana* of these cliffs!" he said.

"*Prana*?" Lew said. "You mean the air?"

"Well, yes," Sharma said, looking at Lew with laughter in his eyes. "You could call it *air* for lack of imagination."

"Trismegistus calls it the aether," Lew said.

"Same thing."

"But what is the significance of aether or *prana* over plain air?" Lew asked.

"Air is a molecular mix of gases," Sharma said. "Nothing more. *Prana* is that and the subtle medium of consciousness giving life. The universal vibration of the cosmos is transmitted through the *prana*, which pervades all things, all times, and all spaces. *Prana* is the breath of Brahma, the uncreated creator of the Universe."

"Oh," Lew said. "*Prana*, or aether, then, is the Asklepian wave."

"Enough talk," Sharma said. "Now we meditate." He sat down on a smooth surface facing the valley. He assumed the lotus posture of deep meditation. Looking up at Lew, he gestured for him to sit. Lew found the rock hard, and he was not nearly so limber as Sharma. His tight jeans added to the difficulty, but he was able to affect a reasonable imitation of the other's position.

"Close your eyes," Sharma said. "Count the breaths for a while. But not for too long. You must realize that breathing is not an object for observation, but that you *are* the breathing. Then relax and repeat the mantra internally to yourself."

"What mantra?" Lew asked.

"You will know," Sharma said. His breathing quickly became deep and slow.

For Lew it was different. He was aware of his discomfort and shallow, fast breathing for a long time. But gradually his body softened and he began to feel a steady rhythm to it and a pleasant peace. The mantra came from the rhythm of his breath. In the space between the inbreath and the outbreath he felt a vibration which began to resonate independently of his breath. The sound was *aum*, and it grew until that was all he heard or felt.

It was wonderful at first, this little aum that pulled him to deep relaxation and marvelous peace. Deeper and deeper he went. But then an anxiety began to grow. The aum was too big, the vibration too strong; he was afraid to surrender any more of himself to it. When it was small, smaller than he, it was fine, but now it threatened his own individual existence. The aum was the Universe.

It was the green of the valley, the smells of it too. It was the awe-inspiring, terrible beauty of life, hidden from most mortal eyes. It was his search for that beauty, and his hope that the Universe would someday validate his existence, finally make him whole and enable him to lead an authentic life. Pure being, pure beauty beyond which nothing could ever exist. Lew immediately perceived the seamless whole of it.

But, he realized with a sinking feeling, this placed him squarely in the nothing, in the realm of non-being, because he was still afraid. Afraid of what? It made no sense. Why couldn't he simply relax and merge with the blissful unity of the Universe? It was a paradox. The Universe was one, a seamless whole of being. The cosmos. He knew *intellectually* that he was a part of that cosmos.

But intuitively, he saw himself as the one thing which did not belong. Reality *would* have formed a flawless, seamless whole if it were not for the undeniable fact of his own, reluctant existence. His very own life seemed to be the one imperfection which threatened to destroy an otherwise perfect world. He felt a horrible longing for obliteration, for death.

He opened his eyes in panic. The entire landscape was alive, shimmering, vibrating with the aum, the universal mantra. He looked at Sharma, whose eyes were also open and looking back into his. He saw a curiosity in those eyes, as if they were asking, "What is wrong?" His panic grew; he could feel his heart racing. Unable to speak, his mind screamed "help." Sharma's face softened, and Lew imagined that he saw understanding and compassion there. This enabled him to regain a little control over his terror.

The terror, he began to understand, was the natural terror of being a self. Self implies a separation, and separation from the ground of being is a scary thing. But what was this *self*? he wondered. The fascination of this question served to further alleviate his fear. He saw it as the supreme mystery, the question that fuels a life.

Sharma smiled and nodded, almost imperceptibly. "Like all of us . . ." he said, exhaling, "like all of us."

"How?" Lew whispered, exhaling, too, and realizing that he had been holding his breath.

"Actors," Sharma said. "Actors all of us. Alienated islands in the pulse of life. Cut off somehow. But not completely. And relax, Lew—no matter how flawed you find yourself, you are far too small to threaten the perfection of God." He looked closely at Lew, who was running his fingers sensually over the rock surface of the cliff. Lew's face was flushed, and, filled with a new euphoria, he uttered an involuntary sigh.

"Yes," Sharma said with impish authority, like a comical guru. "To a male the universe is female."

Lew was so overcome with the sensual ecstasy of the moment that this remark failed to register at first. Then a dim recollection began to dawn. Where had he heard that before? He looked closely at Sharma, imagining the face without the beard, a little fuller, a little younger perhaps. Sharma's eyes were laughing in silent recognition.

"Alan," Lew whispered. "No, it can't be."

In the moment of recognition Lew felt his whole being vibrate in harmony with the universal aum, an ecstasy that transcended all ecstasy. He knew that he would suffer anything to experience that feeling again. But before it was over it was broken by a violent rumble. They both turned to behold a terrifying image. It was a black beast the size of a panther. The rumble was actually a deep, throaty kind of growl. The awful thing bared its fangs, about to spring.

"Felix!" Lew shouted. The cat stopped, confused. The sounds changed subtly from menacing growl to puzzled purr.

"What is that?" Alan shouted.

"My cat," Lew said, slowly standing up.

"Mrrrow!" Felix advanced menacingly.

"He's confused," Lew said, softly. "He recognizes me, but I also look like easy prey."

Felix seemed to make up his mind and opened his mouth again, letting loose a fiendish noise. His tail quivered and his back legs tensed.

"I think he's hungry," Lew said.

Lew jumped to his feet and leapt forward, seizing a long, yellow fang in both hands and saying, "Kitty! kitty! kitty!" in a high-pitched voice.

Felix stopped, appeared to relax. Lew shook the tooth as hard as he could. Felix's head swayed to the motion. Rank, hot, cat breath washed over him as he turned to Alan and said, voice shaking, "It's a game we used to play. I don't know how long it will stall him."

Lew slowly released Felix. The big cat seemed temporarily pacified. It sat back on its haunches and began to bathe, licking its right shoulder. Alan and Lew slowly backed away. They reached the path. "What should we do?" Alan asked.

"Let's start back down as quietly as we can," Lew said. "Maybe he won't notice." They had gone about fifty yards, where the vegetation was thicker, offering some welcome cover, when they heard the soft sound of padded paws. "He's stalking us," Lew said. "Walk quietly."

"I am," Alan whispered tensely.

Time passed slowly and the tension mounted. Lew, familiar with the cat's hunting practices, sensed a growing boredom in the stalking noises. Soon they were practically running, and Felix's progress was marked by crashing sounds as the thick flora parted.

When they reached the clearing by the road it became an all-out, frenzied run for life. Alan, with his longer legs, was slightly ahead of Lew. The cat was gaining on both of them.

Alan made it to the Jag and bounded up onto the hood. Lew was not so lucky. Felix gave him a vicious swipe which caught him in the small of the back. With another leap Felix was on top of his master, fangs bared and poised for the kill.

"*Hut! Billi mut kero!*" It was Trismegistus, screaming at the cat in some unknown language. Felix sat up, still on top of Lew, and cocked his head to one side. The cat seemed puzzled. Trismegistus continued to utter words from a forgotten lexicon. Felix began to relax. Soon he was off of Lew and rubbing against the man, purring deeply.

"I know cats." Trismegistus smiled, rubbing the beast hard behind an ear.

Lew slowly got up. "Are you alright?" Alan asked.

"I think so," Lew said, voice shaking. "He kept his claws in. It hurts like hell, though. I took it right in the kidney."

"This cat needs some meat," Trismegistus said. "You guys wait here. I'll take him to the jungle and help him find some prey. He probably just needs a lesson or two."

"Alan . . ." Lew said, when the pain subsided.
"Yes."

"Is it really you?"

Alan laughed. "I think so."

"But how did you get here? I mean, I thought you were . . ." He couldn't finish.

"In Tibet," Alan said. "Yes. Well I am."

"Are what?" Lew asked.

"Still in Tibet," Alan said, smiling.

"You don't remember anything about . . ." Lew asked.

"About what?" Alan asked.

"When was the last time we saw each other?" Lew asked suddenly.

"The day I dropped out of school," Alan said. "We were having coffee in the student union, as I remember."

"And that's the last time. You're sure?"

"Yes. I'm sure," Alan said.

"A person is a good place to hide," Lew said softly.

Alan laughed. "Certainly," he said. "I remember."

"What are you doing here?" Lew asked.

"What are *you* doing here?" Alan said. "You are the last person I expected to meet here. You're older too."

"Yeah," Lew said. "I suppose I am. By about twenty years."

"So what's been happening?" Alan asked.

"You don't want to know," Lew said.

"No, I suppose I don't," Alan said, and then added, "That bad, huh?"

"Not really," Lew lied. "Alan," he said, wanting to change the subject, "how?"

"How what?"

"How, if you are still in Tibet . . ."

"My manifestation here is merely a superficial consequence of a very special kind of meditation practice," Alan said.

"What is that?"

"A sharpening of the mental processes. I focus in on one thought. It doesn't matter which. The point is to hold it, examine it, let it draw other thoughts. A kind of crystallization takes place in which the mind begins to know in a way that transcends all knowing. I can't explain it. No one can. My gurus assure me that my manifestation here is only a temporary phase. When I get better at it, even this place will no longer be a part of the meditation, only pure consciousness, whatever that is."

"You mean to say that you are right now meditating in a Tibetan monastery high in the Himalayas?" Lew asked in disbelief.

"Yes," Alan said.

"Do you retain any memory of it when you stop meditating?"

"No," Alan said. "That's the funny part."

"It is all a bit funny," Lew said. Then he lowered his voice. "So you don't remember anything about . . ."

"What?" Alan said.

"Nothing . . . I feel I know this place!" Lew said. "Like I've always been here!"

"Me too," Alan said.

Suddenly a very disturbing thought occurred to Lew. "Alan," he said, "isn't there some kind of after-death twilight world that the Tibetan gurus have supposedly documented as a real place, the place where the soul resides between incarnations?"

"Yeah," Alan replied. "It's called the Bardo."

"Maybe," Lew said, a creeping terror in his voice, "that's where we are—maybe we are dead."

"Take it easy, Lew," Alan said. "There is nothing wrong with being dead. And that theory won't hold up anyway."

"Why not?"

"Because I'm not dead." Alan smiled. Lew just looked away. Could he find some way to change the past here? he wondered.

"We are in the realm of the possible," Alan said. And then, as if he had read Lew's mind, "You might even be able to rewrite history here."

"It is as if we have stepped out of ordinary space-time," he continued. "Imagine the way an author views the characters in his story. He can get up and walk away from it—he is outside the time of the story. He can change it, rewrite it. By being here you have moved one step closer to your true self. And it is the true self that is the *real* author. The average, ordinary self can see very little of space-time and influence it even less. It goes on forever you realize."

"What are you talking about, Alan?" Lew was completely mystified.

"We have penetrated just a little into the infinite here. There is no end to it, no final, real self. Unless, of course, you believe in *God* . . . and then the infinite collapses into the one, shining eternal moment, which is right now." Alan became suddenly quiet, looking around as if in a daze.

"Oh," Lew said. He fumbled in his jacket pocket for a crumpled pack of Camels.

"A cigarette!" Alan said, snapping out of his awestruck silence.

Lew offered, and Alan took one. They lit up in silence.

A few minutes later Trismegistus came striding back with Felix. "Your cat was out of his element," he said.

"Aren't we all?" Alan responded.

"Speak for yourself," Trismegistus said. "What do you call this creature?" He patted Felix on the head.

"Felix," Lew said.

"Felix? What kind of name is that for a cat?" Trismegistus snorted in disgust. "By the way, I overheard some of your conversation. I have *excellent* ears," he added when Lew stared at him in open disbelief. "Your analyses are quaint. Why does 'here' have to be any 'place' at all? I'll *tell* you why. Because you think the alternate thesis, that it is 'all in your mind,' is an impossibility, an inner landscape larger than life. The implications are too frightening—madness, the nightmare of total self-absorption.

"The problem is neither 'here nor there,' but you. Inner, outer? What's the difference? You think you have to *know*. Just as you have always known that you were on earth, at home, in Australia or Tibet, doing this or doing that.

"Why worry? Why assume that your experience can always be labeled? Don't you see how *limiting* that is?"

Lew glanced at Alan to check his reaction to all this. Some of what Trismegistus said sounded good, but it was also suspicious, a cop-out of sorts. He pulled the pack of Camels from his jacket.

"A cigarette." The alchemist beamed. "May I have one?"

"Sure," Lew said, glancing at Alan.

The alchemist took the offered cigarette and placed it in his mouth, wrong end first; the Camel imprint was between his lips.

"The curse of the camel," Alan warned. Trismegistus shrugged him off, laughing. "Nothing I can't handle."

He produced a long, wicked-looking match and proceeded

to light up. After smoking for several minutes in silence he crushed the butt on the ground and flicked it away with a casual, offhand gesture. He immediately requested another. Lew obliged. "So," the alchemist said after lighting up again, "you two know each other after all?"

Before Lew could respond there was a frightful sound. The discarded cigarette butt was rapidly growing into a gigantic camel, and the cries of the partially formed creature were hideous. The alchemist looked terrified. The camel had risen up out of the smoldering fag to become a towering beast, as large as a house.

It was bearing down upon them. They bolted and ran. Lew heard a scream and turned. The camel, down on its forelegs, had seized the alchemist's foot in its large jaws. Lew stumbled and fell. He lay helpless with fear, watching the grisly scene. The camel was chewing the big man as a cow would chew cud, the blunt teeth crushing bone and tissue, human blood and fluid dripping from the slack lips. Lew was some ten feet away, but the foul breath of the beast washed over him like a wave.

When it finished with the alchemist the camel rose up and turned its attention to Lew, advancing with slow, dumb ferocity. Lew lay shaking as the large head bent toward him. The big, furry yellow hump looked like a mountain.

Unable to run far, Alan also watched with morbid terror. Lew closed his eyes and waited for his agonizing death.

Nothing happened for several long seconds. He opened his eyes to see the awful creature groan horribly and collapse, apparently dead. A death stench issued from its half-open mouth as its stomach continued to gurgle. Suddenly the belly burst open in a flood of digestive juices. Trismegistus pulled himself out of the mess, dripping blood, bits of entrail, and caustic enzymes. He stood for a moment regarding the devastation, still smoking his Camel.

He turned to look at Lew. "The curse of the camel!" he said, slapping his thigh. "That's a good one, wouldn't you say!" He exploded into a belly laugh that caused his whole body to shake. This was followed by a vicious racking cough. The big man's lungs made sounds like echoes in a city sewer. When he finally got hold of himself, he hawked up a large quantity of phlegm, which he flung from his mouth straight

onto the stinking, ruined corpse of the gigantic camel. The
reaction was immediate and intense; soon the dead animal
was a steaming, bubbling chemical soup, which quickly hissed
itself into a noxious vapor that vanished into the air.

Trismegistus, shaking his head, looked down at his cigarette. He flicked it toward the horizon; it flew out of sight.
Looking first at Alan, then at Lew, he said solemnly, "You
boys should put those things down. They're bad for your
health."

"What! How?" Lew was stammering.

"They don't call me 'the three times great' for nothing,"
Trismegistus said with a sly wink at Alan.

"Don't you think that's carrying things a bit too far?" Alan
shot back at the alchemist. Lew was still too shaken to speak.

"Can't you guys even take a joke?" Trismegistus said. "What
is the worst thing that can happen to you?"

"Death?" Lew asked, barely able to stop himself from shaking.

"Death! Pheh! I spit on death." Trismegistus flung a piece
of long, ropy saliva from his mouth. It soared in a parabolic
arc that went out of sight. "No, the worst thing is to lose your
sense of humor. Kill me a thousand times, but just don't take
away my ability to laugh.

"Why do you think they call me the 'three times great'?"
Trismegistus suddenly asked.

"I don't know," Lew said.

"I discovered the written word, many millennia ago. Brought
it into the world. What you take for granted in your countless
newspapers and publications was powerful magic at one time.
It was a language older than Sanskrit, a grammar so elegant
that the syntax alone was more beautiful than the greatest
surviving poetry. The Tower of Babel . . . it really happened.
I erred. Mankind could not handle such power, such beauty.
Modern language is a pitiful remnant.

"Mathematics was the second thing. The geometry of Euclid
was a pitiful echo of the lucid mathematical structures that I
introduced. Theories of number and relation that transcended
logic itself. Oh it was beautiful!

"But all that was nothing compared to the third thing."

"What?" Lew asked. Trismegistus had grown suddenly quiet.

"What the world remembers me for." The alchemist, suddenly gripped with a ferocious intensity, turned back to face Lew. "Alchemy! Not the silly stuff you read about now. Turning lead to gold! Bah! Not even chemistry! No. Something more akin to what you have there in your car." He gestured to the nouancer in the dash of the Jag. "You know what it is really all about, don't you? Not gold, not even magic crystals. But self. Find the ground of your being, make it your own! That would be something! I nearly did it."

"Nearly?" Lew asked.

"That is what got me here, where you find me now," he continued. "But . . . Ah! you don't even know what you are doing! That may be your good fortune. You may actually succeed where so many have failed."

"What are you talking about?" Lew asked.

"Your trip, your journey. What are you looking for?"

"There was a woman . . ." Lew said, remembering the face in the crystal and the mysterious phone calls.

"Of course there is," Trismegistus said.

"And . . ." Lew said, "something about life or consciousness . . ." His voice trailed off.

"Never mind," Trismegistus said, shaking his head. "You may find her here. But I advise against looking too hard."

"Why?"

"Because she is not what you think," Trismegistus said. "She never is."

"Lew . . ." It was Alan. He was standing by the Jag, but the car was visible through his body.

"Alan!" Lew said. "Don't go."

"Sorry, Lew." Alan's voice was becoming faint. "Meditation's almost over. We will meet again. Can't you tell me something about the future? Something good?"

The words pierced Lew like a knife and he struggled not to let it show. "We will all be together again, Alan," he said, "just like old times." His voice broke, but his friend was already gone.

Trismegistus was eyeing Lew with a penetrating gaze. "So he is the one, eh?"

"What do you mean?" Lew shot back defensively.

"You know what I mean. He's the one you murdered. Your best friend, no doubt."

Lew was staring at his shoes; anger and shame surged through his body.

"No need for that, Lew. You can't afford it now. Come on. Let's get going. I'll drive this time." Trismegistus opened the rear door, spoke a few words to the cat, and Felix climbed docilely into the back and curled up on the seat with a deeply contented purr.

"We have it backwards as usual," Trismegistus said, after a few miles.

"What?" Lew asked.

"The particulate precipitate of thought," he said, pulling the crystal out from the nouancer. Most of the dried blood had flaked off.

"Crystallized nous?" Lew asked.

"Nous! Hah!" Trismegistus said, sliding it back. "I suppose."

"But that's right, isn't it? I mean intellect or idea is crystallized thought, isn't it?" Lew asked.

"Yes. You could say that. I was just laughing at the pretentious term, 'nous.' Philosophers and others of my profession have made a rather big mystery out of an obvious thing."

"What?"

"Crystallized thought. Or 'nous' if you like—The philosophers' stone, some call it. It is *more* dense than matter. Not less. We generally think of thoughts as somehow less real, more nebulous than things. That's because most of our thoughts are so pitifully vague and impoverished. But get one pure idea! Then you have something that transcends anything physical. Thoughts are composed of nouons, the elementary particles of consciousness. It takes a singularity to produce a nouon. A singularity exists outside space-time; it is no longer in the universe.

"The device that this thing powers . . ." Trismegistus pointed to the panel housing the crystal.

"Nouancer," Lew said.

"Whatever you call it . . . It filters and processes enough nouonic pulse to jump the gap between potentiality and actuality. You probably regard your former life as the actual, the real."

"Yeah," Lew said. "It was real."

"Nothing is real," Trismegistus said.

"Nothing?"

"Not completely. Some things are more real than others. What you are headed for is the source of it all, where potential is more real than reality." Trismegistus looked at Lew.

"I don't understand," Lew said.

"No one does. Look at it this way. There is the world that most people regard as real. But it is only one instantiation of the possible. The possible exists. It is all written. That is the source of your imagination. In a very real sense the figments of your imagination are more real than . . ."

"What?" Lew asked.

"Than anything you could possibly imagine." Trismegistus laughed. "But seriously, the possible is sometimes far more real than the actual."

"How do you know?" Lew asked.

"How do you know *when*, you mean?"

"Yeah."

"For that there is only one guide. Experience. You have to live it. But you will learn nothing if you do not fully cast yourself into the wave."

"What wave?"

"The Asklepian wave, the wave that carries all the information of life and consciousness. It is always changing, and you can never know for sure what is real. But one thing is certain—unless you fully commit yourself, you are sure to miss it. The ride I mean. It is like surfing. The waves can be big, dangerous and scary, but you can't get a really good ride on one unless you fully give yourself over to it."

"What do you mean all things are written?" Lew asked.

"Everything that has ever happened. Everything that ever could have happened and will or might happen is recorded in Akasha, the great cosmic Hall of Records. The Asklepian wave originates there. It is broadcast from Akasha throughout the universe. It is via the wave that the possible is realized in countless worlds."

"If you could get there," Lew said, "Akasha, I mean, could you change the past? I mean if all possible pasts are recorded there, could you . . ."

"Bring your dead friend back to life?" Trismegistus said. "I wouldn't think too much about that if I were you. But I suppose you will get a chance to find out."

"What do you mean?"

"That is where we are headed," Trismegistus said. "Eternity Road ends at Akasha."

Lew had not been paying any attention to the road, but when the alchemist said this he looked out the windshield. They were moving at a great speed. It seemed as if the entire landscape were distorted, elongated in the direction of their trajectory. He looked at the speedometer—the needle was quivering at the top end. Trismegistus gave him a wicked-looking smile. "Slow down!" Lew screamed.

"Too late for that," Trismegistus said as he reached over to turn the nouancer on. Again the interior of the Jag was filled with a loud roar, like the amplified sound of a sea conch held to the ear. But this time it was not soothing.

"You want to save your friend?" Trismegistus shouted.

Lew nodded.

"Then forget about him. Think only of yourself. Then . . . well, who knows? Anything can happen!"

The roar resolved itself into music. Again Lew had the impression that it was the unheard music behind all music, the very form of music which makes music possible.

6

Postcard Proof

Pamela woke with a piercing scream. "That was no dream," she said, breasts heaving and soaked in sweat, "that really happened." The vivid nightmare was still fresh in her mind as she rose shakily and went to the bathroom. She slipped her panties down and sat, resting her head on her knees.

In the dream Lew was riding down a cobblestone highway

at an incredible speed. The man driving was dark and gaunt. There was an eerie, compelling music from the radio, if it was a radio.

That was the really strange part. The radio kept getting farther and farther away from the passengers. The faster the car moved, the faster the dash retreated ahead. She was seeing it through Lew's eyes and he was staring at the radio as if down a long corridor.

"What's happening?" Lew screamed.

"We are almost there!" the driver shouted back.

"Where?"

"The Hall of Records. Akasha."

"But we are being sucked into the nouancer." That is what Lew called the radio.

"Of course. Where did you think it was?"

Lew was resisting, trying to hang on, but he was being pulled out of his seat, and so was a very large cat. Pamela recognized it as a giant version of Felix, Lew's pet.

"Let go!" the driver said. "Let it take you!"

"But what about you?" Lew shot back.

"I'm not going anywhere."

"Why not?" Lew said, turning to look at the driver.

"Because"—the words were spoken by a grinning skull—Trismegistus had reverted to his earlier form—"I'm dead!" This was punctuated by a spine-chilling laugh.

Recalling the sound of the laugh made Pamela shiver as she dabbed between her legs with a sheet of toilet paper. She stood, pulling her panties back on.

Too shaken to go back to bed, she started toward the kitchen but stopped abruptly as another image from the dream came back. The dead man had spoken to her, but the scene was jumbled in the typical fashion of dream recollection. Alan was there too, a young, bearded Alan dressed in Indian clothing. He was off in the distance, fading into the horizon and smoking a cigarette while the skeleton spoke to her with a sense of urgency. What had the thing said? "Check your mail . . ." or something like that. It was holding a postcard between skeletal thumb and forefinger. The bones cracked as the elbow joint opened, extending the arm. The card came into view, practically under her nose. The postmark was from Tibet.

Pamela went to her file cabinet, grabbed a handful of Alan's faded postcards, and carried them back to the kitchen table. She brewed a cup of tea and sat down, where she had been working. She took a sip and spilled some tea on one bare breast. "Ouch!" she jumped, but it did not really burn. Pamela preferred to approach her mathematics as naked as possible—the purity of it seemed more tangible that way.

Her fountain pen lay open on top of the coarse, yellow paper on which she liked to write. Ink stains had formed underneath the equations which represented her last attempt to solve the canonical singularity problem. She held one of the postcards and idly studied the still-growing ink blots, enjoying the sight; the random black forms seemed the perfect contrast to her precise notation. She put the card down next to the tip of her pen, directly underneath her work.

What she saw immediately interested her. Alan had often included bits of Sanskrit in his cryptic messages, with little translations. She had absently set the card down upside down. Some of the symbols, which looked like Sanskrit characters right side up, looked curiously like mathematics upside down. She studied the writing more closely. Mere curiosity turned to astonishment. Under her intense scrutiny the symbols begin to resolve themselves into the next, and last line of the solution to her problem.

Her heart was racing. She realized that she had been holding her breath, and gasped. She looked at the clock on the wall—5:00 A.M. The first light of dawn was barely visible. She was afraid to look back at the table, sure that she had imagined the whole thing. But when she did, it was still there: the solution to her problem on a postcard mailed years ago from the high Tibetan Himalayas. She quickly tore off a sheaf of fresh paper and began to copy the entire solution—this, she was convinced, would earn her recognition as the world-class mathematician she knew herself to be. It was long overdue, something for which she desperately yearned, even as hope of its attainment had slowly but surely faded.

After she finished she went to the bedroom where Alan lay in his half-dead state. She just sat there watching his breath for a few minutes. She thought of all those postcards he had sent, hundreds of them, in the bottom drawer of her file cabinet. For two years after Alan had left she had thrilled to every one. Slowly they had become a painful reminder of a lost passion, then mere curiosities, and finally irrelevant. Suddenly they had a new significance.

She looked more closely at Alan. It appeared to her that his head nodded, an almost imperceptible motion that seemed to say "yes." But on closer examination he was no different, and any motion, real or illusory, was no more to be detected.

7

Akasha

As his flesh peeled away the alchemist stretched a bony hand into the vastness that now extended ahead and retrieved the crystal from the distant nouancer. He handed it to Lew, saying, "You might need this." Lew managed to get it into his pocket a moment before he and Felix were sucked violently into the void.

Lew felt a terrible pressure on his head, as if something were squeezing the bones of his skull from all possible directions. He was moving extremely fast, and when he looked in the direction of motion he could see the gleaming front panel of the nouancer growing larger and larger. It was pulling them in. Felix let out a low, feline wail.

Trismegistus's last words were still ringing in his ears. "Outlaws, Lew. Remember that. We are all outlaws!" The skull grin was all too vivid in his mind as the pressure and speed increased. The nouancer had grown so large that it towered over Lew and Felix as they hurtled toward it. They were headed straight for the empty slot that housed the crystal.

Just as he thought his head was about to implode, they zoomed through the hexagonal opening. Lew had a sensation of immense space and absolute quiet. All the pressure was gone and he was floating in the eternal moment. "Ah," he sighed, and started to relax. Then, with a sickening nausea, the bottom fell out, and Lew, for the brief moment before unconsciousness overtook him, knew absolute terror as he began to fall an infinite distance into the infinite void.

He awoke to a curious, wet scraping sensation on his cheek. Felix was licking his face. *That's an odd thing for a cat to do*, Lew thought. He opened his eyes and immediately closed them. A hot, white sun shone directly overhead, giving off an intensely painful glare. He rolled over and stood up. It was hot, hotter than Texas asphalt in August, hotter even than a Delhi summer. He was sweltering in his black denim jacket. He quickly removed it along with his shirt. The heat explained Felix's licking; the cat was drawn to the salt of his sweat.

It was a vast desert of burning white sand as far as Lew could see. Then he turned around and gasped at the sight. A massive, domed structure stood before him. Engraved in bold letters above two huge gold doors set in the smooth stone face was the word, "Akasha," and underneath, "Hall of Records."

To either side of the building Lew could see nothing but blue. The library was a little above where he stood, so he had to work his way up the loose, hot sand to get closer. Walking around to one side of the building, he realized that he was on the shore of a vast ocean. And there was nothing more to be seen. A long crescent beach that stretched to the horizon in both directions, an unbroken desert, endless sea, white-hot sun, and the library.

Felix at his side, he walked down to the water. It was salty. The sun was so hot that he was already beginning to feel weak. He put his shirt back on and returned to the giant doors. "We have to get inside, kitty," he said. Felix rubbed against his thigh and gave a distressed "mrreoow."

There was no visible mechanism to open the doors, so he leaned against them and pushed. The effort left him panting and extremely faint. *No sense getting heat exhaustion*, he thought. He decided to sit down in the sand and wait for the sun to move. It was high noon, and Lew reasoned that soon the building would cast at least a small shadow and he could cool off and try something else.

But the sun did not budge. At first he thought his sense of time was distorted by the heat. But still the sun did not move.

Their situation was growing desperate. Felix lay motionless, mouth open, tongue out. Lew was getting dizzy just sitting down. He got up and moved back to the doors, pounding on them, "Let us in! We're dying out here!" He could hear the ringing echoes of his blows on the inside, but nothing else.

Felix was again at his side, sniffing the doors and growling. "Take it easy," Lew said, rubbing the big cat's neck. "We'll be OK." But he did not believe it. Lew was sure that another half hour in that heat without water would kill them both. The cat became fixated on a section of stone next to one of the doors. It was clawing the limestone, marring the smooth surface. "Felix!" Lew barked. "Stop it!" For some reason Lew was afraid of defacing the structure. On reflection it seemed ridiculous—who was there to care? The cat, heeding his tone, stopped scratching, but hissed when Lew bent to examine the vandalism.

Then he saw the reason for the cat's interest. There was a hole, now surrounded by claw marks, in the stone. Lew was thrilled when he realized that the hole was hexagonal, about the diameter of the crystal. He quickly picked up his jacket and pulled out the crystal.

It slid in easily, a perfect fit. Lew pushed on the doors again but nothing happened. He strained and nearly passed out from the effort. "Damn!" he shouted. "Open up!" Still nothing.

They both collapsed on the sand. Lew was too weak to get up again. Felix was making disturbing gurgling noises, sounds Lew had never heard from a cat. And the sun was blazing with what felt like renewed intensity. *What am I doing here?* he thought. His thoughts became confused, disconnected. *A person is a good place to hide . . . hide me where it is cool . . . are we dead yet . . .*

Why am I here? Sheila, I never got to . . . see you, love you . . . where are you? Lew dragged himself to his feet, determined to retrieve the crystal and try to catch a glimpse of Sheila in its reflective surfaces one last time. He had trouble locating the hole—he was seeing double and everything was shimmering as if it were a mirage. Finally his fingers found the smooth, faceted end and he slowly drew it out of the stone.

He could see no form in the crystal, only the broken white light of the merciless sun, but he could hear noises, sounds like giant gears slowly turning and metal scraping against stone. They were slow, heavy, ponderous sounds, and he was so disoriented from heat exhaustion that it took him several seconds to realize that the doors were open. What finally brought him round was the blast of cool air that was spilling out from the interior of the library.

He quickly went inside, and the doors began to close. Suddenly he realized that Felix was still outside, too weak to get up. He managed to drag the poor cat in just before the doors slammed shut. The beast was still alive, but breathing very rapidly and shallowly. Lew, drained from the effort of dragging Felix inside, scanned his surroundings for any indication of water; the sight that confronted him was so confusing that he collapsed in a dead faint.

He came to with a burning thirst. Felix was nowhere to be seen. He slowly sat up, rubbing his head and calling, "Felix! Here kitty, kitty!"

"Mrroow!" The resonant reply echoed across the cool marble floor. Lew followed it, working his way past long rows of cabinets. They were the kind of file cabinets libraries use for manual card catalogue systems. The fine, polished wood and shiny brass fittings of the cabinets stretched farther than Lew could see, but there was a break in the monotonous rows, and that is where he found Felix, looking magnificently regal and lying in front of a large pool in the center of the building beneath the dome. It was some fifty yards in diameter with a splendid fountain in the center. The water was cold and tasted better than anything Lew could remember drinking.

Thirst quenched, Lew once again surveyed the library's interior. The domed ceiling was at least two hundred feet high. It was decorated with vivid paintings that rivaled Michelangelo's immortal Sistine chapel. Every scene perfectly captured a spiritual or philosophical motif. Lew could instantly relate to each one. In fact he felt that each picture was an artistic rendition of some struggle in his own life. Some of the paintings were so erotic that Lew was overcome with a burning sexual passion just from looking. Others evoked the longing to find a place, a home. And there was one which he could not bear to look at for long. It depicted a murder. The artist had given the victim a special look of horror, clearly evoking the violation of trust and friendship that the murder entailed.

The rows of card files were not really infinite, as it had first appeared to Lew in his initial state of heat exhaustion. They stretched radially for perhaps one hundred yards in all directions from the circular pool—the fountain formed the hub of a wheel in which the card file rows were the spokes. Lew walked down one row, in a direction some ninety degrees from that of the entrance.

He stopped and opened a file. The craftsmanship was truly remarkable. The wood grain shone with an amazing depth; Lew could lose himself in the wavy swirling patterns. The brass fittings sparkled with a near-crystalline brilliance. The drawers opened with a fluid motion that was absolutely silent. He pulled a card at random. The cards were creamy white and the typeface particularly elegant. Lew read, "*Castanada—influence of on Slack's employer, A study of the impact of the works of Carlos Castanada on Roy Phelps.*" Lew immediately began scanning other cards. All referred to subjects or people in his life. Some were familiar and some were not. It made sense, given what the alchemist said about the library. It contained all things possible. Some had actually occurred, like his ex-boss reading Carlos Castanada, others had not. Some might also refer to future events that might or might not happen.

The one thing which he did not understand was the central theme of all the books on file—he, himself, Lew Slack. What about everyone else, all the other creatures and things in the universe? Weren't they as important? Where were all the other stories? It was a creepy feeling to be in a library devoted to oneself. Lew could not imagine that in his short, rather shallow existence, there could be enough stuff to fill a library. But from the looks of it, all the minute details were documented. And if all possible events, past and future, were recorded, it just might fill an entire library.

The call numbers made no sense. And where were the books? Lew took a card and continued down the row. It ended and he stepped out onto the black marble floor about ten yards from a white wall. There was an ornate, gold-lettered sign on the wall. It read, "Stacks," and hung over an arrow which pointed to Lew's left. He followed to find a stone stairwell. As he descended there was a notable change in the air.

It took on a musty quality different from the cool crispness of the file chamber. It was warm and soothing, with a rich organic quality that lifted his spirits.

The stacks of books seemed to go on forever. Whereas the domed file room had clearly finite dimensions, Lew could detect no end to the rows and rows of books which confronted him.

There was a strange, blue-green glow coming from the direction opposite the library's entrance. Searching for the source of the light, he worked his way past several rows of books. It was difficult since the stacks were not laid out in any recognizable pattern. The books were of all shapes, sizes, and colors. He gasped when he found the source of the illumination. The underground wall of the library, which faced the ocean, was transparent, giving a spectacular submarine view. It was the only wall in evidence; the maze of books looked to be infinite in all other directions. It had an inward concavity; Lew assumed that it followed the crescent shape of the shoreline above. For this reason the view along the plate glass curved gently out of sight in both directions.

There was a row of finely crafted wooden desks facing the underwater panorama. Each desk was equipped with a comfortable padded chair, pen, and paper. Lew sat down at the nearest one and was instantly hypnotized by the wonderful sight. Sea creatures of an astonishing variety swam past. Enormous whales mingled with giant squid. Tiny, brilliantly colored minnows followed the erratic motions of exotic jellyfish. It was the most peaceful thing Lew had ever seen. A beautiful harmony of life merging, diverging, and flowing in the source of all life, the primeval ocean. His head began to nod as the soothing calm lulled him to the edge of sleep.

Lew woke to an acute hunger. His head was resting on the desk—a small pool of saliva had dripped from his mouth onto the surface and had already begun to compromise the beautiful finish. He rose from the desk and stretched. Felix was perched on the desk next to Lew's, gazing with ferocious intensity at the swimming sea creatures.

The cat growled when Lew rubbed it, but made no threatening moves. Apparently Trismegistus had taught it that humans were not appropriate prey. "Sorry, Felix," Lew said. "You can look, but don't touch. I'll see what I can find." Lew began aimlessly to wander the stacks. The books themselves were not exclusively about him. He found several that dealt with subjects like science, religion, or philosophy.

He sat down to look at one. The floor was covered with a heavy, thick Persian carpet. The patterns were the most beautiful Lew had ever seen. They integrated every conceivable color, from the most garish to the softest pastel tones. And the designs seemed a perfect synthesis of two contradictory themes. On the one hand they never repeated, but they were held together by a common pattern that was never seen yet always sensed as the supreme unity that inspired the weaver through the entire process of creation.

Lew read sitting cross-legged on the soft carpet. It drew him in as no other book he could remember reading. The text was a long poem about beings from another world who lived on thought. Having no need for physical nourishment, they spent all their time creating new recipes of metaphysical truths. Entire chapters of verse were devoted to the preparation of such mental feasts. Each one was more savory than the previous. Often a new "dish" would be prepared from two older recipes that were actually two supreme truths about the Universe that seemed to contradict each other. But the poet, who was the master chef, would always find a way to resolve the contradiction and show how the two were really only lesser ingredients in a greater truth that was tastier, more satisfying to the mental palate, than anything previously experienced.

Lew identified with the protagonist, a young man who understood little of this, yet had an insatiable appetite. He devoured cosmic truth after cosmic truth, and remained always hungry. The ending was rather tragic; he lay starving to death trying to piece together one last great revelation.

Lew dropped the book. "That really happened," he whispered to himself. His stomach was growling and his hunger was rapidly becoming the center of his universe. This was also true for Felix, who was following Lew with the nervous intensity of a hungry cat.

"Maybe there is a *real* cookbook around here somewhere, Felix," Lew said. Most of the books were quite old, bound in the style of a bygone era, when the physical aspects of a book were taken as seriously as were the literary. They felt good to touch and hold. He opened a medium-sized volume bound in green fabric with a pleasing rough texture.

The passage, which concerned a luncheon conversation, immediately captured him. "I'm telling you that everything is interconnected. Take this taco for instance . . ." a man named Jim was saying.

"I will," Lew said—he had so completely identified with the other character that he became that character. He grabbed the taco out of Jim's hand and began devouring it.

"Hey!" Jim said. "That's mine!" He reached over to grab it but Lew turned away, stuffing it into his mouth. Picante sauce dribbled down his chin and onto his shirt. "What's gotten into you?" Jim asked, and grabbed some fajita meat from a steaming plate.

There was an unnerving, beastly sound as Felix pounced on the table, tipping it and sending all the food crashing to the floor. The cat immediately started devouring the beef. Jim rose and backed away, terrified by the animal. Lew and Felix just ignored him and continued to eat.

Satiated, Lew looked up and inspected the room. It was a small dining room, adjacent to a modest kitchen. Thirsty, he went to the refrigerator and got a beer. Before he could open it, the front door flew open. It was Jim and someone else. The newcomer had a rifle aimed at Felix.

"Don't shoot!" Lew yelled, positioning himself between the barrel and the cat.

"Get out of the way!" Jim said.

"This isn't really happening," Lew said, pleading.

"The hell it isn't," Jim said, approaching him. He grabbed Lew by the lapels of his jacket. Lew resisted and Jim punched him in the solar plexus. Felix growled and leaped at Jim. There was a blast as Jim's friend fired his gun.

Lew lay on the thick rug trying to get his breath back. Finally he was able to sit. Rubbing his sore stomach, he called out to Felix. "Mrroow." The cat came around from the other side of the stack and rubbed against him, apparently alright.

"I guess we got out of there just in time," Lew said, scratching Felix, who responded with a deep purr. He looked down at his shirt, which was still stained with sauce. He rose painfully to his feet. Suddenly Felix froze, and at the same moment Lew thought he heard the sound of a book closing.

"What was that?" he whispered—Felix's long, black whiskers were twitching rapidly.

He followed Felix in the direction of the sound. The stacks were a labyrinth. Rows seemed to stretch endlessly in one direction, only to take sudden right-angle turns. Aside from the glass wall looking out to the sea, there was no visible end to the maze of bookshelves winding apparently into the infinite.

He would have missed it if Felix had not stopped in front of him, ears pricked and tail quivering. A book lay, facedown, closed on the shelf, as if a browser had forgotten to return it to its proper place. He started to pick it up when he saw the cup. It was a cup of tea, half-empty. Lew picked it up. He immediately put it down and looked behind him. The tea was warm, steam still rising from the surface. He listened very carefully, but no more sounds disturbed the complete silence of the library.

"We are not alone, Felix," he said. The cat paced between the stacks, already bored with the hunt for the phantom browser. Lew took the book and followed Felix, who was prowling aimlessly. It was not long before he realized that they were lost. His sense of direction was gone, so uniformly irregular was the layout of the stacks.

Looking around with a growing sense of panic, he was relieved to detect a greenish blue glow coming from only one direction. The light was coming from the underwater vista. Even so it was not easy winding his way back. There were no ends to the rows of books, only twists and turns, so Lew was forced to follow many false leads before he breathed a sigh of relief as he emerged next to the peaceful marine panorama.

The title of the book that the mysterious tea drinker had left behind was *Strange and Distant Episodes*. Lew put it down on one of the desks and went back to the stairwell. The walk up and entrance into the beautiful, domed file room felt like an ascension to heaven, so open was the room compared to the claustrophobic labyrinth of the stacks. The finite dimensions of the file room felt more open than the infinite maze below.

Adding to his sense of delight was a new discovery. A few yards on the other side of the sign that pointed the way down to the books was a small room. In one corner of the room was an old telephone booth. But what immediately caught Lew's attention was the giant coffee urn. The thing was silver and topped with a gold replica of the winged helmet of Mercury, messenger of the gods. There were clean cups and real cream. The coffee was delicious.

After a satisfying cup he followed a radial row of card files back to the pool. The fountain in the middle shot some twenty feet toward the magnificent dome. Lew stripped and dived into the pool, swimming to the center, where the spray buffeted his body. The turbulence propelled him to a calm section of the pool, where he floated on his back and let the eddies slowly turn him.

He was again awed by the beauty of the images above. One in particular caught his eye. A man was chasing a woman. The surrounding scenery was lush, tropical-looking, but also evoking the green feeling of an old growth temperate forest. *The garden of Eden*, Lew thought. The figures seemed alive. Lew thought he saw the woman's beautiful breasts move just a little as she ran, and the face seemed to turn slightly toward him. With a painful longing he recognized the face of the woman in the crystal, Sheila. He lay there, floating for several minutes. It was only the accidental inhalation of water that brought him out of his reverie. When he looked back the figures were as beautiful as ever, but they seemed less alive.

He swam slowly to the pool's edge and climbed out. The cool air made him chilly, and so he dressed before he was completely dry. Looking at the taco sauce stain on his shirt, he realized that the books in the library were more than books. They were somehow doors—doors into other stories, other lives, worlds, and possibilities. "If that is the case," he mused, looking up, "maybe there is a book that will let me into *her* world. There must be."

How could he find the book? The library itself seemed to house books of endless variety on an endless number of subjects. But the card file appeared to be restricted to him, Lew Slack. Therefore, he reasoned, if Sheila were ever to be a part of his life, even as only a *possibility*, the book which told that story should be listed. With a growing excitement, Lew set out from the pool, scanning the index, in search of the S's.

8

First Person Singular

Pamela, dressed in her most professional suit, closed her presentation to the American Society of Mathematicians with the following remarks, "So the applications of the canonical singularity group extend far beyond mathematics. Clearly my result ties together several loose ends relating to the general relativistic gravitational theory of black holes or *singularities* as they are called. But the more exciting implications of my work relate to psychology and philosophy. All things are interconnected, including the very essence of personal identity. But the mystery of personhood has eluded the very best efforts of scientists since the beginning of civilization. My work, I believe, points the way for a serious scientific investigation of the self, that mysterious entity which we all call 'I.' "

She stopped and lowered her head. She had never presented a paper before such a distinguished audience. These were supposedly the best and the brightest. The hall was silent for several, long moments. Then there was a smattering of polite applause. When Pamela looked up and out at the audience her gaze was met by confusion, amusement, and derision. Some were openly laughing at her. But worst of all there were no questions. That was the kiss of death in such an academic forum. No questions meant utter rejection. She picked up her papers, mumbled a quick "thank you," and hurried from the podium.

A few of her friends tried to put the best face on it. "That was very . . . interesting," Jane Castle, the president of American Women in Mathematics said. Pamela was fighting back

97

hot tears. She knew her work was controversial, but she had mistakenly assumed that the quality of the mathematics, excellent by any standards, would stand on its own.

She was trying to work her way out into the lobby, but it was slow going. She could hear bits of idle conversation, "Can you believe it? . . . What nonsense . . . I alway said that mathematics was a man's field. This just proves it . . ."

She was almost to the door when someone tapped her firmly on the shoulder. She ignored it and pushed her way out. In the more open space of the lobby she allowed herself a few tears. She was dabbing at her eyes when a voice said, "Dr. Fine?"

She turned around slowly. "Yes," she said, confronted by a man in his forties, wearing an expensive suit with a paisley bow tie.

The man paused, noting her red eyes before he spoke. "I guess they gave you a pretty cool reception in there. I tried to catch up to you but you were too fast for me."

"Oh, it's nothing, I expected it more or less," she lied.

"Even so it can be unnerving when it happens. Allow me to introduce myself. I'm Elliot Pritchard, director of the Manhattan Institute for Advanced Mathematical Research." He extended his hand.

"Oh . . ." Pamela lost her composure for a moment. The man standing before her was the head of the most prestigious academy in her profession. When she finally did take his hand she said, "*The* institute?"

"Indeed. I read your paper in the *Proceedings*."

Pamela's pulse quickened. Her paper had recently been published in the *Proceedings of the American Mathematical Society*.

"I am very impressed with your work. As you know there has not been much interest in singularity groups, but your result here looks as if it may open up the entire field. First-rate, really. Congratulations."

"Thank you," she managed to say.

"I understand you are working at a *community* college?" His thinly veiled distaste at having to pronounce the words was quite obvious.

"Well, yes. Actually I am between jobs at the moment," she lied.

"Listen, I was very much intrigued by your paper. Do you

suppose we might get together sometime? How long are you in San Francisco?"

"Just until the proceedings are over . . . until tomorrow, I mean."

"Well in that case . . . what about dinner tonight?" Elliot asked, some unease in his voice.

"I don't know. I was going to do some sightseeing . . . but actually I am awfully tired. Maybe a nice quiet dinner would be just the thing," she said quickly.

"Good." He smiled. "Meet you down here about seven?"

The dinner went well, and when it was over Pamela had an offer for a position at the institute. It was a dream come true for any mathematician. "Of course I can only offer you a three-year contract at the moment," Elliot said, "but there is an excellent chance that we can arrange something on a more permanent basis. Particularly if your work continues to show such promise . . .

"I don't know what to make of all the more-exotic trappings of your work, but the mathematics is the best I have seen in years. Tell me seriously, do you really buy some of that other stuff you were talking about?"

"It is too early to tell if there is anything to it really," Pamela said, "but yes, I take it seriously."

"That took a lot of nerve to say some of those things in front of a crowd like that," he said.

"Or a lot of stupidity," she said. He started to laugh, but the seriousness in her tone made him stop.

Only one thing marred Pamela's excitement on her flight back. That was Alan. Specifically what to do about him. She could not leave him, but how could she move a half-dead, unconscious man over a thousand miles? How could she move him to a Manhattan apartment? *Damn you, Alan Fain!* she thought, *why couldn't you turn into a vegetable someplace else?*

Cline solved the problem by building a special case. A long polymer box, it resembled a coffin. He designed it to be well ventilated while hiding the contents, which made for an interesting placement of air holes. The trip was nerve-racking.

Pamela rented a truck. She drove in constant dread of being stopped and searched. While she knew such a thing was highly unlikely, it would have been difficult to explain the contents of Alan's carrying case.

The worst was unloading. The men who hauled her furniture up the stairs to her third story apartment were visibly curious and uneasy at the strange box. "What's this?" one of them asked her directly.

"Oh that," Pamela said. "That is a special incubation chamber for . . . growing herbs."

The two men just looked away. Pamela directed them to the spare bedroom, where they set on the floor. "Thanks," she said.

"Sure. It is kind of dark in here, isn't it?"

"Oh. Yes, I guess it is." She said, trying to usher them out as quickly as possible. "I'll have to buy a grow light."

"Be careful," the other man said.

"Huh? What do you mean?" Pamela blurted more loudly than was warranted.

"Oh, nothing." The man was obviously taken aback by Pamela's defensive tone. "I've been reading that the DEA is keeping track of who buys that kind of stuff. You know, to try and bust people that want to grow dope at home . . . Not that—I didn't mean to imply that . . ."

"Thanks," Pamela said. "I'll be discreet."

After they left she could not bear to be alone in the place, so she took the subway uptown and wandered Times Square. Somehow the sleaziness of Forty-second Street made her feel better. The ugly reality of New York contrasted sharply with the reality of her work and promising new position in life.

That promise had begun to fade by the end of her first month. Pamela gazed out the window of her corner office at the institute. She was worried. She had been unable to make any significant progress in her research. There was no pressure, at least not yet. But she was beginning to doubt her abilities, to wonder whether or not she belonged in such an exclusive community.

She never got tired of the view. It was a midtown office building, and she could catch the afternoon sun gleaming on the gilded crown of the Chrysler Building.

"Pamela?" she turned in her ergonometric swivel chair to see Dr. Pritchard standing in her door.

"Hello, Elliot. Come in." He was as well-groomed as ever and wore a maroon bow tie. Pamela liked his ties. They made her more comfortable somehow.

"How are things?" he asked, looking out the window.

"Oh, fine," she lied.

"I don't mean work," he said. "Are you enjoying New York?"

"I love it. It's a dream come true for me. Really."

"Yes," he sighed. "One gets attached. I don't know if I will ever be able to leave."

"But why would you want to?"

"I've always had a fantasy of living on a ranch out in the high plains of Wyoming, far away from . . . all this." He gestured to the traffic below.

"Oh," she said. "That sounds nice."

He laughed a little ambiguous laugh; hard to tell if it was directed at her, him, or both of them. "Listen, I have two tickets to the Met tonight. Do you like opera?"

"Well . . ."

"It grows on you," he said. "Ever been to the Met?"

"No."

"You need to go. At least once. It's part of the experience."

She didn't say anything. Pamela had a rare gift. She could let conversations lapse without feeling the compulsion to talk, say anything, stupid or not, like most people.

"The city, I mean," he said awkwardly. "Part of the New York experience."

"Yes," she said, thoughtfully. "I suppose it is. Alright. I'll go."

The show was unbearable, an unending barrage from a shrill soprano. Halfway through the second act, he leaned over and whispered, "Had enough?"

Her expression was all the answer he needed. Soon they were in the lobby.

"Sorry," he said. "This is an aberration. Believe me."

"I'm afraid I don't know much about opera," she said.

"I know a great espresso bar in the Village. It's practically straight out of the fifties: beatniks, Kerouac-style rap, and jazz, and they have wonderful cheesecake."

Pamela smiled. "Sounds perfect."

It was. They lingered for hours, drinking coffee and listening to entertainment from the fringe of life.

"So tell me," he said, trying to sound casual and not succeeding, "how is it that an attractive woman of your abilities has managed to remain single?"

"It's a long story," she sighed.

"Care to talk about it?"

"No."

"I'm sorry," he said, hearing the pain in her voice. "It's none of my business, I know. It's just that I like you. I . . ." He stopped, very embarrassed.

"That's OK." She placed her hand on his. "It's just too complicated for me to talk about right now. Coming to New York, working at the institute—it is just what I needed. Some things I need to put behind me is all . . . and I like you, too."

"Can I get you a cab?" he asked her later, when they stood on the street. It was cold. Pamela pulled her long, down-filled coat tightly around her.

"No thanks. I'd like to walk for a while."

"But it's late," he said. "I mean it's not safe," he added when she failed to say anything.

"Oh, I know my way around here," she said. "I feel safe enough."

"Why don't we have a drink?" he suggested. "At my place. It's not far. We can walk there."

"I don't know. I kind of wanted to get some things done tomorrow. And it's already late."

"Forget about work," he said.

"Yeah." She smiled.

His place was like his wardrobe. Tastefully eccentric. There was a large sofa and a coffee table, circa early sixties in his living room. A Dali print hung on the wall opposite the sofa.

He poured wine while she sat looking at the lazy clocks in the print. "Dali's surrealism seems almost quaint, these days," she said taking her wine.

"I suppose it does. Life itself is stranger. Is that what you mean?"

"Something like," she said, dreamily. "Something like."

A long silence followed.

"How did you get into mathematics?" he asked.

"When I was in school, everyone was experimenting with life," she said. "You know, yoga, meditation, drugs. One of my best friends just vanished one day. He went to the East to seek enlightenment . . . or something.

"I just never could understand it all. All the feverish seeking, all the bizarre methods people were using. Still . . . I sometimes think that was better than what the kids are up to these days."

"Which is?" he prompted.

"Nothing." She laughed. "They all seem so bored. At least we weren't bored, or if we were, it was extravagant boredom!" She made a gesture of gay abandon with her arm, spilling some wine on the coffee table.

"I'm so sorry!" she said.

"It's nothing."

"No. This is a really fine piece of furniture. A real collector's item. Let me wipe it up."

"No really . . ."

"I insist. Where are your paper towels?" She got up.

"They're in the kitchen."

She returned and cleaned up the mess. It was only a few drops.

"The stain would have added character," he said as she sat back down.

"Nonsense. You must take care of your things. I mean . . . oh I must sound ridiculous." She set her glass down.

"Not at all. You don't seem ridiculous at all. Tell me more. You were about to describe your early interest in mathematics."

"Well, I just couldn't see that any of those things people were doing were real. But I was as interested as the rest. Then I took an abstract algebra course. I knew I was good at math, but it was then that I saw what I thought everyone else was looking for, except that I saw it in the pure, metaphysical reality of mathematics. Do you know what I mean?"

"I think I do," he said softly. She was gazing at him intently. He was fascinated by her look.

"And it was real! Not some dream to be had on a short-lived drug trip or a story to be bought from a ripoff guru. It was real, right there for the asking. So I took it, and . . ."

"And the mathematical community spat in your face," he said.

She was taken aback, but only for a moment. "Yes. That's right. Until now, anyway."

"Until now," he said, and leaned toward her. She did not resist his kiss.

It was a long kiss. Afterward they had more wine, in silence. When he took her in his arms again, she pressed more closely against him. He slipped his hand inside her shirt. She sighed, and did not resist. Her nipples grew stiff under his caress.

Pamela wore a plain wool skirt and nylon panty hose. He put his hand on her knee, and she uncrossed her legs. Then he slid his hand slowly up her thigh. He reached up and slid his hand underneath the elastic waistband. She gasped as his hand went lower. Suddenly an image flashed in her mind. It was the image of a sharp, hard crystal sliding into the side of her lover, mortally wounding him, blood freely flowing onto her kitchen floor.

"Unnghh!" she cried out, the breath forcefully shot from her diaphragm. She stood gasping, smoothing her skirt.

"I'm sorry!" she cried. "I can't! You must think me an awful tease. I mean, I want to really. I'm not like this! It's just that I can't right now. I want to so badly! But I just can't."

"Pamela . . ." He was standing beside her, trying to hold her, but she wouldn't let him. "I'm sorry, I guess I shouldn't have . . ."

"Don't say that," she said. "It has nothing to do with you. I have to go now." She grabbed her coat and left under his protests that it wasn't safe, that he should get her a cab.

Pamela stared out her apartment window overlooking Gramercy Park. She wanted to go walk there in the cold moonlight, but people said it was dangerous in the dark. It was 2:00 A.M., a time when she sometimes came alive, or at least a part of her did, a part that lay dormant during the hours of the day.

She knew something that night. She did not know how she knew it; it seemed a rather preposterous thing, but she knew it. Her fate, Alan's eventual demise or recovery, and Lew's adventure had something to do with her work. Her mathematical research. The unexpected revelation on Alan's postcard, twenty years after the fact, in upside-down Sanskrit, had been no coincidence. She knew that at the time of the occurrence. But now she knew it with a clarity that had been lacking. Not only was it not a coincidence (coincidences like that just do not happen), it was part of a larger story.

She had to work. Work as she had never worked before. For Alan and for Lew. But most of all for herself. Because it was plain to her that night, looking out at the world, that if she were ever to be free of both of them, if she were ever to start a new life, her own life, a life that she desperately wanted, it would only come through a resolution of the drama that included poor Alan lying half-dead and Lew (wherever he was). That resolution was intimately tied to her work.

In a way it made sense. Or it made sense in a way that she did not understand. Lew had talked of taking a journey into the unknown, a metaphysical journey. Alan had set off on just such a trip when he left her for the Orient, so many years ago.

In fact she had done the same thing with her mathematics. But, of the three, she was the only one who had precise control over what she did. Possibly that control had something to do with the possibility of Lew's return.

She was not deeply concerned with saving either of the two men. She had loved Alan for most of her adult life. She now saw that love as a quaint thing, an artifact for the files of her romantic past. She had loved Lew in a different way. She had never seen Lew as the bold gallant that Alan had represented to her. She knew Lew too well for that, his pettiness, his selfishness, and his absurd dreams. Her love for Lew had been an affair of compromise, an accommodation to reality, the way things *were* as opposed to the way she might have liked them to be.

But she now saw even her plans to marry Lew as just another curious chapter in the unfolding story of her life. A chapter that had ended. But she also saw that they were still bound together, caught in a web that transcended the plans or ideas of either of them. Before she could move on to the next phase, before she could find freedom in the next chapter of her life, she had to resolve the present adventure.

She could only do that by trying to understand something of what had happened to Lew. For Pamela there was only one way to do that: mathematics. And while she had control over the mathematical structures that might bring some connection to Lew, that control depended on precise manipulation of highly refined, abstract mathematical objects.

That sort of work, as any good mathematician will confirm, demands uncompromising dedication. Pamela had seldom been able to muster the kind of concentration that mathematical research at that level required. She had gone as far as she had because she was brilliant and could often find little windows of opportunity to let that brilliance shine through.

But much more was now required. For the task that lay ahead, Pamela was going to have to work with an energy and concentration that pushed the boundaries of human limitations.

The full realization of that filled her with a new kind of peace. It was a peace laced with excitement. And a little fear. But it was for a good cause: her life.

The next morning, Elliot Pritchard came around to see her. "Hello," he said sheepishly. "You know I didn't really mean for things to move so fast last night . . . really . . . I guess I owe you an apology."

"No you don't," she said.

He could not read much in her tone. It made him even more uncomfortable. "Well, what I mean to say is . . . I mean we don't have to . . . I'd like to go out with you again. Just go out—you know?" He was turning red and shifting from one foot to the other as he leaned against her doorjamb.

"I'd like to. Really. But there are some things I have to take care of first."

"Oh?"

"Personal things. That's all. Unfinished business, I guess you could say. Once it is over—then we'll see." She smiled. It was a real smile, which threw him into an even more befuddled state.

"Does it have anything to do with work?" he asked.

"Yes. Yes it does. I realized last night that I have got to

spend all my time and energy on my research right now."

"We are very patient here at the institute." He said quickly, "We don't want you to feel any pressure to produce. I know that sometimes it takes years for one good idea to surface, one good paper to get published. We are not like the rest of the academic community in that respect. Believe me. You wouldn't be here if we did not believe in you, if we did not have confidence that you will eventually succeed."

"Oh it has nothing to do with the institute," she said.

"But I thought you just said that it was your work . . ."

"It is. But right now my research is an intensely personal matter . . . I can't really explain. But I just know that until I solve the automorphic singularity conjecture, I will not be free in any way, personally or professionally. I really can't explain any more than that.

"But when I have got it I will know."

"Know what?" he asked, baffled.

"What I can do with the rest of my life." She smiled again.

He left, perplexed. He knew that for some, maybe most, a mathematician's work was an idiosyncratic thing, a personal thing. But Pamela had carried it to a new level. The thing that bothered him the most was the strange peace she had projected. The woman was obviously driven, completely possessed by her work. But by giving in to that drive, she had found peace. He did not want to admit it, but he was actually jealous. It was the combination he had sought and failed to find, the perfect equilibrium between passion for work and the serenity needed to follow through on that passion. Pamela had found it. He wondered how long it would last for her. Before she burned out. Or would she be lost forever in the metaphysical world of logic and abstract structure?

He hoped not. For purely selfish reasons. The previous night had ignited another passion he had thought long gone. But it was there and still growing. He resolved to leave her alone for as long as he could, to let her work. But he did not know how long that would be. Love has its own timetable and Elliot was on that schedule.

Pamela brought her old postcards into the office. Her sharp mind had begun to piece things together. Time had been transcended in a subtle way by the old shoe box of epistles from an exotic land. Many years ago Alan had sent information that was only now relevant. It held the key to his fate and Lew's.

Pamela understood just enough of the kind of esoteric Buddhism that Alan practiced in Tibet so as not to be too surprised. The goal of the yoga that Alan went in search of was the transcendence of all worldly limitations. These included time. So if Alan had succeeded at all, he might have had access to the future. But why, she wondered, had he not told her of this? Maybe whatever he had discovered was something that he did not understand himself; maybe the information was in his subconscious only.

No matter. Pamela was convinced that he had coded that information into his correspondence. It was information that could lead to her solution of the automorphic singularity problem.

It would also vindicate her assertion that singularity groups had applications beyond mathematics. She knew that there were those at the institute who thought Elliot's decision to hire her was a lapse in judgment. They were waiting for her failure to use as ammunition against Elliot, to get him removed as director. She sometimes thought they might be right. How could her equations shed any light on the mysteries of the soul?

But the picture was beginning to come into focus. Lew and Alan both had always been seekers after "it," that elusive notion of pure, unsullied self. Alan had let the chase lead him to the farthest, highest corner of the earth that he could find. Over the years, Lew had all but abandoned the quest. But now, these many years later, they were both back in the thick of it. And it was going to take a woman with brain, pencil, and paper to get them out of it.

She laughed out loud. How absurd it was! And if anyone were to ask her how she knew, she would have to answer "feminine intuition." Maybe there was something to it after all. It didn't matter, though. All that mattered was her work. She opened the box and began searching the cards with the strange postmarks, searching for clues to a most-perplexing and deep mathematical problem.

The exposition of the automorphic singularity map would

bring her entire body of mathematical work into focus. She surmised that Lew's adventure could take one of two turns. Either he would be swallowed up forever in progressively deeper layers of abstraction, or his experiences would come into focus, that is, he would recognize himself in whatever new place he found himself and bring his adventure to a crisis.

Knowing Lew, Pamela understood that the first option was the more likely. Lew was an incurable romantic, bright, but his mind lacked clarity. Whatever the manifestations of his new reality, he was far more likely to go chasing dreams than analyze. He could be trapped forever in deeper layers of dreams from which ultimately there would be no escape.

If she could solve the mathematical problem, she might bring about a singularity, a point in consciousness outside all space and time, a point at which it would be possible for Lew to step back through the door.

How Alan had managed to see her problem years ago was a mystery. She reasoned that his meditations in Tibet had somehow given him access to the same space that Lew now roamed. He might have even met Lew there. But he had, either consciously or unconsciously, unraveled the mathematical key to the place and given that information to Pamela years before she needed it.

By afternoon she had succeeded in discovering that the search would not be easy. She had been through all the cards and examined the script, English and Sanskrit, from all possible angles. There were no more equations waiting to leap out. Whatever was there was more subtly coded. She went for coffee.

The institute offices were comfortable and attractive, the perfect blend of corporate conformity and academic eccentricity. She was beginning to feel that she was actually where she belonged, for the first time in her life.

"Dr. Fine?" It was the front office secretary.

"Oh." Pamela was startled, having been lost in thought as she poured cream into her coffee. She spilled a little on the rug, a strange-colored blend of turquoise and pastel pink.

As she bent down to wipe it up the secretary said, "Some new mail for you." Something in her tone of voice caused Pamela to stand back up quickly.

"Thank you," she said.

"You may not want to thank me when you look at the post-mark," the secretary said. "People make jokes about the mail being slow, but . . ." She handed the postcard to Pamela.

It was yellow with age. The postmark was some twenty years earlier, and it was from Tibet. "Oh my God!" Pamela gasped. It was from Alan. Addressed to her home, it had been forwarded to the institute.

"They wanted a dollar for postage due," the secretary said, "but I told them that they had a lot of nerve, considering it is twenty years late. Are you alright?" she asked. Pamela was leaning against the wall, just staring at the card. "Yes," she said. " . . . really. It's just that I never expected to see another one of these."

"Neither did I. Let me make you some fresh," the secretary said, taking Pamela's cup, from which she was about to spill coffee all over the rug. "This stuff has been on the burner all day."

After struggling in her office with the new postcard for two hours, Pamela made a decision. She could find no more clues in any of the cards, including the new one. Old doubts began to set in, even the haunting suspicion that she was delusional. Worst of all was her inability to make any significant progress with or without the help of Alan's old communications.

She had to bring someone else in on it. She did not know if she could trust Elliot, but there was no one else. It was with a trembling voice that she said on the telephone, "Elliot, can you please come to my office? There is something I have to show you."

He was incredulous at first, but when she showed him the one card that had led to her breakthrough and how it fitted so perfectly with her computations, he said, "Well I don't see how you can fake a postcard like that. Or why you would want to unless you are completely crazy . . ." When she lowered her eyes he quickly added, " . . . which I doubt very seriously."

"There is something else," she said, making another quick decision.

"What is that?" he asked.

"Can you come over to my place for dinner tonight? I'd

like to cook some *real* enchiladas for you. You Yankees don't really have a clue when it comes to Mexican food."

"Well, sure." He smiled. "I'd love to. Should I bring anything?"

"Just a healthy suspension of disbelief," she said enigmatically.

"That was great," Elliot said. "You are right. I've never really appreciated the subtleties of . . ."

"It's OK, Elliot," Pamela said, "you don't have to . . ."

"No, I mean it. They were delicious." Pamela seemed uneasy. It put Elliot on reserve, so that what he said sounded insincere.

They moved to Pamela's small living room. "I'm surprised you got such a big place," Elliot said, "Manhattan real estate being what it is . . . and our salaries being what they are."

"Well, I needed a spare bedroom," Pamela said.

Something in her voice made Elliot afraid to ask why.

"I've got to show you something," she said after an uncomfortable silence. She rose from the sofa and walked toward the spare room, motioning for him to follow.

"You know what I said about the cards?" she asked at the door.

"Yes." Elliot's heart was beating faster than he liked.

"I lied about one thing. Alan, the man who went east to India and Tibet? Well, he came back a short time ago."

"Where is he?" Elliot asked, but she did not answer directly.

Instead she opened the door. It was dark. The room was illuminated by a single low lamp at the far end. Pamela walked toward the light and stopped in front of a long, coffinlike box.

"Pamela . . ." Elliot said, "I'm not sure that this is such a good idea . . ."

She seemed not to hear. Instead she was unscrewing the bolts on the box. When she was done she said in a near whisper, "Come here."

He obeyed as she was removing the lid. He leaned over and looked inside as she placed the top against the wall. "Pamela," he said, annoyed, "if this is some sort of joke . . ."

"Joke?" She looked inside and gasped, "Oh my God! Alan . . . what happened?"

Elliot was already backing away, trying to think of a good excuse that would allow him to leave gracefully. Pamela just stood there staring at the well-cushioned, but completely empty interior.

9

Checked Out

Lew had no trouble finding the index card. "*Sheila—nouspace feminine counterpart of Lew Slack*," the card read. He pulled the card and ran down the stairwell. Before he dashed off into the stacks he had the presence of mind to take pen and paper in order to make a map. His previous experience had shown how easy it would be to become hopelessly lost in the labyrinth.

Felix seemed to have no trouble. As Lew meandered about, taking notes and making a schematic, the big cat would be at his side as often as not, but he never had trouble finding Lew when he was bored or wanted petting.

Lew could make no sense of the library's cataloging system. Each book was carefully numbered, and the numbers went more or less in sequence, but no sooner would he think he was on the right track than the next twist in the maze would bring him to a new sequence, and he would have to begin all over again.

This went on for several hours and he had penetrated so deeply that the green glow from the seascape was no longer visible. Hungry, thirsty, and tired, he knew that he needed to start working his way out of the maze, if only to get a drink of water from the fountain. He had kept a careful schematic of the layout. His training as computer programmer helped immeasurably in that regard. He had been able to devise a binary code that accurately reflected each turn he had taken. The result was an efficient program of the tiny section of the library he had explored. Lew was certain it would lead him out.

But following the program to get out proved to be a tedious, slow business. What Lew was doing, in effect, was executing a computer program inside his brain. The irony of the concept was not lost on him. It was twofold. It was a peculiar reversal of the ordinary. Normally the computer is a machine and the data is really only a set of signals existing inside the machine. But this exercise turned that concept inside out. The database was the physical structure, the library itself, and the computer was he, a living creature inside the database.

And the second irony was the reversal of the common notion of artificial intelligence, the simulation of human intelligence on a computer. Lew always thought it impossible to program intelligence as we know it into a computer. But the reverse of that, the simulation of computer functions by the human mind, was a new twist, one that so far had received almost no attention in earthly scientific circles.

He could see why. It was an enormously time-consuming bummer. He had to stop every ten yards or so and consult the program. That entailed binary procedures which even the slowest computer could execute in nanoseconds. But it took Lew at least a second or two. Those seconds quickly added up, and he was completely exhausted before he was halfway back. He knew that he needed to stop and rest in order to avoid making a mistake that might get him hopelessly lost.

He made one more calculation, which told him to turn left. He rounded the corner and stopped, stunned by what he saw. It was a mirror. Either he was lost or someone had recently placed it there while he was exploring deeper in. He checked the numbers and quickly determined that he was not lost; he had indeed come this way, but there had been no mirror to be seen on his way in.

It was an old-fashioned, oval mirror held in place on a stand that allowed it to pivot on a horizontal center pole. The carving on the wood border was ornate, depicting vines, flowers, and various organic forms, some of which, on closer inspection, were quite erotic. And the glass was clearer than any glass Lew had ever seen. It reflected with a luminosity all its own that enhanced anything in its field, making colors brighter and shapes much sharper, better defined than the originals.

Lew stood looking at his reflection, awed by details of his personage which he had never before seen. After several minutes of this he sat down to rest, leaning his back against the base of a bookshelf. He nearly dozed off, but a movement from the direction of the mirror roused him.

He turned to look and gasped out loud. A naked female form was facing away from him in the mirror. Her figure was exquisite, hips at a slight angle, rounded buttocks, and slender back rising to delicate yet strong shoulders set off by a cascade of blond hair. He quickly looked behind, but there was no one there. Her reflection, however, was still quite evident. She turned to the side and pulled a book from the shelf. When he saw her profile Lew instantly recognized her as Sheila, the woman in the crystal, the one he so desperately sought.

It was intensely erotic to see such a beautiful, nude female body in a library. She held the book slightly below her bare breasts. She read for a few minutes with a puzzled look on her face and then put it back, at the same time turning to face Lew.

"Sheila," he called to her, "I'm here." Apparently she could neither see nor hear him. She walked in his direction, growing larger in the mirror. She stopped for a moment, her hips looming large just in front of Lew. His eyes were drawn to the blond curls between her legs, which instantly disappeared. She was gone, appearing to walk out of the mirror into nowhere.

Lew continued to stare for several minutes, hoping that she would reappear, but all he saw was his own reflection, which now seemed paltry and pitiful. He looked for the book which she had held and found one that matched what he saw in the mirror. It was a sex manual. It was so detailed and vivid that Lew grew flushed from the reading. Just as he remembered the danger of getting too involved in the library's literature and had determined to close the book, he felt himself drawn in to a sex school narrative.

"Girls," the instructor was saying, "this is a man." There was nervous giggling as the young women, in various states of provocative undress, looked on. "Note the narrow hips." The instructor, also a woman but older, ran her hands down the sides of Lew's naked pelvis.

"Note the body hair." She gently pulled the sparse black growth around Lew's nipples. "Turn around, please," she said to Lew, who obeyed instantly. "The buttocks are noticeably less rounded, more compact. You see how the tissue is more muscular, less fatty. Watch." She slapped Lew's butt, giving him a firm spank that did not hurt so much as stimulate. She put her hands on Lew's shoulders and rotated him so that he was again facing the audience.

She placed her hand on his genitals. Her touch was soft yet commanding. Lew felt the blood surge to his nether regions. "And this," she said with a tone that hinted at amusement coupled with quiet resignation, "is his penis." This brought a louder chorus of tense tittering. "Now girls," the instructor warned, "none of that. This is all quite natural. And you must pay attention. Note the growth." She released Lew's half-erect member. There were expressions of open curiosity from a few of the students.

"How big does it get?" one girl asked shyly.

"That depends," the instructor replied, "on the state of arousal and on the individual. Some may get quite large— perhaps ten inches or more." There were some worried gasps at that. "But this specimen—hmm," she took hold of Lew's penis and squeezed it. "I should think he is a little under the average— coming in at slightly less than six inches when fully stiff."

This distracted Lew.

"Dear, dear," the instructor said. "Seems to be taking a while." She squeezed harder. "Mary?"

"Yes, mum?" A petite brunette wearing bikini panties and nothing else answered.

"Could you please come up here and give us a hand?"

"Well, I . . ." She blushed and lowered her head.

"It's quite alright, Mary. Now get up here. That's a good girl. Sometimes a little visual stimulation helps. Would you take over here please?" She offered the penis to Mary, who blushed even more deeply. "Mary, how are you going to learn?" the instructor said in a more severe tone. Mary's eyes met Lew's as her fingers folded around his penis. They were reticent but full of curiosity.

The instructor was fully dressed in a conservative business suit. She proceeded with a slow, but extremely elegant strip-tease. Lew again felt himself growing hard. When she was down to bra and panties she instructed Mary to move her hand in a stroking motion. Mary, quite embarrassed by this, obliged, eliciting a low moan from Lew. This caused her to stop and let go.

"No, no darling," the instructor said, "that is quite a normal response—you are doing a good job." The instructor removed her bra and approached Lew with a writhing, erotic motion that sent him into a sexual frenzy. She stopped just short of letting her nipples brush his chest. She removed her panties, and drew them slowly across his face. The scent of her vagina was warm and sweet. Lew sighed. She winked at him, dropped her panties, and proceeded to lie down on a sofa in front of him.

"Mary," she said, "release him and get the ruler." Mary did as she was told and stood next to Lew, holding a wooden ruler. "Measure him, silly girl!!" the instructor said. Mary bent and held the ruler up against Lew's penis. "Well?" the instructor said, impatiently.

"Six and one-eighth inches, mum," Mary said.

"My my," the instructor said. She was reclining, legs drawn up and pulled to the side. "I underestimated. Well that is actually *good* news, although I'm rarely wrong about these things. Bring him here, Mary." As Mary led Lew to the couch, the instructor stretched out her legs and slowly spread them open. Her labia were glistening with moisture. Mary watched wide-eyed as Lew knelt on the couch and bent to kiss the downy pink furrow. "Now watch closely, girls," the instructor sighed. "This is an extra which I hadn't counted on."

After a few moments of this, she said, "Mary, we are running out of time. Period's almost over—unnh, ummm. Please direct the subject's penis to the appropriate place. You know what I mean."

Mary reached between Lew's legs and, grabbing his penis, pulled him up so that the tip of it was just nestled in the right spot. The instructor reached around and put both hands on Lew's buttocks and slowly pulled him in. "Ooooh," she said softly.

Lew followed her rhythm and soon they were moving with rapid abandon.

"The body just takes over girls—oh! oh! OH!—that's the most important lesson to learn—and ah! ah! AAH!—learn to

read the male signals so that you don't get left in the lurch—
OOH! GOD! OOOH! YES! OH MY! COME ON! OH!"

After her orgasm, she whispered to Lew so no one else
could hear, "OK baby, you can come now. Thanks for being a
good sport." Lew responded, like a good student. At the same
moment the bell rang, and the young women quickly gathered
their things and left.

Lew found himself lying naked, facedown on the thick,
Persian carpet. He got up slowly and dressed. When he put
the book back on the shelf he was careful to memorize the
location. He felt certain that this was a book he would want
to read again. The mirror was gone and so Lew resumed the
laborious execution of the program to find his way back out
of the stacks.

When he finally emerged in front of the underwater sea-.
scape a few hours later, he was exhausted and extremely
hungry. "I wish I could find a safe eating book," he said.
He thought he imagined a warm, spicy odor. Then he heard
a peculiar sound. It was coming from a direction farther down
the glass wall, but out of sight. Lew followed it and found
Felix loudly lapping a large bowl of cream. "Felix!" Lew said.
"Where did you get that?"

The cat just looked up at him and hissed briefly to warn
him off the cream. "Sorry," Lew said. "Don't let me bother
you. I've only fed you since you were a kitten."

Then Lew saw the source of the aromas. There was a steaming plate of curried rice on the desktop next to Felix. Lew
loved Indian food. He was halfway through the meal before he
noticed the stack of fresh-baked, Indian flatbread and a glass
of red wine. They were stashed in a large, square cubbyhole
on the desk. The wine was an excellent cabernet. Lew guessed
California.

"Ah! kitty-kat," Lew said, finishing the wine and wiping up
the last bit of pungent sauce with the last bite of bread, "that
is more like it, eh?" Felix just stretched out on the rug and
closed his eyes. "Good idea," Lew said. He lay down next to
the cat and fell asleep.

Whoever was leaving the meals seemed to know Lew's
favorites. He would periodically find delicacies like barbecued

chicken with a side of steamed broccoli and a chilled mug of bock beer, or pasta with fresh mussels and glass of fine Bordeaux.

Try as he would he could not catch his mysterious benefactor in action. Sometimes he would hear the sound of a book closing or footsteps coming from the stacks, but search was to no avail; the maze was so dense that tracking a person through the myriad twists and turns was virtually impossible.

There were no clocks in the library, and the lighting never changed from the soft pastel glow that seemed to emanate from everywhere and nowhere—the light was perfect for both reading and sleeping. Lew tried to keep track by counting meals, but eventually time was forgotten, replaced by the more nebulous category of simple duration. Lew just knew that he was there and had been there for a period of time somewhere between short and long.

He made regular forays into the stacks trying to decode the call numbering system in order to find the book that he hoped would take him into an imagined paradise, the world of Sheila. The desk which he had claimed was piled with the papers that were the results of these explorations. They were filled with binary code and schematic diagrams. The work was extremely frustrating. On several occasions he thought he finally had it, the big picture, only to discover that the new pattern was still only a part of the whole.

To break the tedium he would drink coffee and stare out at the sea, watching the gliding graceful rays and brilliantly colored fish. These times were the most relaxing, meditative hours Lew had ever experienced. And he frequently swam in the bracing waters of the pool in the catalogue room above. Often he would float and stare up at the domed panorama, always finding something new there, something else from his life.

For excitement Lew would read. But that proved to be so dangerous that he did it less and less. Some of the books seemed innocuous; he could read them as ordinary texts. But if a scene or idea moved his emotions or intellect even a little, he was liable to get trapped inside the narrative. When that happened he could not control the getting out. Only when the tension was resolved, or a great danger threatened, could he reassert the distance between himself and the literature. There were some close calls.

The worst was when he had gone back to his favorite, the sex manual. He had found a chapter on extramarital relations which seemed exciting and provocative. In it he was making love to a mistress when the woman's husband came home. The man pulled a pocketknife. Lew was standing naked while the irate husband took vicious swipes at his most vulnerable areas. Lew took a nasty cut on the forehead before he was able to break away. It looked as though the wound would leave a permanent scar above his right eyebrow. Afterward he had resolved to leave the book alone.

But some time later Lew woke after a long sleep thinking about the sex manual. The smell of tandoori chicken lingered from the empty plate on the nearby desk. He contemplated going for a cold swim, but found himself instead retracing the path to the book. He no longer needed to consult his program notes of the stack layout and soon found himself approaching the right spot. The carpet seemed to be alive, the pattern more beautiful than ever. But when Lew examined it he could identify no obvious change. He realized that the design was both more differentiated and more unified.

The book was lying open on the rug. This surprised Lew since it was his practice always to return it to its proper place on the shelf, but he gave it no serious thought. He picked it up. The scene on the page before him looked promising, a ménage à trois, so he began reading.

But something was wrong. Lew had expected from his initial reading to find himself alone with two women. But instead he found another man present. There was something familiar about the intruder. A pair of loose, pajama-style trousers were discarded on the floor, and the young man in question stood wearing only a long Indian shirt which failed to conceal his state of arousal.

"Oh my, look at the tent," one of the women laughed, pointing at the shirt. She was tall, dark, slim, and beautifully naked.

"He certainly comes well equipped," the other, more buxom one, said. "Who goes first?"

"Alan!" Lew said loudly, when recognition dawned.

Alan was momentarily disoriented, as if he could not place the direction of the new voice at first. His eyes finally focused on Lew. "What are you doing here?" he said, "This is *my* scene."

"Oh boy," the blonde with the large breasts said, "I guess there's no waiting." She approached Alan.

The scene resulted in a resentful Alan and a puzzled Lew able to function at less than desired capacity.

"Don't worry, honey," the willowy one said to Lew at one point, "we all have our slow days."

Shortly after that the two found themselves facing each other back in the stacks, book still open on the floor. Lew put it carefully back on the shelf while Alan dressed.

"You!" Lew said, buttoning his shirt. "How . . . ?"

"Give me a break, man," Alan said. "It gets pretty lonely there at the monastery. I'm not supposed to do this sort of thing"—he gestured at the book—"but I can't see that it hurts anybody . . . right?"

"So you are still . . ."

"Practicing my meditations," Alan finished for Lew. "Yeah. The monks know when I've been indulging. I can tell by the way they look at me, but I don't think they care. We all have our needs, you know."

"Yeah," Lew said, "Sorry if I spoiled things."

"Maybe we should work out a schedule," Alan said. "I'll take Mondays and Wednesdays."

When Lew took Alan up to the catalogue room, Alan was surprised. "Wow! Did you do this? This is far out!"

"What do you mean, 'did I do it'? " Lew asked.

"This room was never here before," Alan said. "I've been here several times, but there was never anything but the infinite maze of stacks."

"Well *I* certainly didn't do it," Lew said.

They were standing in front of the fountain. Alan looked up at the dome. "Lew! All the pictures are about you. This must be your place. And look, 'The curse of the camel!' Far-out, man!"

Lew looked to the lower reaches of the dome, where Alan was pointing. It was a scene which had hitherto gone unnoticed. It was a parody of the famous Sistine chapel rendition of God reaching out to touch Adam, thereby imparting the gift of spiritual life. In place of God there was a skeleton with white-boned arm extended in the classic pose that Michelangelo had made so famous. Adam's role was taken over by Lew, who stretched to receive a burning Camel cigarette, lit at the wrong end, the end opposite the Camel trademark. Lew recognized the skeletal figure as Trismegistus, and the deathlike grin on the fleshless mouth seemed overly garish.

Lew took it in for several moments and then said, "Alan, people don't say things like that anymore."

"What things?" ·

" 'Far-out' and 'man.' "

"What do they say?"

"You don't want to know."

"I *do* want to know," Alan said with intense curiosity.

" 'Awesome' and 'dude.' Things like that."

"Really?" Alan sounded serious. "That's terrible."

"I told you so, man."

Looking back in the same general area of the dome, Lew saw a picture which, although seen before, made him extremely uneasy in Alan's presence. Two men were fighting. One was about to plunge a sharp hexagonal crystal into the side of the other. The faces were all too familiar. Alan was drinking from the fountain. Before he could look up again, Lew said quickly, "You want some coffee, Alan?"

"Coffee? Real coffee?" Alan's eyes brightened as he straightened up.

"Yeah. It's delicious. Come on."

"This is great," Alan said when they were seated below, watching a giant sea turtle. "At the monastery they only have Nescafe. I keep trying to tell those crazy Buddhists that it is not the same as real coffee. Either they don't understand or they are just having me on." He took another sip and sighed.

"So it has been you all along," Lew said.

"Me what?" Alan asked, breaking out of the peaceful reverie inspired by the coffee and cool, relaxing vista.

"The meals. All the food I have been eating. And the sounds I hear from time to time. Books closing, footsteps . . ."

"Maybe the noises, but I don't know anything about food," Alan said, puzzled.

"Somebody's been leaving me food," Lew said, voice rising. "Grilled shrimp, barbecued chicken, lasagna . . ."

"Wait a minute!" Alan said. "I haven't seen food like that in several years. If I did, I would eat it myself."

"Then who . . ." Lew stopped suddenly. "Alan, you hear that?"

"Yeah," Alan said. But it was only Felix. He came into view pacing down the long concavity of the glass wall in front of the desks.

"Alan, look," Lew said. When Felix got closer a large drumstick was plainly visible, clenched in his sharp teeth. The cat growled a low warning as he passed by the two. He went a few more paces and flopped on the floor, where he began tearing into the meat in earnest.

Suddenly Lew had a thought. "I've never explored very far down that way," he said, indicating the direction from which Felix had come.

They walked for at least two miles. The slow curve of the glass and row of desks seemed to stretch on forever. "Sooner or later we will have to circle around back to our starting point," Lew said.

"Except I get the feeling this goes on forever," Alan said.

"How can it?" Lew asked. "The curve has to make a loop sooner or later."

"Higher dimensional geometric manifold," was Alan's only reply to this.

Alan, who was slightly ahead of Lew stopped. "Look at this," he said.

All the other desks had been empty. This one was piled high with books and notes. Lew picked up a book titled *Confessions*. Alan started to warn him, but was too late. The first sentence drew Lew in like a magnet.

"I must write of these things, lest the weight of them on my conscience prove ultimately too much to bear. Not that writing them will change anything nor will it lessen my guilt, but sometimes the only solace is in disclosure.

"I adhere to no strict chronological order, although I will try to give the earliest events first, and then proceed to the more recent. But there is absolutely no guarantee that precedence in the telling is reflected in fact. My memory is not so good. Some things will come to me only after much self-prodding and will be set down strictly in the order in which they arise.

"When I was a schoolboy life was sometimes very hard. I was a reasonably popular child, having many friends with whom I enjoyed a certain amount of influence. But I was by no means the smartest, fastest, strongest, or biggest of my school chums.

"Sometimes they would tease me and call me names. My best friends! It hurt so badly. I always felt helpless in the face of such taunting. I had no recourse, no way to get back.

"But as I said, I was really rather well placed as far as schoolboys go. There was another lad, a small boy, who had no friends. At least none that I knew of. He was very shy, very quiet, and extremely smart. He always made the highest grades in the class.

"I could tell that he wanted to make friends with me, but I would have nothing to do with him. Not because there was anything particularly unpleasant or disagreeable about him. I rather liked the poor fellow, but he was not popular with my friends, the ones who sometimes tormented me, so I could not justify returning this fellow's overtures toward friendship.

"One day he suggested that we walk home together. Our families lived only a few blocks from each other, so we went the same way. At first I said no, just out of principle, but then when I saw him walk on rather dejectedly I ran to catch up with him.

"'Wait,' I said. 'Sure, let's walk.' My feelings were confused. All at once I liked him, felt sorry for him, and resented him for being a threat to me and my social position at school. How dare he make me feel guilty!

"We walked along, talking about school and boyish things like guns and planes and rocket ships, until we reached our juncture. I don't know what came over me. I really had not planned it. I was not a violent type. But something in me erupted. 'Bye.' he said. 'See you tomorrow.' He was smiling. Happy that he might have a friend at last.

"I saw his extreme vulnerability. Without a second thought I socked him right in the breadbasket! Knocked the wind out of him. I watched him crumple to the sidewalk. He gasped for breath. Tears welled in his eyes, but he could not cry until he got his wind back. 'Bye,' I said. 'See you tomorrow.' And I walked away.

"The next day he was more quiet than usual. At recess he approached me. 'Want to play catch?' he asked, nervously.

'No,' I said and ran off to play baseball with my friends, leaving him alone with a ball.

"That afternoon he was waiting for me outside the school. 'Hi,' he said.

" 'If you try to walk with me, I will slug you again,' I said.

" 'Why?' he asked, fighting back tears.

" 'OK,' I said. 'I won't.'

"He smiled and started to walk with me.

" '*If*,' I said, noticing my friends watching us, 'you carry my books.'

"At first he was surprised, then reluctant. But finally he said OK. We walked and gradually he seemed to forget that I had humiliated him. He became quite friendly, and I actually enjoyed our conversation. He was really interesting, with good jokes and stories to tell.

"Again we came to our intersection. He handed me my books quite innocently. 'Bye,' he said.

"I put my books down. 'Just a minute,' I said, and began to roll up my sleeve. I made it obvious what I was going to do.

" 'But you said you wouldn't,' he stammered.

" 'I lied,' I said, and whammed him again as hard as I could. His books went flying and he hit the ground hard, skinning his chin. He was able to cry even through his cramped lungs. It was probably the most pathetic, forlorn sound I have ever heard.

"I think I ran away from the horror of it, from the horror of myself.

"He never spoke to me again. He became even quieter at school, never playing with anyone, never joking. I did not bother him anymore. Sometimes at recess I would see him watching me, sitting alone, and I would feel something strange, something hard and sad, but then I would look away and find myself back with my friends and our jabber, taunts and jokes. His family moved away sometime after all this and I never saw him again. I forgot about him.

"Except sometimes at night when I am about to fall asleep, I hear him crying or see him watching me, lonely and small, and I cringe. My whole body jumps like I want to crawl outside myself.

"But I cannot, and every word, even to this very day, every word is torturously true."

While Lew was immersed in *Confessions*, Alan was browsing the other papers and books on the desk. He found some equations which interested him, kept him busy for several minutes. Then he found the book which Lew had picked up earlier, *Strange and Distant Episodes*. Years of training in the yogic techniques of mental concentration made it possible for him to actually read without being drawn through the literary doorway into the actual narrative of the text. He came across a disturbing passage. It concerned him, twenty-odd years later wandering the slums of New York City in a semicomatose state. He grabbed a pen, copied down a New York City telephone number from the text onto a sheet of paper, and ran quickly upstairs to the coffee room and entered the telephone booth.

He quickly picked up the phone and dialed. "Pamela?" he said, when he heard someone answer.

Meanwhile, Lew finished reading the passage, and the book fell from his hands and landed with a plop on the desk amid all the other books and papers, remaining open at the last page of the shameful story. He was shaking and crying. It was a story that he knew too well. An incident from his past which he had ceased to think much about, except late at night when he could not sleep. It was his story. He was the bully. And now there it was in black-and-white, the ugly truth about himself which he could never change no matter how much it hurt to remember.

Before long Alan appeared and said, "I have some good advice for you, Lew."

"What?" Lew asked sadly.

"Avoid books titled *Confessions*. Especially in a place like this"—Alan had his hand on Lew's shoulder—"unless you want to die of shame and guilt."

"But you don't know the half of it, Alan!" Lew practically wailed. "The things I have done!"

"And I am sure I don't want to know. Spare me, Lew. You think you have a monopoly on shame and regret? It is just your towering ego that torments you, unable to accept that it is not perfect."

When Alan could see that Lew had calmed down a bit he said, "Now take a look at this. Your mystery is solved."

It was a sheet of paper, a handwritten list. "Preferred Foods," was the heading. Listed were most of Lew's favorite meals.

"Garlic soup!" Lew exclaimed. "It's been a long time since I had that!"

"Well somebody plans to make it for you again," Alan said.

"Who?"

"I have no idea, but whoever it is wants to know you better. All these books are about you. Someone is researching your entire life, Lew."

"Why?"

"Don't ask me. The thing that I find more interesting is the mathematics."

"Mathematics?"

"Yeah. Don't you remember? It was my major when I dropped out of school."

"Oh yeah, that's right. You were on to something if I recall," Lew said.

"Well, it was Pamela really," Alan said. "She was doing some highly original work. It was too advanced for me." He got a faraway look in his eye. "We never told anyone, Lew. But we were in love. I mean *really* in love."

"I know," Lew said.

"How . . ."

"She told me years later," Lew added quickly.

"What happened to her?" Alan asked with an urgency.

"Well she . . ." Lew began.

"Never mind," Alan said quickly. "Better that I don't know." He became very quiet.

Lew looked at the papers of equations which interested Alan. They reminded him of something. "What is all this?" he asked.

"Well that's the interesting part," Alan said. "It looks like the natural extension of the stuff that Pamela was working on . . ."

"Singularity groups, you mean?" Lew asked.

"Is that what she ended up calling it?" Alan mused. "Yes, it makes sense. *Singularity* groups. The stuff she was doing related to identity, or singularity if you prefer—how one thing can exist *as* one thing and still be tied into everything else. Anyway this stuff"—he gestured to the papers—"is far more advanced than Pamela's initial work."

"She eventually got a Ph.D. out of it," Lew said.

"It figures," Alan said, wistfully. "She was the smartest one of us all, you know."

"I know," Lew said, "I know." Alan was beginning to fade out. "Do you have to go?" Lew asked.

"Afraid so," Alan said. "It is back to Nescafe and the disciplined life of the monastery."

"Sorry about spoiling your threesome," Lew said.

"Yeah. Well don't wear it out," Alan said, "I'll be back. Save some coffee for me, too." With that he was gone, leaving Lew alone with the unseen researcher.

Lew felt that the investigator was not far away, but he could hear nothing. He copied several of the equations and started back.

The equations were significant because they provided a clue to the puzzle he had been trying to solve, the library's indexing and filing system. Alan's recognition of singularity theory in the equations made Lew realize that he had seen it all before.

The diagrams that he had been able to put together had already convinced him that the layout of the stacks was that of a relational database. The design, in fact, was essentially the same design he had programmed for the professor into the nouancer. But it took Alan's remark to make him see that— just as Alan had provided the singularity equations that had resulted in his breakthrough in programming the nouancer.

He sat, working feverishly for several hours. Without the aid of a computer it was extremely tedious to piece it all together. But having done it before made the job manageable. He was writing a new version of the same program that had originally activated the nouancer. This program, he was convinced, would allow him to navigate the entire maze of stacks, and find the one book that he so badly wanted.

Finally he was convinced that he had it. He rose and stretched. His neck and shoulders were extremely stiff from the intense work. He gathered his papers together and organized them as a computer would, that is to say, as a sequence of executable, binary instructions.

In the process he was struck by several thoughts at once. Alan had said that the card file catalogue room was a new addition to the library. And it, unlike the rest of the library, was centered around him, Lew Slack. All the indexed books in the file related to his life. And the program that corresponded to the index, the search and retrieval system, was identical to the program which he had put into the nouancer. That program corresponded to the radial setup of the card files.

One thought closed in on him with clarity. Try as he would, he could not escape the conclusion that the filing system was not only patterned after his original program—it actually *was* that program. That meant that the file room was actually inside the nouancer.

It was consistent with the data. He had seen it happen, his being sucked into the interior of the nouancer. And the professor had said that his possession of the crystal would set up a sympathetic resonance between his life and the Asklepian current. That sympathetic resonance was manifested in both the indexing of all the books pertaining to him and the beautiful pictures on the domed ceiling.

These thoughts reverberated in his mind as he set off to find the book that would take him to Sheila. He pulled the sheaf of papers from his jacket. If his analysis were wrong, he could get lost in the stacks, lost to wander forever in the infinite possibility of all the stories that could be told. He began the laborious process of executing the program on the only computer he had, his brain.

The search for Sheila's book took him deeper than ever into the stacks. He had no idea how many hours of winding and stopping to calculate the next turn in the maze it took. But finally, tired and thirsty, he found himself in a stack with the right sequence of call numbers. With pounding heart he followed the codes on the book spines to the right spot. He stopped, knowing that the book was right in front of him. He scanned the shelf for several seconds, refusing to believe his eyes. Between two books that came right before and after the one he sought in the sequence of call numbers there was an empty space on the shelf. He frantically searched the adjacent shelves in hopes that it had merely been misplaced.

All he found were two blond hairs on the rug. He picked them up and held them close to his face for a few moments, overcome with nervous exhaustion.

The way out was as slow going as the way in. Lew had to run the program all over again in his head—this time in reverse. When he finally emerged from the stacks he was exhausted, both mentally and physically. His mind was filled with dark thoughts as he ascended the stairwell and headed for the fountain to quench his insistent thirst.

The book was checked out. Never before had such a simple fact caused him to feel such deep despair.

10

Sex and the Singularity Girl

"Do you have a photo of the individual, Ms. Fine?" the police officer asked. Pamela started to say, "That's *Dr.* Fine," and thought better of it. She had anticipated this question with some anxiety. "Yes, this is a picture of him." She handed the New York policeman a faded photo.

"This looks rather old," he said.

"Well, yes. Actually it is over twenty years old."

"Do you have anything more *recent*? It occurs to me that he might have changed since this was taken," the officer said with thinly veiled sarcasm.

"I'm afraid not," Pamela said. "But you should be able to recognize him. The face is older of course."

"Of course. Now you say that Mr. Fain was your . . . room-mate?"

"Yes, that is correct."

"Was there anything more to your relationship?"

"What do you mean?" Pamela said, her voice rising.

"Any intimacy. Did you have sexual relations for example?"

"That is none of your concern," Pamela snapped.

"Alright, Ms. Fine. I need as much information as possible. Did he have a girlfriend?"

"No."

"Boyfriend?"

"No!"

When she left she did not have much confidence that the police would be able to help her locate Alan. Cline had insisted that they design the box so that it could be opened from the inside in case Alan regained consciousness. Apparently that was what had happened and it could have been at almost any time since they had shut him in.

Elliot had not taken it well. He avoided her now, obviously convinced that she was a little crazy. She found it impossible to concentrate at all—even her most recent work looked unintelligible when she tried to get back into it.

She was making an attempt, several days after the disastrous dinner, when Elliot appeared in her office doorway. "Hello," he said.

"Oh hi," she said tensely.

"I just thought I would see how things are going."

"Depends on what things," she said.

"Well tell me about the good ones," he replied.

"That may be a little difficult," she said, a dark look descending across her brow. "I just don't know anymore . . . I just . . ."

"It's alright, Pamela, you don't have to put on a show for me. Any news?"

"News?"

"About your missing friend?" This question in itself made Pamela brighten a little. Either he was humoring her or he half believed that there was a missing person.

"No. The police weren't much . . ." Just then the phone rang.

"Pamela?" The voice at the other end was weak as if the call came from a bad connection overseas.

"It's Alan."

"Al . . ." She started to say and caught herself. Elliot had already started to back away. She cupped her hand over the receiver and said, "No, Elliot, stay . . . please?" She motioned him into her office. He hesitated and then came in and sat down opposite her desk.

"Yeah. Alan Fain," the voice said. "Not the one you might think either."

"Where *are* you?"

"Well that is a little difficult to explain. I'm in Tibet, actually."

"Oh. That explains the bad connection," she said.

"No, it doesn't. I'm calling from a library which you may have read about. It's called Akasha. Anyway the reason I am calling . . ." his voice faded out.

"Alan?" Pamela said. "Alan, hello?"

"Listen, I had better make this quick. I don't know how long this connection will hold. I have done some research here. Or someone else has, really. Anyway, I came to learn that you are looking for me there in New York."

"Yes! Where are you, Alan?"

"I am *here* in the library. You are talking to me as I was. Don't ask how, but this conversation is bridging a fifteen-to-twenty year gap in time as well as a spacial dimension which I can't even begin to comprehend. Anyway you will find Alan, the Alan you are looking for that is, down along the Bowery. And I suggest you hurry. He is pretty bad off."

"The Bowery?"

"Yeah, and one more thing, Pamela. You know the singularity problem that you are trying to solve?"

"Yes?"

"There is no time to waste. Solve it if you can. It is extremely important to all of us. But I think you know that already."

"I guessed it."

"So long," he said. "And listen, Elliot is a good guy. You could do a lot worse. I'd move with all deliberate speed on that front too, if I were you . . ."

"Alan, how . . . ?" The connection faded out completely, leaving only a dial tone.

"Your friend?" Elliot asked.

"Yeah, that was Alan," Pamela said. "Elliot, I know it's a lot to ask, but could you please come with me? I must go try to find him and it is not a very nice area of town."

* * *

The urine stench was the worst. Oddly Pamela was not afraid of the people. They were mostly so weak or compromised by alcohol or other drugs that she could not imagine any real threat.

"Pamela, it is getting dark," Elliot said.

"Just one more alley," Pamela said. "He said we would find him here."

"Why couldn't he just come to you?" Elliot asked.

"I don't know," she said tensely, trying to see through the long corridor of trash and human castoffs.

She saw a foot protruding from behind a dumpster. The shoe looked familiar.

"Oh my God, Elliot," she said as she bent closer, "it's him. Help me, please."

"Is he alive?" Elliot asked, as they pulled the ashen, emaciated body out into the fading daylight.

"Yes, thank God he is still breathing," Pamela said.

They rode back in Elliot's car, Pamela cradling Alan's head in her lap in the backseat. Carrying him up to her apartment, they drew some curious stares. Elliot assured her that the onlookers had seen worse.

They stretched him out on the bed in the spare bedroom. "He needs a doctor," Elliot said when he saw the hole in Alan's side.

"No!" Pamela said. "A doctor can't help. Listen, the only thing that will save Alan is for me to solve the singularity problem. You have got to believe me. You must think I'm crazy but . . ."

"He should be dead," Elliot said after a closer inspection of Alan's wound. "In fact I am not sure he is really alive, but . . . Yeah, I do believe you. I don't know why, but I do."

"Then you will help me?"

"How?"

"To solve the singularity problem? I can't do it alone. I need another mind."

"I'll help you," he said, with a note of resignation.

"I need something else too, Elliot," she said.

"What is that?" Something in her voice caught his attention.

She led him into her bedroom and slowly removed her dress. Standing naked before him she said, "I'm as good a mathematician as you are."

"I know," he sighed. "Better, if truth be told."

"I have a better grasp of logic than most men will ever have," she said, approaching him. "But men are still good for something." She pressed her body close to him.

He wrapped his arms around her. "But what about the singularity problem?"

"Fuck it," she said, tongue playing in his ear.

11

A Paradise Born

As Lew approached the fountain, his deep despair was suddenly swept away at the sound of water splashing. Someone was swimming in the pool. As he drew near he caught a glimpse of blond hair and a shapely bottom with contours vaguely familiar before it slipped out of sight, under the water's surface. The intruder was swimming gracefully underwater. Her movements reminded Lew of dolphins he had seen; she seemed so at home.

Suddenly she surfaced, her back to him, and climbed slowly out of the pool. She seemed awed by the surroundings, looking up at the ceiling and down the rows of card files. She went over to one and began fingering the brass fittings and running her hand across the wood surfaces. "So beautiful," she said, "such loving craftsmanship."

"Yes," Lew said, "it is."

She was not surprised at his voice and slowly turned around to face him. Her body was the most perfectly beautiful human form Lew had ever seen. She stood a few inches shorter than he. Her legs were smooth and straight, meeting at the fair tuft which Lew had seen in the mirror. Her hips were full and off-set by a slender waist and flat stomach. The blond hair that fell across her shoulders stopped just short of firm breasts that looked both proud and tender. She was staring at him with a smiling, open curiosity.

"Hello," she said.

"Sheila?"

"Yes, Lew. It's me. Let's go for a swim!" She stood on the pool's edge and executed a lovely shallow dive.

Lew removed his clothes hurriedly and jumped in after her. He could not keep up. She swam like a fish. He chased her around the pool several times until she finally let him catch her. He took her in his arms and kissed her. She pushed him away and stood there watching him as he leaned against the pool, trying to catch his breath. Then she looked up at the ceiling and laughed.

He followed her gaze to see an extremely graphic depiction of himself engaged in sex with a different woman. She was dark, powerful, and oddly familiar.

"What are you laughing at?" he asked.

"I'm sorry," she said. "Is that how you do it?"

"Do what?"

"You know, silly," she said shyly, approaching him. "Is it?" she asked, looking back at the ceiling.

"More or less," he said.

She came close and pushed up against him.

"Lew, make love to me now. We haven't got much time."

"Why not?"

"She is going to call me back."

"Who?"

Sheila looked back to the dark woman on the ceiling for her answer.

"But I wanted it to be different, Sheila," Lew said.

"It will be. But not now. Just make love to me, Lew, hurry." She put her arms around his shoulders and wrapped her legs around his waist. "Oooh!" she gasped. It sounded to Lew like a cry of pain as well as pleasure.

When it was over she got out and lay for several minutes by the pool. Lew, feeling suddenly self-conscious, put his clothes back on. She got up and started back toward the stairwell.

"Where are you going?" Lew asked, following her.

She ran to the coffee room and went immediately to the telephone booth. He followed and found her talking to someone, "You will come won't you, Lew? Please come?" He recognized the telephone call that he had received.

"Who were you talking to?" he asked after she hung up.

"You, silly."

"How? It is not possible. I mean I am here."

"And there," she said, gesturing to the room below and the stacks full of books.

"But a telephone?" Lew said.

"Why not?" Sheila said. "I have to go now, Lew."

"Where?"

"Back."

"But why? I wanted us to . . ."

She had already started running down the stairs.

Lew ran after her. "Where are you going back to?" he yelled.

"That's for you to figure out," she said, disappearing into the stacks. She obviously knew all the twists and turns, giving her a decided advantage over Lew. Soon he had lost her and could follow no more.

And he was lost. Fortunately he still had the program with him. He pulled the sheaf of papers from his jacket. He did not know if it was accurate enough to get him out of a random place inside the stacks. But it was his only hope of finding the way back. Once again he began the laborious process of executing the program on the only computer he had, his brain.

He was not so deep inside the maze this time and so he was out in less than an hour. His mysterious companion had left a steaming plate of pasta with shrimp sauce. Famished, Lew began shoveling great forkfuls into his mouth as soon as he could sit down at the desk. Watching the fish and sipping the white wine his benefactor had provided served to calm Lew a little. The stress of finding Sheila only to lose her again had taken its toll on his nerves.

He ate the last bit of garlic bread and pushed the empty plate to one side. Then he poured himself another glass of wine and leaned back in the soft chair, propping his feet up on the desk. *Where could the book, the door to Sheila, be? Who would want it other than me?* A possible answer flashed into his mind.

Alan said that the books they had found on the library phantom's desk were all about him. Someone was researching his, Lew's, life. Therefore, it stood to reason that the missing book might very well be there, on the mysterious researcher's desk.

Lew jumped to his feet and went running back along the concave row of desks in front of the never-ending, always-changing, undersea panorama. He was there in under twenty minutes, panting and searching the desktop. He found several books detailing various aspects of his life, and others on the mathematics of the singularity problem that so interested Alan, but not the one he wanted. He was about to give up when he remembered the drawer. He opened it up and there it was, the long-sought book. He picked it up. It was bound in a light blue fabric that had a soft, velvety texture.

He was about to open the book when he heard something. It was Felix rounding a nearby turn. The cat came up to Lew and rubbed its big head hard against his thigh, issuing a deep purr. The pressure put Lew off-balance for a moment.

When he regained his footing he opened the book and began to read. Felix made a lonely feline cry, "Mrrooowriip!"

Lew and Felix were back in the Jag, cruising down Eternity Road. This time they were alone. Lew rolled the window down and took several deep breaths. *What is it about the air?* he wondered. It imparted a certain quality. It seemed finer-grained somehow, more *rarefied*. The nouancer was tuned to a talk show. Someone was being interviewed, "The ancients suspected that there was a substratum, a substance which pervades everything in the universe." Lew turned up the volume.

"What do you mean?" the interviewer asked.

"Well, if you regard the cosmos as *one thing*, as many did and still do, then you have a problem. Clearly, it is also many things. So if it is also one thing, a *Universe*, then there must be something common to each individual, instantiated part. That's where the aether comes in. Some of the early philosophers identified it with air, but that soon became an untenable position. So the existence of aether was postulated. Aether is finer, more subtle than air, so it can pervade everything, from the smallest subatomic structure to the biggest galactic cluster. In Eastern traditions of yoga it is known as 'prana,' again something like air but with the added quality of life, both mental and physical . . .''

Having heard it all before, Lew switched it off.

The air, or aether, was beginning to affect him. Breathing it made him feel more connected, more in tune with the macrocosm above and the microcosm below. It was more than invigorating. It was exciting and intellectually stimulating.

After a few hours of driving he pulled onto the shoulder. He let Felix out of the back and headed off in the direction of the stream. The grass was tall and lush. Lew noticed insects for the first time. Big, vicious-looking beetles and some butterflies.

He came to a wide, babbling brook. He followed it a way until he found a place where it narrowed. There was a waterfall about ten feet high, which emptied into a shady, deep, inviting pool. Lew quickly stripped and dived in.

The water was bracing; he emerged with a yelp, but it felt good. He swam to the waterfall and sat underneath it, letting the clear spray buffet his head and torso. It was pure delight. Lew threw his head back and laughed.

There was a sudden black flash in front of him. Lew jumped up and lost his footing, falling back into the pool. He emerged to see Felix on the flat limestone with a large fish speared on a long, sharp talon. "Damn! You crazy cat!" Lew exclaimed. Felix, ignoring his master, flopped down with a soft thud to feast. Lew was careful to find a place on the rocks as far from the beast as possible. He lay down, letting the delicious rays of the sun dry his naked body. Soon he was asleep.

A soft pressure on his chest woke him. He opened his eyes to see the cat's big, black paw pressing into him. Felix was asleep. Lew stirred, causing the cat to shudder and purr before resuming its catnap. It was late afternoon; soft colors came through the lush foliage. Lew rolled out from under the cat's paw and stood, facing the stream.

A pair of eyes stared back at him from across the water. He saw a look of cool appraisal, and then they were gone. A hint of rustling leaves and a glimpse of a firm, bronze breast and an arm carrying a bow and then nothing; the forest was silent with the calm of waning day.

Where had he seen a figure like that before? The question nagged at him. His body felt warm and vibrant. It was the aftereffect of the evening sun on his skin and something else—the water. He knelt by the waterfall and took a cool drink, cupping his hand under the spray. It was water alright, but like the air it had a subtle, refined quality that sharpened the senses and braced the spirit. When he stood up again he felt more relaxed and awake than he could ever remember feeling. There was a soft glow in his genitals; not a burning sexual desire but a sexual differentiation that was insistent yet reassuring. The energy flowed up his spine to the crown of his head, where it manifested as potential ecstasy.

Lew was aware of all this in an instant, and then, like the form on the other bank, it was gone. A breeze blew upstream, bringing a slight chill. He found his clothes, and as he was zipping his jeans, Felix rose and stretched his long body. The cat turned to face Lew and gave a huge yawn, showing his long, slightly yellowed fangs. "Nice kitty," Lew said, putting on his jacket. Felix came up to rub against him. "Come on, let's go." Felix followed silently as Lew began walking back to the car.

Lew found some dried beef and a loaf of coarse bread in the Jag. There were also some huge, two-fist–sized onions. After he ate he lit a cigarette and watched the sun sink between two steep, green hills. He opened the front door of the Jag, turned on the nouancer, and sat down at the edge of the road, leaning his back against the front tire. He could see birds flying in the last rays of the sun. They were large, more gliders than fliers.

"Evolution, fact or fantasy?" a voice from the speakers said. "Nothing can really change, now, can it? Because if it did, it would no longer be itself. In other words nothing could have an identity or an integrity of being at all. So evolution is impossible . . ."

Lew tuned out the voice and watched a great solitary bird fly into the last remaining ray of light streaming up from the spot where the sun had gone down.

Suddenly something flashed in the sky. It was a small, bronze gleam arcing upward from the wood. It ended abruptly, precisely where it met the bird. There was a sharp cry of pain, or was it ecstasy? The wings folded, and the bird fell with a curious, restful momentum. It happened so quickly that Lew doubted his senses. He turned up his jacket collar and watched the darkness begin to roll in.

Soon they were moving again, driving with only the Jag's big headlights penetrating the darkness. Felix was curled in back, sleeping. Lew grew drowsy and before long he fell into a daydream. He was outside in a tropical paradise, reclining on a magnificent golden sundial. A yellow sun blazed overhead; the shadow of the sundial cut across Lew's lean, tan body. Rich, luscious scents and brilliant colors assailed his senses. Warm sweat beaded on his chest. There was a rustle in the foliage. Lew raised up on one elbow and turned his head to face in the direction of the sound.

The colors seemed brighter in that direction. Birds with enormous beaks perched on the limbs of great fernlike trees. Beneath the branches of one such tree the smaller ferns and foliage suddenly parted and a woman stepped into view.

She wore a cloth around her hips. She stood with her weight on one foot, the other slightly arched, the classic posture of the nude. Her breasts were bare. She carried a wooden bow in one hand; the wood was intricately carved in an organic motif of vines, flowers, and mythological creatures. A leather quiver of arrows hung from one shoulder. She was supple, muscular. Her hair was long and auburn, cascading about her shoulders. The breasts were firm and full; the nipples pink with a hint of moisture clinging to them. Subtle, enticing aromas emanated from the spot where she stood. She turned her gaze to him, her large blue eyes betraying no sense of fear. Two recollections leapt into his mind. The first was a book cover he had seen—it seemed so long ago. The second was Susan. This woman had Susan's face. Then he remembered where he had seen her before. It was Psylene, the illustration on the cover of that silly book, *Goddess Power*. Only now it did not seem so silly. Lew realized he was naked and instantly reached to cover himself.

The image faded and Lew was drawn into the music playing on the nouancer. It was classical. The complex scales and modulations were soothing. Lew closed his eyes and relaxed. He felt pulled by the piece, pulled into the harmony behind all

harmonies. He was just a node in a vast net in which all nodes
were related in ever more intricate ways with the passage of
time. Flow of time was the music and Lew let it move his
being through the network of being, increasingly enraptured
by the beautiful complexity.

As rapture built to ecstasy it became too much. The piece
was building to climax, the point at which all the various
complexities would be resolved into one song, a universe.
But each time Lew was convinced that it was going to happen, the music became more complex, more of a multiplicity.
Instead of resolving into one theme, the many previous themes
became mere instantiations of a grander one with a complexity
of exponentially increased order.

Lew's calm turned to extreme tension as he strained to hold
the music together—it was he! He was the center, the one node
upon which all others depended. But it was terrible! The burden was too much too bear. It was infinitely great. He longed
for release into . . . anything! His heart raced and he felt sure
it would rupture.

Suddenly the sounds changed to free jazz improvisations.
It was a blissful release from the ecstatic classical harmonies.
Then, as if in response to his still-pounding heart, the music
changed again to a thumping rock beat. It was the Doors'
music, the rock group of the 1960s that derived its name from
Aldous Huxley's book, *The Doors of Perception*. Of course
Huxley, the genteel, radical writer/philosopher had got
the phrase from the works of William Blake, another visionary.

"Keep your eyes on the road and your hands upon the
wheel!" the lyrics went. It was a driving song, "Roadhouse
Blues." Lew braced himself and gripped the wheel. A glance
at the dash showed the fuel gauge hovering just above empty,
but it didn't matter to Lew.

Nothing mattered except the beat that was driving him on.
Felix slept, oblivious to it all, in the backseat. "Why couldn't
I have been a poet/rock singer like Jim Morrison?" Lew muttered. He was willing to forget, for the moment, that Morrison
had died young, a bloated alcoholic, unable to write any more
poetry.

But the lyrics of Morrison had him completely transfixed.
He imagined what it must have been like to live the life of

a rock poet. To sleep until two or three in the afternoon and then to show up casually at the studio where all the tools of your trade would be waiting. Musical instruments. Sound room. The best of both worlds, an artist, yet a man who commands respect from the established power structure. Instead of the insulting drudgery that most mortals have to face each day! "Damn!" he exclaimed and emerged from his thoughts.

The night came alive around him again. He blinked and looked at the speedometer. Ninety! The Jag was barreling down a dirt road—he must have taken a wrong turn during his vivid daydreams.

He braked—too hard. Then the car began to slide sideways. He struggled to regain control, but the surface was gone. There was no more road. The Jag was skidding on muddy, semiswamplike terrain.

They did not roll; the car simply sank its right tires into the quicksand and came to a stop standing up on its side. They were sinking. Felix was scrambling to get out the open rear window. Lew tried to restrain the cat, but a vicious hiss warned him away. Felix was out in a few seconds. A crescent moon had risen, and in the faint light Lew could just make out the cat's desperate thrashing motions in the bog. But he had no trouble hearing the wet, sucking noises of the deadly mud as it tried to pull the beast under.

The car was going down fast. Sounds were still coming from the nouancer. It was eerie, creepy swamp music. Music that made one think of vampires prowling the bayous of Louisiana at midnight. A voodoo voice whispered, "Watch out for the she-devil . . . yeah man!" Lew shut it off. He grabbed the crystal, stuffed it into his jacket, and began climbing out the window.

Lew knew that quicksand was real, but his only experience of it had been in movies. At first it felt like ordinary mud, but soon it became apparent that the bottom was very deep. How deep? He could see the car still sinking. Maybe it would hit bottom and then Lew could cling to the wreck until daylight and devise a possible means of escape.

Motion was difficult. He was soon up to his waist and, just as in the movies, any attempt to free himself caused the stuff to grab and suck more viciously. He held still, watching the car. His terror grew with every inch of metal that disappeared from sight.

Finally it appeared to stop. The right rear quarter panel and a section of the trunk were still visible. Lew slowly started to propel himself to a place where he could seize the bumper. His efforts were painfully slow and they caused him to sink to chest level, but finally he was there. He reached out and grabbed with slimy hands. It was difficult, but he managed to get a grip. It felt solid enough. He began to pull himself up.

A nauseating slurping noise emerged from thick mud bubbles that burst around him. And the stench was overwhelming. Sulfurous and foul, it smelled of rotten eggs and long dead things. He barely had time to let go before the car slid with an easy, sexual fluidity out of sight.

He pushed himself up and back, barely escaping the gaping hole which closed around the vanished vehicle. Lew tried to lie on his back, to see if he could float. It was impossible; the stuff was closing in tightly around his chest. He could barely move his arms.

He thought of Felix. "Kitty! Kitty!" he called out. "Here, kitty, kitty!" The only sounds were the insect sounds of the swamp. *Poor Felix*, Lew thought.

Then he heard something like padded footsteps, not far away, and a familiar, "Meeoww!"

"Felix!"

"Meow!"

It sounded as if the cat were pacing nearby. If that were the case, Lew reasoned, then he was not far from solid ground.

The stuff was closing in on his shoulders. He kept calling and the cat kept answering. Felix wailed, obviously wanting his master to join him. *How did he get out?* Lew wondered. He tilted his head back to keep his mouth out.

But he was still sinking. The moon shone high above; he could see what looked like cypress branches in the silvery light. He thought he heard music. What was that old blues/rock song?

> "*Going down, Going down.*
> "*Going down, Going down,*
> "*Down, down, down, down, down . . .*"

Only his nose and forehead remained above the surface. And he was still going down.

On the assumption that he was facing death, Lew tried to make the most of it. But nothing of any particular interest transpired—no scenes from his life flashed before his eyes. It was just him and the dense swamp in the deep darkness. It was filled with sounds. Strange birdcalls, and the rustling of creatures as they went about their nightly business. It was beautiful, like a symphony.

That realization was what brought on the terror. Why had he, for most of his life, missed the beauty that he now saw so clearly! It was about to end, and this was all the glimpse of living that he was going to get! Lew panicked. His lungs heaved; they were unable to draw breath, the pressure of the quicksand was so great. He kicked, but there was little motion to be gained. With his last gasping spasm he felt the deep mud pull him harder. It closed around his nostrils with agonizing slowness. Then his eyes. The last thing he saw was another pair of eyes, which he took to be Felix's, flashing in the darkness as he disappeared.

Morning broke on the swampy delta where the river fanned out and Felix the giant cat lay in lazy contentment. There was a half-eaten animal carcass beside him, a large, unlucky lizard. Flies were buzzing over the remains.

Lew's mind was filled with visions of death and sex. A long, postmortem dream. He feared its end, the blankness that lasts forever, the eternal nothing. The dream was familiar. She came again, the powerful dark creature with the bow. She led him to the clearing where the giant sundial cast its shadow. She laid him across the big brass arm and removed his shoes. She undid his belt buckle and loosened his jeans.

She started doing things with her mouth. Lew was afraid that he would be impotent; after all he was dead or dying. But death, he found, was a powerful aphrodisiac. He could hardly believe the sensations surging through his body.

Lew lifted his head just a little to see Psylene (it was difficult to think of her as Susan) reach behind and loosen the cloth wrapped round her thighs. It fell to the ground revealing a magnificent set of hips that quickly became the center of Lew's shrinking universe.

Lew felt a smooth, sliding sensation which reminded him of his slow slide to death beneath the quicksand. But now terror was replaced by sharp pleasure.

She was good. Lew rode the waves of pleasure to unbearable heights several times, but each time she used hidden muscles to stop him from going over the edge. And with each wave the pleasure was more intense, until it became so fierce that pleasure was indistinguishable from the terror of death beneath the bog. Once again he felt certain that he was going to die soon. With the final wave he would cease to be. The desire for release and the dread of oblivion created something in between, an insane ecstasy that burned with icy heat.

She moved faster. This time there was no stopping. "No! Noo!" he moaned. Beads of sweat dripped from her heaving breasts onto his chest. He reached up to grab them, fondle them with both hands. It built with agonizing slowness, yet inexorably mounting to the conclusion he dreaded. His life was going to erupt, explode, and flow out of him. There was nothing he could do but give in to it, let it go, let it flow.

It felt like a small rupture followed by a tidal wave. Lew tried to stop it, but he no longer mattered. The wave pushed him along like a piece of driftwood. He felt his soul flow out on a white-hot stream of lava from an undersea volcano.

Then nothing. Just as he knew it would be. Nothing. Stillness and nothing.

It was really the "little death," as the French say. It emptied him of everything, even peace. The quiescence which he felt lacked depth. It was the closest thing to pure nothingness he had ever experienced. When he finally woke it was like climbing out of a deep, dark well. His eyes had been open and blinking for several seconds before he was aware of the fact that he was seeing again.

He lay on a shiny metallic surface. The morning sun reflected golden light from the brass structure. His body was covered with thick mud, most of it dry. He raised up on one elbow; his denim jacket, plastered with mud, made his movements even stiffer than they would have been from his great fatigue.

With slow amazement he recognized the great sundial from his daydream. The clearing was just as he had imagined it; brightly colored birds perched on the branches of great cypress trees. The giant arm of the sundial was also stained with mud, some of it still wet and pungent with the odors of the swamp.

The swamp! He remembered dying, being swallowed by the quicksand. And he remembered an encounter with a female. Was this death? It felt too much like life, like waking up with a severe hangover.

He tried to stand, and tripped. His jeans were a dried muddy mess and down around his ankles. He remembered the woman towering over him and . . . oh yes! The memory of what had happened next sent a shiver through his naked loins. A cursory self-examination convinced him it had been no dream. But how? Where was he? In another world below the bog? Was this yet another bizarre, unexplored layer of reality?

He stopped the questions and stripped off his clothes. They were too cumbersome. Wearing only shirt and running shoes, he walked to the edge of the clearing. There was a path into the thick wood, which he began to follow.

It wound through forest and vegetation that Lew found absolutely pulsating with life. The short hike of about half a mile left him invigorated.

It ended when he emerged onto a rocky bluff. The view of the valley was spectacular. The river and road were clearly visible, only a few hundred yards below the spot where Felix stood. They both ended in a large delta, the swamp which appeared to stretch on for miles, to the other side of the valley. Lew could see the place where he had driven haphazardly straight into it. Muddy skid grooves were visible. And then Lew saw Felix, napping in the sun.

"Kitty! Kitty!" he called out.

Felix appeared not to hear for several seconds. Then he rose and gave a long, lazy stretch. Lew called out again, and Felix appeared to notice his master for the first time.

"Mrroow!" The cat began bounding up the trail to where Lew stood.

"Nice kitty!" Lew rubbed Felix behind the ears. Then he noticed the footprints. They were smaller than his, and made with a smooth sole, possibly a leather sandal. They led up from the swamp along the path Felix had just traversed. They were deep, as if the person had been weighted down, carrying something.

Simultaneously Lew thought he caught a scent, the same powerful, exotic scent from his vision of the sundial and the woman. It was gone as soon as he noticed it. But it chilled him. Had she rescued him only to seduce him? And why? Who was she?

Higher in the forest, Psylene arrived at her lodge. She hung her bow and quiver outside on a peg, beside the heavy, wooden door with the brass fittings. She pulled on the great ring, and the door swung outward with a loud, tortured creak.

Inside it was both light and dark. The cabin had many windows that let in ample sunlight, but there were corners where dark shadows fell, making it difficult to discern all the contents of the place.

She went to a crafted wood cabinet and opened the door. Bottles and vessels of different sizes and colors lined the shelves. Psylene extracted a small, clear glass vessel with bulbous base and a long, narrow neck. She squatted down and put the smooth neck of the bottle between her legs. Then she pushed it up and inside. After several contractions a cloudy, white fluid flowed out into the round receptacle. She deftly extracted the bottle and walked to a long, narrow table in the center of the room.

Psylene's lab bench was a curious blend of disarray and orderliness. Glassware littered the surface. Carved spatulas and strange alchemical apparatuses lay cast about the table, indicative of some work in progress. A large, ornately worked metal cabinet stood in one corner.

She lit a glowglobe in the center of the bench. This was done by merely passing her hand across the top, which activated an unseen current of energy not conducted through any visible wires. The light was a smoky yellow, which suggested a metaphysical source by its very color and density. The glowglobe was supported by a short iron pole that had been worked into a double-coiled spiral suggestive of mating serpents or the DNA molecule.

Setting the bulbous vial with its congealing white liquid on the bench, Psylene walked to the large metal cabinet which stood in the corner opposite the door. The legs of the cabinet were steel. They had been cast to simulate cat claws. The door of the cabinet was nickel which had been engraved with images of animals and humans engaged in all manner of sexual activity. There were stags copulating with women, women with men, men with does, and even creatures of apparently alien origin so depicted.

She pulled down on the ivory handle, which was carved into the likeness of a phallus. The door opened and white vapor poured out. It was a refrigeration unit.

She took out a small vial stopped with a cork. The contents appeared to be a few drops of frozen blood. Going back to the bench, she carefully set the vial on a small bronze stand. She found a small globe, much like the one which illuminated the bench, and placed it under the stand. She passed a finger over the opening in the miniature globe and it immediately exhibited a warm, orange radiance.

She removed the stopper from the vial in the stand, and kept close watch, monitoring the heating process. Satisfied that the blood was reacting properly, she turned her attention to the long-necked bottle. She quickly took the vial from the stand and poured the warm red droplets into the bottle with Lew's semen. Placing the mixture back on the stand, and heating it further, she lifted the bottle and peered at the contents every so often, shaking and coercing them into a more homogeneous mixture.

At a precise point in the thermodynamic action, known only to her, she removed the mixture from the heat and passed a finger over the globe, causing it to go dark.

She let the mixture cool until it had a viscous, almost rubbery consistency. Then she grabbed a mortar and pestle from the bench and proceeded to crush several large, dried mushrooms into it. She poured the mixture of blended blood and semen in with the fragments and ground the pulpy, gooey concoction until the particles of fungus were extremely fine. Using one of the spatulas from the bench, she scooped most of the stuff into a smoky blue bottle with rectangular sides. She corked the new bottle and placed it in the refrigeration cabinet.

She looked about, seeming more relaxed than when she arrived. Leaving the vial and bulbous, long-necked bottle, with their respective residues of blood and semen, discarded on the table, Psylene retired to her couch of red velvet. She was soon dreaming, breasts rising and falling with the slow regularity of sleep.

Lew dried his clothes on the rocks in the sun. Then he beat the mud free from the denim. The process made his jeans and jacket remarkably soft. And the clothes felt clean despite their recent submersion in the bog. There was still a trace of the smell, but the sun had mellowed it so that the aroma was now actually pleasant, a sweet, musty, organic scent.

Lew went back to the clearing with the giant sundial. It really was a beautiful piece, about thirty feet in diameter. The sweep of the arm cast a sharp shadow. Lew was content to sit and watch as it slowly moved, marking the passing day. Felix seemed restless. He kept rubbing against Lew and wandering off back toward the swamp.

Lew, on the other hand, felt drawn by the wood. The air, or aether, of this place was wilder. Just sitting there he felt waves of energy pulse through him with an almost sexual rhythm. He noticed that the path continued past the sundial deeper into the upper wood. He stood up and walked toward it.

Felix was beginning to make disturbing guttural noises. He was clearly afraid. When Lew advanced toward the trail that led deeper into the wood, Felix became extremely agitated, growling and attempting to block his master's way. Lew cuffed him behind the ear and the cat retreated, head held low.

The wood was dense, the path crowded with vines and huge trees that came right to the edge of the trail. Occasionally a fallen tree blocked the way and Lew had to climb over a massive trunk.

He advanced about a half a mile into the wood, his cat stalking him. He stopped to look and listen. The sounds of life were like music. Music in tune with the life within him. Lew again felt euphoria bordering on ecstasy. Felix did not. When the cat caught up with him he wailed in pitiful fashion, signaling existential feline distress.

"What's wrong, kitty?" Lew asked, rubbing the fur on the cat's neck.

"Mrrooow!" Felix gave a violent start backward and stopped, his back arched, fur along the spine standing straight, and horrible deep hissing noises emerging from his open, fanged mouth.

At the same moment Lew heard a rustle of leaves and vines to his left. He turned to see a strange but familiar woman emerge before him on the trail.

"Kitty is disturbed by the overabundance of nous in the aether here," she said. Lew was more impressed than ever by her bearing, the wonderful breasts, strong wide hips, and slender waist. He tried to smile, remembering their recent encounter, which he now knew to be real, not a dream at all.

"Don't flatter yourself," she said, anticipating his grin. It was a painful rebuff.

This woman obviously had no interest in him as a man.

"What do you mean, too much nous?" he asked, trying to conceal his wounded ego.

"Nous, *mind* if you prefer," she said simply. "The aether here is quite dense with intellect. Nothing is immune. Surely you have noticed."

He started to answer but she cut him off. "Animals who are not used to it, like your cat-beast, find the transition to higher consciousness difficult. He will be happier in the lowlands, by the swamp."

"It was you who rescued me, then?" he said. "I mean last night."

"Yes, and your precious cat, too. I hate to see things wasted. I had immediate use for you. And as for your pet . . . all creatures have potential value."

She strode forward and grabbed Felix by the scruff of his neck. The poor cat wailed loudly as she raised him to eye level. She spoke some unfamiliar words in a guttural growl which Felix seemed to understand. When she let him go he bolted. "Don't worry. He will be fine. I've sent him back to the lowlands of the delta, where he will be more comfortable. You can stay if you like. You may find something special here. But be careful. You are free to eat what fruit and vegetables you need, but do not hunt. You are a guest."

"But Susan," Lew said, "surely you remember me!"

She laughed. Then she walked up to him, boldly. Her nipples were nearly brushing his chest. She was shorter than Lew, but he felt as if he were looking up into her eyes

when she spoke. "I am Psylene now. What I remember is
insignificant compared to what I have become. I am mistress
of this world."

She started to leave, but turned to face him again. "And
Lew . . ." she said.

"Yes?" Lew was mesmerized by the face, which he thought
he had known so well. Susan was still there—but just barely. Her new persona was something much greater. The easy
familiarity mixed with utter strangeness thrilled and terrified
him.

"My best advice is that you leave immediately. But since I
am almost certain that you won't, please remember that whatever happens I don't really want to hurt you. On the other
hand, you have probably got it coming." She turned again and
quickly disappeared in the dense foliage.

Lew's earlier euphoria was quickly turning into a weak despair that made him want to cry. His intellect told him that he
should turn back and join Felix, but his intellect was not his
master. "You may find something special here." Her words
echoed in his mind. He suspected that she knew what she was
talking about.

Several days later Psylene removed the blue bottle from the
incubator. She took it to her bench, where she found a magni-
fying glass. Eyeing the contents through the glass, she smiled
at the sight of little white filaments beginning to grow up the
sides of the container.

Later that day she planted the contents in damp soil, not far
from the giant sundial. She carefully tamped the earth, rich
with decaying vegetable matter.

As the days passed and the bitter memory of his second
encounter with Psylene started to recede, some of Lew's initial excitement returned. He never wandered more than a few
miles from the sundial, and he saw no more of the mistress
of the wood.

He did find a delightful stream which cascaded toward the
valley floor. The water was sweet with the intoxication he
had previously experienced. It was more heady, stronger. The
air and water of the place made his body feel alive with an
independence which sometimes frightened him, threatening to

overpower his entire consciousness. He found several varieties of edible fruits and vegetables. Eating became a new, intensely sensual experience.

Sometimes, in the early morning hours, when he awoke on his bed of leaves, Lew would feel an impending sense of danger, an urge to flee the place and rejoin his cat. But those feelings always faded with the eating of some new, exquisite fruit, and they were entirely forgotten as he bathed beneath the spray of a small waterfall or swam in a pool.

One such morning he was brought violently to consciousness by the flash of lightning and the deafening crash of a thunderbolt. Then he was pelted with a torrential downpour. The water was so thick as it came lashing out of the sky that he found it difficult to breathe at times. The storm lasted for several hours. When it was finally over he stripped and hung his clothes out to dry on the arm of the sundial.

The next morning he was surprised by the spectacular growth of fungus all around. The rain had brought out an astonishing variety of beautiful, multicolored mushrooms. Some were as high as his waist, with caps several feet in diameter. The smells were rich and pungent.

Lew was tempted to eat some of the more savory-looking varieties but he was afraid of being poisoned or worse. He imagined that some of the toadstools contained powerful mind-bending agents that might send him on a one-way trip to some new, more bizarre layer of the universe.

Within a few days all the mushrooms had cast their new spores and were gone. All but one.

It continued to grow and exerted a powerful attraction. It was not just the odor, which reminded Lew of sex and all the most delicious and exotic foods he had ever tasted. It was the shape. It appeared to be an ordinary mushroom, except for the size—within a week it was nearly as tall as Lew. But there were subtle curves and crannies on the stalk which seemed almost feminine to Lew.

He found himself spending time near the thing, sometimes losing himself in contemplation and reaching out to caress it. He would then catch himself and quietly issue a reprimand. "It is just a fungus," he would whisper, "just a fungus."

Contemplating the fish darting in a pool one afternoon, he began saying, "I love this water, these fish." The motion of

the fish seemed something which took place inside himself
as well as in the natural world of wood and stream. Only on
reflection, when the moment was over, did he realize that what
he felt was peace; the kind of peace which had always eluded
him, yet when experienced was understood to be completely
simple and immediate.

He wandered back to the mushroom, which had ceased to
grow, although it still underwent subtle changes each day. It
was now only a few inches shorter than Lew. If he stared long
enough, he could almost detect human features in the cap. But
it was like seeing forms in clouds—they were never there for
long.

The stalk was something else. He reached out to caress it.
The curves and depressions there were beginning to acquire
human form and texture.

He had done this before, always feeling a little ashamed,
guilty. This time his advances grew more ardent. He thought
he felt the fungus shudder, a cool vegetative protest against
his hot, animal passion. He quickly withdrew, keenly aware
of his highly aroused state. He looked around quickly, suddenly afraid that he was being watched. He saw nothing but
a large bird perched nearby. It cried out what sounded to Lew
like a taunt before it flew away.

Lew's slumbers became more fitful after the incident. His
dreams were full of erotic images; often he would awake in
a sweat. His desire grew more insistent with the passing of
each day. He tried to avoid the mushroom, successfully doing
so for a few days.

But finally it was unbearable, and he approached the small
clearing in a state of extreme excitement. He emerged into
the clearing and gasped. The cap was smaller; the rudimen-
tary features of a female face were almost certainly visible
there. The stalk was now a clearly defined female body. It
seemed to lack something, as if it were only the pure potential
of woman.

This time Lew's advances were answered by an unmistakable tremor that shook the entire fungus very slightly. Again
Lew felt slightly ashamed as his caresses grew more intimate. It was as if he were violating something sacred—the
mushroom was so completely defenseless and so purely vir-
ginal.

But he could not stop himself. He was transported to new heights of feeling and psychic excitement by the powerful sensations. Finally there came the defining moment. What was left of his conscious mind told him to cease, to leave the mushroom and the wood forever. The idea of rape had always disgusted him, and Lew felt that what he was about to do was very close to rape. He felt that he had no right.

It made no difference. He was beyond the realm of "right." Only passion and need were left. "She" had begun to respond. He quickly looked up to see what looked like lips slightly parted in what was not quite yet a face. He also saw an expression of pain, and it appeared that the primitive eyelids were starting to roll back. Then Lew lost all consciousness of anything but their lovemaking. The rhythm seemed to come from without, in the forest, as well as from within. It grew faster.

He thought he detected Psylene in his peripheral vision, watching him, but he did not care. Soon he saw only images in his head. Vast polarities out in the cosmic aether, coming together, separating, in a dance that was profoundly erotic.

When he did open his eyes to look up, it was into another pair of eyes, that seemed to grow more sentient each moment. Strangely, Lew thought of the professor. He closed his eyes and saw the old face clearly. The man seemed to be saying something about memory, about how all learning is really only a recalling of what we already know.

"Is that why I can understand what comes over the cosmic radio?" Lew asked the old man, thinking of the nouancer. "You said that the brain is a receiver and a decoder. It tunes into the Asklepian current that carries nous, the essence of mind, life, and consciousness."

The professor laughed. "If you want a scientific explanation—but let us just say that a mind, appropriately disposed, in the presence of its appropriate object, *will* understand. Language is just an interface between mind and object."

The professor picked up a big yellow pitcher of lemonade. Lew held out a glass while the professor poured. The yellow liquid coming out of the pitcher seemed connected with the yellow sun high overhead in the sky. *I'm not dreaming*, Lew thought. *This is real*. It also seemed connected with the energy surging through his body.

Simultaneously with that thought his glass was filled, but the professor just kept on pouring. "Stop!" Lew protested as the lemonade began to flow out of the glass and over his fingers. Soon it was flowing all over the ground. It ran up the trees and through the forest.

The professor was laughing. "Don't worry," he said. "There is plenty."

Lew opened his eyes. The forest was filled with an old rock tune, "Mellow Yellow," by Donovan. Lew had an immediate intuition that he did not need the nouancer in these woods; the pulse of nous was so dense that it needed no additional amplification or refinement. He passionately kissed the mushroom lips, and they returned his ardor, wet and hot.

He could no longer tell if his eyes were closed or open. The forest flowed with yellow. Betty Boop, the cartoon character, blew him a kiss from her perch on a tree. He was filled with embarrassment as she continued to watch him with giant eyes.

Lew's embarrassment became white-hot. The burning yellow from the lemonade went incandescent—the wood flared with a burning white heat. So did the creases of Lew's own brain. In fact it was difficult to separate the two. It kept flowing in and out, white light, the white light of the Buddhist void, the white light of cosmic consciousness, universal bliss. It was Lew, and it was flowing out and in, covering the entire universe as he melted into bliss.

"Finally," he muttered, "I've gone white. Take me home." He slid down the body of his fungoid lover and melted into the earth.

Lew drifted through layers of being from the pure, radiant, clear light and then back down to the organic unity of the wood. He was the ground, and the trees, and the birds, and the sky, and the water rushing down to the delta. It felt as though he lay there without a self for eons.

When he opened his eyes it was a painful experience. Not just for the sunlight which blazed overhead, but for the resegregation of self and world. He was again Lew Slack, not the universal white light, not the organic whole of the earth. He felt an inexorable pull away from the *one* into separateness; the fibers of his nerves screamed as they were irreversibly uprooted from the ground of being and bliss.

But there was no choice. Soon he was looking at the sun and sky, an independent entity once again, alone and searching. He was naked. He propped himself up on one elbow and gasped.

There before him, still tenuously rooted to the earth by strands of fungoid mycelia, stood the most beautiful woman he had ever seen. It was Sheila, the woman who had called him—how long ago? It seemed forever.

She was covered with a thin membrane, the last remnants of her fungoid nature. *I would travel across the galaxy to find you*, he thought. *Does she love me?* he wondered. *Does she need me? Will she take me?*

Her eyes opened, tearing the thin membrane seal. Her face was fully formed and fully new, graced with an expression of embryonic wonder. She stepped forward with a soft shredding sound as her feet pulled away from the filaments which still clung to the earth. A few white strands, mixed with dark soil, clung between her toes.

She looked into his eyes with smiling passion. "I do," she said.

Lew stood and took her in his arms, a naked embrace of his Eve in Eden.

12

A Paradise Lost

Lew had the feeling, when he looked at Sheila, that he had never truly *seen* a human being before. She brought to life the ancient description of the human creature: *animale rationales*, the rational animal.

Her eyes were full of the fire of intellect. But she was clearly an animal, an organic creature of earth and feeling. When she spoke, emotion trembled upon her lips. Her breasts were lusty. This was a sexual being who knew no shame; her life was an erotic life as well as a logical one. The two blended perfectly, without discord, creating something that transcended both. This, Lew thought, was what a human was supposed to be. This was a *real* woman.

He thought that what he had seen, before in his world, were mere shadows, projections, hints of the potential person that resided in each of his brothers and sisters. Never before had he beheld a man or a woman.

And this woman was perfection. When Lew thought something was funny he could see the laughter in her eyes before he laughed. Often she completed his thoughts before he could utter them. At times he felt that they shared memories.

"How did you call me here?" he asked her one afternoon. She was seated, her back resting on the bole of a great cypress. Lew lay with his head in her lap, looking up into her blue eyes. Her long, wavy blond hair fell across her breasts and lightly caressed his chin.

"On the telephone . . . in the library," she said.

"But you did not yet exist."

"Oh," she laughed. "Time is such a funny thing, isn't it?"

"Do we really only exist in a book? I guess if that is the case, then time between inside and outside the story would be a meaningless concept. After all, I can read any passage of a book at any time regardless of . . ."

She touched a finger lightly to his lips. "Ssh! None of that matters."

"But is this just a story? Sheila, it feels more real than anything else I have ever known! I . . ."

"All things are stories," she said simply. "Nothing exists outside a story."

He saw that she was right. He could not conceive of any part of his life without putting it into a story of some sort.

"Come on!" she said, suddenly jumping up. She began running through the forest. Lew ran after her, laughing in delight, full of lust and love as he followed her streaming hair, and beautiful, naked body. She led him to the place by the sundial where his clothes still lay. They were settling into the fertile earth; rain, soil, and decaying vegetable matter had begun their work.

He no longer cared how it had happened, how he was there with her. He only cared for her and the eternal present. He pulled her to him, and kissed her. She put her arms around his neck and pressed her warm breasts against his naked chest. They were covered with a thin layer of perspiration from the recent exertion.

"You also said that you were carrying my child, our baby," Lew said, letting his hands slide down the curve of her back. He squeezed lightly and pressed her to him. Her flesh was soft, yet taut with well-developed muscles.

She returned the pressure. "Not yet. We'll have to work on that," she said in a hot whisper to his ear.

They did. It was always different. Sometimes pure hot passion, wild abandon, sex for the sake of sex. Sometimes it was slow and cool, almost clinical. He would examine her every curve and crevice with objective curiosity that was utterly insatiable. At those times he felt as if he were a scientist preparing a paper for a research journal. Sometimes she would take charge with her supple hands, employing lubricating agents from plants that yielded sweet, oily liquids. Sometimes it was so gentle as to bring tears to his eyes; then it felt religious, like worship. At other times it was violent and hard, although he never hurt her nor she him.

Lew had a new acute sense of time. It had nothing to do with hours or days. It was a kind of organic time from which he was normally disconnected. Their forest paradise was always undergoing subtle changes. Lew's sense of smell in particular brought him into harmony with these. But even his taste, appetites, and thoughts were part of it, the seasonal flux. It was spring when Sheila stepped into his life. Summer came with delicious, vibrant smells and shifting shadows.

Sheila was changing too. Her individuality grew stronger. Lew loved her more for it, the independent personality that sprang from somewhere inside her seemingly limitless potential. But every now and then her initial expression of embryonic wonder would return, reducing Lew to a state of near-religious worship.

They roamed the forest freely. Lew never cared where they were. Sheila knew it better than he did. She could always find new and more delicious fruits and vegetables to eat: a particularly tangy root or a sweet berry that exploded in the mouth with flavor that defied description. She was particularly expert in the fungi. Lew learned that they were not to be feared. Some of the most treasured delicacies of the wood were mushrooms thriving on the fertile, fecund forest floor.

He almost forgot that they were not alone. He never saw Psylene, and though they often passed her lodge, it was never noticed. Psylene's home seemed to grow from the ground, and the trees, vines, and giant ferns grew so as to integrate themselves with the structure. One had to know exactly what to look for, and where to look, to find the brass door ring. And Psylene, herself, knew well the art of not being seen.

The smells gradually became sharper, more focused, and Lew felt the flow of life begin to ebb slightly. He sensed the approach of fall—and something else—Sheila was pregnant. "Why didn't you tell me?" he asked, joyfully patting her slightly swollen belly.

She just laughed and ran away, leading him on one of her delightful chases. The forest leaves were slightly turning; there was the hint of a new coolness in the air. It was bracing, invigorating.

He caught up with her and grabbed her around the waist. Looking into her eyes he saw something that he had never seen before. For the first time her face did not completely cheer him.

It had never occurred to him to ask her if she loved him. Things were so perfect. Never any doubt. Not like the usual situation in relationships, where when one says "I love you" it is for one of two reasons: Either the asker doubts being loved or doubts loving.

There was never any of that between them. Just pure experience of man-woman bliss.

But that first fall day, Lew sensed that something new was present, something that threatened to intrude on their perfect world. "Sheila?" he asked. "What is it?"

"I don't know. I just caught a chill. Like . . . nothing I have ever known."

"Is it the baby?" he asked.

"No. You do want it, don't you?" she asked suddenly.

"I want it almost as much as I want you," he said, meaning it. It wasn't that.

It was something else. But he didn't quite know what.

One thing he did know for the first time that day. She did not love him. At least not the way he loved her. He loved her in so many ways. But so much of his love was love born of his need. She answered his need like nothing ever had.

But Sheila had never known need the way he had. She had only known fulfillment. And the thing that disturbed him most about what he saw in her eyes that day was the simple fact that for the first time she was looking beyond him. What did she see? Could he lose her? Surely it was inevitable that she would grow and change.

"What did you see just now?" he asked her.

"I don't know. What will happen, Lew?"

"What do you mean? When?"

"When you leave me."

He experienced a physical feeling of fear deep within his gut. "I'll never leave you," he managed to say.

"Lew, I'm afraid."

He held her in his arms. Had he looked over her shoulder and through the foliage, he would have seen a door. They were standing right outside Psylene's house. She was watching through a window.

It was a brief, small moment, but things were never the same after that. Lew still loved life in the forest, and he loved Sheila more than ever. As the days grew cooler and shorter he began to feel pain. It was a pain made worse for its brief absence from his life. For a short time Lew had actually known the joys of life free from burden, free from fear, free from worry about the future.

Even so what he had with Sheila in the forest was better than anything he had known in his former existence. The new anxiety was completely mysterious; he had no idea what it was he feared. But he would find himself sitting by the stream, watching the spray as it gently pounded the moss and ferns, thinking about life without her, worrying about her safety and his great need of her. Sometimes he would snap out of it and curse himself for obsessing over a future that might never come. But the very thought of it, the realization that it was a possibility, put the perfect peace of the recent past forever just beyond his reach.

None of this prevented him from enjoying the coming winter. He delighted in the cool freshness of the air. Bathing was shorter and more of a challenge, but more invigorating for the chill of the water. There was no need for clothing. The new season was distinct, sharp yet gentle. At night they would curl together under a tree and sometimes cover themselves with leaves or grass. A soft warmth came from the earth, and when Lew woke to the morning sun's first light he actually welcomed the feeling he got from the frosty air as he stood stretching his limbs.

Sheila was getting bigger throughout. At night Lew would listen to the new heartbeat. It made him feel good, almost as if the new anxiety were just an illusion. "What will we call him?" Sheila asked one night.

"How do you know it will be a he?"

"I just know." She pressed her back more firmly against him. It caused a stirring between his legs, which caused her to giggle. "Oh Lew."

"Oh what?"

"You know," she said and rolled over to kiss him.

They made love. It was getting more awkward with her size, but somehow that just added to the erotic intensity.

Afterward she asked him again, "What will we call him?"

"Maybe we should let him pick a name."

"But it will be years before he is old enough," she said.

"Yeah." It made him sad. Very sad suddenly to think of years. He did not want to be reminded of time, not time as he had known it before. *That tyrant of hours and days that sucked the life out of you!* he thought.

Sheila sensed it. "You won't be here then," she said. "Will you?"

"Of course I will!" he said grabbing her roughly. "I'll never leave you! Never!"

"You're hurting me." She pulled away.

"I'm sorry." Lew let her go. "But don't talk like that. I will never leave you.

What could possibly make me go?"

"I don't know." She said it with just the right inflection to indicate that it was precisely what she did not know that would tear them apart.

Sheila went into labor the next morning. It was a hard labor. Lew made a pallet for her, and attended her constantly. She knew what herbs, flowers, and roots were needed to relieve her pain. He gathered them and prepared the compounds according to her precise instructions.

It was not enough. Night came and she was still laboring hard. He nursed her through the night, trying to remember what little he knew about childbirth. He helped her to breathe slowly and deeply, and continued to give her the medications she requested. But by morning it was clear that something was wrong.

"Lew," she whispered, pale and weak, "I'm afraid. We are losing the baby."

"No, Sheila," he said.

"I can feel him," she said, placing her hand over her womb. "He is not moving so much."

Lew listened, putting his ear to her flesh. The little heartbeat was not as strong. It was agony. He was so helpless. Sheila looked awful. Her pulse was rapid and her breathing fast and shallow.

"Sheila," he said softly, "it will be alright. I know it."

"No," she said. "Something is wrong. I can't bring the baby, Lew." She started to cry.

Lew went all numb. He could see that she was dying. They were both dying. It was such a natural thing, he thought. Finally it struck him full force. How weird it is, the process of birth. Everyone he had ever known came into the world that way. They were grown inside another human and squeezed out through a narrow canal by a death-defying process.

Everyone but Sheila, he suddenly realized. Was that the problem? That Sheila had not been born at all? Was the one person who seemed most human to him *really* human? He had never thought to question it before.

Not knowing what he was doing, he took her in his arms and stood. She felt so frail, so light for a woman full of child. He began walking. It seemed to help. She curled against him and said, "That's nice. Walk me. Rock me. That's nice, Lew." But still he felt her slowly slipping away.

He walked a long way, just wandering aimlessly. He stopped out of tiredness and despair. She was no longer talking. Her eyes were closed and her breathing very tenuous.

He stood facing what looked like a thicket of trees. Something caught his eye—a metallic gleam. The sun, rising to its zenith, caught a piece of metal, a brass ring and the momentary, reflective flash caused him to blink. He stared at the spot. Was it a door?

It opened with a swift, sure movement. Lew instantly saw that it was a cabin which he had been staring at. It was like one of those pictures for children, the kind that you look at to find hidden objects. But this was no picture. This was Psylene's house, and she stood fiercely in her doorway, breasts proudly displayed and legs spread in a firm stance beneath her powerful hips.

"Good," she said. "You have brought her. It is earlier than I expected."

"She is dying," Lew said, hollowly.

"Bring her in!"

Lew obeyed.

Psylene quickly cleared her lab bench. "Lay her there." Lew put Sheila down on the flat wood surface.

Psylene quickly felt for pulse, listened to her breathing, and then she put her hand inside Sheila. The patient squirmed and murmured a little at the intrusion.

Psylene began lighting heatglobes and assembling flasks, powders, and liquids. Soon she had a suppository ready which she inserted. After several minutes Sheila opened her eyes. Some color came back into her cheeks.

Psylene leaned over and kissed her on the mouth. Sheila looked up into the woman's eyes and smiled.

It made Lew sick. Not because he had anything against a woman kissing another woman. Lesbianism had never troubled him at all. It was the look he saw in Sheila's eyes. It was a look he had thought was for him alone. Before he could agonize further, Psylene began barking orders at him.

She sent him to the refrigeration cabinet, where he retrieved a small bottle of frosty cream. Psylene rubbed it over Sheila's abdomen. Sheila began breathing harder. The contractions were getting strong again. Psylene rubbed some of the stuff between Sheila's legs.

"Alright," she whispered in Sheila's ear, "he is ready to come and you are ready to bring him. Push him out. It will hurt until you cannot bear the hurt. But then you will feel a deep pleasure beyond pleasure, and you will be glad."

Sheila pushed. She screamed and pushed again. And again. Lew watched, completely fascinated by the seemingly impossible event. Then he came, slippery and squished, but whole and lively. His first act was to squirt a warm, yellow stream right into Psylene's eye.

Lew laughed. Psylene wiped her face and picked up a shiny scalpel from the table. She put the baby on Sheila's breast. Then she lowered the blade to its tiny head. "No!" Lew yelled and moved swiftly toward her. Her free arm shot out and caught him right in the solar plexus, sending him instantly to the floor where he struggled vainly to get up. He managed to rise to one knee, gasping for air that would not come. He watched helplessly as she made a crescent-shaped cut just above the baby's right eyebrow. It was small and did not seem to cause him any pain; he lay calm and watchful throughout the process.

When Lew was able he went to Sheila's side. "Sheila," he said, taking her hand. She looked into his eyes, and Lew was stunned. It was as if she had never known him, as if he were merely a friendly stranger, a man she no longer recognized.

"What have you done to her!" He turned to the other woman.

"Saved her life and delivered her baby," Psylene said calmly, watching him.

Lew looked into those steely cold eyes, and then back at Sheila who was oblivious to all but the child, his child. He bolted, ran out the door, furious, confused, and afraid.

He got lost. When he finally stopped running he felt quite stupid. He had never bothered to learn much about the forest. It had never mattered before. It was getting dark. Lew tried to retrace his steps but it was impossible.

He did find the stream, and recognized a favorite pool. He drank, and went for a swim. For the first time he was really cold in the forest. In the twilight he followed the water downstream until he came to the clearing with the sundial.

His clothes were nearly buried from the natural action of rain and earth, but he found them. The crystal was still in his jacket. The cotton was soiled and soft but did not feel dirty. After shaking them and beating the dirt particles out he quickly dressed. His jeans and denim jacket were more faded and softer than he thought possible; the earth had tempered them, but strangely the fabric was not rotten; it was still strong, as if the fibers had absorbed something living from the ground, something gentle and vibrant. His running shoes were spongy and light.

He lay awake for hours, exhausted and grief stricken. The initial shock had been too great to absorb, but now it was beginning to sink in. When he finally did sleep it was a deeply troubled slumber that left him tired and drawn when morning came.

Lew wandered for days, trying to find the cabin, to find Sheila. He ate and slept little. Often he would call her name, to be answered only by birds and the wind in the trees.

Finally, tired and hungry, he stumbled upon a clearing, where Sheila sat in front of the cabin, nursing the baby. It was such a pristine, peaceful scene that Lew could not bring himself to step forward for several minutes. When he did finally walk up to her it was with a sense that he was somehow intruding, committing a sacrilegious act.

"Sheila," he croaked, in a voice hoarse from hunger, fatigue, and desperate calling.

"Lew." She said his name in a neutral tone, as if stating the mere fact of his existence. "You look tired."

"Oh Sheila." He fell at her feet, crying. "Come away with me."

"Away?" She sounded perplexed at the word, as if it had no real meaning.

"Away from her."

"Psylene?"

"Yes!" He sat up, staring intently into her eyes. "She is dangerous. Don't you see? That was the problem from the beginning. I didn't realize it at first! But we were never alone. Let's run away. Far away, where we can be alone again, where we can be like we used to be! Sheila, please!"

He was tugging at her arm. It put her off-balance and the baby fell away from her breast. The harsh noise of the strange man scared the little creature and he started to cry.

"But I can't go," she said.

"Why! Why?" he nearly screamed.

"I belong here."

"You belong with me!" He pulled her roughly to her feet.

"Lew, you're hurting me." The baby was wailing pitiful-ly.

He dragged her through the forest, not knowing where he was going. She was still a little weak from her labor and unable to resist much while attending to the baby.

The woods suddenly seemed a hostile place to Lew; he wanted to get out. He increased his manic pace. It began to rain. Hard. Lew was oblivious to the sheets of water pelting them. Lightning split huge nearby trees, and the thunder was deafening. Finally, soaked and exhausted, Sheila collapsed, unable to keep up.

"Lew," she cried, "you're hurting us."

Something in her voice got to him. "I'm sorry," he said. "But we have to get away, that's all." He tried to find shelter but there was not much to do except huddle underneath a tree and hope that the lightning did not find them.

Lew was utterly miserable, completely unable to provide even minimal protection for his woman and child. Meanwhile the baby cried and Sheila pressed against him for warmth, nothing more. Lew tried to kiss her once and was pierced to the heart by her indifference to his advance.

"I'm sorry, Sheila," he said finally. "But don't you see? We have got to get away."

"And where will you go?" It was Psylene. She walked straight toward them, looking as comfortable in the storm as they were miserable.

"You!" Lew exclaimed, standing. "What have you done to her? She is mine. You had no right."

"She is yours?" Psylene laughed. "I suppose you could say that she is yours in the same way that a lump of clay could claim the pot which is molded from it."

"What?" Lew was stung hard by the open derision.

"She is *mine*," Psylene said, quietly.

"How?"

"I made her. I took your seed and made something better than you could ever hope to make, a perfect female. The experiment was a success. Now I want her. And she wants me. You may go."

Lew looked at Sheila, who was looking with love at the other woman.

"Look closely, Lew," Psylene said, "You may recognize something."

Lew continued to stare hard into those eyes he had come to love so dearly. "I took your seed." The words of the woman echoed in his mind. "Your seed, your seed, your seed!"

Through the violent storm Lew saw that he was looking into a mirror. Sheila turned to look at him. It was with a silent, screaming terror that he recognized his own features in the other face. It was just him and her, nothing else existed for the moment. He felt himself fuse with Sheila and lose any sense of sexual differentiation. It was death, or rather prelife that he experienced for an instant. In that instant he understood that, in a very real sense, all energy was sexual energy—life itself was born of the separation of opposites and their struggle to come back together. He felt himself drawn into a vortex where male and female merged. His masculinity was being consumed. The sensation was one of exquisite bliss tinged with terror.

He pulled violently back and found himself standing, breathing hard, heart throbbing. Once again he was a lone man. He was still looking at Sheila.

"She is you," Psylene said. "You have been fucking yourself." She laughed at the joke. "Still—your passionate love *is* touching. But that is over. I have no further need of you. You may go."

"Susan," he said. "Why?"

"Why?" she said. "Why not? You had all the power before, playing with your little computer . . ."

"But Susan, we were both at the mercy of the system! I was just a programmer . . ."

"Who happened to make twice as much money as I did!" Psylene interrupted. "But none of that matters now. Do you think I still care about any of that? Sheila is my creation. She stays with me. I'm sorry if you can't accept it. What was it you said to me that day? 'It is one rough old world out there'? I guess it is—only now it is my world."

The brief union with Sheila had stirred deep energies within Lew. Determined to reclaim his lost female side, the woman-creature born of his own passion, he reached into his jacket and pulled out the crystal. A lightning bolt hit not ten feet from where they stood. The eerie, white electric light illuminated his thrusting hand as he sought to bury the crystal deep in Psylene's breast.

The same flash saw Psylene reach behind her and draw an arrow with a motion swift and sure. Her arm shot out to meet Lew's. The tip of the arrow caught his right arm just above his hand. She drove the sharp, brass wedge through his wrist and into the trunk of the great cypress tree.

There was a dull "thunk!" as the point dug in. The tendons of his wrist snapped back up into his forearm. Lew's now useless fingers fell limply open and the crystal dropped to the ground with a light bounce. Sheila picked it up, and the little baby grabbed for it. It all happened in a silent flash.

Lew's scream was drowned by the huge thunderclap that followed. He yanked the arrow out and grabbed his wrist.

"That was stupid," Psylene said. "Please leave now, Lew. I spoke the truth when I said I didn't want to hurt you, but you gave me no choice."

Lew was whimpering with pain and staring at Sheila, who was watching her baby try to grip the crystal in his tiny fingers. "What about him?" he said, nodding toward the baby.

He felt a strange kinship with the little thing. He did not want to leave it.

"He can do as he pleases when the time comes," Psylene said. "Now please leave."

"Give it back," he said, "and I will leave."

"Give what back?" Psylene asked.

"The crystal. It is mine. Give it back."

"If you still want it you may have it," Psylene said. "Look."

Sheila was still holding the crystal, but it did not look the same. She was speaking into it, saying, "Who are you?" Lew remembered with a shock his first glimpse of her on the evening of the day that the professor had given him the crystal. It seemed an eternity ago that he heard her speak those same words in his garage apartment.

The crystal was dissolving in her hand. The raindrops mingled with its melting and the clear liquid seeped through her fingers. She held what remained of it up, offering it to him. The expression on her face was full of pity, even sympathy, but no regret.

He tried to take it, but the hand he stretched forward was useless so she set it gently in his palm underneath his twisted fingers. He held it up to his face and watched as it continued to dissolve, mingling with the blood from his wound. The colors refracting from the shrinking facets seemed more brilliant; they drew him with a strong, sharp magnetism. For a moment he was lost in the beauty. He saw his face, reflected in its surface. He looked tired, older. Suddenly he realized that the face he saw *was* older, and getting older even as the crystal was shrinking. The hair went to gray and then to white. The eyes grew deeper, and wiser. It was a face he knew. *Where . . . ?* he wondered. Just as he thought he recognized a familiar old friend, the crystal vanished—there were only a few drops of liquid left in his palm. He tasted them. Ordinary water and blood, nothing more.

"Crystallized nous?" Psylene said, with a hint of sarcasm. Lew remembered his teasing Susan about her book, *Goddess Power*. She was taking the same patronizing tone with him now.

"But Susan," he said, barely above a whisper, "I never really hurt you." He held his mangled hand up for her to see.

"Yes, Lew, I am sorry about that." Her voice was sincere but flat, as if there were nothing more to be said.

Lew slowly turned away, right hand dangling, blood spurting onto the rain-soaked ground. He felt that Sheila's dead love was reborn in him. Even if she were his image reflected in a sexual mirror, he did not care. Union with Sheila had become his life, and that union was over.

So when he got to the stream he hardly hesitated. It was swollen from the downpour which had not abated. The waters rushed downstream in a torrent. It had become a raging river, careening across rocks and boulders through treacherous rapids. Lew raised his face to the sky and got a mouthful of water. Then he hurled himself into the river. The vicious waters felt like justice on his body as he was swept relentlessly downstream.

A dispassionate, instinctive drive to survive caused him to hold his breath underwater and snatch a breath or two when he was thrown to the surface. The current bounced him off hard surfaces and carried him deep as the channel widened. He was soon out of Psylene's forest; the stream had reached the valley floor and was about to rejoin the main river there.

A will to live slowly crept back, but it was too late. Exhausted, bruised, battered, and weak from loss of blood he tried to swim but could not. The water was very deep, and even though the current had slowed, it was still bouncing him against the shoreline with great force. With only one good hand he could not get a solid grip on anything.

A particularly heavy blow against a boulder knocked the wind from his lungs. He could not draw a breath, and he felt his body begin to sink for lack of buoyancy. He flailed his arms about to no use; he was going down.

Something black flashed by, and there was a sharp pain in his ribs, like death. Lew let go his life, not ready to die but unable to live. His body went limp and his world dark.

There was buzzing—incessant buzzing. *The vibrations on the interface between life and death*, he thought. He tried to sink farther into the blankness to escape the noise, but it just got louder. And the stench. There was an awful smell, reminding him of the swamp that had claimed the professor's Jag and nearly taken him. "I wish it had," he murmured between parched lips. He felt wet heat all around. The sun was blazing on his head.

Opening his eyes was a tremendous effort. He immediately shut them at the sight of what he took to be his dead and mangled body. He assumed he was a dead soul lingering in some tenuous connection with what remained of his human form. He tried to force his mind away, into the void of space or whatever afterlife awaited him.

No success. The buzzing was louder still and the smell so strong he could nearly taste it. He opened his eyes again. It was not his body that lay before him. Rather it was the half-eaten carcass of some other poor creature. Lew could not tell what animal it had been, a quadruped of some sort, but the hind section was all that remained and the fur was matted and discolored by the humid, heat-hurried decay. That was the source of the sound. Flies were buzzing all around the mess, having a wonderful time.

Lew hurt all over. He felt weak and sick. His back was propped up against something, and his legs stretched out in front of him, almost touching the rotting carrion. He was beginning to suspect that, yet again, he was not dead.

He saw that he was on a large flat area of silt and river debris. It was more solid than the swamp, being farther downstream. The river had gone down considerably since the storm, but it still rushed swiftly by, full of mud and debris just a few yards away. Apparently the river fanned out into a large swampy delta and then slowly re-formed itself into a free-flowing current. Lew was at the downstream edge of the swamp, and the silt plain was the result of the creeping movement of the quicksand bog that lay farther upstream.

Lew rose to the cracking sounds of creaky joints. "The Jag!" he exclaimed after he turned around. He was looking right at the professor's car. It was what had supported his back when the buzzing, stench, and heat had pulled him back to consciousness. The car was half-buried; the trunk and rear quarter panel were sunk into the silt and the hood and front section jutted out at a thirty degree angle. The body was beginning to rust, but the sight cheered him a little. The slow movement of the swamp must have pushed it to its present position, he reasoned.

He walked around the car. It was clearly no longer drivable, even if he could free the thing—which he could not. He thought he saw another dead animal not far away and went to investigate. It looked like the other half of the mysterious beast. Lew got up to it and was startled by a guttural growl. He half expected the carcass to rise up and attack until he saw the source of the new noise bounding toward him.

"Felix!" he shouted. The large cat came up to Lew and rubbed against his side, causing him to wince. Lew realized in his pain that Felix had pulled him from the river, ripping his side in the process. Felix returned to the other half of the dead animal and tore a piece of flesh to eat.

The cat had brought down an animal after saving Lew, ripped it in half, and given one piece to his master. But Felix was fiercely protective of his own portion, issuing menacing growls to warn Lew if he ventured too close to the cat's foul feast.

"Nice kitty," Lew said. Felix came back to rub against him, purring deeply. Lew started to cry. "Nice kitty."

He went back to the Jag and reached out to open the front door. His hand banged useless against the rusting metal. He looked down to see the shriveled claw that his fingers had become. The wound in his wrist was caked with clotted blood and silt. The physical pain was only a dull ache; Lew sensed that the silt had an analgesic quality. But the memory brought sharp emotional pain.

With his left hand he clumsily pulled open the front door of the Jag. The interior was muddy and mold grew on the leather seats. He absently reached over and switched on the nouancer. It sputtered to life. Without the crystal the music was full of static, unfocused. It faded in and out.

Lew let it play anyway. The white noise seemed to help. He was beginning to remember too much. Sheila. The perfection that they had known. His desperate desire to love her the way he had never loved anything. And even when he had finally come to understand that she was really he, himself, it had not mattered. Knowing that it was all within him, this love, this passion, did not weaken the desire. It had nothing to do with knowledge. Knowledge is a thing of time and separation.

What he had with Sheila had been outside of time altogether and completely integrated with every facet of his experience. It did not matter what she was or was not. What mattered was his inconsolable loss.

In the morning his pain still cut like a knife, but oddly it seemed to suit him. He examined himself in the rearview mirror. It was not the white-haired visage he had seen in the vanishing crystal, but he had aged. *I'm really not so young anymore*, he thought. His bones felt a little more . . . well, just a little more. So did his muscles and joints. The morning chill charged him. Thoughts of Sheila or Psylene triggered feelings that were too powerful, too threatening. He had to shut them out before they completely consumed him. *They are too dangerous*, he told himself. It was a liberating thought. An odd kind of liberation consciously to turn away from feelings out of necessity. He was a man, nothing more. So what if his past was full of a pain that defied description? So what if he was a crippled and crooked man? He was still a man on the road. The fuzzy music drifted in louder. *It kind of suits me*, he thought again, *this older, hollowed-out shell of an existence*. He was ten pounds too light from malnutrition and exhaustion, but his appetite was returning and he began to scan the shoreline for signs of fruit trees and edible plants. He had a strong desire to spit into the wind, which he did, watching the saliva arc up and down.

He actually laughed. It was not a hearty laugh. He was still too poisoned with grief and hate for that. But it was sincere, bubbling up from a place inside that he had not even known about. It was a place at his center where the essence of his identity as a man lived. It was a real laugh and, as such, the most miraculous thing he could imagine feeling. It was gone as soon as he recognized it. He looked at his cat, who was watching him with an intent look of expectation. Lew thought it looked a little like worship, reverence of the beast for the rational beast.

"Come on, kitty!" he said, not knowing where he meant to go or what he meant to do.

"Meeooww!". Felix responded with a lively feline sound and motion.

"Come on, kitty! Let's go!"

"All men are outlaws. Outlaws all, outlaws all." Lew heard or thought he heard these words whisper forth from the incessant static of the nouancer. They were dry, raspy-sounding words, as if they came from a parched shore on the other side of the river of life.

13

~~~∿∿∿~~~

An Extraordinary Singularity

One of the advantages of working at a high-powered place like the institute was the lack of prescribed duties or working hours. The faculty taught no classes; they were expected to do only one thing—research.

Pamela and Elliot came into the office less and less. This was a source of gossip among their colleagues and the staff, but they were not breaking any rules. "I'm putting my position as director on the line, you know?" Elliot said, late one night as they were working on the singularity problem. They were working later and later, sometimes staying up all night and sleeping into the day.

"So no one is forcing you," Pamela said.

"I wouldn't be here if I didn't believe in what we were doing," he said, hurt by the coldness in her voice. "You are onto something big here. I know that. But it took a lot of political maneuvering for me to get where I am. I just . . ."

"I'm sorry, Elliot." Pamela removed her glasses and reached across the kitchen table to touch his hand. "Maybe we are pushing too hard. Maybe we should slow down a little."

"No." A weak, raspy voice broke from behind her.

She turned around quickly. "Alan!" He had not moved since

the day they rescued him from the alleys of the Lower East Side.

"You have got to hurry." His eyes were half-closed and glazed over. He could barely stand.

They helped him back to his room. He refused to lie down. "It is starting to come back to me now," he said.

"What?" Pamela asked.

"Akasha. The library. Lew . . . and me. We were there, and . . ."

"There where?" Pamela prodded.

"Doesn't matter where," he said, fighting to stay conscious. "The point is that Lew will not be able to get back unless you solve the problem. They need the equation to navigate . . . or else they will be lost forever, and I will . . ." His voice faded out completely and he collapsed back on the bed. They covered him and went back to the kitchen.

"What is he talking about?" Elliot asked.

"The singularity problem. I made the case in my presentation to the society that it relates both to the physical nature of black holes and also the psychological or philosophical nature of self. Remember?"

"Of course," Elliot said. "How could I forget? They practically laughed you out of the hall."

"Well that is what he is talking about," Pamela said. "Unless we solve the problem soon he will die, and . . ."

"What?"

"I won't be able to live. Not really, I mean. I can't start a new life until all this is behind me. A new life with you." She smiled at him.

"Then let's get back to work," he said, fighting fatigue. Something else bothered him more than the pervasive tiredness. It was the feeling that he was caught up in something beyond both his ability to control and understand. That was not an easy thing for an ordinary mathematician to accept. Pamela not only accepted it—she seemed to thrive on it. But then Pamela Fine was no ordinary mathematician.

14

An Aethereal Empathy

"Outlaws all. Outlaws all." Lew was whispering these words to himself as the open book slipped from his hand. He looked up to see a giant octopus staring at him with a probing eye. Felix was pacing on the carpet, restless and disoriented, a few yards away. He slowly raised his crippled hand to verify with his eyes the paralyzed, clawlike feel of his fingers.

He turned away from the plate glass, unnerved by the cool appraisal of the octopus. Sitting back in his chair, he looked at the maze of books before him. "So many stories," he murmured.

Swiveling back around, he looked down once more at the page before him. With an angry frustration he thrust out his left hand and slammed the book shut. The desk was still littered with other papers and books, evidence of an unknown person who was probing into the life of Lew Slack.

He noticed a journal that had not been there before. It was the one book which did not relate either to him or to the mathematical singularity problem. It was a handwritten, personal journal of someone who called himself Pascal.

He opened it and began to read.

"There is one thought that helps me when I begin to feel distant from life and the unknowable purpose for which we were all created. I imagine that the particular moment, with its perceptions and awareness of being, is all that I have ever known or ever will know, and I ask myself, 'For this alone would I choose to be?'

And the answer is always, 'Yes!' In looking up at the naked branches of a winter tree, fading into crooked interlacing twigs, or in seeing the lines in the palm of my hand as I write this, for either sight alone, I would choose to live. For that would I step out of nothingness—and return a moment later to nothingness—without question. And could I, from the void, contemplate what had happened, I would shudder with amazement and delight. Yet every moment of life is such.

"But still something is missing. I suppose it is for this reason that I find myself here writing these words. For why would I have left my home and risked all if it were not to fulfill some need? I do not understand what it is that drives me, but I suppose that should come as no surprise. How can the creature ever hope to fully understand itself? The great philosopher was wrong when he said, 'Know thyself.' It was an impossible task that he set before humankind, the pursuit of which can only end in despair. No, the only real hope lies in trust, faith. You must nurture that faith until it is strong enough to give you strength and courage enough to cast yourself completely into the wave of time. Then you can truly ride the wild surf, which is where it all begins. Surfing that wave we can transcend time. My work here in the library leads me more and more to the conclusion that time is really not so important, perhaps ultimately irrelevant. Life intends to take all of time into itself eventually, not to negate the slow beauty of hours and days—we need not lose the sunrise nor the dead of night—but to defeat once and for all the tyranny of the clock."

Lew looked up to gaze out the plate glass window in front of him. The slowly undulating currents on the other side were hypnotic; the ripples, eddies, and convolutions reminded him of watching the patterns caused by cold cream mixing with hot coffee on a winter's morning. Pascal's words had stirred him. For the first time it occurred to him that he might never leave the library; he could be trapped forever in a maze of endless possibility. A large, phosphorescent fish swam by and turned to eye him. It lingered, tail fin flapping against the tidal current for a few moments, and then swam on. He continued to read.

*   *   *

*"And so there is really nothing left for me but to pursue
my work. The filing system here in the library seemed an
impossible riddle at first. When I arrived I knew almost
nothing of electromagnetic theory or modern physics.
But my understanding of biology, naturally, was far
superior to anything yet achieved on earth.*

*"Terrestrial biologists have such a pitifully narrow
definition of 'life.' They retain a stubborn, willful blind-
ness to the simple truth that the entire universe is alive.
And they have no conception of how 'ordinary' biological life spreads throughout the cosmos.*

*"Nouons, the fundamental particles of thought, radi-
ate throughout the cosmos in an aethereal medium,
the Asklepian current. These particles actually travel in densely packed, single-coiled, helical molecules
which are the precursors of life. They travel by 'feeding on light.' That is, light from a stellar source sets
up a rotation along the molecule's helical axis. This
rotation, in the opposite direction of the helical twist,
actually propels the structure through the cosmic aether,
just as a ship's propeller moves a vessel through water.
When such a molecule strikes a planet with a suitable
biosphere then the planet is 'fertilized.' By a process
not well understood, the superdense nouonic structures
give rise to DNA, the basic structure of life as we
know it. DNA is simply the planet-bound analogue
of the nouonic structure. DNA exists in atmospheres
and oceans, in bounded biospheres, while the nouonic
life/thought structures exist in the unbounded aether of
the entire cosmos. Thus life and consciousness are intimately bound together, are in fact the same thing, and
they exist, at least in fundamental form, throughout the
entire universe.*

*"Because of pervasive 'electromagnetic chauvinism,'
none of these fundamental truths about life and intelligence are understood by terrestrial scientists. Only
when I began to educate myself in these electromagnetic disciplines did I begin to see the relation of the
Asklepian aether and nouons to the organization of the
library. I had long suspected that nouons and the nouonic*

molecular life precursors originated in superdense points of space. These, I was thrilled to discover, have a theoretical basis in the physical concept of black holes or singularities.

"Relativistically these are described in terms of gravitation. But algebraically these singularities are best analyzed by singularity groups. And it so happens that singularity groups are powerful cybernetic tools. That is they allow one to design enormous database systems and extremely efficient searching algorithms.

"I was handicapped for a long time in my search for the key to Akasha's labyrinth of volumes because I was using the wrong model. I was trying to get at it through numerology. But the library is an information matrix. One needs an information-processing science to make sense of it.

"I knew of no such science. My methods were based completely on organic modes of synthesis and integration. What was needed was an analysis of differentiation. I finally came to the conclusion that this library is a binary structure which will yield its secrets only to a science of feedback, recursion, iterative loops, and information processing. The singularity algebras proved to be the key to the design and implementation of a map, a program, that finally gave me access to the wealth of information buried deep within the stacks."

So, Lew thought, *Pascal discovered computer science all on his own, without the aid of even a simple computer*. And he had applied the theory of cybernetics to the library to reach the same conclusion as Lew, namely that the structure of the library database was to be found in the algebra of singularity groups. But Lew had not done any of this on his own. He had needed the help of Pamela, Alan, and the professor. Pascal's was no mean feat of analysis.

Pascal had drawn maps of the library's data structures in his journal. They corresponded more or less to Lew's rough sketches. But Pascal was an artist as well as a scientist. The maps were beautiful to behold, transforming the analytic reality of the library's design into an intricate visual feast of symmetry and color.

Lew was lost in this beauty when a voice said, "What's going on, Lew?"

Lew jumped to his feet and turned around. It was Alan. "Oh it's you," he said.

"What happened to you?" Alan asked, noting Lew's crippled hand and his emaciated condition.

"Nothing," Lew said softly. "Paradise lost . . ."

"Oh that . . ." Alan said. And then, as an afterthought, he added, "Let's get some coffee."

"On another sexual foray?" Lew asked as they ascended the stairs.

"Yeah."

"How did it go?"

"Not so good this time. Got into a bummer of a scene where a girl and her mother wanted to mess around. I just couldn't go along with it. They tied me up and spanked me." Alan rubbed his butt and winced.

There was something new in the coffee room. It looked like a big, old-fashioned Wurlitzer jukebox, the kind that one would see in a soda fountain of the 1950s.

"Great!" Alan said as they approached it. "The *Religious Experience Jukebox*. I love this thing!" He ran his hands over the curved glass top.

"I need some help here," Lew said. It was difficult pouring coffee left-handed.

"That hand looks bad, Lew. How did it happen?" Alan said pouring two cups.

"I'd rather not talk about it," Lew said, scanning the selections on the jukebox. "We've heard the Hindu; let's try the Buddhist."

"That's old hat for me," Alan said, "but I'm game."

The machine was coin-operated and Lew could find no change in any of his pockets.

"Try this," Alan said, fishing a coin from his *coorta* and flipping it to Lew, who instinctively tried to catch it in his right hand. He succeeded only in knocking it to the floor.

"Sorry," Alan said, "I forgot."

Lew retrieved the coin. It had strange markings that looked as if they should be familiar but weren't. Lew thought that it could pass for legal tender in any land in any era. He dropped it in the slot and punched some numbers.

An ancient, haunting kind of music began to play. It was unlike anything Lew had ever heard, but it made him think of deserts, blazing suns, and, above all, a burning passion for life. The music drew him in, and Lew became one of God's chosen people. He was overwhelmed with visions of a violent, fierce love that burned him to the marrow. For generations he flowed through the seed of his tribe and walked in perfect obedience to this love, this holy covenant.

But then something alien, something foreign began to creep in. He began to feel strange desires that tempted him away from the path of righteousness. Raw sexual lust devoid of love, hunger for power, and insatiable greed began to consume him. And with these desires came shame and guilt. It was a guilt of cosmic size in precise proportion to his former position as one of God's favorite sons. *Better that I had never known God*, he thought bitterly.

Retribution was total. He was swept away, punished and destroyed as if he were a cockroach in the king's kitchen.

This basic theme was repeated several times in various guises. Lew lived it in many eras and many nations. Finally, all that was left was an overwhelming sense of guilt, a burden that was too much to bear. He had fallen out of the holy covenant too many times and his unrighteousness was impossible to cleanse. He prayed to God for a miracle, the miracle of righting a wrong that no mortal could ever right.

Just as he thought his prayer was about to be answered, and he sensed the approach of a peace and redemption greater than any for which he could have hoped, the record was over.

"Lew," Alan said, "you really screwed up."

"What do you mean?" Lew asked, still hovering on the brink of an impossible salvation.

"I mean you punched up the wrong disk. That was the Jewish selection! That was about as Buddhist as Ronald Reagan. Damn! I thought I was going to die from guilt."

"But the ending part," Lew said hesitantly. "I liked that."

"Yeah, I guess," Alan said, still disgruntled, "if you go in for that sort of thing."

"Does it go on?" Lew asked. "I mean the ending was so good. Isn't there a flip side?"

"That would be the Christian," Alan said, "and I am just not up for it. Besides, I haven't got any more money."

*   *   *

They went for a swim in the pool. Lew was terribly anxious that Alan would look up and see the picture depicting his murder. Lew himself was not surprised when the first image he noticed on the domed ceiling was that of a powerfully built, dark, bare-breasted woman banishing a man from her wooded domain.

"You know, Lew," Alan said getting out.

Lew was struck by the red marks on Alan's butt. *It must have been some spanking*, he thought.

"Sometimes," Alan continued, "I think we are just avoiding things by retreating into places like this."

"What things?" Lew asked.

"I don't know. Life, I guess. Maybe it is a desire to change things, to change the past even," Alan said. They dressed in silence and sat down, leaning against the marble side of the pool.

"Can you change the past?" Lew asked, tentatively.

"Sure," Alan said, "but it's tricky."

"What do you mean?"

"I mean that you have to escape desire. That is the essence of Buddhism, you know. Blow out the flame of desire and you enter nirvana, which is release from all sorrow. But that implies acceptance of everything as it is with no desire to change it. Now nirvana is a state in which anything is possible. So if you are in that state you *could* change the past or even the future, but only if you had absolutely no desire to do so. So it is tricky, you see?"

"I guess," Lew said, sounding very depressed.

"Why? What do you want to change?" Alan asked.

"Nothing," Lew said. "Oh everything! I don't know. It is too confusing."

"I get the impression that there is something you are not telling me, Lew," Alan said, looking up at the ceiling. If he saw the picture, he didn't indicate it.

"It is not easy, Alan," Lew said.

"Well don't worry too much about it," Alan said. "As far as changing the past goes, it is a little like reading the texts in the library. I have learned through my yogic discipline to withhold desire. So I can read most of the texts without getting captured by them—unless I want to." He rubbed his sore butt. "Now if you could somehow control your desire precisely enough to enter into one of the stories down there,"—he gestured below—"but still retain a core of indifference to the outcome, I think you could actually rewrite a page or a chapter of history. But it would require a supreme mastery of the will. You would have to let yourself want something within the story enough to enter into it, while at the same time not care about the outcome at all. Might actually be impossible." He began to fade.

"Do you think it might be possible?" Lew asked quickly.

"Maybe . . ." Alan said, flickering more dimly, "and maybe not . . ." He was gone.

Lew went back down, intending to read more of Pascal's journal. The spicy smell of Indian eggplant greeted him as he walked out onto the plush carpet, but there was still no sign of the cook.

Lew realized at once that he was ravenous. He tore into the soft flatbread and rich curry like a crazed beast, spilling bits of food and fragrant sauce on himself, the desk, and the floor. Felix, who was napping nearby, stirred at the manic energy of Lew's eating, sniffed the air, and rolled over.

Hunger satiated, Lew walked the distance back to Pascal's desk. He scanned the journal's entries for any information on Pascal's identity or point of origin with little success. He did find a reference to the author's mother. It was a poignant scene where Pascal left home, never to return.

"She approached me with a brave look on her face. She was still so beautiful.

" 'Take me with you,' she said.

" 'You know that I cannot,' I said, trying to control my voice. I wanted to weep. I think she knew that I would never come back. There was a solitary tear inching slowly down her cheek.

"I touched the teardrop, and it clung to my finger. Carefully opening the pocket of my jacket, I put the tear inside and buttoned the pocket flap, saying 'But I will take your little tear with me, and when I get too lonely I will take it out and gaze into it so deeply that I will see your reflection.'

" 'Oh, son!' she cried and flung her arms around me, holding ever so tight. I think she believed my little tale, although I did not.

"The amazing thing is that it turned out to be true. Her tear solidified and began to grow, the way a seed crystal grows in solution. I can see her face so clearly this very moment in it. We both knew that I could not stay with her forever. Even so . . ."

The entry ended. There was little else to indicate anything of a personal nature about Pascal. There was a reference to his interest in the healing arts. Apparently he believed in an esoteric method which employed something which he called the empathetic aether. Lew read.

"I found that certain fungal extracts, when mixed with human genetic material had remarkable healing properties. I was able to synthesize one of the more potent blends in my laboratory. I called it the empathetic aether.

"A young man happened to present himself to me with a gangrenous foot. This was extremely unusual for the simple reason that my mother and I seldom encountered anyone in our isolated existence. It was also an excellent opportunity. I had him produce for me a portion of the binding for his wound. This I took to a small vessel wherein I had dissolved a minute quantity of the synthetic aether. Submerging the dirty binding, soiled with blood and dead, infected tissue, I asked my patient to describe his symptoms. He groaned in pain at first. Then, after a few moments, he said in near disbelief that his suffering was ended. I advised him to remove the rest of his bandage, and he was amazed to find that his foot was completely restored.

"The empathetic aether heals through the medium of the Asklepian current, the same medium which pulsates with the life-giving energies of nous, the universal consciousness."

Lew's eyes were tired. He got up slowly. He was surprised at how light and springy he felt. Except for the hand his body seemed renewed. Feeling the need for a special kind of comfort, he was about to go in search of the sex manual when he heard footsteps behind him.

Lew knew that it was Pascal. He had assumed that he had Pascal to thank for the meals and something else. The hypothesis had formed in the periphery of his mind that Pascal and the professor were one and the same. So he was surprised at the face he beheld when he turned around.

It was not the face of the professor, although, as with the professor, he had the strange, uneasy feeling that he should recognize this man. He was younger than the professor— Lew estimated about fifty-five. He was dressed in clothes that resembled Lew's outfit, soft cotton jeans and a black denim jacket. His were cut more elegantly as if they were hand tailored, and the jacket had a military look; it was narrower than Lew's, with sharp lapels, and it sported epaulettes.

"Mr. Slack, I presume." Pascal extended his hand.

"Yeah," Lew said awkwardly, holding out his clawed fingers and then hastily pulling the crippled hand back.

Pascal still had his hand out. "Maybe I can help you with that," he said.

"How?" Lew asked, looking with despair at the scar and bulge where the tendons of his forearm were ripped and knotted. He knew that the nerves were severed as well as the tendons.

"Well," he said, taking Lew's right hand in his, "it would have been better if I had been able to treat it before the wound healed. But the empathetic aether has remarkable properties. We may be able to restore some function."

It was then that Lew realized why he thought he should recognize Pascal. Lew was looking at the man's face and he could practically see the flash of the knife that had carved the crescent-shaped scar just above Pascal's right eyebrow.

15

~~∿∿∿~~

Center of Impossibility

"Something is missing, Elliot." Pamela looked up from her pages of calculations, took off her glasses, and rubbed her tired eyes.

"What do you mean?" he asked.

"We are so close to the solution. I know it. But we are not on the right track. There is something we have overlooked—the key to the whole theory, and I just don't know what it is."

"How can you be sure?" he asked. "We have made a great deal of progress, and I agree that we are close." But underneath his optimism he knew she was right. They were barking up the wrong tree.

Later in the evening, after Elliot had left, Pamela went in to check on Alan. He seemed almost aware of her presence, though there was nothing definite she could identify to indicate a change in his usual state. If anything, he looked worse, less color and more gaunt.

Suddenly he opened his eyes and looked straight at the ceiling.

"Alan?" She leaned close.

"Singularities," he said in a voice that sounded like a chant. "I remember now," he continued. "I was *with* Lew."

"With him. With him where?"

Alan gave no sign that he saw Pamela. But he did answer. His answers were like those of an oracle responding to a priest

185

in a temple. "In the library where all things are recorded. All things possible, both past and future."

"How?" she asked. "How do you mean you were with him."

"Tibet—practicing my meditation. There is a way to go there—where Lew is now. Now means nothing there. Outside of time, like the author of a book is outside the narrative.

"Lew is there—in the *library outside of time*. Our lives and times are the books. I could not remember. Until *now*." Alan hissed the word "now." It frightened Pamela. She touched his forehead, but he still gave no sign that he saw her, except that he continued to respond in a resonant monotone.

"What has this got to do with us, Alan? I don't know what to do," Pamela said.

"Lew is there not under his own power, but by other means. All life and consciousness are waves. Asklepian waves. Wave-particles. Nouons, the quanta of our very essence. Existence—now—mediated, made possible and actualized on the Asklepian wave—from the smallest to the largest. Lew and the nouancer can receive and amplify the nouonic signal.

"He programmed it! He did it! The key to the software was singularity algebra. Singularity algebra!" The tone of Alan's voice did not change but the volume was greater. He was still staring straight up, as if he saw something hovering just below the ceiling.

"Can he get back the same way?" Pamela asked.

"The program is not powerful enough for a return trip."

"But you?" Pamela asked. "You got back."

"One-point! One-pointed concentration! Lew cannot do this! He does not have the skill—years of practice, years of meditation are required. It does not come easy. Each moment Lew becomes more mired in the overwhelming potential of possibility.

"Only one way back for Lew. No *turning* back. He must go forward. He must go beyond the possible. He must penetrate the *im*possible."

"How?" Pamela asked, but she already knew.

"The singularity groups now isolated represent only potential singularities. Possibilities. The possible is too limited. Final analysis! Only one *real* singularity. Center of impossibility! Ultimate paradox! Only real reality lies in that which is

utterly impossible to conceive. Funny this way." Alan laughed.
It was a rasping, wicked sound that made Pamela shudder.

"Find the characteristic equation of the ultimate singularity," he continued in his droning voice. "Then Lew can program the nouancer to penetrate to . . ." He became suddenly silent.

"Where?" Pamela tried to look into his eyes, but her gaze was met with a deep emptiness. "Where, Alan, where?"

"Where is not here. Take a gamble, bet it all—one throw of the dice. Simple choice, pure chance—yes/no? There is no place like that. No place like that. No place like home, no place like home . . ." Alan's voice trailed off, and his gaze became more glassy.

"If I solve the characteristic equation of the ultimate singularity, how can I get it to Lew?" Pamela could see that she would get no more answers. Alan's eyes had closed, and his breathing had slowed back down to an almost imperceptible movement.

Pamela went for a long walk. Alan's strange pronouncements had the ring of truth. There could only be one singularity. Anything else would be an oxymoron. But the impossible?

"Why not?" she mused. The mystery of personal identity seemed like an impenetrable impossibility. And so did the secret of gravitation. There had to be a singularity in the heart of the impossible. It was that singularity which underwrote all the myriad worlds and beings of the universe. And more. Scientists had speculated for years that black holes were doorways to alternate realities. Some of those alternate realities, she now felt sure, were impossible realities—at least impossible for her to conceive.

The singularity equations which she had so far discovered simply were not powerful enough to describe this ultimate mystery. They only played around the edges of it. With them one could begin to explore the possible, as apparently Lew had, but that was all they would do, and it was not enough.

She was stuck. *I have got to make something happen*, Pamela thought, *but how*? Alan had started to babble before he had slipped back into his coma. She tried to remember what he had said about gambling, chance, and binary choice. One approach would be symbolic logic, but Pamela felt sure that would not

work. The field was too narrow, too stymied by its own sense
of limitations. She required a more dynamic approach.

Where, she wondered, *could I really investigate the logic
of the impossible as it relates to choice—choice and chance
on a grand scale*? It came to her in a crazy flash. But that
was how most of her breakthroughs occurred.

She went back home and packed a small bag. Then she
called Elliot.

"But I don't understand," he protested. "It sounds crazy . . ."

"Of course it does," she answered. "But I'm not going to
make any more progress here in New York. Can you check
on Alan? You've got a key."

"Sure, but . . ."

"I'll call you in a few days," she said, in a hurry. "By then
I should have some idea of how things are going. Bye."

It was late so she caught a cab to Kennedy Airport. They
were about to seal the hatch when she arrived breathless at the
gate. "They said that you could ticket me here!" she gasped.

The flight attendant was inclined to tell her that it was too
late and she would have to wait until morning, but something
about Pamela's intensity made her change her mind. "Normally I wouldn't do this, but . . ."

"Oh thank you!" Pamela said with an enthusiasm that raised
eyebrows of those within earshot.

"Will this be a round-trip?" the attendant asked.

"No."

They sealed the door behind her, and Pamela took her seat
to the hostile stares of passengers convinced the flight had
been delayed because of her.

They were right, but the plane took off only five minutes
behind schedule at 12:07 A.M. The captain assured them that
a favorable tail wind would allow them to more than compensate in the air, and they would still arrive at the prime hour for
blackjack. Of course that is really any hour in Las Vegas.

16

An Imaginary Son

"You . . . !" Lew said, swallowing hard, eyes bulging.

"I believe we have met." Pascal smiled. "Shall we say . . . some *time* ago—for want of a better expression."

"But you were . . ." Lew stammered.

"I know," Pascal said. "Indeed I was. But I have spent some time away. A rather long time actually. Obviously I could not stay in the forest. It was a wonderful place for a child, but as a man—well, to live in paradise with one's own mother and her . . . *designer* is a little too claustrophobic, bordering on the incestuous really."

"How is . . ."

"My mother? She is the image of happiness, you may be disappointed to hear, but it is the truth."

"I'm not disappointed," Lew said glumly. "I just wondered."

"Naturally. My story has been somewhat more complicated. As you are no doubt aware, Sheila is not exactly human, strictly speaking. A pure creature of potential, really, an imaginary being. So I am quite literally a child of the imagination. I am far more *actualized* than she, so my needs are not so easily satisfied, which is why I spent the better part of thirty years roaming the galaxy."

"How?" Lew asked.

"In a spaceship, of course."

"Where would you get a spaceship?"

"My peculiar status gives me a freer access to the volumes contained here. There are fine spaceships to be had if you know where to look. Also fine cuisine from all cultures of all eras. I trust the food has been satisfactory?"

"You didn't cook it yourself?" Lew asked.

"Where would I do that? There are no facilities. No, I get the various dishes straight off the page. I was rather conservative in my selections, limiting them to those things which I knew you would like. But you really should try some of the more exotic fare which is available, ancient Sumerian crocodile philones for instance, or an authentic Siriuan cheesebread."

"Why"—Lew began searching for the words—"all this?" He indicated the desk, littered with Pascal's research material.

"Naturally I wanted to find out as much about you as I possibly could," he answered.

Hearing this made Lew extremely uneasy. He could not possibly relate to this older, more sophisticated man as his son.

"Yes, it is rather awkward, isn't it?" Pascal said, noticing Lew's discomfort. "But in a very real sense we are both children of the same father."

"Who is that?" Lew asked.

"That would be the essence of you yourself, Lew Slack. We have a great deal in common on that score. But as to the precise nature of our relationship—it is probably best not to worry too much about it.

"Now the mathematical research. That is the really interesting stuff. Because that may lead to a real beginning."

"Beginning of what?" Lew asked.

"The great leap into the impossible!" Pascal said, eyes shining. "That is all that is left for me, and I am eager to get on with it.

"You see, I explored the breadth and depth of the cosmos. I even plunged straight into the center of the galaxy seeking the ultimate singularity." Pascal paused, obviously cherishing some memory. "But," he continued, "as glorious and grand an experience as that was, I discovered that what I seek is not to be found there."

"What do you seek?" Lew asked.

"Would you like some tea?" Pascal asked suddenly.

"Tea?" Lew said, confused by the abrupt change of subject.

"Everything in this universe, including tea, has infinite significance, especially here," Pascal said.

He disappeared into the maze of stacks and returned with a woven bamboo tray on which sat a beautiful china teapot, two cups in saucers, a silver creamer, and a bowl of sugar cubes. "This Darjeeling stuff is the best," he said, setting the tray down on a desk. Lew pulled up a chair and sat down while Pascal poured.

"You can actually go into a text and retrieve things?" Lew asked. "Spaceships and tea, I mean?"

Pascal laughed at the juxtaposition. "Yeah. Spaceships and tea. My specialties. Yes, I can do that. It comes with the territory more or less."

"What do you mean?" Lew asked.

"Well I am a child of both worlds, am I not? The actual who is you, and the potential whom you also know very well." Pascal gave Lew a rather lascivious look that seemed inappropriate.

"Sorry, Lew," Pascal said. "I meant no offense. Anyway I can move rather comfortably in both realms and so am able to provide excellent teas like this."

"And spaceships," Lew mused out loud.

"Indeed," Pascal said, pouring cream into his tea.

Lew began to relax. It was as if all the uncertainty and anxiety of his adventure were suddenly transformed into a palatable sense of cool excitement and intellectual ease. They sat in silence, watching the underwater scene just a few feet in front of them. Beautiful fish and strange life-forms darted past. One bizarre creature with a single eye in the middle of a pentagonal body stopped to look at them. Lew felt an eerie tingle as he returned a seemingly sentient, cyclopean gaze. Then it vanished into the depths.

Finally, when the tea was cool enough to sip, Pascal spoke. "You would not believe!" He paused and then in a long, forceful exhalation said, "No one who has not done it can imagine what it is like to sail in the emptiness of space. The icy cold, the solar winds, the nouonic pulse of life coursing through your veins—no, not even your veins! It gets down into the molecular structure of your cells—the very code that is your life is energized by it! Inflamed by it!" He became abruptly quiet, sipping his tea and looking out.

"Where are we?" Lew asked.

"Wrong question," Pascal said, taking up his tea again.

"What's the right one then?" Lew snapped, suddenly irritated.

Pascal laughed. "I don't blame you. It is a damn frustrating thing. And it is also a very ambitious project." He looked out the window; the water seemed suddenly possessed of a slow fury.

"Which is?" Lew finally prompted.

"To get to the center of it all," Pascal said.

"But where is that?" Lew asked. As far as he knew, astrophysics had no such concept as a geometric center of the Universe. *Does Pascal have access to an exotic science which postulates such a thing?* Lew wondered.

"It must be out *there*," Pascal said, gesturing toward the underwater depths with his teacup.

Pascal turned to face Lew, carefully placing the cup back into its fitted indention in the saucer. "You know, I think maybe I am looking for God." He said this with a curious expression, at once comical, self-absorbed, and euphoric.

Lew felt suddenly embarrassed, as if he had been made privy to some intensely personal thing that he should not see. He lowered his eyes and nervously shifted in his chair. He put his cup down and jammed his hands into the pockets of his jeans. Finally, to break the silence, Lew spoke. "Well surely you will find Him, God that is . . . at the center." It sounded more like a question than a statement.

Pascal laughed. "Ah, Lew. The ancients were obsessed with centers. They constructed elaborate cosmologies of concentric spheres. Center after center. Then science gave us new centers. Atomic nuclei, galactic cores, and centers of gravitation. But there are centers and there are *centers*. The ancients wanted absolute geometric centers, the modern scientists want theoretical ones. Vanity, vanity. And all of it is vanity."

"Ecclesiastes," Lew mused. He remembered the professor and felt guilty, as if he should be taking notes. Pascal was talking about the sort of thing the professor was interested in, the kinds of questions that had inspired project Asklepios in the first place. *But what the hell!* he suddenly thought. The professor's theories! What did he care about that foolish old man and his half-baked ideas anymore—after what he had been through.

"Maybe the center I seek is neither geometrical nor theoretical," Pascal said.

"Then where is it?" Lew asked.

Pascal's eyes had taken on a faraway look. They came back into focus. "Maybe it is not so much a where as a 'who,' " he said.

"But now look." Pascal's tone of voice suddenly changed from passionate longing to military precision, very business-like. "Our meeting here is no accident. It just may be that together we can push on—leave this place. I'm sick of this library with its abundance of information. You can read your entire life story here if that is what you want. But I prefer to live it, not read about it. The time has come for action!" He ended this quick speech with laughter that sounded a little mad. But in spite of that, Lew could not stop himself from joining in—the spontaneous levity was contagious.

Pascal proceeded to question Lew on the particulars of his adventure so far. He didn't seem to care for many of the personal details although he did smile strangely when Lew claimed utter ignorance as to the identity of the professor, the old man who had started it all.

Pascal was interested in the hardware. He was extremely tense when Lew finished describing the nouancer. "Where is this marvelous machine now?" he asked through clenched teeth.

"I don't know," Lew said, reluctant to divulge what he really thought.

"You have no idea?" Pascal pressed.

"Well I do have an idea, but it sounds ridiculous, I . . ."

"Out with it, man! How could anything sound ridiculous anymore?" Pascal practically shouted.

"Well," Lew said, "I think that somehow the nouancer was transformed into . . . into the file room upstairs."

"Yes!" Pascal said. "Of course! I should have guessed it myself. The filing system is based on the singularity algebra, is it not? The very same system which you programmed into the nouancer?"

"Yeah," Lew said.

"Well . . ." Pascal was deep in thought. "This could be really interesting. It just might work."

"What might work?"

"We need that device, Lew. We need it for the final leg of the voyage—out there!" Pascal pointed with his cup toward the window, where the gray-green waters moved. "It would be a hopeless mission without the right equipment."

"What equipment?"

"A reliable guidance system. Without it one would quickly become lost in the infinite depths of consciousness—or I should say *un*-consciousness. But with your nouancer—we have a chance."

Pascal rose from his desk, lost in thought. "Let me show you something," he said.

He led the way back into the stacks. Lew followed. After several twists and turns Pascal stopped and pulled a dusty old volume from the shelf. He opened it, indicated a passage, and began to read. Lew read along with him, and in a matter of moments found himself standing outside a set of heavy iron doors set in stone. Pascal opened the doors, and they descended a steep flight of stone steps into a dark chamber. Then Pascal passed his hand over a glowglobe illuminating the place with the same smoky yellow light Lew had seen in Psylene's lab. The scene was eerie and surreal.

As his eyes adjusted to the light, Lew watched the dim outlines of a vessel take shape. Lew was struck by two things immediately—the thing seemed simultaneously antique and futuristic. It reminded him of artistic interpretations of the *Nautilus*, the atomic-powered submarine from Jules Verne's classic *Twenty Thousand Leagues Under the Sea*. The prow of the ship was an elaborate hermetic caduceus, a single serpent coiled around a staff. The sides were lined with circular portholes. It was constructed of a steely blue-gray metal, not shiny but strangely luminous in the light.

"What do you think of her?" Pascal said with obvious pride.

"It's beautiful," Lew said sincerely.

"She's ready to go, stocked with provisions. Let me show you below."

They entered a narrow hatch in the top of the vessel and went down into the ship. Lew's sense of antiquity, the gilded age of the nineteenth century to be precise, was more powerful below deck. He had expected to find sparse, cramped living quarters, like the interior of a German U-boat from World War II. Instead he found soft velvet chairs, a lime green upholstered couch that ran alongside the portholes. There was a small dining room next to the galley, where Pascal had stored frozen meat, dried herbs, spices, tea, and coffee.

The mate's sleeping quarters were small but sported a bed with silk sheets on a polished wooden frame. Cabinets in the head were expertly crafted hardwood with brass trim.

The captain's quarters were cleverly designed to give the illusion of great space, a challenge since the ship was small, no more than fifty feet in length. The stern navigation room featured a large brass wheel, captain's and navigator's chairs, compass, maps and charts strewn everywhere.

The ship looked well used and well maintained, and Pascal obviously was her captain, checking everything and pointing out small details that Lew would otherwise have missed. It was during this tour of the sub that Lew realized Pascal's black denim jacket and jeans were cut in a distinct nautical style. The effect was that of a ship captain's uniform.

"I have dreamt for a long time now of taking her out into the sea of nous," he said. They were seated in the captain's quarters, Lew on a short, plush sofa, and Pascal in an overstuffed reading chair. The brightly colored velvet cushions were illuminated by a green glow from the globe in the ceiling.

"Sea of nous?" Lew asked, looking down at the Persian rug.

"Yes. That is the ocean outside of the library. That is where eternity lies. It is truly the cosmic ocean. But I have not dared," Pascal said.

"Why?"

"Because deep in those waters lies the impossible. The library, wherein we find the records of the possible, is a tiny place in comparison. The vast sea is an awesome cauldron of infinities—infinities of an order impossible even to conceive. Without a means to navigate her, to find the center, any voyage into those depths would be a one-way journey to infinite fragmentation, absolute dissolution," Pascal said.

"Dissolution of what?" Lew asked.

"Self. Dissolution of self. But paradoxically the ultimate nature of self also lies in the depths of those waters. The ultimate singularity, the center of impossibility which girds the entire Universe, is out there. But we need a way to find it. That is where your device, the nouancer, comes in. That is the essential hardware. But we will need one more thing."

"What is that?" Lew asked.

"The software. To that end I have been investigating the mathematics of singularity groups. I am close to solving the singularity problem, but the final equation still eludes me. But once I have it . . . together with your nouancer, then we can make the plunge. Our chances of success are excellent," Pascal said.

"Our?" Lew asked.

"You don't want to stay here forever do you?" Pascal asked. "Haven't you had enough of reading the endless possibilities of your life into existence?"

When Lew did not answer Pascal said, "Well, never mind. Come here. It is time we took a look at that hand."

Lew went to Pascal and held out his hand.

"Damned hideous piece of butchery!" Pascal said. He probed the wrist and forearm, feeling for the ends of the severed tendons under the scar tissue.

His examination finished, he looked up and said, "I can't promise anything, Lew. The nerves and tendons are all separated. But with the empathetic aether I may be able to restore some function. I'll have to open up your arm again—pull it all apart—where it has healed. It's going to hurt."

Pascal went to an antique wooden medicine cabinet on the wall and got a small, green glass beaker. Into the beaker he poured a few grains of a white crystalline powder. "Concentrated"—he smiled—"my greatest discovery!" He filled the beaker with water from a white ceramic sink stained with tea and chemicals. The stuff dissolved quickly and Lew detected an aroma, just a trace, that made him think of childhood memories and dreams long forgotten.

But he had little time to savor these reveries. Pascal took his arm in one hand and brandished a gleaming, stainless steel blade in the other. "This will hurt quite a lot," he said. With one long stroke of the blade he laid bare the inner workings of Lew's forearm.

Lew screamed.

Pascal stuffed a piece of gauze cloth into the new wound. He quickly removed it and left Lew, walking back to where the beaker stood. A heavy vapor rolled over the beaker's rim and fell to the floor, sending steamy tendrils across the plush carpet. He dropped the bloody swath into the solution.

Instantly Lew felt a soothing tingle in the raw nerves of his mangled wrist. He watched dumbfounded as tissue knitted and the wound closed. The long dendrites of motor nerves shot out and found their respective stations; tendons joined and flexed; it was over in a matter of seconds, leaving a distinct scar.

"Try it," Pascal suggested.

Afraid of more pain, Lew was cautious at first. But the pain had subsided, so Lew tentatively wiggled his index finger.

"Excellent!" Pascal exclaimed. "Try a fist."

That was more disappointing. Lew could not get his fingers all the way closed. But he could touch each finger with his thumb, and when he picked up a pen he found that he could write; it was awkward and slow, but the script was legible.

"We could not have hoped for better results," Pascal said. "Be patient. Some of the stiffness will work itself out. I doubt that you will ever have your former dexterity, but with physical therapy you should be able to restore most function."

Lew was crying. He had not really had time enough to grieve for the loss of his hand, and the prospect of a minor disability seemed more real than the former paralysis. But there was something else that triggered a deeper emotion. Lew was thinking of another hand that had once spilled a glass of wine, and another scar that he now recognized as his own. "Thanks," Lew said. He closed his eyes. The image of a white-haired visage filled his mind, and he was overcome with the recollection of that which he now knew he had always known.

17

~~~~~~

Lady Luck

It was the middle of the night, and Pamela was still blasted by the sunbaked asphalt and concrete as she stepped out of the airport. "Sure is hot!" she said to the cab driver.

"Hmmph!" The man just laughed. "That's Vegas. First time?"

"Yeah," she said.

"Just don't go outside. That's the trick. No one does, you know?"

"Does what?" she asked.

"Goes outside. That's not what this town is about. There's nothing natural in Vegas. It is all artificial. Live it or live *with* it."

"What?"

"Just an expression," he said. "Something my *attorney* used to say. Doesn't make any sense."

"Oh."

"Where to?"

"The Aladdin," she said.

"That's a good medium-priced place. Right on the strip too. Vacation?"

"I suppose," Pamela said.

"You're not sure," he said. "That's good. You'll probably have a better time that way. Trying to have fun and relax is the best way to ruin a holiday, I always say."

Cruising up the strip, Pamela was dazzled by the neon lights. "Amazing," she said.

"It's not real," was the driver's only comment.

When they pulled up to the Aladdin, the driver said, "Stay away from the slots. In fact don't gamble is my best advice. You can't win, you know."

"I hope to get lucky," Pamela said, giving him a $50 bill.

"That's what they all say," he said, fishing for change. When he looked up Pamela was walking into the hotel with her one bag. He started to call out to her but caught himself. *What the hell*, he thought as he drove away, *maybe she will.*

Pamela's theory was quite simple. It hinged on the distinction between plausibility and probability. The probability that she could quickly find the solution to the singularity problem was very small; there were just too many leads, most of them blind alleys. Only one would pay off. But it was *plausible*. Improbable as it was there was no reason why she should *not* get it.

The odds were stacked against you in Vegas. Every card table, slot machine, and roulette wheel gave the customer the short of end of the deal. The driver was right. You could not win. Yet they continued to flock to the casinos, thousands every day, just to offer themselves up in sacrifice to the gods of the odds.

Why? Because as unlikely as it was that you would win, it was plausible, eminently plausible. Plausibility has a strong hold on the psyche even though in the normal course of events the plausible loses when it goes against the improbable. Pamela's work, while it had not yet solved the singularity problem, had resulted in an interesting corollary. She thought she had a system of equations which, if applied correctly, could turn things around, give plausibility the edge.

She hit the blackjack tables first. Vegas likes a winner. For a short while. One winner among all those losers sets up a feeding frenzy. Pamela's table was soon buzzing with activity, and onlookers were crowding to get a glimpse of the petite redhead who knew the cards.

"And the lady's a winner again, folks." The dealer shoved a stack of chips across the table. He also looked up at the mirror which concealed the one-way glass in the ceiling. It was a signal to the goons above that something was wrong. The customer was doing too well. Maybe it was time to check her out.

Pamela did not notice the signal, but she sensed that it was time to move on—she was drawing too much attention to herself. She stepped out into ovenlike heat and the absurdly bright night. A well-dressed man in a blue suit followed her.

She lost at Caesar's. Seeing this, the goon was about to leave, assuming that it was just an unusual run of luck—not impossible after all. But then he noticed something which immediately put him back on her tail. Pamela sat down at the bar, pulled a sheaf of yellow papers from her purse, and began studying them with intense concentration.

"Hi, Steve, what's up?" a waiter asked the goon in the blue suit as he took a table not far from the bar.

"Club soda," Steve said, eyeing Pamela intently.

"Working, huh?" the waiter said. "OK."

"Uh, Bill?" Steve said to the waiter.

"Yeah?"

"See that woman over there, in the green dress?" Steve pointed at Pamela.

"Yeah."

"I want you to get a look at those yellow sheets of paper."

"You're out of your territory, Steve," Bill said.

"Look," Steve said, irritated, "this could be important. I guarantee if it is what I suspect, your people will want to know about it pronto. I'm doing you a favor, Bill."

Bill went behind the bar and asked Pamela, "Can I get you anything else?"

She was writing furiously on the back of one of her papers and did not even look up.

"Excuse me, Miss. Can I get you anything else?" he asked again loudly.

"Oh." Pamela looked up, obviously quite distracted from the breaking of her concentration, "No . . . no thanks. I'm fine."

"What was it?" Steve asked, taking his club soda.

"I don't know, Steve," Bill said. "She's got a bunch of papers with stuff like I've never seen before."

"What kind of stuff?" Steve shot back.

"I never was any good at math, but it looked like equations and things. Real complicated too. She was writing new ones down like crazy . . . didn't even hear me at first."

"Thanks, Bill." Steve gave the waiter a $100 bill. "That's for you."

"Thanks a lot, Steve!" The waiter beamed as he walked away.

Pamela hit the tables again and started to win. Soon she had a brand-new audience, and her table was jumping. Steve was no longer watching. He could be seen back at the bar making a phone call.

After a short stint at the Flamingo Pamela was satisfied. Her theory was corroborated, and she was confident that all she needed to do was apply it to the singularity problem and the solution would fall right out.

Meanwhile in the Aladdin a small conference was taking place. "How much has she won so far?" a large, greasy man asked.

"About $10,000," Steve said.

"Let's not do anything just yet," the greasy one said. "She may just cash in her chips and leave. If she is smart, that's what she will do, and ten grand is nothing to get excited about. I don't want a stink."

"But, I'm telling you, Martin," Steve said, "she has a system, something brand-new!"

"How do you know that?" Martin shot back.

"It is just a hunch, but . . ."

"Fuck your hunches," Martin said. "I don't want any unnecessary trouble. Just keep an eye on her. Now get out of here and leave me alone."

Pamela ordered a steak and egg special and pondered her situation. *With just a few more hours of playing, I could rake in twenty or thirty thousand more*, she thought. On the other hand, she practically had the solution, and time was running out for Alan, and possibly Lew.

She left the Flamingo and started back for the Aladdin but stopped suddenly. *Fuck it*, she thought, *let's make some money!*

"Taxi!" She flagged a cab.

"Where to?"

"Take me downtown," she said.

"Any place in particular?" he asked.

"Blackjack," she said. "The best blackjack tables."

*　　　*　　　*

It was 5:00 A.M. when Pamela unlocked the door to her room back at the Aladdin. She was exhausted. *I should get a reservation back*, she thought as she went into the bathroom.

She came out wearing only bikini briefs and started toward the telephone. She turned on the light and froze, choking back a scream. There were two men sitting in the chairs by her bed, coolly appraising her body. One man was young and trim wearing a blue suit. The other man, dressed in Bermuda shorts and golf shirt, was older and fat. The young one got up and walked quickly to the door, positioning himself in front of it and folding his arms.

"Good morning, Ms. Fine," the fat one said. "Please put your dress back on. We have to talk."

Pamela ran back into the bathroom and locked the door. She quickly dressed and began searching for an alternate way out. There was nothing. The bathroom faced the hall. She sat on the tub, trying to remain calm.

After about fifteen minutes she heard a voice at the door. It sounded like the younger man. "Please come out, Ms. Fine. No one is going to hurt you. We're from hotel security. We only want to ask you a few questions."

"How do I know you are from security?" she asked.

"We have identification."

"Slide it under the door, then," she said.

"OK. I lied about that. We don't have any identification, but we are with the hotel. That much is true. I promise you that no one will hurt you. Now please come out."

"No," Pamela said. "Hotel security is supposed to keep people out of my room, not come barging in on my privacy."

"I'm afraid you don't understand the situation, Ms. Fine," the man said. "This is Las Vegas. Things work a little differently here. We had to do it this way in order to be discreet. Discretion in matters like these is paramount."

"Bullshit," she said.

The fat man nodded at Steve, who backed a few paces from the door and then slammed his shoulder into it.

Pamela jumped and screamed softly. The door held.

It took two more tries, but finally the door flew open and Pamela stood facing the man in the blue suit. "Please don't hurt me," she pleaded, voice shaking. "What do you want? I've got money . . ."

"I know," Steve said. "That is what we want to talk to you about. No one wants to hurt you. Now please come out and sit down." He took her by the arm and led her out into the room.

"I'm Martin Sable, Ms. Fine." The fat man stood up and extended his hand as she entered the room.

"That is *Dr.* Fine," she said. Pamela found the big man unhealthy-looking and repulsive.

"Please sit down." He gestured toward the bed.

"My partner is Mr. Steve Rucci," Sable said. Pamela refused to take his hand and remained standing. "Steve," the fat man said, "get Ms.—I mean *Dr.*—Fine a chair."

Steve left the room and returned with another hotel chair. Pamela waited until both men were seated before she sat down. "Who are you?" she asked the fat man.

"I have a major interest in the casino here," Sable said. "Steve is head of our security operations."

"Is there a problem?" Pamela asked.

"We were hoping that you could enlighten *us* about that," Sable said, suddenly looking less benign and staring straight at Pamela.

"No problem as far as I'm concerned"—Pamela did not flinch—"except two strange men in my room who have no business being here."

Rucci, angry, started to speak. Sable cut him off by laughing suddenly. It was not a pleasant sound. "I heard you say you have money, Dr. Fine. May I inquire how much?"

"None of your business."

"But you see, that is the problem," Sable continued. "It *is* our business when it is *our* money."

"I won it," Pamela said. "Gambling. It's not yours anymore."

"You seem like an intelligent woman, Dr. Fine," Sable said. "I admire doctors. One saved my life once. I was injured. Shot actually—could have died, but that surgeon was so good. It hardly left a scar. Care to see?" He started to lift up his shirt. Pamela was disgusted by the rolls of white fat underneath.

"I'm not that kind of doctor," she said quickly.

"What kind of doctor are you?"

"I'm a mathematician," she said.

"Oh! Now that is something," Sable said. "Well then"—his

voice got suddenly ominous—"as a mathematician maybe you can tell me how a lady who knows nothing about gambling, a lady who has never even been to Vegas, wins over $100,000 at blackjack in less than four hours."

"I got lucky," she said.

Sable laughed louder and the sound was uglier than before. "You hear that, Steve. She got lucky." He was wheezing, the laughing had aggravated his emphysema. After he coughed up a wad of phlegm, which he spit on the rug, he pulled a pack of cigarettes from his pocket.

"Care for one?" He offered the pack to Pamela.

"No thanks," she said, "and I would rather that you did not smoke in my room."

"Well," Sable said, lighting up, "it may be your room, but it is my hotel. So fuck you." He exhaled a cloud of smoke in her face.

Pamela got up and turned to leave. She had not taken three steps before Steve grabbed her by the shoulders. He pinched her hard and led her back to the chair where he pushed her down roughly.

"I'll sue you bastards," she said, breathing heavily.

"Sue away," Sable said. "Meanwhile we will prosecute for felony conspiracy. You are the one in trouble, Ms. Fine. But we don't want trouble. We will even let you keep some winnings. Say ten percent. But in exchange you must tell us how you did it, give us all documentation of your methods, and promise not to come back for a few years. I think that is fair."

"I want to make a phone call," Pamela said.

"I don't give a fuck what you want, you little cunt!" Sable got suddenly livid. "I just want my money, and if I don't get it, your cheating little ass is in for it! Maybe I should spell it out. You want to call your lawyer! You got no rights here! We own the police. They work for us. We own the courts too. Vegas justice doesn't give a shit about your rights. Justice here means keeping you safe while you roam the casinos shitfaced on booze, gambling your hard-earned money away. As long as you do that, everybody in this town is your friend. But you fuck with the odds and you are one lost, lonely, little slut in one of the most mean-assed places on the planet. Understand?"

"Yeah," Pamela said, voice steady. "I think I do. Now I want to make a phone call."

They kept at her most of the day. They even ordered room service, eating breakfast and lunch in front of her. Pamela went hungry; they gave her only water.

"You have nothing on me," she said, about three in the afternoon. "You can't prove a thing. If you keep me here much longer, my husband will start to worry. And I don't know about Vegas, but the New York Police Department might get curious as to my whereabouts."

They finally let her make the call. *Please answer, Elliot,* she prayed silently as the phone rang.

He was home. After she explained the situation to him he said, "OK, Pamela. Sit tight. I know some people here who might be able to help. Sounds to me like they are just trying to intimidate you. I'll call you back when I know more. And, Pamela?"

"Yeah," she said.

"I checked on Alan today. He is looking worse than usual. I don't think he can last much longer. Whatever it is you have planned, there is not much time."

"OK, Elliot. Bye." Pamela sighed. She was exhausted and hungry.

Within an hour there was a phone call for Sable. He went downstairs to take it, leaving her alone with Rucci. "Sorry about all this," Rucci said, after Sable left.

"Spare me," she said.

"No really, you need some food." He got room service to bring Pamela a plate of chicken.

She was still eating when Sable came back. "You can go," he said abruptly to Pamela. "But don't let me see you in my casino again. Ever."

Pamela stared silently at the two men until they left. Then, exhausted as she was, she packed her bag and headed for the airport.

At the terminal a man came up behind her. It was Rucci. "Listen, I really am sorry about all that back there," he said. "I have a proposition. You and me could make some dough. If you cut me in I can handle things at this end. No one needs to know. You were just too dumb—I mean naive, but I know all the angles. A little here a little there. We could easily pull a couple hundred grand a year. What do you say?"

"I say fuck you," Pamela said, resisting the urge to spit in his face.

"Why you little . . ." Rucci raised his fist and almost slugged her, but stopped when he realized that the airline counter attendants were all looking at him.

"Buck up, Steve," she said to his back as he walked away, "everybody gets lucky sooner or later!" She was shaking as she boarded the plane.

Elliot met her at the airport. "Thanks, Elliot," Pamela said.

"Sometimes it helps to know a senator," Elliot said. "But apparently you ruffled some large feathers. You are advised to stay away from Vegas for a while."

"Don't worry," she said.

"This is it Pamela!" Elliot said in amazement when she showed him the equation back at her apartment. "It is so obvious, but I would have never found it. How did you do it?"

"Luck," Pamela said.

18

The Miserlou

According to the ship's clock Pascal kept Lew inside the sub for two and a half days pumping him for information on the software that programmed the nouancer. "It is just as I expected." He looked up from the maple desk where they were working. "We are only lacking one equation!"

"What equation?" Lew asked.

"The one that ties it all together, describes the whole set of singularity groups," Pascal said.

"And then what?" Lew asked.

"We can make the final plunge," Pascal said.

"Plunge where?"

"The center of consciousness, the origin of life, man!" Pascal nearly shouted. "It's what I set off into the cosmos for initially. But I was young and foolish. I assumed you had to journey to the stars. It is both easier and more difficult than that. Easier because the path is right there before you all the time, but more difficult because without a way to navigate one would be helpless, lost in the void . . ." His voice trailed off.

Lew was not surprised when the next thing Pascal did was suggest tea.

Tea always capped the captain's deeper reveries. Lew had started thinking of Pascal as captain because he clearly was the captain of the ship.

"We should give her a name," Pascal said, setting the tea down on top of the papers filled with esoteric mathematical calculations which littered the desk.

"Give who a name?" Lew dropped a sugar cube into his tea.

"Our ship of course!"

"Oh." Lew was not yet comfortable thinking of the ship or Pascal's plans in terms of "our."

"We could name her after you," Pascal said, leaning back in his chair.

"No . . ."

"Yes that's perfect, the N.S.S. *Slack*!" Pascal laughed.

"What's the N.S.S. for?" Lew asked.

"Nouspace Ship of course."

"I don't like it," Lew said.

"You have a better suggestion?"

Lew thought furiously. For some reason he felt it essential that he come up with an acceptable alternative. "How about *Miserlou*?" he said finally. The title of the classic old instrumental surf song was the only thing that presented itself.

"Yes," Pascal said softly. "That's even better. *Miserlou* it is. You're a fan of surf music, too, then?"

"Yeah."

"She really is just a sophisticated surfboard, you know," Pascal said. "That is what it is all about. Always and ever-

more. Surfing the waves of possibility. Catch a good ride and
you can shoot the pipeline all the way to the center of impossibility. And then . . ."

"Then what?" Lew asked. Pascal's obsession with impossibility made Lew nervous.

"I don't know." Pascal grinned. "That's the beauty of it.
None of us can know. It is only on the cusp of the unknowable that we reach the beginning."

"The beginning? Beginning of what?"

"Who knows? But all this is prelude," Pascal said, sweeping
his hand wide to indicate the vast cosmos. "All of reality, all
of possibility—it is all mere prelude to that great beginning
of which we have as yet seen only vague glimmerings—
glimpsed through a glass . . . darkly." He stopped talking; an
expression of profound peace crossed his brow—but only for
a moment.

"All singularities are connected," he went on, excitedly.
"They all hook up, being both everywhere and nowhere at
once. Gravitational centers are physical manifestations of the
singularity phenomenon. Individual selves are the psychic
manifestations of the same thing. But all those centers, those
singularities, are only relative. The singularity algebra which
you programmed into the guidance system of your nouancer
navigates these relative cosmic centers quite well. Akasha, the
library, is one such center.

"The next level up, however, requires a more advanced
theory. All my research indicates that a single equation exists,
one which describes the nexus in which all singularities merge
in a confluence of awesome majesty and beauty. It is that
equation which we need. From what you have shown me here
these past few days, I am convinced that your programming
skills are more than adequate to translate that equation into
navigational software for the guidance system. But until we
have the equation, we are stuck."

"Stuck?" Lew hated the sound of the word.

"That's right. There is no way back, Lew. We can only go
forward."

"I can't get home?" Lew asked.

"Home? Where is home?" Pascal said, finishing his tea and
staring at the paisley print patterns on the curved wall of his
chambers.

* * *

"What do we do now?" Elliot asked Pamela. They were seated at her kitchen table. Both of them had exhaustively checked and rechecked Pamela's final equation, and both were satisfied. It was the essence of singularity theory expressed in one elegantly simple, precisely balanced mathematical equation.

"I think we should show it to Alan," Pamela said.

"Why?"

"I don't know. But I think we should, before . . ."

"Before he dies?" Elliot finished for her.

"Yeah." Pamela got up slowly and started walking back to Alan's room. Elliot followed.

Alan was clearly dying. His breathing, still slow, was now irregular, and his color had turned from pale to sickly yellow.

"Alan?" Pamela gently pressed his shoulder. "Can you hear me?" He did not respond. They tried to rouse him, elicit some sign of consciousness for over an hour. Finally, exhausted and afraid that their very efforts were weakening him, they went to bed.

"Make love to me, Elliot," Pamela said, sliding her thigh over his and pressing into him. Opening her legs a little more she rubbed against him.

"Are you sure you want to?" he asked. "You haven't slept in . . ."

"Sssh," she breathed into his ear. "Just do it. I need you."

She felt like a teenager—it was all awkward groping and fumbling. She was so tired. Elliot ended up doing most of the work. Out of the corner of his eye he thought he saw someone watching, but when he looked there was no one at the open door.

They were interrupted by a loud crash.

"What was that?" Elliot asked.

"It sounded like it came from the kitchen," Pamela said.

They quietly put on robes and crept toward the kitchen.

"Oh my God!" Elliot got there first.

"Alan!" Pamela screamed. He was lying by the overturned table on the kitchen floor, a piece of yellow paper crumpled in his hand. She knelt by his side and put her hand on his forehead. Then she touched his neck, pressing on the carotid artery. She pulled the paper from his cold fingers and stood up.

"I'll help get him back to bed," Elliot said, weakly.

"He's dead," Pamela said hollowly. "Look at this." She handed him the paper. It had the singularity equation on it. "Well, he saw it," she said, " . . . He saw it." She repeated this to herself a few times before her words were finally choked off by sobs.

Alan's meditation was going well. That morning, his guru had insisted that he do a particularly long session. The old Tibetan monk seemed intent, more serious than usual, as if he knew something that Alan did not. But Alan had learned not to question the masters too closely, especially when it came to idiosyncratic behavior—it generally turned out that they did know something.

He felt himself drift into a particularly empty space. He was very familiar with the Tibetan doctrine expressed in their Book of the Dead, the *Bardo Thodol,* that after death the soul wanders in various realms before it enters a new womb and is reborn. He had never experienced the Bardo realm directly in his practices, although his teachers claimed it was possible to do so in meditation without actually dying.

The space he was in felt like what the monks had described. There was a radiant white light giving a blissful, pure peace. He tried to merge with it.

But something was wrong. As soon as he attempted to get closer to the white light, he was engulfed by multicolored lights of various hues and intensities. They were too distracting. Some seemed friendly, almost familiar, and others seemed positively inimical.

Out of one of the friendly colors came a face. It was the face of an older man which he soon recognized as his face, twenty-odd years more mature.

"Hello, Alan," Old Alan said.

"Hi," was all he could think of to say.

"The after-death plane is real," Old Alan said.

"Is that what this is?"

"Yes."

"But I'm not dead," Young Alan said.

"No, but I am."

"Does this mean that I will die?"

"Did you ever doubt it?"

"No, but . . ."

"Never mind. You must do something. It could save my life, and Lew's," Old Alan said, with an intense look.

"What?"

"When the Bardo experience wears off, go to Akasha. Find Lew and show him this." Old Alan held out a sheet of coarse yellow paper with a mathematical equation written on it. "If you act quickly, it may be in time to prevent me from getting reborn."

"You don't want to get reborn?" Young Alan asked.

"Not yet." Old Alan faded back into the purplish red glow from which he had come.

Alan floated in and out of various realms, some of which were quite pleasant. He sat atop a mountain at the center of the Universe for some time. The view was fantastic. It turned out that the mountain was a giant spinal column and the Universe was really a man sitting on top of a mountain at the center of the Universe, and that mountain was another spinal column of another man who sat . . .

He soon grew tired of that. He remembered the paper which he had stuffed into the pocket of his *coorta*. Looking at the equation, he slowly drifted off the mountain and began to feel the now-familiar contours of Akasha, the Hall of Records, take shape around him.

He found himself in an unfamiliar area of the stacks. There was a book which lay open before him. Hoping for some new erotic adventure, he picked it up. It appeared to be a science fiction story about a submarine named the *Miserlou*. He was about to put it down, but the description of the sub's plush, antique interior was too vivid. Soon he was aboard, peering out the portholes amidships. It appeared to be in dry dock, in some sort of damp cellar.

He heard noises coming from the direction of the bow. Cautiously he set off down the corridor. The well-polished hardwood floor stopped at a thick Persian carpet which marked the entrance to the captain's chambers. Alan looked up to see two men. Lew was seated, his back to Alan. The other man was dressed in well-tailored jeans and black denim jacket. The jacket had the cut of a naval officer's coat.

"So we meet again," Pascal said.

Lew turned around. "Alan! What are you doing here?"

"You should stop asking questions like that, Lew," Alan said.

Pascal came forward extending his hand. "How is the foot?" he asked.

"Fine," Alan said, dancing a spontaneous little jig.

"So he is the one . . ." Lew started to say.

"Yes," Pascal said. "Alan was my first human patient and the confirmation of my hypotheses about the empathetic aether."

"I went walking in the mountains barefoot one day," Alan said. "The Sherpas do it all the time. I slipped on a glacier. It tore up my foot real bad. The monks tried everything, but when it went gangrenous, well . . . I was lucky to find the doctor here."

"Care for some tea?" Pascal said.

"No coffee?" Alan asked.

"Certainly. Colombian or Tauresian?" Pascal smiled.

"Well, I'll try the Tauresian," Alan said. "It's not flavored is it?" he asked as an afterthought.

"Of course not," Pascal said, busying himself with the coffee-making apparatus.

Soon Alan was seated in one of the captain's overstuffed chairs, with a steaming mug in his hands. "Man, this is far out!" He said, taking a sip.

"It's the peculiar dodecahedral, vector space symmetry of the secondary constituent alkaloid molecules," Pascal said. "The flavors take on a multidimensional quality."

"Better living through chemistry," Alan said, taking another long sip.

"I have to ask you something, Lew," Alan said, when his mug was about half-empty.

Something in the tone of Alan's voice made Lew tighten up. He felt like squirming in his chair. "Yeah, what's that?" he said.

"I've had the feeling that there is something I should know, something you are not telling that is related to your being here and all . . ." He looked up from his mug, straight at Lew. When Lew did not volunteer any information Alan continued, "For example, when you made the trip here was I . . . ?"

"Were you what?" Lew finally said.

"Was I alive?" Alan asked, exhaling deeply.

"You were in Tibet for a long time," Lew said, his voice shaking.

"For a long time. But I came back, didn't I?"

"Yeah, you came back."

"And what happened?"

"It's kind of complicated," Lew said.

"But whether I was alive or dead—that's not very complicated."

"There was an accident," Lew said.

"And I was killed?"

Lew just nodded.

Alan got very quiet; he appeared to be studying the patterns on the wall hangings. "The *Miserlou*," he said finally. The word came out like a deep sigh. "That must have been your idea, Lew. Right?" He smiled.

"Yeah."

"That is where it's at you know. Surfing, I mean. We are all surfers on the waves of reality, the tides of time . . . My teachers back at the monastery use the surfing metaphor. They are more worldly than most people realize. If I had it to do all over again, I would . . ." Overcome with emotion, he could not finish. His eyes filled with tears and he looked from Lew to Pascal, as if searching for something he knew he would not find.

"What, Alan?" Lew pressed. "What would you do?"

"I'd go out to California and ride the waves, become a surfer, follow the seasons and the waves around the world for the rest of my life."

"*The Endless Summer*," Lew said softly, remembering the name of the movie that told the story of surfers who did just that, followed summer around the world searching for the perfect wave.

"The story doesn't *have* to end," Alan said passionately.

"Indeed it does not," Pascal, who had remained silent through the emotional dialogue, said. "Lew and I are making plans to embark on the final stretch of the endless journey, which ends, naturally, at the grand beginning of the never-ending saga of which all of this is only prologue."

"In the *Miserlou*?" Alan asked.

"She is a beauty, isn't she?" Pascal beamed.

"Yeah," Alan said. "Pretty fancy surfboard. I take it you're going out into the sea of nous?"

"Yes," Pascal said.

"Those waters are dangerous," Alan said. "None but the most advanced of the Tibetan gurus have ever attempted it. Very few have been able to navigate the depths of infinite possibility. How are you going to . . ." He stopped to look at Lew.

"How are we going to navigate successfully, avoid complete and total dissolution?" Pascal said.

"Yeah," Alan said. "I don't know about you, but frankly I doubt Lew's proficiency in such matters. I mean it takes years of hard dedication, meditation, and then even if you are lucky . . ."

"We are going to rely on an artificial navigational system," Pascal explained. "I've done a great deal of research into the mathematical basis for mapping the infinite potentialities we will encounter. Lew's skill in translating my equations into binary, computable code will enable us to program the mathematics into a precise guidance system. Unfortunately the final solution to the singularity problem eludes me. I am convinced that there is an equation which will extend the range of our system beyond the merely possible to the center of impossibility, the central singularity where . . . well, where we want to go."

Alan remembered the paper. "On my way here this time, I made a slight detour. You remember asking me if we were dead, Lew? If this nouspace, the library and all, was possibly the Bardo, the plane of existence between death and rebirth?"

"Yeah," Lew said.

"Well I don't understand the precise relationship, but the two are not so very far apart. I entered briefly into the Bardo state—it can be done through meditation. I met myself there. A much older self, but clearly me. He is not keen on getting reborn just yet." Alan looked at Lew, who was trying hard to avoid his friend's piercing stare. "And he gave me something to pass along. I'm not sure, but I think it might be of significance to all three of us." He pulled the yellow sheet of paper out of his *coorta* and handed it to Lew.

"I think you should look at this," Lew said after briefly

looking at the equation. He handed the paper to Pascal.

It took Pascal only few seconds to confirm what he hoped he would see. "This is it!" he said. "This is the solution! All we need to do is program it into the system and we are ready to set off on the greatest of all voyages." He became quiet with a silence that was filled with unspoken dreams.

"I hope . . ." Lew said, "I hope that maybe we—or I—can . . ."

"Help me?" Alan asked.

"Yeah," Lew said.

"Anything is possible now," Pascal said brightly. He was already up and brewing another pot of tea.

"Make mine coffee," Alan said.

"Yeah, me too," Lew echoed.

19

The Egg and the Tear

Lew wandered over to the small bookshelf built into the *Miserlou*'s wall next to Pascal's desk. He absently grabbed a book. A thin layer of dust, which did not seem dusty, fell in a fine powder. Lew brought his fingertips to his nose to smell the bits that clung there. The pungent odor excited him; it seemed to carry a message that was both ancient and eternally new, a message of pure life that transcended any quest for meaning or search for answers.

It was the same book which he had found next to Pascal's teacup in the library, *Strange and Distant Episodes*. He opened it; the pages felt creamy, yet there was a fine-grained texture to them which he liked very much. Before he could begin reading, Pascal brought him his coffee.

"This is the most incredible . . ." Lew said after his first sip.

"And it just keeps getting better," Alan said, sighing with satisfaction.

"People would fight wars for coffee like this," Lew said.

"They have," Pascal responded. He was going through the pages of calculations and programming notes that he and Lew had compiled over the last few days.

"All you have to do," Pascal said, looking up from his desk, "is rewrite the last program, the subroutine which controls the relational search algorithm. This equation"—he held up the yellow sheet of paper—"will give you the function. It should be a simple matter to translate it into code."

"Damn!" Alan said.

"What's the matter?" Lew asked, but he could see just by looking that Alan was beginning to fade out.

He was struggling to finish his coffee, but it appeared to be a losing battle. "When are you guys going to set off?" he asked.

"As soon as possible," Pascal said.

"So this is it, I suppose," Alan said, looking at Lew. "*Bon voyage.*"

Lew could not bring himself to say anything as he watched, knowing that it might be the last glimpse he ever got of his best friend.

After Alan was gone, Lew again picked up the book. All the stories and descriptions seemed familiar; each page contained some reference that seemed especially relevant. "We really begin the journey when we begin to meet ourselves in various new guises. Perhaps a chance meeting with one's own aged, future self, or union with a sexual opposite . . ."

"Why me? Why my story!" Lew threw the book down on the desk where Pascal was still working, studying flow charts.

"Why not? Isn't that where we usually wind up?" Pascal said with a smile. "In the middle of our own story, that is?"

"Is that where I am?" Lew asked, a nervous hysteria creeping into his voice.

"Calm down," Pascal said. "That is where we all are."

"One thing that I do not understand about this project," Lew said, trying to regain a grip on whatever reality was still available.

"What is that?"

"We have the information necessary to program the *Miserlou*'s guidance system, do we not?"

"Now we do. Thanks to your friend and whatever other agencies might be involved," Pascal said.

"But the hardware is still lacking, the nouancer I mean. What good is the software if we don't have a machine on which it can run?"

"You already know the answer to that," Pascal said.

"The file room, you mean?" Lew said, remembering the beautiful domed room with the black marble floor, exquisite ceiling, and fountain.

"Of course. The file room is the nouancer," Pascal said.

"How does that help our situation? It is many times bigger than the entire *Miserlou*."

Pascal reached over and picked up the book Lew had been reading. He found a chapter entitled, "The Temple of Self," and handed it back to Lew. Reading, Lew recognized a description of the domed file room. Before he could pull back he found himself once again inside the place, looking up at the vivid representations of the scenes from his life.

He thought he was alone, but he heard a soft splashing. He walked down a radial row of file cabinets to the fountain. It was not a splashing noise, but a slurping one. Felix was eagerly lapping at the cold water. Lew could not restrain himself; sensing that this might be his last visit, he stripped and dived into the pool. The water sent a chill through his entire body that communicated both an excitement and a sense of dread, a fear of that which was unknowable. He swam for a long time, diving to the bottom of the pool and sprinting vigorous, freestyle laps. Finally, exhausted, he just lay down on the cold marble. Felix was pacing nervously close by.

He was looking up at the dome, and, as had happened so many times before, he saw a picture which he did not remember seeing. It was an egg, the shell of which was highly decorated with images and scenes reminiscent of the dome itself. The shell was cracked, and from inside the egg there came streaming forth another set of images that echoed and even merged with those on the surface of the shell. Lew studied the picture for several minutes. The artistry was subtle and seduced the viewer into participating in the illusion that the inside of the egg was indistinguishable from its outside. In fact the sense of it was that inside and outside are really misleading terms and that all reality exists on the interface of some larger, incomprehensible duality. Inside/outside, positive/negative, male/female—these are all merely secondary echoes of a larger cosmic division, and as such, they are constantly intermingling, merging and transforming themselves one into the other.

This feeling grew to become an overpowering intuition as Lew lay naked on the floor. He stretched up his arms toward the dome and, to his surprise, his hands reached the ceiling. They seemed to be both inside and outside the structure. Wrapping his hands around the curvature of the ceiling, he pulled down, bringing the images closer. The panorama of his life shrank as it came near. The images came to life, all the figures were moving; the laughter, tears, life, sex, and death merged into a living metamorphosis of form, held in his two hands.

Lew no longer felt the floor beneath him. The radial rows of file cabinets were spinning like the arms of a spiral galaxy. They spun faster and faster, with him at the vortex. He hung on to the living orb in his hands as the dizzying rotation burst into an explosion of light.

There was a loud, hollow, popping sound. It felt to Lew as if the Universe came unglued and all the familiar old categories of reality were momentarily suspended. Then he was aware of a thick rug beneath his feet. He was standing back in the captain's quarters of the *Miserlou*. He was still naked, dripping water on the rug, and in his hands he held the nouancer.

"Excellent," Pascal said. He took the nouancer and set it down on the desk amid the papers. Felix let out a long, low wail. He was standing by Pascal's bed. "Ah, the cat-beast joins us!" Pascal smiled.

Lew found his clothes lying on the rug. Pascal threw him a towel, and after he dried, he got dressed. "What happened?" Lew asked.

"Nothing really," Pascal said. "Your device, the nouancer, has not changed. It is only your relation to it that has changed."

"But, how . . . ?" Lew began.

"You did not think that any of your perceptions were absolute renditions of reality did you?" Pascal asked.

"Well no, but . . ."

"But nothing," Pascal continued. "All we ever experience are images of the Universe. An image is not in itself true or false. Two very different images of the same thing can both be equally faithful representations. You have merely shifted from an image of being inside to one of being outside. Both are real. Or I should say both are equally valid."

"But then where are we?" Lew asked.

"Inside the *Miserlou* of course," Pascal said.

"But where is the *Miserlou*?"

"Come on, I'll show you," Pascal said. He led Lew back amidships and out the hatch of the sub. They emerged into the dark stone cellar that housed the ship. This time Lew noticed that the vessel was mounted on a track that led down into a darker passageway.

"That's the route we'll take to launch her," Pascal said, pointing down the track into the darkness. He led Lew up a different set of stone stairs than the one by which they had entered. They came to a set of large steel doors. Pascal struggled with the locking mechanism for some time. It consisted of a big, rusty wheel, which he had to rotate several turns. The thing was heavily corroded and it moved to the great creaking protests of stubborn, ancient metal. Finally Pascal got the doors unlocked. Opening them required more muscle power. He called for Lew to help, and they both strained, heaving against the resistance.

It was a soft resistance which yielded, but very slowly and only to great force. Lew noticed sand pouring in through the widening cracks. Soon the sand was running in around and all over the two men. The doors finally gave, and they tumbled out into a blazing sun, half-buried by white-hot sand.

Lew stood up, brushing himself; he could barely open his eyes for several seconds, so great was the brightness. When he finally could see, he recognized the sandy shore where he and Felix had nearly died before finding refuge inside the file room. The domed structure was no longer there; it was now inside the *Miserlou* on the captain's desk, reverted to its original form, the Asklepian nouancer.

"Is the library below us?" Lew asked.

"Yes, Akasha is beneath these sands. But look out there!" Pascal pointed to the ocean. The blue-green waters stretched out to a horizon that did not seem to end so much as recede into a higher order of infinity. "That is where we are going!"

Lew got an acute sensation of vertigo at Pascal's words. It felt as though his stomach hit his knees and then bounced back up to his throat. It took all his concentration to keep from vomiting.

"You look a little green, Lew," Pascal said. "Don't worry. You'll get your sea legs soon enough. But right now we need to get out of this heat." Lew followed Pascal back into the damp underground chamber. The coolness was soothing, and he welcomed the finite sense of space, which closed in as they reentered the *Miserlou*. His nausea subsided and Pascal prepared an excellent lunch, consisting of wild rice that grew in the dense patches of dark matter which lie hidden in interstellar gas nebulae and some delicious grilled shrimp.

Programming the nouancer turned out to be a tedious task. Because there were no computers or other digital storage devices, Lew had to enter all the code on the small keys in the front panel. Sections that would normally take only a few minutes to type on a keyboard, took many times longer to punch directly into the machine. When he was finally able to key in the last piece, Lew felt as if he had put in a hard seventy-hour week.

He and Pascal had painstakingly translated the singularity equation into a set of computable functions. It was Lew's job to code these into the nouancer. "If you screw up, Lew," Pascal said, "we are going to be utterly lost out there, and that means complete fragmentation and dissipation of everything that we are."

"Don't worry," Lew said. "I'm a professional." But Lew was worried. He checked and double-checked his entries, but even the best programmer knows that many errors are never detected until the software is rigorously tested. There was no way to test the guidance system. The one and only test would be its actual performance.

When Lew felt that there was nothing more he could do, Pascal installed the nouancer in the bridge of the ship. He linked it to the sub's guidance system. "We are going to submerge ourselves in the deepest depths of the cosmic sea of consciousness," he said. "There is one thing you should know."

"What?"

"The nouancer is linked to the *Miserlou*'s guidance system so the first part of the voyage will be easy—we will be essentially on automatic pilot. But I cannot calibrate the ship's steering to the finer subtleties of the singularity equation. The equipment is just too primitive for that."

"So how do we navigate then?" Lew asked.

"Manually," Pascal said, placing his hand on the big brass captain's wheel. "The nouancer will still be functioning, but we will need to respond to its signals ourselves in order to make the final plunge into singularity."

The installation was capped by the inevitable cup of tea. "Are you ready?" Pascal asked, pouring a few extra drops of cream into his cup.

"Ready? Now?" Lew asked, feeling an empty fear rise up in his abdomen.

"I see no reason to delay any further," he said, fixing Lew with a questioning look.

"Well, shouldn't we discuss . . ." Lew began.

"Discuss what?"

"But this could be the biggest decision of my life," Lew said.

"So what if it is?" Pascal was staring out a porthole into the dusty green light of the sub's chamber. "What indeed . . ."

"Well, one shouldn't just jump ahead into something like that without first thinking about it, I mean . . ." Lew did not know what he meant. He was scared.

"You don't want to stay here do you?" Pascal asked, turning to look at Lew again. "Alone?"

That was what finally did it for Lew. The thought of spending more time in the library was intolerable. The place had too much to offer, too much information. And even when the books were not about himself they seemed too intimate, too full of highly significant details. He wanted to get away, back to a place where things were revealed haphazardly, back to the quixotic process of living as a human with a limited intelligence and limited resources.

The two men had to push the *Miserlou* down the track into

the narrowing darkness. Pascal had activated the ship's exterior light so they could still see when they reached the air lock. The inner doors were as creaky and rusted as the ones which led out to the desert sands. Sweating and breathing hard, they finally got them open and pushed the ship into the lock. Shutting the doors was much easier work.

Pascal and Lew threw their backs into it, and were able to start the unlocking of the outer doors. The big wheel groaned and screamed. When it was open, water began to seep inside. "Come on!" Pascal shouted. They scrambled up the side and into the hatch as water began rushing into the chamber.

With Felix at his side, Lew watched Pascal tightly screw down the main hatch. Looking out a porthole, Lew could see the ocean coming in fast. Soon they felt the sub lifted up off the track. It banged against the roof of the tunnel as the water continued to rush in. The outer doors were thrown wide open from the water pressure. Pascal, seated in the captain's chair, cranked up the engines and steered them out into the shoreline depths.

"Let me tell you a story," Pascal said when they were finally under way.

"OK." Lew was eager for a distraction. The noises of the deep penetrated the *Miserlou*'s alloy hull and reverberated throughout the interior of the sub. They were eerie sounds that conjured up images of a vast world soul, so huge and overpowering that even cognizance of it meant obliteration. Lew could vividly picture leviathans of the deep swimming out there, creatures formed wholly of nous, pure intelligence, swimming in the nous that was dense enough to form a liquid sea.

He recalled the whale songs of earth's oceans, those mysterious sounds by which the giant mammals communicated over vast distances. What creatures made the sounds that he now heard? Were they creatures at all? Maybe there was nothing out there, only an infinite expanse, an expanse so big that in it, one would not even be a point of consciousness; one would be—pure nothing.

These thoughts were full of cold excitement, the kind of thrill that tempts with a deadly terror.

"I have been in the thick of it," Pascal said, seeming to read Lew's mind.

"And . . ." Lew said, letting out his breath, which he had been unaware of holding, " . . . what happened?"

"Infinite potential, flowing through me," Pascal said, in a dreamy tone of voice. "Power surging up my spine, exploding at the crown of my brain and pouring down over my brow, encasing my body with the kind of energy that governs the entire universe. Cosmic consciousness.

"One has to be extremely careful with that sort of thing," he continued. "The temptation is to push it, to claim it as your own, to try to control it. But that path is folly. There is no surer, shorter route to hell, death, and utter defeat. You have to let it flow through and away, you have to let go. You have to let that kind of energy just roll off."

"And did you?" Lew asked.

"Like water off a duck's back," he said coolly.

"I don't think I am ready," Lew said. "I mean I don't think I could."

"I know."

"So?"

"So what?"

"What do I do?" Lew asked, pacing nervously, peering out the porthole into the gray light and the rippling of the dense, deep aethereal waves. The red velvet couch by the shiny brass porthole seemed more scarlet, brighter than before.

"Take it easy," Pascal said. "We still have some distance to go. And I was about to tell you a story."

"Oh yeah," Lew said, sitting on the edge of one of the scarlet cushions.

They were in the sitting room. Pascal pulled down a gleaming chrome-and-brass-fitted periscope from the ceiling.

"There was an egg." Pascal said, looking out the periscope. "And this egg very much wanted to be."

"To be?" Lew said.

"Yes. You're familiar with the verb?" Pascal pulled away from the periscope, and smiled at Lew.

"Of course," Lew said, uneasily.

"Of course," Pascal continued in an ironic tone of voice. "Good verb. By some linguistic accounts it is the archetypal verb, the paradigm of all verbs. 'Is.' And then there is the theological issue."

"What?"

"I am." Pascal said, solemnly. " 'I am' is the proper name of God. Or at least it is the name by which He calls Himself.

"Is, the 'I am' and so on and so forth . . ." Pascal continued.

" . . . Well, as I was saying, this egg wanted very much to be. But there was a difficult question. How to go about it? Should the egg take matters into hand? Should it hatch itself? Bear itself into the world by its own bootstraps so to speak? Or should it wait?"

"Wait?"

"Yes, wait. For all the egg knew, the natural order of things would bring about its hatching in due course. If that were the case, well then, it would be a very big mistake for the egg to try and rush things along. It could seriously screw things up.

"But on the other hand the egg had no idea what to expect. It might happen the very next instant that it would hatch open and step forth, a newly created, glorious creature of the universe. Or it might take billions of eons.

"And then there was the possibility that the natural plan was for the egg to take charge. Maybe the egg was *supposed* to hatch itself out. Maybe it would never truly exist until it exercised its will.

"Do you see the egg's dilemma?"

"Yes."

"Good. It was a difficult one, which it pondered for a long time. Maybe a very long time. But then something happened."

"What?"

"All that worrying placed an inordinate amount of stress on the egg's superstructure. A crack appeared. The egg's inside was no longer completely sealed from the external world. This caused the egg extreme distress, but there was nothing to be done about the crack.

"Even so the egg could not stop worrying about it. Eventually the crack in the egg began to dominate the egg's entire consciousness. Until finally, the egg practically was the crack in its shell. It all but forgot about its dream of coming into existence. It *was*—a crack in its shell."

Pascal stopped talking and sat down on the green velvet directly opposite Lew. After a brief silence Lew asked, "What does it mean?"

"There are several possible meanings." Pascal laughed.

"Give me one," Lew said stubbornly.

"Well, alright. I suppose you could say that the egg's desire to exist was foolish because it already did exist. And you could go farther and say that this foolish desire gave birth to a flaw which eventually came to dominate the egg entirely. That flaw, the crack, is the ego. The ego is the result of a mistake."

"Oh," Lew said.

"But then you could also say," Pascal continued, "that the egg did exactly what it had to do, what it needed to do. The crack is the beginning of the egg's birth and the ego is a window from the outside to the inside. The ego is the interface between deep unconscious desires and the vast universe outside.

"And then you could also say . . ."

"Alright," Lew said. "I think I get the idea."

"Good." Pascal beamed and clapped his hands together. "Now let's have some tea."

In the galley Lew said, "Why Asklepios?"

"Why not?" Pascal said as he put the stainless steel kettle on the stove. The stove was like the rest of the sub, arcane yet curiously modern. It was made of a slate gray, metallic alloy. The metal was finely detailed, a work of art. The gas jets were molded into serpents with open, fanged mouths and operated with smooth, powerful efficiency. "After all we are talking about physics, are we not?"

"Physics?"

"Look out there." Pascal gestured out the porthole over the stove. Lew was again drawn by the undulations of the deep water. "It is really just superdense aether. You are seeing the Asklepian wave," Pascal said. "Asklepios is the archetypal healer, the paradigm of all doctors, the cosmic *physician*. 'Physician,' that is the key word here. You see, physics is the study of matter in motion. It is not coincidence that doctors are also known as physicians, for what is the living body if not an exquisite example of matter in motion?

"So Asklepios, as the physician, is the healer of the universe, all matter in motion is his domain. That wave is essentially where it all starts, from the subtle vibrations that we come to know as consciousness to the more gross physical manifestations that are the subject of pure physics. The doctor, or healer, deals with the entire spectrum. Any good doctor knows that healing requires attention to psychological as well as material phenomena. All I am saying is that they are both ultimately the same." He again gestured to the motion outside in the depths of the sea. "You do see it, don't you?"

Lew didn't answer, and Pascal seemed not to care as he poured the water. He spooned some tea from a tin into the kettle, pausing to sniff it once and saying softly, "Ah yes, that's the stuff."

"What about the crystal?" Lew asked suddenly, when they were sipping tea back in the captain's quarters.

"Crystal?" Pascal asked.

"Yes. The nouancer won't work without it. The crystal is concentrated nous. It is what makes it possible for the hardware and software to amplify and refine the Asklepian signal. I don't have it anymore. I lost it when . . ."

"When I was born," Pascal said.

"Yeah."

"Don't worry, Lew. First of all we don't need it just yet. We only need a very rough sort of dead reckoning until we get deeper. The system can handle that very well right now as it is. We will need it though, eventually . . ." Pascal said this calmly, sipping his tea.

"Then what are we going to do!" Lew almost screamed.

"Don't worry." Pascal set his teacup down and reached into the breast pocket of his jacket. "I have it right here," he said, and pulled out the hexagonal crystal.

"How?" Lew asked. Pascal handed it to him.

"It is a teardrop that I have kept with me these many years throughout all my voyages. It has continued to grow . . . crystallizing more and more of the cosmic aether," Pascal said.

"Sheila's tear," Lew whispered. He looked into the familiar facets and saw her face. But it was an older Sheila, and she was not looking at him. It was the face of a mother letting go of her son. He gave it back.

"So you see," Pascal said softly, "not to worry."

20

〜〜〜〜

This Is It

"There aren't many who have made this journey," Pascal said. The *Miserlou*'s interior was full of strange, soft, pastel light that came from the depths outside.

"What journey?" Lew asked. He had to fight to keep the tremor out of his voice. The sub was also pulsating; the vibration was no identifiable frequency, yet it penetrated everything, especially the body. If one did not fight it, the sensation was not unpleasant, and the result was one of controlled excitement, all biological circuits wide open, in tune, waiting for something to happen—something completely natural and completely unexpected. But if one resisted, tensions began to accumulate—little stresses at first, but they spawned others and grew so that gradually a sense of impending doom began to mount.

"The journey into singularity," Pascal said, pouring himself some more tea. He sat sideways on the green velvet sofa bolted to the wall of the sub and gazed out the porthole into the hypnotic depths of nous.

"What is singularity?" Lew finally broke Pascal's reverie. The tension had become unbearable. He had to talk. Anything to distract him from the nameless fear that was creeping over and into him.

"Well who knows, exactly?" Pascal answered. His voice trailed off as a particularly beautiful refraction of light mesmerized him. "In terms of modern physics I think you can say that the Akashic Hall of Records is located on the event horizon of the central singularity. The event horizon corresponds to that infinite stretch of beach."

"But I don't understand," Lew said. "I mean, if we have crossed the event horizon of a singularity point, won't the gravity of the center, the singularity, pull us in immediately?"

"One would assume so," Pascal said. "Under normal conditions of gravitation that is what would happen. But once you cross the event horizon, there is nothing left of 'normal.' You are, all at once, an eternity away from home and an equal distance from the singularity point. You need a map, which does not exist, or a guidance system such as we possess."

"But," Lew protested, "I thought the nouancer was just a radio. Or like a radio, rather—I mean it was able to receive and amplify the nouonic pulse of thought, the wave vibrations of consciousness."

"So it does," Pascal said.

"So what does that have to do with a guidance system?" Lew asked.

"We are following the nouonic pulse back to the source," Pascal answered. "The algorithms which we derived from the singularity equations are what make that possible. But the programming is not accurate enough to take us all the way in."

"In where?" Lew asked.

"The singularity," Pascal said, "The one-point. The beginning and the end, the alpha-omega, the 'I am.' "

"I have thought at times," Lew said wearily, "that somehow this whole thing was really just a projection of my mind, and eventually I will wake up, as if from a dream."

"Why not?" Pascal said.

"But you talk as if it were all real!"

"Isn't your own mind real?" Pascal asked.

"Yes, but . . ."

"So what if it is, as you suggest, all a projection of your mind? What is your mind? Ultimately that explanation is empty, vacuous—even if it is true, it tells you nothing about reality."

"What did you mean just now when you said, 'I am'?" Lew asked.

"I explained it before," Pascal said. "The name God uses for Himself is 'I am.' That's all. It goes back to what you were saying. Even if it is all just in your mind, your mind is intimately connected to the one principle of being, the 'I am.' "

"So you think that is what we will experience?" Lew asked.

"I don't know what we will experience," Pascal answered. "We will, I hope, arrive at the one singularity. There is just one, you know?"

"Only one?"

"That's right. All black holes are really the same. Once you cross the event horizon there is no more physical space, so it makes sense really. With no space how could two singularities exist separately? We are approaching the single nexus that connects the gravitational density at the center of each star system and each galaxy. We are truly making our way to the center of the Universe. Not many have gone before, I suspect."

Pascal got quiet, and the vibrations continued to build. Lew struggled to control the tremors that had begun in his knees. He was beginning to feel a pulse of underwater waves as they rolled against the *Miserlou* with a frequency of about one a minute. They were getting stronger and with each one Lew could feel their little vessel surge forward.

"Nervous Lew?" Pascal asked.

"Yes," Lew said through chattering teeth.

"We need to go to the bridge."

"Why?"

"We are getting close, and the automatic navigational system can't take us much farther. We are going to have to switch to manual," Pascal said, setting his teacup down.

"But what if . . . I mean maybe we don't want to go after all."

"Listen, Lew," Pascal said, grabbing Lew by the lapels of his jacket, "we no longer have a choice. Either we make the plunge or we wander aimlessly in the cosmic depths forever. There is no turning back."

"Can't we just reverse the guidance system?"

"The event horizon is a one-way gate. Even if we could make it back that far, we could never break through. It is either singularity or . . . this. Forever." He gestured at the depths outside.

Lew shuddered at the realization. It was hard to look out a porthole for more than a few moments. The depths suggested an infinity poised to absorb all finite things and annihilate all separate existence.

He followed Pascal to the bridge. Video screens lined the walls of lustrous, dull, charcoal gray metal. In the center was the shiny brass captain's wheel. There was an upholstered captain's chair in front of the wheel and a slightly smaller navigator's chair beside it. The nouancer was installed in a panel over the wheel. Pascal pulled the crystal from his breast pocket and inserted it into the nouancer. Then he produced two sets of earphones and plugged their two stereo jacks into outlets in the control panel.

"Put these on," he said, handing one set to Lew.

"Can you hear me?" Pascal asked, after Lew had donned the set.

"Yes," Lew responded.

"Good. Now listen very carefully. We are in a spiral trajectory around the singularity. But we can't get any closer on automatic. We are in an asymptotic orbit here, getting infinitely close, but never able to close the gap. So we will have to pilot manually. I've got you jacked into the nouancer. When I switch it on the input will be intense—we are so close. But you can guide me verbally . . ."

"Why me?" Lew asked. "I mean why can't you just jack yourself in and pilot at the same time?"

"Because—the input is going to be powerful. I don't know precisely how it will affect the rational functions. The pilot needs to be fully alert, both mentally and physically. The stuff coming across the nouancer may not allow it."

"Oh," Lew said. "Can't I pilot while you . . ."

"You're wasting time, Lew. Don't you see this is the only thing that makes sense? I am the only one qualified to take the wheel. You will have to function as navigator."

"But how?" Lew asked, despair in his voice. He glanced desperately from vid monitor to vid monitor, seeing the same scene from different perspectives, namely the depths of nous, the ocean of awareness as it grew in density and color, engulfing their tiny ship. Another wave rolled against them. This time the resulting acceleration was greater, and Lew had to fight to retain his balance.

"Just listen. That's all you have to do. You can indicate by saying port, starboard, up, or down, which way I need to turn. It should be unmistakable. We are so close that small variations in our approach angle will effect large changes in the nouonic pulse. I don't know what you will hear. It will be idiosyncratic to your personality, but I'm sure you will be able to note the variations in strength of the signal."

Pascal reached up to the switch on the control panel and looked at Lew, who was still standing. The captain's eyes were full of intensity and question. "Ready?"

Lew nodded, and sat down in the plush, green velvet navigator's chair, letting himself fall into the firm cushions which seemed immediately to conform to every curve of his back. He just wanted to sit for a long time, very quietly. He closed his eyes, took a deep breath, and almost relaxed. Then Pascal threw the switch.

There was a soft "pop" and a huge silence.

"Hear anything?" Pascal asked.

"Not yet," Lew said.

"Tell me if this helps." Pascal turned the volume knob.

The silence just got bigger. "Nothing yet," Lew said. "But . . ."

"What?" Pascal prompted.

"Something is going to happen. Something is out there, and I can hear the silence of it more acutely than I have ever heard anything in my life."

"Well it had better make itself known," Pascal said. The sub was humming with vibration. "We're being compressed by violent centrifugal force waves, intense gravity, and the nouonic drive of the sub. If we don't get a signal to follow soon, we may break up. I'll give you some more volume. And maybe some more treble." He fiddled with the dials on the nouancer.

"There . . ." Lew said.

"What?"

"I heard something."

"Which way?"

"I don't know. Try port."

Pascal turned the brass wheel left a quarter turn.

"No, I lost it."

Pascal rolled back to the starboard side.

"There it is! Stop. Steady. Yeah. Hold it." Lew listened intently. He could barely hear what sounded like music. But it wasn't music. Not music in the usual sense. Rather it sounded like the background to music, the vibrations that support all music, all vibrations.

"God, that's beautiful," he said, softly.

"Good," Pascal answered, "but don't give me a report, just guide us."

"It's a standard blues progression," Lew said, "twelve bar. Here comes the turnaround. That's it, the fifth! Oh man, those are tasty licks. Why did I sell my guitar?"

"What are you talking about?" Pascal asked sharply.

"The sound of a stratocaster screaming through a tube amp with reverb," Lew answered.

"Are we on course?"

"We are beautiful," Lew answered. "Just beautiful."

They cruised for hours. Pascal said nothing because the sea felt calm. They were riding in perfect sync with the waves. But finally he spoke, "Lew. Lew?" There was no answer. "Lew!"

Lew tensed, his reverie snapped. "I never understood music," he said. "I always thought it was just structured vibration. But it's really the expression of the cosmic pulse at the level of life. You wouldn't believe the harmonies that are possible. I've been digging chord progressions that take the concept to a new level. Unbelievable!"

"Are we doing OK?" Pascal asked.

"How would I know?"

"Listen, Lew, this isn't going to work if you don't stay in contact with me. From now on I'm going to interrupt every five minutes. I may deviate from course just to confirm the readings you are getting. It is imperative that we stay on the beam of maximum intensity. Alright?"

"Sure," Lew muttered.

"OK, here we go. I'm going to roll us up a few degrees." He pulled back on the wheel. "What do you hear? Is the signal stronger or weaker."

Lew sat bolt upright, shocked at the intensity. It was a piercing wail that quickly resolved itself into the diatonic frequencies of a musical scale. He could hear the tonic and several other overtones. The sound was not pleasing, but it was certainly stronger.

"Better or worse?" Pascal asked.

Lew hesitated. He didn't like it. "Stronger," he said finally.

"Good."

Pascal's plan worked. Soon the headphones were buzzing with activity. Lew had to turn the volume way down. Still it was nearly too much. The overtones had begun to resolve into voices. They seemed to be speaking many languages at once. Lew could, by listening, focus on any one and, with concentration, understand what was being said.

He heard, "The deeper you go, the farther you hide. Don't let go because you can't hang on."

"Listen, Lew," a voice said.

"Was that you?" Lew asked.

"No," Pascal answered. "Why?"

"It is talking to me now," Lew said, worried.

"Good, stay with it," Pascal answered.

"You heard him," the voice said. "Stay with it. That's me pal. I'm your guide. Hang on to my every word, and I'll get you there."

"Where?" Lew asked.

"Don't ask. And don't worry. There is considerable debate as to the precise nature of singularity. Is it the final realization of self, or the total obliteration of self? Will you continue to exist? Or will Lew Slack wink out of existence as the dewdrop of individual consciousness merges with the vast sea of the cosmic mind? I will not say, nor will I give the slightest hint."

"Why?"

"Because I am you, and thus do not know." Peals of insane laughter pierced Lew's ears. It was nearly unbearable.

"OK?" Pascal asked. "Lew? Lew, listen to me! Are we on course?"

"Yes," Lew whispered.

"You could still stop, you know. It is not too late," the voice said.

Would things go back to the way they were before? I mean before I started on this whole crazy thing, before I met the professor? Lew inquired silently.

"Possibly," the voice said.

Suddenly Lew could not imagine anything worse than going back. Except, possibly, going forward.

"But you will always meet the professor," the voice said.

"Always?"

"Always."

"Why?"

"Because the past must always meet the future. There is no more time. Time is over. Time never really was."

"Lew!" Pascal screamed. "We are going to break up any minute!" The sub was shaking violently, no longer going with the waves. "You have to tell me if we are still on course. I'm not sure I can control it anymore."

Lew had shut the voice from his mind. His heart was racing. He felt that it would burst any minute.

The sound of his throbbing pulse came through the earphones. Intermingled between beats were all the sounds of all life in the Universe. It was trying to get into him and he knew it would destroy him. He was too small, too separate. But the beat was insistent. He sensed that it was slightly stronger to the port side.

"Lew! Which way! Damn! Tell me or we've had it!"

"Port!" Lew yelled.

Pascal threw his weight into the wheel. It would not budge. The *Miserlou* was groaning and shaking. He threw his back into it, to no avail. "Lew! Help me!"

Lew looked up to see Pascal, eyes feverish, veins pounding in his skull.

He got up and grabbed the wheel. Together they struggled. Slowly it turned. A huge wave caught them.

The shaking stopped, replaced by an acceleration that threw both men to the floor. Lew felt his lungs grow so heavy that he could not even breathe. But it was over in a few seconds. Then there was complete silence, a stillness unthinkable, an utter emptiness that was full of all that is, was, and ever will be.

Pascal got up slowly and looked at Lew. His eyes were radiant. He took off his headset and Lew did the same. "Thank you," he said.

"What now?" Lew whispered in the awesome silence.

"This," the captain said with a soft chuckle, full of wisdom and mirth, "is it."

21

~~~~~

Ride the Wild Surf

Lew felt weightless in the awesome quiet. When he stood up it was as if his body just floated erect. Not only was there no sound; there was, it seemed, not even the possibility of sound.

Then Pascal spoke. "Tea?" he asked, face brighter than ever. He looked younger too.

"Tea," Lew said. He felt his voice reverberate throughout the entire ship and pass out into the infinite depths. The entire Universe reverberated to this one word, "tea," before it was absorbed into the silence.

"Yes," Pascal said. "I would like a cup. Will you join me?"

"Sure," Lew said.

When the water was boiling, Lew asked Pascal, "What happens now?"

"That depends," Pascal said, spooning tea. The spoon was solid silver. The handle was exquisitely crafted into the form of a serpent swallowing its tail.

"On what?" Lew said. Despite his anxiety, he felt curiously peaceful. He sank back into the red velvet, enjoying the simple process of breathing.

"On where you want to go," Pascal said, pouring the tea. He handed Lew his cup and then sat down on the green velvet sofa opposite Lew.

"Well I don't know about that," Lew said. "Where do *you* want to go?"

"I want to move on," Pascal said, sipping his tea with obvious satisfaction. "I've been at it too long to do anything else.

This next phase may prove to be the most exciting part of the trip so far."

"What is the next phase?" asked Lew, tasting new, subtle flavors in his tea, flavors which gave him a thrill laced with ecstasy.

"Completely unknown," Pascal said. "As yet. All that . . . back there"—he made an impatient gesture with his hand— "was the domain of consciousness as we know it. Thought, self-awareness, etc. But only the most unimaginative think that intelligence stops with that. That is just the beginning.

"All the structures of ordinary life are designed to reassure and convince you that the mundane world of the thinking individual in society is the end of all existence.

"Nothing could be farther from the truth. And as exotic as nouspace seems at first, if you think about it, you will see that everything you experienced there had its basis in the ordinary world from which you came.

"The next leg of the journey begins the truly new phase, the awakening into a wholly new form of consciousness beyond ordinary thought, beyond traditional categories of self and Universe.

"So you see"—he smiled at Lew—"I can't very well turn back now, can I?"

"No," Lew said, "I suppose not." He was troubled. Pascal's analysis awakened longings in him that he didn't even know he had. But he was afraid. "What if I can't go with you?" he asked. "What happens to me?"

"I can't say for sure. It is dangerous either way," Pascal said.

"Dangerous?"

"Yes. One can always get lost, lose whatever principle it is that keeps you together. I hesitate to call it the soul, but for want of a better word—your soul could fragment into the various levels, or possibly get absorbed in the sea of nous. I don't know. But that could mean the end . . . of you."

Lew put his cup back in the saucer, and set it down. "I'm not like you," he said to Pascal. "I don't know how I got here or where I want to go. That makes it harder for me. I have no definite mission. I'm confused."

"As are we all," Pascal said.

"But you know what you want," Lew said.

"Do I?" Pascal smiled enigmatically. Then he got up and opened a closet. Lew was amazed to see him bring out two long, wooden surfboards.

"I know these are rather old-fashioned," he said. "The newer materials are much lighter, but I am partial to natural substances." He ran his hand along the fine grain of one of the boards.

"What are those for?" Lew asked.

"It's time to catch one more wave, Lew." Pascal smiled. "It's time to ride the wild surf."

"But how . . ."

On either side of the captain's bed there were two cabinets, about three feet square. Pascal opened each one to reveal what looked like small metal air locks. "She used to be a warship," Pascal said. "These are the old torpedo tubes. But we can put them to better use than death and destruction."

Lew felt suddenly inert, unable to initiate any action. "Come on, Lew," Pascal said with a quiet voice of authority that Lew could not ignore. Lew stood, and Pascal presented him with one of the surfboards.

"We are going to shoot ourselves out the torpedo tubes?" Lew asked, after Pascal explained.

"Yes."

"That is madness."

"Possibly, but it is the only way. We are so close yet so far. The only way to actually go the distance now is to strip down to bare essentials. Just you and your board. It has come down to a physical thing, but one which will require complete concentration and precise physical control as well. Technology has taken us as far as it can. Now it is up to us, individually."

"What is out there?" Lew asked, terror in his voice.

"The last wave. The big one. It is going to be one hell of a pipeline, an infinite tube. But you can ride it to the end, shoot that curl into the beginning of the greater adventure . . . if you just don't hold back. That's the most important thing at this point, Lew. I know you are afraid. So am I. But give it your total commitment." Pascal was polishing his board with a soft rag. He handed it to Lew, who began wiping his down out of sheer nervous energy.

"What about Felix?" Lew asked. The big cat, curled up at the foot of Pascal's bed, purred on cue.

"Take him with you," Pascal said.

"Cats can't surf," Lew said.

"You would be surprised," Pascal said. "Don't think in terms of can and can't or should and should not anymore. We are way beyond that. This is the threshold of the land of pure *is*."

"How do these things work?" Lew asked, bending down to examine the air lock.

"We'll crawl in on top of our boards," Pascal said. "There is a button inside. It should be on your left. Just press it and wait. The chamber will fill with water. The pressure is going to be quite uncomfortable for a few seconds. The outer door is pressure activated and it will spring open, which will in turn trigger the release of a massive amount of compressed aether behind you. That will shoot you out. We should hit the surface in a matter of seconds. You will probably have a moment to orient yourself, get your balance. The wave will be waiting for you. Just stay centered, and try to keep in the pipeline. You will see the spot to shoot for. Good luck." He stuck out his hand.

Lew took it slowly. "That's it?" he said. "Good luck?"

"No," Pascal said. "But that's all for now." He began opening his air lock. Lew knelt by his and began unscrewing the wheel. It turned easily, obviously well maintained.

They put their surfboards inside the tubes. Pascal made Felix and Lew get in first, insisting that he could easily close his lock himself. Then he screwed the hatch shut and slid in on top of his board. He turned around in the pitch blackness and sealed his door from the inside. Then, wiggling around to lie flat on his board, he reached up and hit the button.

Lew hesitated a few moments. Felix lay behind him on the board, oddly calm and quiet. With a deep sigh, he reached up and punched the button. The water rushed in, filling the chamber in seconds. Then the pressure built and Lew had to struggle to clear his ears. He was already beginning to feel the need to breathe.

The outer door flew open simultaneously with an explosion of pressure at their rear. The board flew out at terrific speed. Lew had to grip the sides tightly to avoid being swept off.

Felix dug in his claws. They shot forward for what seemed like minutes to Lew. He was beginning to feel his grip weaken from oxygen debt fatigue. *Anything for a breath*, he thought.

The board flew out of the water into blazing sunlight and an infinite expanse of deep blue water. Lew had the sensation of flying, gliding on the board for a few seconds, before they came crashing back down. It was strangely peaceful, nothing like he had expected. He could just make out another figure, Pascal, floating in the distance.

He was about to call out when he realized that the peace was deceptive. They were in the valley of a giant wave. And the floor was dropping out. There was a sinking sensation in his stomach. He looked to his right to see the monstrous wave bearing down. It was taller than the Empire State Building and moving with ominous speed.

They started to rise as the flank of the wave drew them up and in. Lew had surfed only once in his life, but he remembered to try and catch his ride just before the wave broke. The suspense was unbearable. He wanted to try and paddle away, but he knew that would be suicide. The wave would then break on top of them, crushing them out of existence. So he waited.

Finally he saw the beginning of a breaker just ahead. He paddled furiously, fighting the motion up and in. He just managed to get under it, and felt himself shoot forward. He stood up and shifted his weight to fight the pull back down. There was a center to the two conflicting forces, and that center was the middle of the pipeline. It was a precise balance which required all his concentration, plus an enormous physical effort. Every muscle and nerve came alive in the action.

Felix, claws still dug in, seemed to sense what Lew was doing and moved to enhance his efforts. The result was that Lew and his cat were shooting down the longest pipeline in the Universe at incredible speed.

Lew could see Pascal up ahead. He was doing well, keeping inside the tube, long hair flying out behind him, arms extended for balance. Suddenly the aether came alive with music. Surf music. But again it sounded like the surf music from which all other surf music is derived. The thumping lows and wailing highs reverberated to the cosmic beat. It sent chills up and down Lew's spine. Each note seemed finely tuned to his every minute motion.

The music *was* the wave. They were riding the vibrations of pure ecstasy. An electric guitar chord rang out with full tremolo and reverb, sending a passionate ripple throughout the sun, sea, and sky. Single notes of a crystalline clarity sliced the scene with pristine brilliance.

And it was building. Just as Lew felt certain that the music and his ride were about to reach a climax, the wave would get stronger and the pipeline longer. The chords would modulate to a new progression, more complex, yet somehow more simple, than the previous. And always more beautiful.

Yet there could be no doubt that it was all building to something. Something unimaginable, inconceivable. Yet attainable. That was the message in the music—that it could be done, you *could* surf the waves to the very end, which held the promise of a new beginning.

But what was it? Lew looked up ahead to see Pascal still riding, the image of harmony, grace, and balance. And something else. Far up ahead on the distant horizon, the curl of the wave closed in. It formed a hole, a hole in the fabric of time, and beyond that portal Lew could see white light. The closer they got, the more he sensed an awesome beauty, a powerful ecstatic love there that drew him with a longing at once personal and universal.

He felt the vibrations grow to an unbearable fervor. The music could not resolve itself this time. It had to transform itself into something beyond music. The beauty, the intensity was too great. Pascal was bearing down on the portal at the pipeline's end. Just before he sailed through, he stepped back on his board, causing it to shoot up the side of the wave. Then he shifted his weight again, causing his board to trace a splendid hyperbolic arc as it slid back down the wave and through the hole. It had the effect of putting a decisive, personal flourish on Pascal's final plunge into the whiteness. The white light received him with an explosion of brilliant color which sent streams of intricate three-dimensional patterns streaming out into the aether. Lew witnessed an awe-inspiring show of light and form and color. It was over in a moment, leaving only the blazing whiteness up ahead.

Lew set himself more firmly and sped forward. *If I can make it, all will be finally revealed*, he thought to himself. He wanted it more than he had ever wanted anything, to follow Pascal and shoot the final curl, ride the last wave to the end or the beginning. *What will it be like?* he wondered. Images of godhood flooded his mind—Lew Slack promoted to a new station, above all mortals, all those who had slighted or hurt him in the past. *Yes*, he thought, *no more limitations. Absolute power!*

The split-second retreat into daydream cost Lew his concentration. He looked up to see that he was riding dangerously low. He had lost the center. His goal was no more than a hundred yards ahead, but he had lost velocity. And time was running out. The wave was about to break with full force.

Lew guided his board back up, but it cost him more time and more velocity. He knew he had one last shot. This run would either take him through or send him under. He leaned forward. They gained speed again, closing rapidly on the hole. Lew was bathed in the pure, white brilliance which streamed forth from his goal. He felt his entire body become at once younger and lighter. At the same time his mind was filled with ancient wisdom. *Eternally young as spring, always old as the father of time*, he thought.

The music modulated to a minor key and a shattering discord broke the harmony. Lew reached out his hand, and his fingertips brushed against the cosmic radiance at the pipeline's end. Then the wave broke, closing the opening and sending Lew, board, and Felix crashing down.

The sounds were suddenly inimical. Lew heard an unholy peal of insane laughter, which made him shudder even as the waters closed around him with terrifying force. The last thing he heard was a high-pitched mocking wail that repeated one word several times, "Wipeout!"

22

~~~

Those Back Pages

When a wave breaks a certain balance is shattered. Lew felt his very soul ripped to shreds as he lost contact with his board and the force of the dissipating wave sent him down to the bottom. He slammed against something hard and tried to swim back up, but the pressure above was enormous, driving him back down and pummeling him against the packed sand.

He finally gave up, despairing of ever reaching the surface, and prepared to drown. He felt a vicious undertow snag his body and do what he could not do, drag him up from the bottom. It was a twisting, pulling motion that set him spinning head over heels. His feet hit sand just as his head broke the surface. He gulped at the air and took in a significant quantity of foamy spray before his head slammed on the beach. It sent him somersaulting for a dozen or so meters. He lay flat for a moment, coughing up water, before the next wave came crashing in over his head. This one was bigger, and the drag took him back out to sea, where he fought another round with the conflicting forces of tide and wave before getting thrown back against the beach. This time he did not try to rest, but began running as soon as he had room to stand. Still the next wave sent him sprawling on the beach and the backflow threatened to drag him along with it. He threw himself to the sand and dug his fingers in. The sand ran through his hands, and just as he felt his tenuous grip about to give, the last of the water receded. He stood up again and ran as fast and as far he could. His body was bruised and battered, and his lungs were congested with the foamy sea spray. Before he was clear of the tide line his knees gave out and he fell face forward. Lew Slack was all washed up, reduced to so much flotsam and jetsam on the sandy shore of time.

Luckily the tide was on its way out or Lew would have been reclaimed by the sea and utterly drowned. As it was he lay unconscious for hours as the water broke around his limp body. Every so often he would sputter and choke, coughing up some of the liquid that crowded his lungs.

He came to on his back staring straight up at a full moon, twelve o'clock high. He rubbed his eyes, sat up, and groaned at the pain and stiffness in his bruised body. A dark shape sprang to his side. Felix looked more magnificent than ever in the moonlight. "We almost made it, kitty," Lew said, recalling the most compelling sight he had ever seen, that of Pascal artfully shooting the last curl into the brilliant blaze of singularity. "I guess we are done for, now," he added mournfully, feeling his voice choke off with the pain of a loss greater than any he could have imagined possible. *If Pascal were at the beginning, then surely I am at the end*, he thought.

He stood up and surveyed his surroundings. The beach was rocky. He could see that he was extremely lucky to have missed the jagged jetties on either side. Something gleamed in the silvery light on a nearby rock. He went to inspect and found the skag fin of his surfboard. Other pieces of the smashed board were in evidence.

The moonlight was so bright that he could see a considerable distance.

Straight inland there was a large looming shadow. As Lew walked in that direction the vague outlines of a large cliff began to take shape. He found bits and pieces of gray metal strewn along the way. He picked up one particularly large piece. It was about two feet across and appeared to be the fragment of a fin. Turning it over he read the letters, "*Miserl* . . . The *Miserlou*," he murmured. "So she's had it too." Something flashed in the moonlight, directly in his path. It was the nouancer. It was badly smashed, but the crystal was still intact. Lew pulled it out and pocketed it.

He found her at the base of the cliff—or what remained of her. The aft section with the bridge was completely sheared off, as was a small portion of the ship's bow. The bulk of the midsection was smashed sideways against the jagged boulders that formed the base of the cliff. Lew looked up and could not see the top.

He entered the sub through a hole in the front, where Pascal's bed had been. The rest of the captain's quarters was amazingly intact. He collapsed into the green velvet chair, gratefully letting the soft cushions receive his sore bones. Felix followed him in, cautiously sniffing the furniture. He came up to rub against Lew's knee.

"What about some tea, kitty?" Lew said after a long silence, broken only by the distant sound of surf. He rose and went into the small galley adjoining the captain's chambers and was amazed to find the stove still working. Soon he had a kettle boiling and a tin of tea opened. He sipped his tea, pondering his fate. There did not seem to be much left. What else could happen? How could he possibly do worse? He did not even know what to hope for, were there any hope left.

These thoughts, together with the crashing sound of the waves, lulled him to sleep before his cup was even half-empty. Several hours later it was the same crashing sound that woke him up. It was much louder. Felix was pacing nervously. Water was beginning to come inside with each new breaker. "Tide's coming in, kitty!" Lew said, coming wide-awake. The *Miserlou* was beginning to rock as the water rose around its base. Lew saw the book, *Strange and Distant Episodes,* lying on the maple desktop. Without thinking, he picked it up and stuffed it into the waistband of his jeans.

Then he led Felix back out the jagged bow gash. They climbed up on a boulder to see a beautifully intimidating sight. The full moon was still high, apparently motionless. The dark waters were coming in fast, breaking all around with a wonderful crashing sound; the breakers caught the pale light, sending spray after spray of shimmery silver into the darkness.

The water was rising fast. A wave broke around them, the force nearly knocking Lew back into the cliff wall. "Come on, kitty!" Lew shouted above the din. He climbed to higher ground. Felix followed, apparently having no trouble negotiating the steep, rugged terrain.

Soon the *Miserlou* was completely submerged and the tide still rose. Lew continued to climb, but the cliff face got progressively steeper. He had little choice but to climb on. Soon he was on a near-vertical rock face. He had lost track of Felix long ago, and still the water was on his heels, crashing in with what sounded like ever-increasing force. Lew stopped trying to think. He just lived for the next foothold or handhold and the next step up. It went on for hours. Finally, unable to go another yard, he reached up and felt a ledge. When he pulled himself up he saw that it was not a ledge but the top. He stood at the beginning of a giant grassy expanse that stretched as far as he could see into the moonlight. The only visible landmark was a magnificent tree some two-hundred yards off.

As he approached he began to appreciate the gargantuan proportions of the tree. It was over five-hundred feet tall and the branches spread out, casting a moon shadow the size of a football field. The trunk of the tree was at least ten feet in diameter. He sat down resting his back against the huge base. A massive root pushed up the earth on his left, creating a hill over ten feet high. Something moved at the top of that hill. Lew looked up to see a dark feline shape just before it sprang to his side.

"Mrrrooow!" Lew had assumed that Felix was drowned, but the cat had found an easier way up. The beast rubbed against Lew, nearly knocking him on his side. The motion made him aware of an uncomfortable bulge in his pants. It was the book, *Strange and Distant Episodes*. He pulled it out and set it down on the soft grass. "It has come down to this, kitty," he said, "and this," he added, pulling the crystal from his jacket and setting it on the book.

The crystal caught a piece of moonlight and sent a refracted slice of pale color off to a spot next to the book. There was a piece of fruit right where the light had landed. It was an apple.

Lew picked it up and took a bite. It was delicious. He was about to take another bite when he saw a worm crawling through the sweet, white, fruit flesh. The worm gestured to him, beckoned him to bend close, which he did. It spoke in a small voice that was deep and full of authority.

"You have failed to reach singularity. What is left? Maybe you can still erase that which you want to change, but time is running out. Every choice is irreversible. But that does not mean that future choices cannot partially compensate for past ones. However, the farther away you get from any one choice, the harder it becomes to alter the path of destiny. Sooner or later the probability of change becomes effectively zero."

Lew looked up at the great drooping branches of the tree. There was a fragrant, intoxicating scent in the air.

He looked out and was confronted with a vast panorama, a landscape filled with color and form. It was alive, organic. When he looked up into the branches of the tree, the sensation that he was in a living system became more intense. The tree was obviously the nerve center of the network. The branches, which nearly touched the ground and spilled all about him, were full of information and acutely aware of his presence.

He was gripped with terror at the moment he realized that he was engulfed by an awareness much larger than himself, large enough to encompass the entire Universe.

It was that thought, or more precisely that term, "Universe," which saved him from retreating hopelessly into a mindless panic. Uni-verse, one-verse, one song. It was one, and he was part of it.

But he was also conscious of his separation from the system. It was a balance sustained by baffling paradox. He was the Universe, he was not the Universe. Tip the scale too far in one direction and you fall prey to megalomania, the madness of the solipsist. Too far in the other direction produces isolation, alienation, and despair.

Lew felt the tension between these extremes escalate to an unbearable degree. He tried to focus outward. It was the right thing to do. The tension lessened slightly and became ecstasy. He felt it in his spine; it traveled through his nervous system, giving new life and meaning to his whole being.

He was free, free to roam the Universe at will! It was what he was created to do; he saw that clearly now. Everything before had only been preliminary, a prelude to this moment, his liberation beneath the honey-scented branches of the great tree.

With his ecstasy came a sense of others who shared in his liberation. They were there with him, distinct selves that he could experience and appreciate as he had never before been able to appreciate others. All sense of fear, jealousy, hatred, and need was gone. Each self was simultaneously one *with* and one *distinct* from all other selves.

This was joy. This was liberation. This was life as life was intended. Lew prepared to journey outward from the base of the tree. He prepared to enter the Universe as an active, participating particle. He knew that once he left the protective canopy of the tree to bask in the bright light of eternal consciousness, he would never return, and this filled him with even greater joy because he knew that he had nothing to lose and everything to gain.

Just as he was about to take what he knew would be the final step into the realm of pure freedom, he became aware of an unexpected presence, one that did not seem to share in the collective joy.

He spun around to face Alan. But it was a different Alan from the one he had first encountered in nouspace. This Alan was older, and something was wrong with him. He was pale, gaunt, very intense.

Then Lew remembered he was a murderer. Alan pulled his shirt aside to bare the wound in his side, as if reading Lew's mind. The thing was ugly; it had not healed and it seemed dead. The edges were gray, not bloody. It was just a hole. Alan looked like a zombie, one of the undead.

"Just a reminder, friend," Alan said. "A little vision to keep you in line. You were about to get pretty carried away with yourself there. Don't forget who you are, Lew. My pal, my murderer." He flashed a skull-like grin full of joyless pain. Then he laughed a cold, vicious laugh, and Lew realized that Alan was not really there.

And then Lew understood. It was the unfinished business of his past which had kept him from following Pascal just as it now kept him from entering paradise. Would it ever be finished? Would he ever be free? He glanced down at the discarded apple core, and saw the worm slide quickly out of sight into the earth. He distinctly heard the words, "Not yet, little one . . . not yet . . ."

Lew opened the book, and placed the crystal on the creamy page that glimmered in the moonlight. The words of the text and the refractions from the crystal began to merge and flow together. The crystal was emitting a radiance all its own. Lew could not keep from looking at it. In the multicolored light he saw faces, familiar faces. They were actually coming out of the faceted surface of the crystal and forming in the rainbow hues that the thing emitted.

A face leapt from the page and took shape in the multicolored light. It was the white-haired visage of the professor, whom Lew now clearly recognized as himself, much older. "Patience," the old man whispered. Then he saw Pamela making love with a man he did not recognize. Sheila, Alan, and Psylene. There was that beautiful scene inscribed forevermore in his mind of Pascal postponing his final plunge into singularity for a brief moment so that he could exit with his very own signature, a hyperbolic curve going up the side of the wave and then down into a brilliant cascade of form and color. All these images became a beautiful mandala that danced around the crystal. The dynamics of it pulled his attention to the center, to the crystal itself, where he saw his own face.

Simultaneously he realized that the page of text was one with which he was intimately familiar. The words leapt out into the dancing mandala and came alive. They told the story of a man, a computer programmer, bitter and on his lunch break from work. In fact, because of his bitterness, he was taking an extra long lunch break. The moon overhead resolved itself into a noonday sun, and the tree became an ordinary oak, gracing a city sidewalk.

23

〰〰

Distinct Possibilities

"Why so glum, chum?" Lew dimly remembered something.

"I said what's the problem?" the stranger insisted as Lew continued to walk.

"I don't have any spare change," Lew said, looking up to see the white-haired, handsome old face of the professor. "You!" he said.

The professor laughed. Lew realized that he had the crystal, gripped tightly in his right hand. "Here," he said, holding it out to the professor. His fingers involuntarily twitched and it fell to the sidewalk.

Lew flexed his hand while the professor bent to retrieve the crystal. As the professor put it in his pocket Lew again saw the scar on the old man's right wrist that now mirrored his own.

"It will bother you from time to time," the professor said, flexing his hand, "especially when it gets cold." They stood facing each other in silence for a few seconds. "You sure you want to give it back?" the professor finally asked, patting the new bulge in his coat pocket.

"Yeah," Lew said, not feeling at all sure.

"Maybe you're right," the professor said with a wicked gleam in his eye. "Things didn't turn out all that well did they? Maybe next time. The possibilities are endless." With that the professor turned to go.

"Wait!" Lew said. He wanted to ask the man some questions.

"Yes?" The professor stopped.

But all Lew could think of to say was, "Are you *really* a professor?"

"Of course."

"But where?" Lew said, not able to imagine himself as a professor of anything.

"Where?" The professor just stared at Lew with a curious expression.

"What university, I mean."

"The only one that matters," the old man said, looking over his shoulder. He had turned to go again and was off at the rapid clip that belied his apparent age.

"Which one is that?" Lew asked, trying to keep up.

"The University of the *Universe*." The professor laughed. They were both distracted by a vicious shriek.

Lew saw what he thought was a black panther tearing out of the professor's pocket. The animal, terrified at being suddenly on a bustling city street, bolted straight at him. Lew blinked and stepped back to avoid the attack. When his eyes opened he saw only a small, frightened cat.

"Felix!" Lew reached down suddenly, startling the kitty. It bolted straight for the street, full of lunch hour traffic. Lew chased Felix, darting out between two parked cars. A Saab, going much too fast, swerved to miss him, barely avoiding a head-on collision from the opposite lane. Lew scooped up his cat and jumped back onto the sidewalk. Holding Felix, he ran after the professor. But it was too late; the man had disappeared.

Felix was struggling to get free. "I've got to get you home," Lew muttered.

As he walked up the steps to his front door he noticed that his shoes were wet. He took the cat inside and opened a can of tuna. Felix, initially quite disoriented, found reality again in the smell of the fish. Lew changed his shoes and drove back to work.

"What's that cologne you're wearing, Lew?" Susan asked as he walked by her desk. "I love it. Got to get some for my boyfriend."

"Cologne?" Lew asked, noticing that his hair and shirt collar were still slightly damp—he could still smell the surf. "Uh, it's something new," he said, "*nous* or something like that. I forget."

"Where did you get it?"

"No place. I mean you can't. My uncle sent it from France."

"Your uncle from France?" Susan said. Then she smiled at him. There were wild things in that smile, things that took Lew away for an instant.

"Susan," he hissed, "you were there!"

"I was there," she said.

"It really *did* happen?"

"Afraid so," she said, reaching for his right hand. She held his wrist up and traced the scar there. "I really am sorry about that, Lew. Does it give you much trouble?"

"Only in cold weather," he said.

"Still friends?" she asked.

"Sure. Uh, Susan . . ."

"Yes?"

"Do you remember—*everything*?"

She blushed. "Yes, Lew. Everything. You won't tell David, will you?"

"David?"

"My boyfriend," she said.

"Oh yeah. I mean no, of course not. What about *Goddess Power* and all that?"

"What about it?" she said.

"Are you still . . ."

"Dabbling? No, I got what I wanted. I'm quitting my job at the end of the month. David and I are going to Hawaii."

"But it was so . . ." Lew began.

"Real? Yeah, I know what you mean. Even better than the real thing, right?"

Lew was looking around the office, trying to get his bearings. "Yeah. We have to get back there, don't we?"

"Oh Lew, don't you get it? It is all still there. There is *here*. That is the real trick—to bring it back home, right where you always are." Susan got up and went to pour herself some coffee.

"Mind if I join you?" Lew asked, longing for the old days of an innocent cup of coffee with Susan.

"Of course I don't mind," she said. "But you don't have time."

"I don't?"

She jerked her thumb at the big doors to Phelp's office. "He wants to see you."

"Oh," Lew said.

"Where were you?" Phelp's asked as Lew walked in.

"Lunch," Lew said.

"Long lunch," Phelps said, swiveling around in his chair to look Lew in the eye.

"Sorry. Did you need me?"

"No. But we might have." Phelps leaned way back in his chair and folded his hands across his bulging stomach.

"I'll be more careful . . ." Lew started to say and then faltered. "Look," he spoke up again, "you take two-hour lunches all the time."

"Executive privilege," Phelps said, oblivious to his abuse of the term.

"And I suppose tomorrow you will tell me all about power spots and Carlos Castaneda, is that it!" Lew said forcefully.

"Power spots?" Phelps said, surprised.

"Don't deny it. I know you read that Don Juan stuff. You are probably into New Age music, crystal magic, and all that crap too."

This got to Phelps. He did, in fact, own a number of crystals. He slept with one under his pillow. "Lew, what the hell has gotten into you? You can't talk to me this way you know. You just can't."

"Why not?"

"Because I run this place. You work for me." An unwanted pleading tone had crept into his voice.

"Not anymore," Lew said. He got up and walked out.

"Lew, wait! Forget about the lunch. We need to talk, dammit," Phelps yelled after him.

"What is going on?" Susan asked, as Lew emerged.

"I just quit," Lew said, smoldering with intensity.

"Good for you," she said, sipping her coffee. "You know that professor guy was right about one thing."

"What's that?"

"This coffee sucks!" she said and flung the contents of her cup onto the carpet.

Lew was still laughing when he got into his car.

Cline and the professor were having drinks in the basement lab. "So that about wraps it up?" Cline said.

"Afraid so," the professor said. "I would like to stay, but I can't. The time matrix is strained enough as it is. Too many paradoxes are on the verge of breaking the entire fabric of space-time."

"And nouspace?" Cline asked, sipping his cocktail.

"Nouspace can wait," the professor said. "We are, for the time being, still time's slaves."

"What was the thing you were talking about earlier?" Cline asked. "You said that something about all this surprised you."

"Yes," the professor mused. He took a slow drink, enjoying the warmth of the alcohol. "Susan. My old secretary. That was a surprise. I did not remember that part. But of course, strictly speaking, I did not remember any of it, since it had not really happened."

"I still don't understand," Cline said.

"Don't worry about it," the professor said. "Susan's becoming Psylene *was* a real surprise. Of course there are always surprises. Surprises are, in the last analysis, what keep us going."

"One thing that still bothers me," Cline said.

"What?"

"Well, since you are going back to the future, and since we are headed there, does that mean that we are doomed to relive this whole adventure in a series of closed time loops?"

"That is all science fiction," the professor said. "You might say that the very reason I came back was to break old patterns, ensure that we would not get stuck in recursive iterations of the same space-time loop."

"Yes," Cline said. "It makes sense. But I would like to get the theory of it right. We really don't have the mathematics to describe what has happened. Except for Pamela's singularity algebras, I suppose. I must remember to get in touch with her. Maybe we can work it out together."

"Maybe," the professor said. He took another drink. "So long," he said, "and thank you."

Cline tried to reconstruct in his mind what happened next, but it was impossible. The professor neither vanished nor did he fade away. The only certain thing was that the old man was no longer there.

*   *   *

Lew drove home and called Pamela.

"Hello, Lew," she said.

"Pamela, . . ."

"What, Lew?"

"What happened?" he said.

"Are you alright?" she asked.

"Yeah, I'm fine, I think. But what happened?"

"You are back," she said.

"But it is before it all got started. I mean nothing's changed. It can't be, it's not possible."

"It's a corollary to the fundamental singularity theorem," she said. "A bifurcation and reconstitution of the time line. And it may look at first like nothing has changed, but that is only an illusion. Everything is changed."

"But Alan, I mean . . ."

"What?"

"Is he still . . ."

"Dead," she said. "How would I know? I presume not."

"But you remember? I mean the professor, the crystal, the birthday party, and . . ."

"Yes, Lew. All of us who were directly involved in the initial jump across the singularity potential remember. We, in fact, form a singularity group. That is another corollary to the theorem. Our lives are fundamentally different. But for those outside the group the reality changes will be subtle, almost imperceptible." She sighed, thinking of Elliot as she said this.

"When can I see you?" he asked.

"I don't think that is a good idea," she said.

"But I want to marry you," he pleaded.

"Things are different now, Lew," she said. "I expect to be leaving soon. I need to get on with my career."

"I'll go with you."

"Lew, listen to me. You may want to believe nothing has changed. But you know that is not true. We can't go back. I've freed myself from the past. I need to move on. I'm sorry."

"But what about Alan?" he asked.

"What about him?"

"Well, where is he?"

"I suppose you will see him quite soon, and I suppose he will be fine. Now I have to go, Lew. I'm packing."

After she hung up she opened the file with all the old post-cards from Tibet.

She scooped them up into her arms. She hesitated before throwing them into the fireplace. What if she couldn't reproduce the fundamental singularity theorem without those cryptic clues?

"What if!" she said and dumped the whole lot onto the flames. Was it her imagination or did the smoke give off a rich scent of snowy mountaintops, vast oceans, and the musty floor of a primeval forest?

"Pack of Camels," Lew said to the convenience store checker late the following night.

"Is your boss really an ex-marine?" he asked her as she rang it up.

"What?" She eyed him closely. "No, that's just what I tell troublemakers," she laughed.

"How do you know I'm not a troublemaker?" Lew thought as he pocketed the cigarettes and walked out the door.

He carefully pulled a cigarette from the pack as he approached the corner and slowed his pace as he approached a dark alley.

"Need a light?" A voice came out of the alley.

"Sure," Lew said, as the man flicked his heavy metal lighter.

"Good God man!" the stranger said, "You can't do that!"

"Save it, Alan. I've had the curse of the camel, and worse . . ." Lew said.

"You've spoiled my entrance," Alan said.

"I know, Alan. What *could* I have been thinking?" Lew said, offering Alan a cigarette.

"What indeed," Alan said reflectively.

Across town Pamela was drinking tea and pondering her uncertain future when the phone rang. Her heart was beating fast when she answered.

"Dr. Fine?"

"Yes," Pamela said.

"This is Elliot Pritchard of the Manhattan Institute for Advanced Mathematical Research."

"Elliot!" She started to say, and then caught herself. "Oh, hello," she said instead.

"I was reading a back issue of the *American Journal of Abstract Algebra* recently in conjunction with some of my work on automorphic mappings applied to identity rings. Pretty dull stuff actually. But I came across an old article of yours on singularity groups."

"Yes. That was a long time ago," Pamela said.

"Indeed. But very fine work. Some of your conjectures are quite interesting. Have you done any more work in that area?"

"Well some. But I work at a community college. It is not the best environment for research."

"Yes, I understand . . ." Elliot paused, " . . . You know it is funny," he said in an odd tone of voice, "I don't usually say things like this, but talking to you I feel almost as if I know you. A sort of déjà vu."

"I know what you mean," she said.

"Well, I mean . . ." He was clearly uncomfortable. "What I really called about was to discuss the prospects of your coming here on a temporary basis—initially that is. I would really like to explore the field of singularity groups farther. Would you be at all interested?"

"Possibly," she said, smiling.

"What do you remember, Alan?" Lew asked when they were back in his apartment.

"I remember being in the East for twenty years . . ."

"Wait a minute!" Lew said. "What about that book, the *Kybal*, and the professor?"

"Ah yes. Interesting stuff," Alan said, pulling the book from his coat pocket.

Lew grabbed it. He gazed at the cover for a few moments and then began flipping through the pages. *Is this all that's left of nouspace?* he wondered, *a paperback book*?

"And I also remember your trying to *kill* me." Alan smiled.

"So you *do* remember?" Lew said.

"Yeah"—Alan settled back into the soft sofa—"what a trip. What a crazy, far-out trip."

"I told you people don't talk like that anymore," Lew said.

"You crazy sonofabitch!" Alan said. "You actually tried to kill me!"

"But, Alan," Lew said, alarmed. "I didn't mean it. I *swear ...*"

"It was perfectly understandable, given the circumstances," Alan said. "But just one thing."

"What?" Lew asked.

"Don't try it again."

"Sure," Lew said in a humble voice, head lowered.

"Relax," Alan said. "I was just hassling you. I'm entitled, don't you think?"

"Yeah," Lew sighed.

"Man, you take everything so *seriously*." Alan laughed. "You need to lighten up. Now listen, Lew—I've got it all figured out."

"What all figured out?" Lew asked.

"Project Asklepios," Alan said. "Asklepios is the name of the mythic healer, the archetype of all physicians, right?"

"Yeah," Lew said.

"Now why did the professor call it project Asklepios?"

"I don't know," Lew said.

"Because it was a *healing* project, don't you see? I was stuck in the Far East, possibly I would never have returned. I was tripping into nouspace all the time, but I couldn't remember it. The result of the whole project is that I am back. I am restored. I can now put all my transcendental experiences to work—here in the world.

"And that cute, little secretary of yours—what was her name?"

"Susan," Lew said.

"Yeah, Susan. She got in touch with the inner power she never knew she had. No more miserable, demeaning desk jobs for her. She is now destined for a life of adventure.

"And poor Pamela was the most stuck of all. A brilliant mathematician, trapped teaching calculus at a community college. She now has the opportunity to pursue her research at the world's most renowned institute for mathematics. And possibly find the personal satisfaction she always wanted.

"And you ..."

"What have *I* got out of all this?" Lew interrupted, practically screaming. "I have lost my job and my girlfriend! I have a wrist that's going to act up every time it rains or gets cold. I ..." The phone rang.

It was Phelps. "Lew," he said, "we really need to talk. Maybe I haven't been as openly appreciative of your work as I . . ." He was nervous. On the coffee table in front of him lay a crystal which he had purchased that day at a New Age bookstore. There were also several empty beer cans next to the full one from which he was drinking.

"What about a raise?" Lew shot back, remembering what Susan had told him about his boss's plans to promote him at the end of the month.

"Well, as a matter of fact I was planning to upgrade your position to that of *Programmer II* in a few weeks. That's a ten percent raise," Phelps said, "but I can make that effective immediately, if you will just reconsider . . ."

"I'll come in tomorrow," Lew said. "We'll talk about it."

"Great! . . ." Phelps said. Lew cut him off by hanging up.

"What's the matter?" Alan asked, when Lew remained silent.

"You were talking about Asklepios, how we all got restored—healed in some way?" Lew said.

"Yeah."

"Well, I just got a ten percent raise," Lew said, sourly.

"Congratulations," Alan said with a deadpan expression.

"Congratulations!" Lew echoed. "I risk my life many times over, suffer the slings and arrows of, of . . ."

"Outrageous fortune," Alan prompted.

"Yeah," Lew continued. "And I get promoted to a *Programmer II* position. The irony, the absurdity, the . . ."

"Think of it as *sublime* irony, Lew." Alan smiled. "You should quit that job anyway."

"How can I quit?" Lew asked. "I won't have any money."

"You still have the $10,000 from the project," Alan said.

"I hate to tell you this, Alan," Lew said, "but ten grand won't go very far these days . . ."

"Never mind," Alan said. "I have the solution to all our troubles."

"What is that?" Lew asked.

Alan pulled a vial from his coat pocket and handed it to Lew. It was a small green bottle, archaic-looking, with a cork stopper. Lew recognized the empathetic aether that Pascal had used to heal his hand.

"I swiped it from his desk in the sub," Alan said, "the . . . what was it?"

"The *Miserlou*," Lew said, suddenly filled with a romantic longing to have one more shot at the wave.

"Yeah," Alan said, "the *Miserlou*. Anyway, this stuff will come in quite handy. I've got plans."

"Plans?" Lew asked wistfully.

"Yeah. I didn't know how screwed up things were until I came down off the mountaintop, back to civilization. You guys have done a pretty good job of destroying the planet while I was gone. The entire global ecosystem is in jeopardy."

"I know, Alan," Lew said, "but what does that have to do with . . ."

"Let me finish!" Alan said, excitedly. He grabbed the vial from Lew's hand.

"The whole nouspace thing and that stuff about surfing the waves of mind was kid stuff compared to what we can do with this."

"What?" Lew asked.

"We can begin to *heal the planet*," Alan said. "I'm talking about an eco-war to reclaim the globe for life and the living!"

"Oh," Lew said.

"I'm telling you, Lew, it is going to be all-out war—war between the forces of greed and death and the forces of life. It is that simple. Until now the good guys have been losing. But with this . . ."

"Just a minute," Lew interrupted. "Do you want something to drink?"

"Sure," Alan said.

As Lew got up to go to the kitchen, Alan suddenly remembered something.

"The professor asked me to give you this," he said, pulling a sealed envelope from his inside coat pocket. "It is for both of us, but he told me to wait until I found you. Apparently there was some doubt about that."

"But here I am," Lew said, taking the envelope. He went into the kitchen and found the bottle of cheap red wine just where he expected.

He returned to the living room with the bottle and two glasses. He poured the wine, handed a glass to Alan, and sat down at his desk, where he picked up a long, wooden letter opener made of Indian sandalwood and slit the envelope. The paper was coarse, light brown, and gave off a musty, sweet scent. Felix jumped up onto the desk, where he stretched out with a lazy yawn. The cat batted once or twice at the paper with outstretched paw before settling into a deep catnap.

The script was in dark blue ink. The professor's handwriting was impeccable, elegant and smooth flowing. Lew read out loud,

Dear Lew,

Time has many mysteries, not the least of which is the relation between past and future. Time is more like memory than anything else. Or maybe it is more nearly correct to say that memories are patterned after time. Time is perhaps the mold from which memory is cast.

However it works, the past is not an irreversible given, engraved in stone. Like memory, it is constantly revised; it grows, changes, and evolves. In so doing it changes the future. Our memories grow with us, and things that were once opaque become clear; we understand and act directly from a newborn memory.

You must have sensed it a thousand times. The present is the only real time. Yet the past and future are real too. The present, then, is the result of an eternal dialogue between the past and the future.

Or something like that. The present is the only "real" time, but not one of us actually lives there. We all live in the past or the future or some strange hybrid of the two.

So—what was the point? If I had not come, you would have sunk deeper into your life of quiet desperation and would never have found the inspiration to break free.

And surely I would not exist either. In a sense, our two times would have collapsed into each other at the point of your miserable capitulation to the mundane world